FORGOTTEN MILE

MATT
AMERLING

This work contains quotes from:

Network. Writ. Paddy Chayefsky. Dir. Sidney Lumet. Perf. Peter Finch. Metro-Goldwyn-Mayer, 1976. Film.

Springsteen, Bruce. "Thunder Road." *Born to Run.* Columbia Records, 1975. CD.

The Gaslight Anthem. "Great Expectations." *The '59 Sound.* SideOneDummy, 2008. CD.

Bush. "Glycerine." *Sixteen Stone.* Trauma Records, 1994. CD.

The Upanishads. Trans. Juan Mascaro. London: Penguin Books, 1965. Print.

All works used with permission.

Cover photograph by Matt Amerling

Cover design and author photograph by Erin Amerling

ISBN: 1517623529
ISBN-13: 978-1517623524

FOR MEME

CONTENTS

SIDE A

SIDE **B**

FROM THE AUTHOR

I first started writing *Forgotten Mile*, along with another completely different book, a year after I originally published *The Midknight* in 2005. Anyone who has read *The Midknight* may recognize the character of Jade Saha as she had a minor role in that story. Nearly all of my characters I write are created with a particular look in mind and, of course, I take inspiration from actors (i.e., *The Midknight's* Jesse Sands was originally seen as a Jesse Eisenberg; or, as of 2015, Asa Butterfield or Thomas Mann. Vanessa was always a *Roswell*-era Shiri Appleby; or, as of 2015, Olivia Cooke, a dark-haired Elle Fanning, or Maia Mitchell). In 2006, when I imagined Jade for this story, I pictured a *Firefly*-era Morena Baccarin. However, I had to soon shelve the story as having kids, getting a new job, moving to a different state, and attending college can merit such a delay. But as soon as I graduated, I set out to finish one of the two stories I started. I wanted to do something completely different from my first book, so I chose to focus on this story – originally entitled *Undiscovered* – and began to continue writing from where I last left off: after the three chapters I'd written all those years ago. As time has marched on, my vision of Jade changed from Baccarin to Indian actresses Pooja Hegde (who I actually envisioned while writing this) or Priyanka Chopra. For the part of the main protagonist, Tom Frost, I pictured someone like Robert Buckley (The CW's *iZombie*), Jesse Spencer (FOX's *House*), or Mike Vogel (*Cloverfield*).

One of the main characters which was most important to this story, however, has always been the music. My first novel had a soundtrack consisting of particular songs integral to the mood and action of that story. So, for this book, I had the same thing in mind. What started as about a twenty-song soundtrack soon grew into a massive four-and-a-half-hour-long saga! In fact, whether it's the mood and/or the lyrics, each song which makes up this vast soundtrack has a reason for being where it is in the story, at that moment. The lyrics correlate to what is going on – or has happened – in the story, and each song that headlines each chapter also has a particular lyric which fits to the theme of that particular chapter. There are also some very difficult, very subtle homages in the book, with some characters named after characters in songs, and some references to movies.

My original idea for *Forgotten Mile* was to write my version of a romantic comedy because I think the genre is so exhaustingly formulaic. But as I wrote the story, it started to transform into my version of a "man-in-search-of-himself"-type drama; although, it's the type of drama that women and men could both enjoy. I also wanted to make Jade a major character this time around, with her own story, and not merely some romantic interest for the protagonist. It wasn't just romantic relationships and the mix of good and bad that I wanted to address while writing this story. There were also prominent themes of family and unconditional love, as well as expectation versus reality, that I really wanted to address. I don't want to expand or explain anymore on what the story is about, what it means, or how one character or moment affects others because I leave that up for the reader to decide. Whether you can find deep meaning in what happens in the story, or take it simply at face value, either way, I hope you find it entertaining. So, without any further rambling, read on ...

SIDE Ⓐ

"Our lives are not our own. We are bound to others, past and present, and by each crime and every kindness, we birth our future."

--David Mitchell, *Cloud Atlas*

I.

"I had skin like leather
and the diamond-hard look of a cobra
I was born blue and weathered,
but I burst just like a supernova
I could walk like Brando right into the sun
And dance just like a Casanova"

--Bruce Springsteen
"It's Hard to Be a Saint in the City"

Tom Frost had never felt so nauseous in his life. As he knelt down on all fours, wiping his mouth with a handkerchief from his tuxedo jacket, he thought about the last time he was this sick. It had been when he was a freshman in college – the morning after his first major party – and he had awoken to a heavy hangover fueled by two glasses of red wine, five beers, and five shots of whiskey. However, this sickness wasn't because of a heavy night of drinking. This uneasiness in his stomach came purely from nerves. Tonight, he and his show were competing for an Emmy for "Outstanding Structured Reality Program." The prominent show was something he had dreamed up as a senior at University of Delaware while majoring in criminal justice and minoring in television production.

Heartbraker was a show that each week had a desperate spouse hire Tom as a private investigator who followed their significant other to see whether or not that person cheated on them. If they were cheating, Tom would report this to the victim, and then all of those involved would confront one another and resolve their problems on the air. It was part reality show, part talk show. Of course the only times they would air a case was when a spouse *was* caught having an affair. It was an emotionally driven series that caught a lot of audiences' attention – whether it was because they generally liked the rage and sadness that was showcased from the victim, the cheater, and/or the mistress, or because each scene was so tragic that it attracted people the same way a motorist would stop to watch a horrible car wreck. Either way, people found some enjoyment out of it; and now, Tom Frost – being producer, host, director and editor – was up for a prestigious award because of it.

He looked down at the smelly brownish-orange vomit swirling in the toilet, disgustfully winced at the sight and stood up as he flushed it down. Tom warily stepped over to a mirror and rested an arm on each side of the sink in front of him like pillars holding his frame up from collapsing in the sink basin. He shifted a hand to turn the right water handle and the cold liquid rushed into the sink with all the force of a miniature waterfall. He placed a hand under the stream and splashed the cool relief onto his feverishly hot face, rubbing some of the water into his acorn brown hair.

Amidst the grand décor of the polished white and grey tiles that coated the men's bathroom in the Nokia Theatre,

Tom looked up into the mirror and saw the heavy bags under his almond-shaped, lentil brown eyes. It had indeed been months since he last had a decent night's sleep as he had taken on a workaholic's life and pushed his every limit just to keep the show interesting and fresh. The months of constant interviewing and staking out dirty motel rooms and editing footage with hosting segments had left him exhausted and in drastic need of a vacation. But now it had all paid off. Well, it would pay off ... if he won the Emmy.

His only real competition was an island survival competition show named *Outcasts*, a show called *Roomies* about five spoiled young adults that are forced to live together, and some insanely superficial show called *Marriage/Money* in which a group of girls all fight over a man they think is wealthy, but in truth, only makes a minimum wage annual salary. To Tom, even if *Heartbraker* wasn't his show, he still would think that it was the better of the category. He thought it was practically a sure thing that he was going to win. Glaring into the mirror, Tom remembered most of the sadness that his clients had to face in order for him to get this far. And now, it was his night. He had ridden high on a wave of other people's misery and his future now depended on the next announcement.

He could hear the famous female actress presenter from the auditorium. "And the winner for Outstanding Structured Reality Program is—" The dramatic drum pounded a steady stream of loud booms as the tension built within Tom Frost.

"—*Heartbraker*!!! Produced, created and hosted by Tom Frost!" The star presenter shouted above an instantaneous sea of applause.

3

Tom's lips curled into a shifty smile as he stood up straight and checked his overall appearance in the mirror one last time before taking the stage. Now he was a force to be reckoned with in Hollywood and that meant his stock had just rapidly increased. He adjusted his black bow tie and raced out the restroom door into the auditorium. The bright, hot spotlight encased him as he strode down the red carpet aisle toward the stage.

The proud thirty-two-year-old producer stepped up onto the stage and gave the female actress presenter a kiss on her cheek – noticing it was the same beautiful actress that he had had a one night stand with after a Golden Globes post-party two years before he had gotten married. He grabbed the award statuette from her hands and grasped on tightly as if he were some jealous kid claiming a toy that was never his.

"First off, I'd like to thank my crew for all of their tedious, dedicated work. Also, thanks to the wonderful network that carries us. Couldn't have done this without everyone's support there. And, finally, I'd like to thank ... my wife, Maggie, who is the most beautiful and most supportive woman I've had the pleasure to know." Tom glared into the audience to see his stunning wife – a beautiful woman who slightly resembled the actress Rachel Weisz, with porcelain skin accentuated by red, pillowy lips, dimples, and orange-red hair which practically looked like fire, falling over one side of her face, covering one of her grayish-blue eyes, reminiscent of Veronica Lake. Her soft face was nearly covered with tears and she mouthed the words "I love you" back to him. "Thanks, Maggie, for always being there for me. I hope ... that I can someday give to you what you've given me these past two years. I love you." He raised his award and addressed the crowd. "Thanks."

With a quick turn, raising his statuette to the crowd and a flash of a beaming smile, Tom whisked himself off stage and was escorted by the curvaceous blonde, twenty-something trophy girl to a small press room where he was to be interviewed. An ecstatic energy pulsated through his body, coursing through his veins even faster than before. When Tom started the reality show two years ago, he never imagined – even though it's what he had been striving for – that he would actually win a major award for it.

Four steps up onto a blue winner's platform and all he could see from that point were bright lights and a sea of cameras. Several reporters were shouting his name, trying to get his attention for the first question. Above everyone else's voices, he strained to listen for one in particular: Jen Desmond. Jen Desmond was a famous newscaster for WPNX Channel Six news – and his ex. They had dated for a long time before she dumped him to focus more on her career. Although he was no longer in love with her, he still longed to have something to rub her nose in. And tonight was the opportune moment. Tom had everything: a beautiful wife, a new home in the Hollywood hills and, now, an award-winning television program that he created, hosted and produced.

He filtered the voices as best as he could, hoping to hear hers. Then, it came to him. "Tom! Tom! Tom!"

Tom's eyes followed the trail of the voice to the right corner of the room and saw her standing there, arm raised with reporters' notebook in hand and that determined glare in her eyes. Her eyes. Of all the traits with which Tom remembered, it was her eyes that stood out the most. In fact, most men who gazed longingly at her picture would get caught up on many of her assets, but her eyes were always the clincher which caught their attention. Famous for a rare condition known as heterochromia iridium that left her right eye a hazel color and her left eye a sky blue color, Jen's eager eyes now purveyed that determination when her mind was fixated on anything.

"Yes," Tom said, pointing to her. "Miss Desmond."

Although the young, vibrant, slender blonde reporter was beautiful – a former Miss San Diego – Tom's view of her was jaded by their sordid past. Jen had been prominently featured in most men's magazines (*Maxim*, not *Playboy*) as well as having done a stint as the St. Pauli Girl beer spokesmodel the year before her venture into broadcast journalism. She was lusted after by most of the men that saw her model photos. However, if those men knew her the way Tom knew her, they wouldn't be so eager to imagine being in bed with her rather than their actual wives. When they were together, Jen's only concern was with her career. It wasn't until after they split that she became a trusted friend to Tom. She even gave him good reviews for his new reality-based show. And because of that, they were rather good acquaintances. Still, that wouldn't keep Tom from bragging about his new status as Emmy award-winning producer and creator.

"Congratulations on your win," she projected with her signature smile.

"Thanks."

"How do you feel about the critics out there who have poked fun at your show and those who said it has reached a new low in American television?"

This wasn't the type of question Tom was expecting from a "friend," and her face expressed no awkwardness from asking it. However, he knew it was her job to ask the grittier, no-holds-barred type of questions. That was how she got where she was today.

Tom took her question in stride and held up his shiny, golden statuette. "The evidence speaks for itself," he casually replied, trying to mimic a nonchalant demeanor of James Dean and Steve McQueen. Some members of the press laughed at his response. "Reality programming is a field of tough competition nowadays because of its popularity. There are shows popping up everywhere and most don't last."

"If people truly didn't like my show," Tom continued, "they wouldn't be watching it and I wouldn't be standing here tonight, holding this trophy. I think my show is a staple in today's society."

The casual, calm fluidity of Tom's answer left Jen satisfied with his answer but wanting more. She had been the one to dump him but, from time to time, still felt a strong sexual attraction, specifically times like now when his talent and self-esteem were at an all-time high. Her eyes swooned at her ex-lover and she wanted to rip off his clothes and take him right there at the podium. After all, it had been a long time since she had found a lover as good as him. From what she remembered, he did have nice sun-browned skin, a ruggedly handsome face and, not to mention, his slightly toned body.

"Next question," His voice snapped her out of her mental imaging and another reporter shouted a question.

"How does your wife feel about you working on a show

that breaks up many relationships and marriages?" a reporter from a rival TV station voiced.

"She feels great! She supports me in all that I do. We couldn't be happier," are the words that came out of Tom's mouth, but what he really thought was: *How dare you question me and my wife's relationship in front of all of these people, you little, pretentious shithead!* "Next question."

"What do you see in store for the future of your show?" one of the reporters voiced.

"I have to admit that a lot of people – including myself – didn't think the show would carry on this long, let alone be nominated for such a distinguished award. So I'm not exactly sure where we'll go next with the show. A lot of critics have been condemning reality shows – especially those that can get as nasty as my show. However, as long as the people want it, I'll be delivering it to them. I have no doubt that next season will be an even bigger and better season for the show."

Tom noticed one of the award show's producers signaling for him to move off the small stage. The handsome Frost waved to the audience of reporters and said, "Thanks, ladies and gentlemen."

Tom stepped into a little trophy room where they took his prop trophy and gave him the actual trophy, which had his name, the year, and the name of his show engraved into the golden base. He exuberantly continued backstage into a restroom and quickly searched the stalls for anyone's presence. When Tom knew for certain that he was alone, he jumped up and down like a little kid on his parents' bed, making hushed screams of excitement.

His jumps grew higher and he began spinning his body around in mid-air like a top. Through one of his jumps, he heard the creaking of the bathroom door and saw two men in tuxedos entering. Their faces were a little bewildered and a little freaked out by the sight they were witnessing. Tom's feet planted firmly on the ground, his back to them, and he closed his eyes in embarrassment, thinking that maybe they didn't see him.

"So anyways," one of the gentlemen continued talking to the other man. Tom slowly opened his eyes and ducked into a stall as the two men walked up to the urinals. He closed the door and sat down on the plastic seat, laying his anxious head in his hands.

Tom could hardly contain his excitement and all of his fears of failure left his mind and body. A high-pitched ringing instantly broke the brief calm, making Tom slightly jump off the toilet seat. He grabbed for his cell phone in his inside jacket pocket. Looking upon the display screen, he noticed it was his parents. They were probably calling to congratulate him.

He hurriedly accepted the call and placed the phone to his ear. "Hi! Mom! Yeah! Yeah, you saw it right. I won!"

The thirty-two-year-old intently listened to his mother rave on about his success and how great he was at his job. No matter how much she adorned him with praise, he tried to not let it get to his head too much. However, the more positive reviews he got on his show, the bigger his ego expanded.

"Of course, Maggie's ecstatic! I just won the Emmy, Mom! Our lives are gonna get better from this point on!"

Tom Frost's mother had always been a naturally

concerned woman. Ever since her only son had announced his desire to produce television, she had become worried that he would starve and remain unsuccessful. Although, despite her concern, she and his father always supported Tom and showed their pride in all that he accomplished. Now that his father was ill – could hardly do any physical labor on account of his recent heart problems – Tom was making this money not just for recognition but also to pay his father's bills. But tonight's win wasn't about his father. Tonight was a paramount moment in Tom's career and he hoped both of his parents were proud.

"How's Dad doing? Did he see it?" Tom raised his voice above the rising voices in the bathroom. He listened to her excuse, then said, "Oh. Sure. Yeah, maybe you can show it to him online."

As his mother spoke on the other end, Tom held his open ear closed so he could try and hear what she was saying.

"I'm not sure what happens next," he answered her. "I just got done with my quick press meeting backstage. I guess I go back to my seat with Maggie and, after the show, we're gonna hit the town!" Some more noise flowed into the bathroom and Tom shouted, "Mom! Mom! I'm gonna have to call you tomorrow. It's getting crazy here! OK. Tell Dad we said hi and we'll talk to him tomorrow. OK? Alright. Take care. I love you. Bye."

Tom hung up his cell phone and nearly jumped again in uncontrollable excitement and pride, but, realizing where he was, he adjusted his tux jacket and stepped out of the stall and back into the craziness of the backstage.

The moment he emerged from the restroom, he was

escorted back to his seat and sat down with a long kiss for his wife, Maggie. Even with tears filling her eyes, she still was as radiant as ever. She gave him another kiss on his cheek and whispered into his ear, "Congratulations, baby. I love you."

"So where should we go to celebrate?" Tom asked his wife.

"Doesn't matter to me. It's your celebration, so you pick."

Tom sat and thought about it while other announcers up on stage read off the next batch of nominees for best actress in a miniseries or movie made for television. The more he thought about it, the bigger the smile on his face grew. He would now be famous and making the kind of money he had wanted for so long, which meant the possibilities for his career and his social life, would be limitless.

"I hear Nobu in Malibu is nice," Tom replied with an intoxicated smile.

"I thought you'd want to go to one of the post-award parties," Maggie said with a hint of surprise.

"Screw it. That's work and I can go to work tomorrow. Tonight, I spend time with the most beautiful woman in the world."

His wife's face slightly contorted to a shocked look although Tom failed to notice; he was too preoccupied in the dreamy state of his future.

Maggie Russell had known Tom Frost since high school. They had met during the summer while both working at an amusement park in Delaware, and the first time he laid eyes on her, Tom had fallen in love. At first, they were friends and that's all Maggie thought of Tom. He, however, fell more in love with her every time he heard her talk. Even though he wanted more than the mere friendship she wanted, he kept his romantic feelings at bay just so he could spend time with her.

Two years after first meeting – and after a few one-night stands and a brief fling Tom had with Miss Desmond – Maggie kissed Tom and they soon became a couple. After college, they were married. All of her friends always wondered what exactly had turned Maggie's feelings of Tom from platonic to romantic and she would say, "He's passionate about what he wants to do with his life. And he's one of the best people I've ever met."

Tom was still passionate – if not obsessed – about his career, and things between he and Maggie only seemed to be getting better. He had been subjected to a lot of poor-paying internships and bosses' bullying personalities to get where he was now. The sense that he could now do anything was overpowering him and he couldn't help but feel a rush of energy course through his veins.

Tom looked over to his wife. Through everything, she had been by his side. When he was depressed or frustrated, she held him and told him everything would be fine. Her compassion was one of the things that he admired most about her. Maggie hated her lithe frame and stringy muscles, but Tom loved every inch of her apple blossom skin. Every day, her feline-like walk and eyes attracted him even more.

He leaned over and kissed Maggie's long, slender neck and she giggled. Even though Tom's career had often taken him away from their home – he spent most nights at the studio, editing for the show and setting up arrangements for the next episode – Maggie was still so happy for him. Maybe now that he had accepted some achievement for his work, Tom might ease up and they could settle down a little more.

Once they entered Nobu, Tom was surprised to see his best friend, Dylan Vaughn, and Dylan's fiancée, Lucia, waiting at a reserved table with a bucket of chilled champagne awaiting them. The Leroy song, "Good Time," was playing in the background. Tom had known Dylan since college when they both became roommates at their fraternity. Even though they had never kept up communication with the rest of their frat brothers, they still became closer friends. Soon after college, Tom had gotten married to Maggie and Dylan had gone off to make a name for himself as an entertainment agent before Dylan approached Tom about a job with the show. Tom had never been good at talking to people. No matter who he met, he always seemed to say the wrong thing or say it in the wrong way. That was the reason that – despite his looks – he always screwed up when it came to meeting women.

Dylan was the exact opposite. He was the ultimate mix of *Leave it to Beaver*'s Eddie Haskell and Don Draper from *Mad Men*. Everyone who met Dylan seemed to love him. That is why Tom agreed to give him a job as co-producer. About two years ago, Dylan met Lucia and proposed. He figured that she was as sexy as any Spanish girl he had met out in L.A. and since it also seemed like everyone he knew was settling down, maybe it wasn't such a bad idea getting married.

Dylan Vaughn was an extremely good-looking man and didn't have any problems getting women, although he was very particular about the kind of women he got mixed up with. His smooth, handsome face, straight dirty blonde hair and piercing blue eyes were the perfect bait for any attractive young women. Up until Tom had met Maggie, the two college buddies used to be the biggest "lady-killers" on campus. When it came to knowing the quickest way to get the ladies to drop their panties, Dylan and Tom were the experts.

However, ever since Dylan had proposed to Lucia Torres, Tom knew that his friend didn't need any other women. Lucia was one of the most beautiful women Tom had ever seen; she had come from a middle-class Spanish family. Her mom, who was a light-skinned African American, and her dad, who was Spanish, were still happily married, and she had an older sister, Rita, and a younger brother, Carlos. Dylan didn't know much about family life himself; his parents had divorced when he was sixteen-years-old and he always had secretly swore that he wasn't going to ever let love get the best of him. But, like Maggie, Lucia was no ordinary woman. Like Maggie, Lucia had a skinnier, "classic beauty" face. Unlike Maggie, however, Lucia was a voluptuous woman with caramel skin, all the right curves in all the right places, long, gorgeous dark brown hair, a small, sexy mole – like Cindy Crawford's – directly above the left corner of her upper lip, and brown eyes that could make even the slightest glance so very sexual.

At first, Maggie didn't know whether to trust Lucia or not, but after all of their outings together, they had become the closest of friends and were now inseparable. Maggie greeted Lucia with a big hug and a huge smile. Dylan reached out his hand to shake Tom's hand but, in his excitement, Tom merely grabbed a hold of his college pal and gave him an enormous hug.

"It's about time you got here," Dylan exclaimed. "We were beginning to wonder if you two would ever show up!"

"Well, us *Emmy winners* have lots of important places to be," Tom joked back.

"It's so good to see you!" Lucia said as she still hugged Maggie. Then she turned to Tom and gave him a hug, saying, "And congratulations, Tom!"

"Thanks, Lucia," Tom greeted back. "You look stunning tonight."

"Thanks," she retorted.

"So!" Dylan cut the small chit-chat short. "Where are we going from here?"

"Dylan!" Maggie cut in. "Let's forget about that for one night! Tonight is a night to celebrate Tom."

"Hey," Dylan raised his palms in defense. "I just see this as a major career move. Besides, it's my way of celebrating."

Tom looked upon his wife and best friend arguing and simply shook his head in amusement. "Don't worry, Dylan. You'll be the first one I call tomorrow morning."

Dylan looked at his flashy Rolex wristwatch and said, "It *is* tomorrow."

"Yeah, I know. I meant the *other* tomorrow."

The ladies laughed at Tom's small joke as Dylan brushed off the statement, raising a champagne glass. "I'd like to propose a toast."

Tom, Maggie and Lucia raised their glasses as Dylan said, "To Tom. Here's to you and here's to me; forever friends may we be. But if we happen to disagree, *fuck* you and here's to me!"

They all tapped glasses and laughed at Dylan's lewd,

amusing toast as each one of them drank. Dylan leaned over to Tom and whispered, "We'll talk more about this later."

Tom gave a slight nod and sat upright, when Maggie leaned close to him, gave him a soft, wet kiss and whispered, "I love you. And I'm so proud of you."

Ever since he married her, Tom knew his wife supported him but lately she had seemed slightly more stressed out in wanting him to back off from his work. She wanted a baby and he knew it was time to start the family that he and Maggie had talked about so many times before him starting the show. Still, though, Dylan was tenacious when it came to business – especially if there was major money to be made. And while Maggie could be swayed to remain patient, Dylan could not.

"Don't worry, Dylan. Let's order some more drinks first, then we can talk business," Tom stated.

Dylan leaned back near his fiancée with a pleasurable grin gracing his face, noticing that they needed more drinks, and quickly ordered another round. Tom looked to his beautiful wife and recognized a bit of discomfort in his willingness to talk business on a night of celebration. He leaned closer to her and briefly kissed her, then pulled back to say, "Don't worry. I won't let it go on for more than fifteen minutes." He wrapped her hand in his and continued, "I want to spend this night with *you*."

Maggie immediately smiled her usual warm grin and gave her husband an approving nod. Tom gave her a longer kiss and then turned to Dylan, asking, "So what do you have in mind for this season?"

"Well, I was thinking that because it's still so early in the show's run that you need to mix things up a bit to keep the viewers' attention. Since the next major landmark of the show will be the fiftieth episode, and it will be the season finale, I was thinking that we could shoot the entire episode live. What do you think?"

"How would we shoot a live episode?"

"Instead of you having all those graphics flashing across the screen, we'd have the camera primarily on you and the victim throughout most of the broadcast. We could also cut between you and the suspect cheater. I'm tellin' ya, Tom! This would grab the nation's attention and be more emotionally driven. People would love it! It would be *the* water cooler discussion piece each week."

In all modesty, Tom loved Dylan's idea. Nevertheless, he didn't want his friend to know that he loved it *that* much. Otherwise, Dylan might charge him a huge percentage of the income for the idea. So, Tom did what any cautious television exec might do: he kept his cool and brushed off the idea.

"That sounds like an OK idea. Tell ya what, let me think about it and get back to you in two days. How's that sound?"

The waitress brought the group their drinks and Dylan raised his glass off her tray as if he were already toasting the idea. "Sounds great to me."

The waitress placed Tom's martini in front of him and he raised his glass to quietly clang against Dylan's. "Good." The both of them smiled and took a drink. Tom gulped down his Belvedere vodka and dry vermouth with a comforting ease and said, "Now, no more shop talk. The night's still young and we've got *a lot* of celebrating to do."

"I'll drink to that," Lucia chimed in as she took a large

gulp of her dirty martini. Tom leaned in closer to his wife and she smiled even bigger, happy that her husband's work had paid off and that he was so happy.

The friends all partied and danced into the early hours of the morning and the next thing Tom knew, he was waking up naked to an annoying, uninterrupted buzzing of an alarm clock. Being under his covers, he couldn't see it, but he knew it was his alarm because it was the only noise he knew of that could wake him up. He reached out of the covers and could feel his bones crack and ache as he pounded on the top of the clock to turn it off. Quickly, he sank back into sleep.

As his thoughts drifted off into darkness, Tom began to see various faces and he knew each and every one of them. They were the clients on his now-award-winning show that had found out their spouses were cheating on them. These were not just his imagination getting the best of him but actual memories of clients' faces. Each face he saw hit him like a blow to his gut, the emotion intense and excruciating. There was no relief or gratitude in their expressions; it was pain and anger and hopelessness and fear. Their faces were inescapable. Each rushed through his line of sight – first very slow and then speeding up. The multitude went through his mind so quick that he thought he may have a panic attack were it not for his dreaming.

Tom's eyes shot open and he immediately reached over to Maggie's side of the bed and felt a vacant spot where her body would usually be laying. She was gone but that wasn't much of a surprise; she usually woke up before he did. His sleepy eyes peered upon the green numbers of his clock and saw them turn to 10:01 a.m. For a brief moment, Tom panicked, thinking it was a work day, but then his nerves quickly soothed when he realized that it was Sunday. He laid his head back down on the fluffy pillows and drifted off into another uneasy sleep.

* * *

Two hours passed but Tom's hangover hadn't dissipated much. He was still slightly tired but he had already slept away the morning and noticed Maggie still wasn't lying next to him. He arose out of bed and put on a blue bathrobe before going into the bathroom and splashing cold water on his face. His eyes began to sharply focus on his image in the mirror and he looked absolutely dreadful; he looked as if he had just been through a hurricane and his body felt like it as well. Tom began brushing his teeth and hurriedly finished before moving toward the downstairs to search for her. The house was a spacious mansion – or "McMansion," as some people called them – located in Hollywood Hills. The walls were a barren white with occasional prints from the likes of Roy Lichtenstein and Jack Vettriano. Most importantly to Tom, the big screen television was an 80-inch; it was Tom's pride and joy. The kitchen appliances were chrome, adding to the cold feel of the residence and when he reached the downstairs wide-open, black-and-white tiled kitchen, he found a yellow sticky note with black scribbling attached to the refrigerator.

Tom stumbled, still half-awake but mostly hung over, to the fridge and read the note. "Hey baby! Didn't want to wake you. Went to the mall, probably be back around two.

Love you, Maggie."

He looked to the microwave clock and saw the time in blue numbers, 12:19 p.m. The thought of Maggie shopping for about five hours – and the money spending that would ensue – made Tom shudder. The last time she had gone out for that length of time, she and Lucia had spent close to a thousand dollars on a posh lunch and four outfits for Maggie. He figured he'd give her a call and make sure she wasn't going too crazy with the money.

Tom picked up the phone and dialed her cell phone. It rang four times before he heard the usual cute voice recording: "Hi, you've reached Maggie. You know what to do." Then came the beep. He didn't leave a message; she must've left her phone in the car.

He put the phone back on its receiver and figured now was as good a time as any to get a shower so he went back upstairs, to the bathroom, took off his clothes and turned on the warm stream of water pouring from the showerhead.

By the time Tom had stepped out of the shower, he heard his phone ringing and quickly wrapped a towel around his waist to race to pick it up before the caller hung up. He snatched up the phone and said, "Hello?"

"Hey, Tom," it was Dylan. "Did I catch you at a bad time? Still recoverin' from last night, huh?"

"No. I'm fine. What's up, Dylan?"

"I was thinking about what we were talking about last night. You know – about kicking the show up a notch? Do you have time to talk now?"

"Sure. What's up?"

"I was thinkin' about that idea I had last night. The live

fiftieth episode. I think the show being shot live will definitely be what it needs to keep the audience wanting more."

"I don't know about this, Dylan."

"C'mon, Tom!" Dylan immediately cut him off. "You don't think I'd steer you wrong, do you?" There was a brief pause and Dylan continued, "You know I wouldn't screw with you like that! I've only got you and Maggie's best interests in mind."

It was true that Dylan had always been a good friend to Tom. Ever since they knew each other freshman year of college, Dylan had always seemed to look out for Tom. Nevertheless, something seemed amiss about Dylan and his offer. He hadn't ever sounded this needy or pushy before. Something must have been wrong.

"Dylan, is something wrong?" Tom asked suspiciously.

His college buddy chuckled at the thought and answered, "No. What would be wrong? Why would you ask that?"

Tom was hesitant to answer but concisely said, "You just ... seem ... I don't know. You seem ... more pushy than usual."

"Pushy!?" Dylan exclaimed, almost taking offense to the comment. "How am I being pushy!?"

"You've never put a deadline on *any*thing for me before and – what? All of a sudden, it's so urgent that you need a response right away for a show that's not even gonna air for another few months?" There was no response from Dylan but Tom could hear his breathing had grown slightly faster. "What's going on? Just tell me."

Dylan tensed up and knew that he was taking a huge

professional risk by admitting his troubles to one of his business partners, even though he may be his best friend. To Dylan, admitting weakness (or problems) was never dignified, let alone a respectable quality, and he didn't want to lose any respect from his co-worker and best friend. Still, he felt that he at least owed it to Tom to be honest. He took a deep breath, released it and spoke.

"I don't know how to tell you this, Tom. But the ... network is breathing down my neck. Since they received word that your show won, they've been bustin' my balls to get you to commit to givin' the show even more of an edge."

Tom couldn't believe this! He was the one who had fought to get this show produced and put on the air. He had to practically beg for the network to back it and air it. And now that it was an award-winner, rather than kissing his ass (which they should be doing), they were criticizing him and telling him the show could be better.

"Can't you just tell them to wait forty-eight hours and you'll get back to them?" Tom asked, dumbfounded.

There was a pause on Dylan's end as he furrowed his brow and furiously scratched his head in desperation. "The problem with that is – I can't." Just as Tom was opening his mouth to ask why not, Dylan carefully tried to explain. "Ya see – *shit*, Tom! I didn't want you to know about this."

"About what?"

"Before I started representing you, I made a lot of mistakes with the company."

"What do you mean 'mistakes'?"

Dylan blew out a long sigh of frustration and hesitantly answered, "Before I was *lucky* enough to represent you, I made some bad deals that could've ended my career. In order for me to keep my job, they put me on probation and said if I screw up again, they'll fire me. I hate to do this to ya but I *need* this, Tom. I need you to take this step with me and take the show live so I can keep this job." Dylan noticed his friend's hesitant, worried glare and added, "It's only for the one episode. I promise."

Tom heard a key hit the front door lock and silently watched as Maggie strode through the door with a few shopping bags in her arms. Her soft aquamarine eyes met his brown eyes and he knew that if he decided to take his show to this level - even for just one episode - his wife would not be too happy about it, even though they could definitely use the extra money. But his best friend needed his help. Especially since Dylan was engaged to be married to a sweet woman like Lucia, and Tom knew from personal experience how pricey weddings could get. Besides, he couldn't let Dylan lose his job over him.

Maggie flashed him one of her usual smiles which always seemed to lift his spirits and bring him to his knees all at once. Tom returned a small smile, not sure what to make of this predicament.

She placed her bags on the ground, the smile Tom had come to love and know since high school still beaming at him, and moved closer to him, her arms welcoming him with an endearing hug. He felt even worse when she did things like that. It made him feel all the more like a jerk when he had to make decisions of which she most likely wouldn't approve. Over the phone, he could practically hear Dylan's heart pound and feel his sweat pouring down his brow. As Tom felt the warmth of his wife's embrace, he knew what he had to do. In the long run, Maggie would be thankful for the amount of income that they would earn from this decision and the show would benefit as well. Besides, Tom couldn't even begin to think of himself as being the reason why his best friend lost his job – a job that he knew he loved.

He let out a long sigh, rolled his eyes and said, "OK, Dylan. Sign me up. I'll do it."

A loud *yaaahooooo* came roaring from the other end of the line, which made Maggie somewhat jump at the unexpected sound, and Dylan's excited yet exasperated voice said, "You won't be sorry, Tom! I promise this is gonna change all our lives for the better! We'll be rich, famous and havin' networks beggin' us to develop shows for them! I'll be in touch with you again after I've told them. We should plan on getting together tonight and go over any plans. See ya!"

Dylan's phone loudly clicked off, making Tom's head jolt away from his earpiece and then casually hang up his phone. He peered down at Maggie once more and knew that it would be tough telling her what he had just agreed to do. Her rich lavender scent and soft hair touching his skin made it all the more difficult to confess.

2.

"So now I'm goin' back again,
I got to get to her somehow.
All the people we used to know
They're an illusion to me now.
Some are mathematicians.
Some are carpenter's wives.
Don't know how it all got started,
I don't know what they're doin' with their lives"

--Bob Dylan
"Tangled Up in Blue"

Estella Margaret "Maggie" Russell never thought she would ever get married - let alone to Tom Frost of all people. Back in college, she knew she wanted to get married, settle down and have kids *someday*. Hell, that's what almost every girl wanted. But she knew there was a lot more fun to be had, men to meet and a life she had to carve out for herself first. She had gotten involved with guys while at college but made sure that any relationship didn't become too serious. When she first entered high school at fourteen, she made a conscientious decision not to go out of her way to get into a relationship and while she dated a few guys - even became intimate with one of them - she was more concerned with having fun. Her red hair and dainty figure attracted quite a bit of attention from men, a majority of which just wanted to get her in their bed.

It wasn't until she had met Tom Frost during the summer before they started college that she had met a guy who didn't just want to get her in to bed or make her one of his possessions. Tom was a sweet guy who never got jealous like most of the other jerks she had dated. He had asked around about her and knew she was a wild spirit and dated a few other guys – he even heard some sexual stories from one of the guys she had dated. However, unlike most guys, he was able to look past all of that. He saw something in her that made her special and she felt it when she was around him.

Maggie, as she had been called by her closest friends, very much liked that Tom saw that special quality within her, but she couldn't pretend to feel something that wasn't there. The truth was that Maggie simply didn't care for Tom in a romantic sort of way. As much as she hated to fall into a cliché, it was true that Tom was like a best friend to her.

She continued dating guys and hanging out with Tom in their final months of spring semester their freshman year. Their times together were full of many ups and downs and just when she thought their friendship was in danger, Tom's phone calls and emails to her began dwindling until she didn't hear from him at all. At first, she welcomed the space; she could go out with any guy she wanted and do whatever she wanted with him without feeling guilty over how Tom may react. However, after a few weeks, she began wondering where Tom was, what he was doing, and who he may be meeting – or dating.

When Maggie asked around to their friends about Tom, they just said that he started going out on a few random dates with different girls, but was now seeing some blonde named Jen; that's all they knew about her. Maggie honestly felt relieved that Tom had finally seemed to meet a woman who liked him as more than a friend. She smiled and the idea fit comfortably into her mind. After all, that wouldn't hinder their friendship. Tom was good to his friends and never seemed to neglect them so Maggie wasn't worried about being dropped from his life.

But then, a month went by. And then another. Then, another ... until she didn't hear from him at all. She didn't even see him on campus, which wasn't too hard since his dorm room was on the outskirts of campus. She tried calling his dorm room but always got his voice mail or no response at all. She emailed him but got no replies. She even tried to visit his room twice, but there was no one there.

Maggie's curiosity had finally boiled over and she simply had to know why she hadn't heard from Tom at all in the past couple of months. She knew he wasn't like the other jerks on campus who ignored a girl 'cause he didn't get her in bed. There had to be some kind of rational explanation. And since she couldn't get one from Tom himself, she'd get one from someone who was closest to him: his best friend, Dylan.

After knocking on Dylan's door and not getting a response, Maggie had resorted to pounding on it. She knew *someone* was there; Love Seed Mama Jump's "Pauper" was blaring from inside the dorm room. She pounded again.

"I'm coming!" A voice yelled. "Damn!"

The door swung open fast and a head with tussled hair popped through the crack. "*WHAT!?*"

Seeing Maggie in front of him, Dylan calmed himself and stood up straight, opening the door wider to reveal his wearing nothing but a pair of boxer shorts. "Oh, Maggie." He ran a hand through his rustled dirty blonde hair to make it look somewhat neat. "What's up?"

A random sorority girl with equally messy hair, wearing a slinky, wrinkled black dress, walked out of Dylan's room and down the hallway.

"I'll call ya later, Brooke!" Dylan shouted to her as she raced down the stairs without trying to be noticed.

Maggie looked from the girl's back to Dylan with a disgusted glare. Dylan picked up on her look and shot back a look of his own – as if to say, *Hey, I can't help it if the ladies love me.*

"So ... to what do I owe this honor, Miss Russell?" Dylan asked amusingly.

By that time, Maggie's disgust had faded and her curiosity had taken over. "Dylan, have you heard from Tom lately?"

"Define 'lately.'"

"You know? At least in the past few days?"

Dylan laughed a bit before cutting it short and saying, "Um – yeah. I was just out with him last night."

"If you were out with him last night, how did Ms. I-Ate-a-Pie-Sorority end up with you back here?" she asked a little angry.

"That's Alpha Theta Pi!" Dylan protested defensively with a humorous tinge as he stuck his chest out.

"Whatever!"

Before Dylan could spout off a harsh comeback, a look of an epiphany hit him and he replied, "*Oooohhhh.* I know what this is all about." He looked her over, then back into her eyes. "You haven't heard from Tom lately 'cause he hasn't been playing his usual part of your little puppy dog – all followin' you around. So, now that you want some attention, you're wonderin' where he is."

As much as Maggie wanted to deny it, when it all came down to it, all of what Dylan said was true. "That's not true!" But she wasn't going to give him the satisfaction of knowing it. "I'm worried about him! I haven't heard from him in months."

"Tom *did* come out with me last night. His girlfriend Jen *met up* with us and she introduced me to one of her sorority sisters."

"Girlfriend?"

Maggie hadn't heard of Tom having any girlfriend. "Yeah. You haven't met her yet?"

Maggie's silence answered Dylan's question and she dropped her head in slight despair, wondering why he wouldn't tell her. Her thoughts were cut short by Dylan's voice.

"I know what you did to him, Maggie." She looked up and her eyes met his.

"What are you—?"

"We all do," he cut her off. "You didn't think he'd catch on one day?"

"Catch on to what?"

"That you wanted to keep him around just when it was convenient to you."

People always say that the truth can sometimes sting and

this time, to Maggie, it certainly did. She never thought of herself as being the type of person who would lead someone on, but, looking at Dylan's groggy face, she realized that she was doing just that. Maggie had to shamefully admit that she liked having Tom - who she knew would always be there for her - around whenever *she* wanted him. What Dylan was saying was right; she was not only taking advantage of Tom, but also taking him for granted. And she felt like a complete selfish bitch for it. She slowly nodded her head in agreement.

"And he told me all about the day he saw you with that other guy," Dylan added.

"What other guy!? I wasn't ..."

"*Alex!* You know? The one you were all giggly and cuddled up next to on the lawn beside Trabant?"

Maggie's face transformed from angered to shocked, her mouth half open. She did remember cuddling up to Alex beside the Trabant Center a few days ago, but she didn't remember seeing Tom. "Dylan, you're lying!"

"Why would I? Go ask Tom if you want!"

Maggie looked down in even more shock, ashamed of how the sight probably made him feel.

"That guy would do anything for you," Dylan continued as Maggie pictured that day in her head. A movie of Tom strolling along on his way back to his dorm room played in Maggie's mind and then, there she was - cuddled up with Alex. She imagined the look of heartbreak and betrayal that must've formed on his face and it made her feel all the more bad.

"You told him flat out that you weren't ready to date or be in a relationship," Dylan continued, "and a few days later, he sees you on his way home from a class, makin' out with Alex!"

Dylan calmed his voice and sounded off, "Maybe you should've just told him the truth. That you weren't interested in having a relationship, or hooking up, with *him*."

Maggie looked back up into Dylan's eyes, a feeling of sad shame in her eyes, as if she were about to cry. "How come he never told me?" she asked.

"I don't know. He's right upstairs. Maybe you should go ask him."

Maggie took in a deep breath and walked up the flight of stairs leading to Tom's dorm room. The hallways of the building always reeked of sweat and what seemed like rotten eggs. Maggie always figured that it was simply the smell of boys since they were the ones who mostly occupied the building. She usually didn't mind it but her guilt and anxiety about confronting Tom turned her stomach and the smell wasn't helping. She started feeling nauseous with each step she climbed, leading her closer to Tom's door.

It was then that the breadth of Tom's feelings for her had hit Maggie. And she put herself in his shoes and could imagine how he must've been so saddened by the sight of her and Alex snuggled up together. The butterflies in her stomach transformed to agitated wasps and she felt as if she was going to throw up all over the cement floor.

She told herself to get a grip and get over it. Tom was, after all, an understanding guy and if he truly cared for her, he would forgive her when she apologized and then maybe they could be friends again, like before. As long as she could remain calm, everything would take care of itself. She just had to pull herself together.

As Maggie picked her right fist up to knock on Tom's door, she thought that maybe Tom *was* the kind of guy she should date. After all, things with Alex went predictably bad and Tom wasn't like any of the other guys she had dated before – he was nice. Maybe she ought to give him a try and –

"Oh, Tom!" a girl's voice moaned in ecstasy through the door, followed by a brief giggle.

Maggie pulled her arm back before she could knock. *Who was that?* That couldn't be the girl Dylan was talking about! To her, they had *just* started dating. They wouldn't be having sex *this* soon.

The curious young woman turned her head and slowly began to put an ear to the door to try and hear more. Sure enough, she heard a bed squeaking almost to the rhythm of Dave Matthews Band's "Crush," and could only imagine what kind of sex was going on in there. She knew this was a private moment and couldn't handle hearing anymore, so she took her ear away from the door, shuffled down the stairs and out the building.

Maybe Tom wasn't as "in love" with Maggie as he said or thought he was; maybe he had gotten over her. And that was all the thinking she needed to do before she unknowingly grew jealous and rejected. She began thinking to herself, *After all the attention and sentiments he threw my way, he just decides to quit like that and go after some sorority chick?*

Her face flushed red with a tinge of anger. *How dare he* – then it hit her. She wasn't angry at him for moving on to some other girl. She was angry that he wasn't doting all his attention on her. She felt like an incredible jerk and decided she would remain friends with Tom but also give him the space he needed to be with his "girlfriend."

A couple of days later, right before school ended for the summer, Maggie was walking home from her history class when she heard a familiar voice call out her name.

She hoped it wasn't who she thought it was. "Maggie!" the voice repeated.

As she slowly turned toward the source of the voice, she bit on her lower lip, slightly closing her eyes, as if she had been caught in the middle of a lie. She was hoping not to see Tom, but, sure enough, life sometimes bites you on the ass when you don't want it to.

"Hi, Tom," Maggie smiled, noticing that he was with a girl. However, she couldn't assume that this was the girl Tom was dating or the one she heard with him up in his room.

"Hey! I haven't seen you around for a long time," he said. "How've you been?"

"Good. I came by your place the other day but you ...," she looked over to the girl and didn't want to embarrass either of them by saying she heard them having sex, so she lied, "... weren't there."

"Oh ... well, I want you to meet someone. Maggie, this is my girlfriend, Jen." Maggie noticed that, as he talked, he put his arm around her and a small dose of that same jealousy she had felt a few days ago had resurfaced and jabbed her in the stomach. "Jen, this is Maggie."

Jen was very pretty – dirty blonde hair; nice, slender yet slightly athletic body; and a nice smile. What stood out most about her, though, were her different-colored eyes: one hazel, one blue. Overall, this girl seemed very nice, which made Maggie wonder if Tom was just your average, superficial college guy, only going after the hot girls.

"Nice to meet you," Maggie shook her hand. "Where did you two meet?"

They both looked at each other with sidelong glances and laughter slowly trickled out of their smiling mouths. Standing close together with Jen, Tom answered, "It's funny. We got stuck on an elevator together."

"What? Where?" Maggie asked, amused.

"Remember that television internship I told you about?" Tom asked.

"Yeah, the internship at channel eight news."

"Well, we didn't know it while we were in the elevator but we were both on our way up to interview for the same position. We didn't talk to each other until - BAM! - the elevator suddenly stopped and the emergency lights came on."

"Ohmygod," Maggie said. "You must've been freakin' out!"

"Yeah, a little," Jen admitted. "But once we started talking, I felt so comfortable." Jen looked over to Tom, who was beaming a smile back at her, and her smile uncontrollably grew longer as she continued, "We talked for hours and kinda just ... clicked."

Maggie's stare looked almost vacant as her jealousy turned to sadness. She wished she hadn't of taken Tom and his affection for granted. Just then, Tom's cell phone rang.

"Sorry, I gotta take this real quick," he said as he put the phone to his ear and stepped back.

Jen turned to Maggie and said, "You like him, don't

you?"

That question snapped Maggie out of her self-pitying trance. She wasn't sure whether Jen's question meant as a friend or romantically and she became nervous that Jen was going to find out her true feelings for Tom. Maggie said, "Wh-wh-what!?"

"You like him, don't you?" Jen unabashedly repeated. "I know he's a good friend."

"Yeah," she answered as if to say, *Yeah, what's it to you and where are you going with this?* "We've been friends for a while."

Jen didn't pick up on Maggie's tone, just the word "friends," and continued in her usual upbeat, but sensitive, way. "I can tell. All of Tom's friends have a really close bond to him. I can tell whenever I meet them."

On the inside, Maggie sighed a heavy breath of relief. This girl was absolutely clueless and Tom deserved a lot better. But then, Jen said something that made Maggie take back what she had just thought.

"Ya know, it's funny," Jen remarked. "Before meeting Tom, I was always going after the wrong kind of guys. They were either jerks who were just looking to get me in bed or guys who I thought I could fix their problems. Those guys seemed to put on this front of being kind and supportive and sensitive. But when I met him, he just seemed so ... genuine. I could tell he didn't have any hidden agenda. We just have this ... connection. I can't explain it any other way."

Maggie looked over with eyes of adoration to Tom, speaking on his phone. Not only was this girl, Jen, really nice, but she was making Maggie realize that Tom was a great guy. And now she was kicking herself for overlooking someone so great that had been right in front of her all this time.

Tom hung up his phone and came back to the two young women. "Jen, that was Jack. He said he'll meet us at the movies in ten minutes, so we better get going."

"Oh, OK." She turned back to Maggie and extended her hand. "It was nice meeting you, Maggie."

Jealous of Jen even more now and feeling a bit sorry for herself, Maggie forced a smile. "It was nice meeting you too, Jen."

Tom came over and gave Maggie a friendly hug, all the while, Maggie was nearly clinging on to him for dear life. He stepped back and said, "Well, it was good runnin' into you. We'll see you around."

"Sure." She watched them walk off together, hand in hand. "I'll see ya around!"

* * *

Still embracing Tom, Maggie looked up at her husband, smiled and said, "Hey, hangover. How'd you sleep?"

"Good," he shrugged.

"You looked so comfortable sleeping; I didn't want to wake you."

Tom knew that there was no time better than now to tell his wife the unfortunate news, so he started with a smile. "I wish you had. Then I could've missed Dylan's call."

"Why?" She backed away and asked, "Is he still bothering you with business stuff?"

"Yeah," Tom sounded exasperated. "It looks like I might have to do this live show for the fiftieth episode."

"Tom. You promised you were gonna slow down after the Emmys." Maggie could see that Tom was just as disappointed and she didn't want to seem like a nag, so she softened her voice. "I thought we were going to try and start a family." Although she didn't mean to, her frustration couldn't help but leak out. "I mean, isn't that still the plan?"

"Of course it is! You know I want a family just as much as you do. But I wanna make sure we've got enough money so we don't have to worry when the baby comes."

Maggie couldn't argue with him on that; she didn't want to be one of those parents who didn't plan ahead for her baby's future. Still, she knew that all the baby would really need was what she and Tom already had: love.

"I can understand you're worried, Tom. But our baby'll be loved. And isn't that what's most important?"

Tom looked long and hard into her delicate eyes and could tell she was on the verge of crying. The truth was: Maggie looked to Tom for support in every way and he liked that she needed him in this way. It wasn't that she was too weak or indecisive to make her own decisions; Maggie had always been a strong-willed woman. Nevertheless, she had needs just like any other woman. She wanted to be loved for who she was, she wanted to be held, she wanted to be treated with respect and she wanted someone who would stand by her side no matter what life threw at her.

"You're right. But right now, we don't have to worry about a baby. So that'll give me time to work on this episode. After that, I promise I'll take a break," he continued, giving her a strong hug, "and then we can start on that family."

Maggie knew this was important to Tom, but for the past year-and-a-half she felt nothing but distance between them. Although they had plenty of bonding moments, there was still an underlying rift between them.

She knew she had deeply hurt him in college, but after they started dating, she thought that hurt had died. Although Tom tried his best to let go of that hurt, there was still that painful knowledge in the back of his head.

"Alright," Maggie hesitantly started, then smiled. "But if my parents ask tonight about grandchildren, you're the one who's gonna have to answer to them."

There are some moments in life when you have an "oh shit moment" – or OSM, for short. The first that Tom could remember was when he was nine and spilled his cherry slushee drink all over his father's brand new, tan leather interior of his car. The next was when he was eleven and he wet his sleeping bag while at his first sleepover. The third was getting caught cheating in high school on a physics mid-term. There were many after that and in college; too many to name. But after college, he hadn't had too many "oh shit moments." He had managed to play it all cool and have pretty good luck ... up until this moment. This was definitely his first post-college "OSM."

Maggie took Tom's silence as a bad thing and instantly asked, "You do remember that we're seeing my parents tonight, don't you?"

"Of course, I do," Tom lied. "But I forget what time we're going over there."

Maggie backed away from Tom's embrace and said, "You don't remember making plans!"

"Yes, I do!"

"No, you don't," Maggie practically laughed. "Or you'd know that my parents are coming over here!"

Tom turned away, mumbling in a whisper, "Damn!"

"Don't tell me you already have something planned for tonight."

"Well ... when I was on the phone with Dylan, he wanted to come by tonight to go over the show."

Knowing Dylan's sense of humor around older people, the idea alone of him spending time with her parents was horrible to Maggie. "Oh, no! There's no way Dylan is coming here while my parents are here."

"It's OK. I'm sure it's nothing too important. I'll just reschedule."

Tom knew that ever since their wedding, Maggie was stern when it came to Dylan being around her parents. Not only did her parents have to stomach his perverted, sick humor, but they also had to look on as Dylan's hand disappeared under the table, where his date's legs were, and his arm was making slow, sharp movements while his date tried her best to stifle her moans of ecstasy. Fortunately, her parents didn't seem to notice what was going on, but the entire incident was embarrassing, nonetheless. Since then, Maggie understandably didn't want Dylan around her parents.

"I'll give him a call now and tell him," Tom said as he picked up the phone and started dialing.

The phone rang five times before Dylan finally picked up on the other end, sounding as if he were fumbling to grasp the phone, saying, "Hello? What!?"

"Dylan, this is Tom."

"Hey, Tom. What's goin' on? I'm looking forward to our meeting tonight."

"Yeah, about that, I'm gonna have to reschedule."

"Reschedule!? Why? What's going on? Is Maggie giving you a hard time about it?"

"No! It's just that ... I forgot we're supposed to have dinner with her parents tonight and it's something we planned long ago."

"Yeah, but, that was *before* you won an Emmy, Tom. We really gotta start planning our next move with the show and your career!"

"I know, Dylan. But I'm not gonna put this off. This is my family!" Tom found himself getting a little heated so he quieted down and said in a softer tone, "Besides, it's my show and it's not like they can do much without me. I promise, we'll meet tomorrow night."

"Tom, buddy. No offense, but – first off – they're not your family. They're Maggie's family. Secondly, if we don't get started on this thing A.S.A.P., we're gonna be left in the cancellation dust with nothing to hold on to except for each other's dicks. Now, again, no offense, but I'm more of a winning-awards, pussy-eatin'-kinda-man myself and I know you are too."

Tom almost had to laugh at his friend because at times like these, that's all he could do. Dylan's logic, although insane, was somewhat right. However, Tom knew he could wait. "Dylan," he almost laughed. "It's gonna be fine. Nothing's happening without me so just calm down, take Lucia out tonight and we'll get together tomorrow."

Unfortunately for Dylan, Tom was right. The network and the other producers couldn't do a thing without his say-so. And there was no way of convincing Tom otherwise. Dylan remained quiet and Tom knew he had won this round.

"Now, I'll see you tomorrow, OK?" Tom concluded.

There was still a silence which Tom took as Dylan being annoyed and throwing his own little temper-tantrum. "See ya tomorrow, man."

* * *

Dylan sat in his black Cadillac CTS sedan convertible (the newest model) as he pressed the phone disconnect button on his steering wheel, ending the call. The warm, southern California wind whipped through his sandy-colored hair as his topless Caddy gunned down a windy side road along the high, green hills of the coast, overlooking the beach, and the radio blared Robin Thicke's "Blurred Lines." Despite the extremely pleasant sensation in his crotch area that Lucia was currently giving him, Dylan wanted nothing now but to go over to Tom's house and yell at him about what a huge mistake he was making. The idea of Tom picking his in-laws over his best friend enraged him all the more. Even the fact that he had just cum didn't lighten his mood.

Seeing a red light up ahead, Dylan Vaughn slammed on his brakes to stop, sending Lucia off of him and flying into the front console, almost accidentally honking the horn.

"Owwww!" she yelled.

This briefly entertained Dylan and made him stifle an uncontrollable laugh as he faked a serious tone, "Damn red light!"

Lucia popped her head up and said, "What the hell!?"

"Sorry, honey," Dylan faked as she quickly fixed her hair only to have it whip back in the wind. "But you were getting me off and I didn't notice the light had changed."

Dylan lied, hoping that the music he had playing in the car was too loud near her ears so that she didn't hear the conversation he had just had with Tom.

"You sure it had nothing to do with Tom canceling your plans for tonight?"

Dylan looked at her incredulously. Those ears; those amazing damn ears could hear better than he had thought.

Picking up on his disbelief, Lucia exclaimed, "I'm not deaf *or* dumb, Dylan."

Dylan released an unmanageable smirk and said, "I know, baby. I'm sorry. It's just that this whole thing with my firm and Tom's show is gettin' me so tense. I don't know why he's being so resistant. He knows that my ass is on the line here!"

Lucia buckled herself back in, rested her left hand on his shoulder and said, "Maybe he just needs a little time with Maggie. Sometimes there's a lot of pressure when you win an award like that and people are waiting to see what you'll do next."

"Exactly! That's why he needs to get on the ball with me right now. So we can have a backup in case this anniversary episode comes back to bite us in the ass."

"I'm sure Tom's feeling just as much pressure as you," she offered. "Just give him this one night. You'll see him tomorrow." Lucia looked carefully at the man she loved and saw that he was truly bothered by Tom's decision to spend time with his wife. She continued to think that maybe this job was more important to him than she was; whereas, to Tom, his wife and family were more important as well as the central answer to all of his decisions. With the likely observation, and feeling that she wasn't as important to Dylan, Lucia bowed her head and quietly said, "I'm sure he and Maggie could use some alone-time."

But it wasn't merely a suggestion of Tom's actions so much so that it was Lucia's suggestion of a way for Dylan to treat her. She longed for a few days where Dylan didn't need a fix in the form of work; when it could truly just be the two of them and there were no needs of his to fix.

"It's called rerun season, Lucia." Dylan could've laughed hysterically at Lucia's inexperience with show business. He couldn't believe that she honestly thought that Tom had time to take a break, no matter how deserved it was. "He can take a break this summer. But while the season is still in effect - and sweeps week is fast approaching - he really has to buckle down."

Dylan looked over to his beautiful fiancée - her eyes close to tears and the corners of her lips curved slightly downward - and could tell that she was upset. Even though he didn't exactly know why, it was a look he was all too used to with women. As far back as high school, girls had often made that face after he broke up with them. He thought of the first girl whose virginity he stole - Teri Kelly. Sometimes, remembering her gave Dylan a hard-on even to this day; her perfectly round ass and breasts (the biggest in their class), those lips that looked and tasted like strawberry Starburst candy, her emerald green eyes and long, feathered blonde hair. When he thought of her, he knew that she would be the sweetest of his sexual conquests as he was her first and she was the youngest age (16) he'd probably ever get. But when she overheard that he was trying to also have sex with her fraternal twin sister, Megan, she decided to warn her sister and then break up with him.

Little did she know that during the process of breaking up with Dylan, he would use his manipulative ways on her and she would end up having amazing, rough "I-hate-you-but-still-find-you-utterly-attractive" sex with him. Afterwards, though, with her hair still in disarray and her clothing completely crumpled, she did indeed break up with him. And that was it. That was all it took for Dylan to know that he had what it took to not only get a girl into bed but also end up using them without even having to make a commitment. Ever since Teri Kelly, Dylan Vaughn was a toxic bachelor; a ladies' man. And he'd been hooked ever since.

Dylan noticed the look of sadness in Lucia's face and knew she wanted him to settle down – like Tom seemed to be doing – and have a family. He knew that if he told her the truth – that he wasn't ready to settle down and start a family but still had more in his career he wanted to accomplish – she would leave him. In fact, settling down and having children was the least of his priorities. The way he looked at it, the minute he had kids, he'd be tied down to a life he wasn't sure he wanted in the first place. Still, it was better to have Lucia than not have anyone at all. So he kept up the charade by asking her to marry him. To Lucia, he was this sweet, sensitive guy, who had a savvy business mind, so that was how he had to act with her.

"Lucia," he said in, what he liked to call, his best "sensitive-guy voice," gently placing his right fingers under her droopy chin and slowly lifting her head up to his gaze. "I promise you we'll have time just for the two of us as soon as this season's over." He made sure his stare boar into her brown eyes and softly, but sternly, repeated, "I promise."

Lucia could always feel her heart begin to melt when Dylan so much as looked at her the way he was right now. And when his calm hand caressed her leg, she was immediately soothed. A comforting sigh almost escaped her lips but she stopped it short by speaking.

"I know," she said. "It just seems so far away, is all."

If Dylan could roll his eyes without Lucia noticing, he would. This topic surfaced one too many times whenever the two of them were alone. He just didn't want to hear about it anymore. Her insecurities were beginning to irritate him but he always remembered how good Lucia made him feel. And he didn't want to lose that; it was what was most important to him. So, yet again, he played Mr. Sensitive and calmed her down.

"I know it does," he affirmed in a supportive, soft voice that didn't hint his actual thoughts or feelings in the slightest bit. "But, you'll see. Once this season's over, we'll have a wonderful wedding. Our families will be there and you'll be beautiful, like always."

Lucia felt comforted by her lover's words and she displayed this by snuggling up as close to his shoulder and chest as possible, her lilac perfume filling his nostrils all too quickly before being blown away with the whipping wind. Dylan rested his head on hers and found the right opportunity to express his true feelings: he rolled his eyes.

3.

"Some love is just a lie of the heart –
The cold remains of what began with a passionate start
And they may not want it to end
But it will; it's just a question of when"

--Billy Joel
"A Matter of Trust"

"All I'm sayin' is: we better be eatin' steak!" Edward Russell grumbled. He looked at his watch and saw that it was seven o'clock. Seeing how he hadn't eaten since 1:30, it was no wonder his stomach was rumbling so loudly and practically doing somersaults.

"I'm sure that whatever they have will be fine, Eddie," Brenda Russell snapped back.

Without swiveling his head, Edward's eyes looked over to the passenger seat where his wife of thirty-five years was sitting. Even though his look might make the usual stranger uncomfortable and intimidated, his wife, Brenda, knew that it was merely a façade and she wasn't intimidated in the least. She had met Edward when they were just a couple of idealistic teenagers and had married right out of high school.

Brenda looked over to her husband; the years had aged him quite a bit - having two kids does that. His hair was beginning to thin and what was once a very dark brown was now beginning to be invaded by varying shades of grey and white. He didn't have many wrinkles but was heavier and his speed of movement showcased his age. His smoker's voice – acquired by smoking since the age of fifteen – was gravelly and scared most of Maggie's potential boyfriends when the girl was younger. But Tom was the one boyfriend who wasn't intimidated by the older man's voice; he thought it gave the man character and made the telling of his jokes all the more funny.

Looking at her husband, noticing his age, only made Brenda notice her age as well. When people saw any picture of her when she was Maggie's age, they often commented on how much Maggie looked like her. Her strawberry blonde hair had grown slightly darker with streaks of light grey poking out in various places. The general consensus of people who said that men age better than women obviously didn't take Brenda Russell into account; she was still attractive, like the actress Blythe Danner. And no matter how much her husband mumbled under his breath or rolled his eyes at her slight nagging, he was still completely in love with her.

"The man's an award-winning producer and he can't afford a good steak?" Eddie grumbled.

"You know that Tom loves steak just as much as you do; it's our daughter who's not big on meat," Brenda said.

Eddie flashed a sidelong smile, slightly raised his eyebrows and mumbled, "Defending the boy."

Brenda chose to ignore his comment. The truth was: she knew she defended Tom. But it was only because she knew he was a good young man and he made a good life for their daughter. How could she not stick up for him? After all, most of her defensive comments were truth. In this case, Maggie *was* the one who often didn't cook – let alone, buy – steak.

While Eddie was quick to blame anyone for any shortcomings they may have – especially his son-in-law – he was extremely hesitant to blame his daughter. But Brenda was different. She knew Tom and Maggie had a beautiful balance going between them where one complimented the other: yin and yang. Ever since Tom and Maggie were married, Brenda had always seen a bit of Eddie and herself in them. She noticed it back when her daughter had first introduced Tom to them as her boyfriend.

The young man had been so nervous to meet them and Brenda could tell by his shaky voice and cumbersome body language. Usually, people like that rubbed her husband Eddie the wrong way – especially if they were dating his daughter. However, to Brenda's surprise, Eddie had found the guy sincere and down-to-earth; two qualities he admired in any person.

She looked over to her husband and saw him sitting in a slouch, driving the car with one steady hand on the wheel and the other hand resting halfway out the rolled-down window. It was these kinds of small moments, the ones that meant nothing in particular, when Brenda realized how much she loved her husband. This epiphany often dawned on her in the most peculiar moments; when he made a funny look or noise he didn't know he was making; or the way he slept facedown as if he was going to suffocate himself at any minute, but was always comfortably fine and the first one up the next morning. There were many minute traits of his that Brenda found adorable and she hoped that her daughter would find the same adorable kinds of traits in the man she married.

"He's a good man, Eddie," she softly confirmed.

"Yeah," Eddie half-mumbled then softened his tone. "He ain't bad."

When Eddie and Brenda's shiny, silver PT Cruiser pulled into the driveway of Tom and Maggie's home, Maggie was racing around, picking up any loose, scattered articles of clothing, papers, magazines or anything else lying around the house. Whenever Maggie's mom came to visit, she always grew self-conscious regarding the appearance of her home. Maybe it was because the slightly displeased look her mother flashed whenever she came in and saw any mess whatsoever. Maggie was never sure why; she simply owned it up to the fact that most mothers were that way.

Truthfully, the only reason Brenda had come out that way was because her mother and her mother before her were both that way. They believed that the way a woman kept her home was an important reflection of how that woman carried herself. And even though Maggie vowed that she would never be that way with her daughter, she probably would turn out that way out of an unconscious habit.

"They're here," Maggie heard Tom shout from the front window in the living room.

Tom's announcement slightly startled Maggie and she accidentally dropped a few shirts, but instantly swooped them back up off the floor and threw the wrinkled pile into her closet.

For Tom, he didn't preoccupy himself too much with the state of their home but anyone would've thought that Maggie was cleaning up for the arrival of the President or some famous movie star; she frantically cleaned and picked up so quickly that Tom swore she looked like that little tornado that the Tasmanian Devil in the *Looney Tunes* cartoons turned into whenever he'd wreak havoc. Whereas most men would probably be annoyed by this cleaning tirade, and turn their frustration toward their mother-in-law, Tom found this side of Maggie cute.

Tom saw the couple headed for the front door and met them there, opening the door for them, as Brenda came through the door first, followed closely by Eddie.

"Hello, Mr. Emmy-award-winner," Brenda chimed, sounding almost like a doorbell, then giving Tom a kiss on the cheek.

"Hi," Tom greeted back, returning a kiss to his mother-in-law. He looked straight from her to Eddie's stoic face. "Hey, Mr. Russell, I got a nice marinated steak waiting for you in the fridge."

Eddie's face perked up into a smile at his son-in-law's surprise. "Ya got any beer?" he asked.

"Sure," Tom said. "I'll go get you one. Mrs. Russell, would you like anything?"

"Oh, no ... thanks, Tom." Brenda studied the not-so-clean state of the couple's house and asked, "Is Maggie running around?"

Tom popped his head out from behind the wall that separated the kitchen from the living room, shrugged his shoulder and said, "You know how she gets when we have company."

Brenda let out a small laugh and asked, "How're your parents, Tom?" She looked around the living room, inconspicuously running her finger along the coffee table to check for dust, and continued, "They must be so absolutely proud of you."

"They're good," Tom said, bringing out two Warsteiner beers and opening them. He handed one to Eddie and took a swig from the other. Tom wanted to tell the truth. He wanted to tell how his father hadn't even watched the event to see him get the award. Tom knew Maggie had most likely told her parents about his issues with his parents – especially his father and how he felt he couldn't talk to the man – but he didn't want to bring it up now. He was in too good a mood. "My dad is ... well ... he's my dad. But, overall, they're doing well."

"They must be so thrilled for you!"

Tom always considered himself a humble, modest guy and hated talking about himself in a self-congratulatory manner, but he couldn't resist this time. "Yeah, they're happy."

Although Tom liked his in-laws, he didn't really like making small-talk with them; he felt the act was a sign of someone who didn't really have much to say but felt like they had to in order to make up for the uncomfortable silences. Brenda Russell was the queen of small-talk. She always had something to say about something – the weather, the President, songs on the radio, you name it ... Brenda had her thoughts.

"Listen to youuu," Brenda dragged out, still gushing over her son-in-law's achievement. "*So* modest!"

Eddie rolled his eyes in slight annoyance at his wife and

her gushing. He always loved her but they were both definite opposites when it came to their approach on life; while Eddie was more of an introvert, Brenda was the extrovert.

"Give the boy a break, Brenda!" Eddie exclaimed. "Go see what's taking Maggie so long." He heard his stomach rumble. "I'm starving!"

Brenda heeded her husband's suggestion and got up to search the main bedroom for Maggie. As she neared the back main bedroom, Brenda could distinctly make out the faintest sound of her daughter sobbing. She neared the source of the crying – the bathroom door off of the bedroom – and noticed it was closed. When she tried to open it, the doorknob wouldn't budge; it was locked.

Brenda grew concerned for Maggie and gently knocked on the door.

The crying immediately stopped and a hushed voice called, "Yeah?"

"Maggie? It's your mother. Are you OK?"

It took Maggie a while to respond but she did. "Yeah, I'm fine! I'll be out in a few minutes."

"A few minutes? Maggie, can I come in?"

Maggie's hesitation was all the evidence Brenda needed to know that something was wrong with her daughter. She waited for any word but there was no sound. After a minute, the single lock clicked back and Brenda knew that she was now allowed to come into the bathroom.

A disheveled young woman whom she hardly recognized sat on the toilet in front of her. Maggie's reddish hair was in disarray and the black mascara that accentuated her blue eyes was running from the tears streaming down her pale cheeks. She looked up at her mother with dread and fear.

"Honey?" Brenda said. "What's wrong?"

Maggie didn't know quite how to tell her mother. Of all people, she would think she could tell her. But the thought of confessing only made her feel more ashamed. So she said the only thing she thought she could say through her sobs.

"I messed up real bad, Mom." With those words, Maggie broke down crying even harder.

Brenda knelt down beside her sad daughter, put an arm around her and said, "Aww, honey, just tell me what's wrong and we'll see if we can't fix it."

If only it were that simple, Maggie thought. She calmed herself and wearily looked straight ahead at the blank white wall, trying to catch her breath, trying her best to gather up enough courage to tell her mother the truth.

"Ya know," her mother began, "Your father and I didn't always get along. We had many problems back when we first started out. No one would think it now ... or back then, for that matter. We were prom king and queen. Got married right outta high school – at the end of July. But we had our problems, even split up for a little while."

Maggie was surprised to hear her mother's admission. This was the first time her mother had ever told her about this. "What happened?" she asked, beginning to stifle her tears.

Brenda beamed a bright, shining smile and gently said, "We found out we were having you." She hugged Maggie and continued, "Things were great from then on, and they have been for the past thirty-one years."

Looking in her mother's eyes, Maggie simply could not force the words out that she longed to now admit to her. She remained quiet and calmed herself until her tears were merely a sniffle and she ripped a tissue from its box, wiping once across her eyes and nose.

"It's OK." Maggie's mood alarmingly shifted from hysterics to tranquility. "I'll work it out, Mom."

"Are you sure, honey?" Brenda Russell seemed most alarmed. "You were hysterical just a moment ago! Are you sure there's nothing wrong?"

Maggie forced a smile upon her face and answered, "Nothing that can't be fixed." She lifted herself off the toilet seat, swept past her mother, opening the bathroom door and said, "C'mon, let's get back to the guys before they start eating the furniture."

Brenda remained knelt down, wondering what her daughter was really hiding from her and her family. She knew it had to be something drastic to cause such a reaction in Maggie.

However, she wouldn't worry about it just now. If her daughter didn't find it important enough to tell her, then she could only assume it wasn't too important. She lifted herself off the bathroom floor and walked into the family room to find Eddie and Tom sitting on the couch, drinking their beers and making small-talk about the Boston Red Sox's latest season. Maggie had quickly composed herself and joined them.

"When do you think the food will be ready, honey?" Brenda asked Maggie.

"In a few minutes," Maggie chimed in. "It's just taking a little longer for Dad's Porterhouse."

Brenda glared at her husband, knowing that his trivial preferences would cause the rest of them to starve, but still preoccupied by her daughter's behavior. What was she hiding? She looked over to her son-in-law and, looking him over, almost felt sorry for him. He had no idea that his wife was hiding something from all of them; something that was significant enough to drive Maggie to tears.

The doorbell rang, snapping Brenda out of her train of thought. "I'll get it," Maggie shouted. She rushed to the door and swung the door open, her face fading from its usually sunny demeanor to disgust as she saw Dylan standing in front of her.

"Hey Maggie!" Dylan shined one of his toothy, shit-eating grins that just made Maggie want to vomit. "Can Tom come out to play?"

Maggie rolled her eyes at Dylan's attempt at humor and pushed the door open wider for Dylan to step inside. "Behave!" she raised an accusatory finger to him. "My parents are here!"

Dylan raised his hands with palms showing as if he were being arrested and laughed out, "It'll be really quick, I promise."

"I bet that's not the first time you've told a woman that." Maggie could barely hold back her smile, turning it into a smirk as she walked by him and into the living room to get her husband.

Maggie entered the living room with an air of urgency and annoyance. And that was all Tom needed to see to know that Dylan was at the door. He arose off the couch and rushed to the front door.

"I'll make sure he leaves soon, I promise," Tom said as he rushed past his wife.

Tom shuffled to the front door and saw Dylan standing

with his phone, yelling at someone about the show staying in the current time slot. "No, no, no, Bill! The ten o'clock spot is ours! If the network tries to push us up to eight or nine, the censors are gonna be on our ass to change our format. If we change the format, we lose the trash that audiences love. If we lose that, we lose the audience. And if we lose the audience, we're done!"

Dylan saw Tom appear and held up a finger, giving him a nod. "Call me back in fifteen minutes with better news or I'll be coming in! And you know how much I hate to come in on Saturdays!!!"

Dylan jabbed his finger onto the off button on his cell phone and slammed it into his inside sports jacket pocket. "Hey, Tom," he greeted, slightly rolling his eyes in annoyance. "Bill was just telling me how since we won the Emmy, the network execs wanna try and move our time slot up to eight or nine o'clock. I'm tellin' ya, Tom – if they do that, we're done for! The FCC's not gonna let us get away with half as much cussing or violence if we're in one of those spots."

Tom stood in silent contemplation, which Dylan always found annoying. Both of Tom's legs were planted firmly on the ground with his right hand up to his face, his pointing finger and thumb cupping his chin, while his left arm crossed horizontally across his torso, his hand holding his right elbow. His brow slightly frowned as he thought of the situation and what might be best for the show. It was only about a minute or so before Tom spoke.

"You're absolutely right, Dylan. Even though I hate to admit that our show's ratings are based on fighting-bordering-on-domestic-violence, not to mention, excessive cussing, it's true. If we move time slots, we're finished. I won't budge on this and neither should you or anyone else on the show. Tell all the execs that."

"Already done," Dylan announced reassuringly, beaming with satisfaction at his own act.

Tom honestly didn't know how to feel about Dylan's take-charge business style. He didn't want anyone else on the show – or at the network – to think that Dylan was the one making the calls. However, Dylan did make good business decisions; Tom was pretty sure that if it weren't for Dylan, they wouldn't have won the Emmy.

"Good," Tom replied almost cautiously. "Anything else?"

"Yeah," Dylan said as he grabbed his smartphone and checked it for messages. "It looks like we have a great 'vic' for the fiftieth episode."

"Good to hear. Male or female?"

"Female. But we have to make sure her story clears. I'll let you know if it does or not."

Anyone in the reality TV business knew that female contestants were a lot better for ratings; their emotions often caused outbursts of melodrama that hooked audiences and kept them just addicted enough to tune in each week. Whether the woman was a flat-out bitch or the wholesome girl-next-door, they made great watercooler talk fodder. Whether over-the-top or justified, reactions of women from reality television were golden for ratings. And ratings were what kept them above everyone else. That's how they won awards and made a living.

The truth was, though, that lately, Tom was unsure if how he was making his living was the most moral way. In fact, while editing the past few episodes, Tom noticed during what they referred to as the "money shot" that his work was somewhat demoralizing. The money shot was the moment in the show when the wronged significant other was shown physical proof – either via video or in person – that their significant other was cheating on them with someone else. When that money shot came on screen, Tom could see it in their eyes. In fact, he'd often pause the footage to see it and focus on it. The soul-crushing defeat of a harsh reality that the real life they had been living with someone they thought had truly loved them was all a farce, a lie that their special someone was sneaking around behind their back. And to make matters worse, it was aired on national television with an audience of at least three billion people watching their heart getting broken. The poor saps; nine times out of ten they didn't even know what hit 'em.

"Is this our only lead so far?" Tom asked.

"Yeah."

"Dylan! You know how much I don't like only having one 'vic' for a show. Especially our season finale of all shows!"

"Don't worry, Tom!" Dylan reassured in his mocking, holier-than-thou voice that Tom simply hated. "Everything's under control. This lead is a sure thing."

"Dylan, you more than anyone knows that, in this business, there is no such thing as a sure thing."

Dylan had to fight from rolling his eyes in annoyance. "Tom, how many times do I have to tell ya? You have to trust me. Why would I take stupid chances if I wasn't a hundred percent sure that they were gonna pay off? I mean, why would I sink a ship I'm sailing on?"

Tom rolled his eyes at Dylan's metaphor. "I know, Dylan." Tom glanced down at the floor, rubbing his forehead. "But I'm sure you can understand why I want this to go off without a hitch."

By the time Tom stared back at Dylan, Dylan was back on his cell phone. He noticed Tom was looking back at him, expecting him to say something. Dylan placed his free hand over the talk piece.

"Don't worry about it, Tom," he whispered as he approached the door and opened it. "I want you to go back in there and enjoy your family. I'll take care of it."

Before Tom could say anything else, Dylan was out the door and already pulling his car out of the driveway. He caught a glimpse of Lucia in the passenger seat, looking back at him with a look of yearning to be anywhere but waiting in that car. Tom raised his hand and gave a slight wave; Lucia's grimace turned to a bright smile as she gave a small wave back.

Outside, Dylan peered back toward Lucia and waited for the person on the other end of his phone to pick up. The person on the other end answered and Dylan smiled as he said, "I just met with him. He's on board." The other person spoke and Dylan said, "Yeah, I told you I'd get his approval. Now let's get this thing going." Dylan eyed Lucia and thought how great she was in bed. Just the look of her was starting to get him horny and he slightly licked his lips like a hungry wolf about to feast on a lamb. His attention drew back to the caller. "Yeah, I'll call you back in a half hour." He looked again at Lucia, who had one of her luscious legs propped up on the door as she was checking for blemishes or spots she missed when she shaved, and the sight made Dylan even hotter for her. "Better make that an hour."

Tom stepped back into the dining room to find Maggie and her parents sitting at the table, about to eat.

"What was that all about?" Maggie asked Tom.

Tom smiled. "You know Dylan. Always thinking business."

"Yeah," Maggie snidely remarked. "Always."

"Are you already starting on the show?" Brenda asked.

"Unfortunately, yes," Tom answered.

"But I thought you had at least three months before you started production again," Brenda said.

"We usually do, but since winning the Emmy, the execs really want us to focus on this fiftieth episode special. There's a lot of pressure to get this show up to the kind of ratings *American Idol* brought in when it debuted."

"Well, that's understandable," Brenda said. "You want to keep the show going for as long as possible. People really seem to like it. But, Tom, you never told us how you came up with the idea."

Tom became quiet as he looked over to Maggie, thinking of that day in college when he saw her lying with Alex on the grass, flirting and kissing. The truth was that that moment was when Tom first dreamt up the idea for *Heartbrakers*. He remembered the pain and anguish he felt by seeing someone he cared about – and with whom he thought he had a relationship – with someone else. Tom felt that no one should be lied to and cheated on when they were doing everything they could in the relationship. And after seeing the popularity with MTV's *The Real World*, and the drama that it broadcasts, Tom got the idea of putting these cheaters on the air so that people could see that there are others who are cheated on, and show how they deal with the knowledge of a loved one being unfaithful. While most ruled it off as intrusive reality television, Tom saw the show as a way of helping out others, realizing that this wasn't some no-name statistic getting cheated on; this was a real person who devoted their life to someone only to see that someone going behind their back, lying to them and sleeping with another. When those people cried, those weren't ratings or statistics to Tom; they were real people whose lives were crumbling apart. Again, he thought of Maggie and that day.

"I can't remember," Tom meekly answered as he looked back to his wife.

All four of them got quiet at the table, leaving a very uncomfortable silence. Eddie looked from face to face and noticed something wasn't right. He saw that Maggie was especially looking guilty or ashamed of something.

"Somebody wanna tell me what the hell is going on?" Eddie asked.

"Oh, Eddie," his wife exclaimed. "Don't be ridiculous! Everything's fine! Just eat your steak."

Eddie shrugged his shoulders and returned to eating his plentiful meal. Maggie looked over to her mother and gave her a slight nod - a silent thank you - for not making Maggie's mysterious predicament public. Brenda flashed a quick smile and returned to eating her meal as if nothing had happened a few moments ago in the bathroom.

A clatter of a fork hitting a plate resonated in the dining room and everyone looked to Maggie, who was holding her stomach. Maggie's pain briefly flashed across her face in a wincing expression before returning to normal as she assured everyone she was OK with a smile. "Sorry," she said. "But I suddenly lost my appetite. I have to go to the bathroom."

She politely excused herself and walked to the bathroom as Eddie glared at Brenda, knowing something was definitely not right. "You were in the back with her a few moments ago, Brenda. What the hell is going on?"

Brenda looked at her husband squarely in the eyes and gave a slight shrug, saying, "I honestly don't know. I don't think she's feeling well." Brenda then looked over to Tom, whose look gave away that he was just as perplexed as the both of them. "Tom. Do you know what's going on?"

Tom leaned back in his chair, trying to think of anything that might be off. Other than Dylan's brief interruption, nothing out of the ordinary came to mind. "No. I better check and see if she's OK. Excuse me."

Tom got up from the table and walked upstairs, through their bedroom, and back to their bathroom. The door was closed. He grabbed the knob and twisted. Locked. He softly knocked on the door.

"Maggie? Are you OK?"

He could hear a distinct noise of Maggie blowing her nose and then the toilet flushed. "I'm ... I'm fine," she answered from behind the closed door.

"Are you sure? You left the table pretty abruptly."

"Yeah. Sorry. I suddenly wasn't feeling too well." The door lock clicked and the door swung open to show Maggie standing in front of him with a smile as she leaned in to give him a quick kiss on the lips. "But I'm better now."

She was walking past him when he grasped her hand

and gently drew her back to him. "I promise after this episode is shot we can start working on making that family."

Tom leaned in and his chapped lips caressed her silky smooth lips, a passionate kiss flooding over, filling them both with a euphoric feeling.

"Maybe we don't have to wait so long," Tom mused.

Maggie leaned back from their kiss and asked awe-struck, "You mean, here!? Now!?"

A big grin graced Tom's face as his hands slid up his wife's legs and back to her butt.

"But ... my parents!" Maggie exclaimed, almost turned on by Tom's audacity.

"We can make it quick," Tom practically begged. Maggie's smile grew so long that she had to bite her lip to suppress a laugh.

"Alriiiiight," she said. Tom turned on the iPod and the middle of The Rolling Stones' "Rocks Off" blasted as he started unbuttoning his pants, and Maggie flung her blouse over her head. "But we *have* to make it quick. And try not to moan. The neighbors complained last time."

"I make no promises," Tom said as he swept her back into the bathroom and kissed Maggie, who began to burst out laughing. He slammed the door shut and locked the door, leaving Maggie's parents to wait downstairs.

Eddie sat at the table, gobbling down his food as if it sat too long, someone would take it away from him. He looked over to his wife and could instantly recognize the concerned look on her face. Muffled rock music sounded from upstairs and Brenda carried on through her concern.

"I guess whatever it was," he spoke through his chewing,

"they worked it out."

"I guess ...," Brenda spoke apprehensively. However, deep down inside, she knew that there was more going on than her daughter was admitting. Brenda only hoped that whatever it was, Maggie would find a way to work it out either with Tom or on her own before either one of them got hurt.

A few minutes later, a disheveled Maggie entered the room, straightening her blouse, with Tom following closely behind her. Maggie's parents noticed the smiles on their faces and Brenda was a little more at ease with her previous concerns.

"Everything OK?" Suppressing a smile as best he could, Eddie looked from Maggie to his wife.

Maggie smiled back with her reply, "Yeah. Sorry we were gone for a while. How's everything?"

"It's great," Eddie said, swallowing the last piece of his steak.

"Did you straighten everything out?" Brenda asked her daughter.

"Yeah," Maggie answered.

Brenda should've let it go and been relieved by her daughter's simple, direct answer, but she wasn't. Maggie had always been a secretive person – even when she was a child. Her older brother, Dave, was popular through school, while she was quiet and shy. She was always distant from her older brother, often because of her feeling as if she couldn't talk to him about her personal life and, therefore, never really bonded with him the way they both would've liked.

Brenda knew that things with her daughter were

anything but alright, but she also knew there was nothing she could do to force the truth out of her. All she could do was stand by her and hope that one day soon Maggie would tell the entire truth when she was ready and comfortable.

Maggie didn't want her husband to drift away from her but she could feel that every day she kept her secret from him, their relationship couldn't help but be distant. There were nights when it all caught up to her and she'd often silently cry herself to sleep. But now, matters had gotten worse. She had to confront her problem and hope that her marriage would survive.

4.

"Now a life of leisure and a pirate's treasure
Don't make much for tragedy
But it's a sad man, my friend, who's livin' in his own skin
And can't stand the company."

--Bruce Springsteen
"Better Days"

Tom arrived at the network studios to see Dylan talking with a small group of men and women who they so affectionately referred to as "suits." These people were the executives – the people in charge of the network and its programming, even though most of them had no clue as to what makes for good television.

Dylan ever-so-slightly peered over one of the suits' shoulders to see Tom walking toward them and he flashed his big, toothy grin and said, "Well, thanks, gentlemen! We'll talk about this later."

The suits turned around and saw Tom approaching them. Tom noticed Dylan leaning in to whisper something to them and then back away, as the rest of them disbanded.

"What was that all about?" Tom asked his friend.

Dylan let out an annoyed sigh and said, "They're still on my ass about moving up our time slot."

Tom became aggravated that they didn't see what he and Dylan saw: a ratings killer to their show which would ultimately and inevitably lead to its death.

"Did you tell them that we can't afford to do that if we want to respect the FCC's wishes of cutting back on the language and fights? And that it'd be a death sentence for the show?"

"Of course I told them that!" Dylan said. "Look, Tom, that's why we need to move on this live feed for our fiftieth episode. It's our only chance at proving to them that our time slot is perfect and that we can get maximum ratings right where we are now!"

Tom thought about it and looked long and hard at his friend, his frat brother he had known for so long and who had been there for him through all his ups and downs.

"Alright!" Tom said. "But only if this lead checks out. We can't afford to screw this up."

"Of course," Dylan assured him. "We're closing on the deal now as we speak."

"Great. Who is it?"

"Let's go to my office and I can show you her profile."

"Alright," Tom almost sounded resigned.

The two walked to Dylan's swanky office, which would be one you might imagine belonging to some Madison Avenue exec in the late 1950s, although polluted with blowup posters of the latest Hollywood young actresses in their skimpiest clothes out of some magazine like *Maxim*. Some were even autographed! The small computer speakers were in the midst of blasting Butch Walker's song, "Synthesizers." Scattered throughout his office were a lot of CDs and pictures of Dylan with different celebrities: his favorite actors and musicians. It made Tom's office, which was similarly decorated in the classic 1950s-style, seem boring. He had no posters, no pictures with celebrities. He did have a nice 5x7 photo of his wife – his favorite of her – in a green field with the sun about to set, her smile just as bright as the sky.

"Wait 'til I show you this loser," Dylan exclaimed. "It's no wonder her boyfriend is cheating on her."

As he often did, Tom let Dylan's remark fall by the wayside and smirked, "Video?"

"Of course," Dylan answered as he grabbed a small chrome remote control, pointed it to the only wall that wasn't a window, and pressed a button. His book shelves parted to reveal a sixty-inch television screen. "I got the profile right here."

Dylan walked over to his computer, silenced the music, then pressed another button on the remote control and a young girl's face appeared on the screen, pretty had it not been for her puffy and red eyes from timeless bouts of crying. The blues of her pupils stood out amongst the deep red in her eyes as she quickly took her stare from the camera, breaking eye contact. The young woman then turned back to face the camera, her bottom lip trembling as she tried her best to get her words out. She was finally able to open her mouth to speak but all that escaped was a heartfelt sob and she dropped her head in despair. She calmed herself after a moment and drew in a deep breath. When her intake was done, she shot her head up and quietly spoke.

"My name ... is Amy," she mumbled out with a soft cry.

"Name's a fake," Dylan spat out.

"Shhhhh," Tom silenced his friend, leaving Dylan to roll his eyes. Tom often had a soft spot for the women on his show. When their client was a man, Tom and Dylan both agreed on how pathetic he was, thinking that men weren't supposed to cry, especially about relationships; they were supposed to take charge. And if a woman was cheating on them, then he should just leave her and find another woman. But, when the client was a woman, Tom's savior-complex went into overdrive. There was a great empathy within him for wounded women that he tried to fix. Tom had always been that way. And when he got out of college and got into television production, he thought of a way to make money off that yearning to help hurt and scorned women. That's when the final aspect of *Heartbrakers* was founded.

"I'm twenty-two-years-old," the young woman continued. "And I think my boyfriend is cheating on me." Her lower lip and chin quivered harder as her eyes squinted and began to flood with tears again.

"Idon'tknowwhatI'mgonnado," she said in one breath before lifting both her hands to her face and hanging her head, hysterically crying. After a minute or two, Amy composed herself enough to talk again. She looked back up into the camera and said through her sobs, "He says he's going to work or out to a bar with his friends, but I know he's said this on days when he never went into work or his friends said they hadn't seen him."

"I love him so much but I need to know the truth." She

dried her eyes with trembling hands and looked directly into the camera with a sudden stoic conviction, her tears abruptly ceased as if there were no tears left. "We're supposed to get married. I need to know."

Her image paused and Tom looked to Dylan who was standing beside the television with a big smile on his face. Tom didn't know if his job was getting old or if it was just him that was getting old, because he actually felt a pang of heavy sympathy for this young woman. Tom had always felt sorry for his featured guests, but, in the past, he could still separate himself and his deep feelings from the subject matter. Although, now, especially with this woman, he felt a gut-wrenching sorrow as if he were the one being cheated on – as if that was him revealing himself on that television screen.

"This chick is gold!" Dylan's smarmy voice shattered Tom's silent thoughts. "If we get this chick on air, I *guarantee* another Emmy."

"You always say that," Tom rolled his eyes.

"Yeah, but last time I was obviously right!" Dylan shot back.

Tom shot his friend that stern look that Dylan instantly recognized as Tom's disapproving stare. Like a melodramatic teenager, Dylan let out a heavy sigh and rolled his eyes. "Let me guess. Now's the time when your dick reverts back into your ass, you grow a vagina, and I have to be the one to convince you that this is a great case!"

"Dylan, can I talk with you for a moment?" Tom stuck his head out of Dylan's office door and looked around like a meerkat to make sure no one was listening in or close enough to overhear their conversation. "In private?"

Dylan also poked his head out and quickly looked around as if he already knew what Tom was going to say and said, "Sure, buddy." He closed the door, crossed his arms and half sat on his desk. Dylan squinted his eyes to give a concerned look and asked, "What's up?"

"I think ... I'm starting to have ... a crisis of conscience," Tom whispered.

And with those words, Dylan's mind began to panic. *Hell*, it started screaming, *this was the last thing I needed.*

"Tom," Dylan nervously laughed. "What the hell are you talking about? *Crisis of conscience!?* About *what!?*"

Tom continued with caution. "I've - listen - I've been having these nightmares lately."

Dylan could see the seriousness in his friend's face and the humor in his face began to fade. "What do you mean 'nightmares'?"

"Well," Tom was searching for the correct words to describe it. "It's more like a clip show of our show. And I see their faces ..."

"Whose faces!?" Dylan interrupted.

"The vics'. *Our* clients'. The people we say we're helping." Tom's voice began to waver a bit. "I see the pain and the anger. And that's all I see."

Dylan placed his hands on Tom's shoulders, slightly squeezing them as if giving a small massage. "Tom. Calm down, man." He squeezed harder with each word. "Take it easy!" He let go of Tom's shoulders and continued. "You can't be freaking out over *every* client we take on. Most of 'em have such screwed up lives that it's really no surprise that they're on our show. Hell, some of 'em probably deserve it for goin' after jerks and sluts."

Dylan chuckled at his own comment and Tom rubbed his forehead to ease his approaching headache.

Thinking that Tom disagreed with his assessment, Dylan defended his remark. "C'mon, Tom! You've seen the people we confront. Most of 'em are scumbag trash or skanks."

Tom was perturbed by Dylan's opinion but that wasn't the reason for his dismay. By this point, Tom's headache had exploded into unrelenting pain.

"You got any aspirin or anything?" Tom ignored Dylan's previous comment. "My head is killing me."

"Yeah, sure." Dylan reached in his jacket pocket and brought out an orange prescription pill bottle. "Take one of these." He rattled two Percocet onto Tom's palm.

"I just need an aspirin, not Percocet!"

"Hey, man. You say you have nightmares? Bad headaches? I'm just tryin' to help you out here."

Tom looked down at the pills and chuckled as he thumbed them around his palm. "Y'know, I was drinking nearly every night to try and stop the damn dreams. And it worked for a while. Now, it doesn't matter. I still have 'em."

"Take one of these, you'll be flying! Take *two* of these and you'll be floating on a cloud gettin' a blowjob from Kate fuckin' Upton!"

"Who's Kate Upton?"

"*Married* people." Dylan shook his head in shame and disgust. "Google her! Just take 'em." Dylan switched his tone to what almost sounded like a dare. "Why the hell not?"

"Yeah, why the hell not?" Tom asked. He focused harder on the little white pills and popped them into his mouth.

About a half hour later, Tom felt like that famous video footage of Neil Armstrong's 1969 moonwalk, bouncing up and down with each step. His head felt almost like a balloon but at least it didn't feel like a jackhammer was burrowing into it. In fact, Tom wasn't feeling much of anything but a little bit of euphoria.

"How's that head of yours?" Dylan asked with a grin when he entered Tom's office.

"Not bad," Tom shined back a small smile. "What's up?"

"I needed to get your final decision about that Amy girl I was talking to you about. For the fiftieth episode?" Tom still wasn't quite sure what Dylan was talking about. "The season finale?"

Tom knew he was high but still couldn't quite understand why his thinking was so muddled. It took him a couple of minutes before he realized who Dylan was talking about. Then, it struck like lightning. "Oh!"

Dylan rolled his eyes as Tom said, "Yeah, yeah! Right!"

Tom stopped speaking, trying his best to remember his conversation with Dylan just an hour ago. He knew he was a bit upset with the show and a suggestion Dylan had made. But what was it again? Tom thought for a couple of seconds, but nothing came to mind. He trusted Dylan and he knew that whatever Dylan suggested for the show must be good for all of their successes.

"Go for it," Tom told him. "Sounds like a good idea."

"I'll contact the client," Dylan held his excitement in as he turned and his grin grew wider and appearing almost sinister. "But first, I'll need your signature on this contract."

Dylan handed the paper to Tom, who read it over, seeing the client's name. Tom grabbed a pen off his desk and signed the paper, then handing it to Dylan.

"Thanks, Dylan," Tom smiled. "What would I do without you?"

* * *

Two years had gone by since Tom and Jen had broken up for the second and final time, and now, here he was, back at his old college town, at the same bar where they had first kissed. The first floor of Klondike Kate's was still the same with the cramped bar and sitting area for eating. The second floor had the same bar and dance floor. Tom's memories from college came rushing back to him. That moment in time seemed another lifetime ago, even though it had only been ten years. He now was based in L.A., working at a new, rising reality TV production company, and his pride couldn't get any higher. So far, he hadn't seen anyone he knew; just the usual bunch of college kids that crowded in every Saturday night – or, as Dylan called it, Sorority Slut Saturday. The DJ had already gotten the themed 1980s night started with A-ha's "Take on Me."

The bar was crowded with its usual capacity of college kids; however, it was all the more packed with college alumni. Tom found it amusing seeing all of these older faces with much younger ones. Then a thought hit him. Was he one of those old faces? He gave himself a mental kick in the ass for returning here for the reunion. Tom had always hated reunions; he didn't attend his high school reunion. But now that he had a job worth bragging about, he welcomed the chance to rub it in with a few of his fellow alumni.

So far, his night was uneventful. There were no old roommates, no former classmates with whom to brag; and the ladies (most of who were of college age) were looking at everyone else but him; it felt just like his old college days. Once again, Dylan was late. Tom glanced at his watch as the opening riff of Bryan Adams' "One Night Love Affair" blared through the speakers. After waiting through half of that song, the bartender finally noticed Tom and asked what he wanted to drink. Tom ordered a Manhattan and within a minute the amber beverage was in front of him, the martini glass hitting his lips. A little excitement arose in him when he saw a barstool open up, and he quickly planted his butt down on the cushion top. He adjusted himself on the seat, leaning from the left to the right, bumping into the person sitting on his left and then his right.

The person on his right snuck a peek at him and was about to turn her head back when she stopped and her glance turned to a stare, wondering if he was the person she remembered.

"Tom?" the woman asked.

Tom looked over and saw Maggie. She was more beautiful than he had remembered her. Her red hair had not diminished and her eyes were still as entrancing as ever. The second their eyes met, Maggie's face lit up with a big smile.

"Hey, you," she said in the same flirty way she had back in college.

"Maggie?" Tom stretched out the end of her name as if he wasn't sure. But he was sure. He knew exactly with whom he was speaking.

"Yeah! Hey, Tom!" She inched a bit closer to him. "I didn't know you were coming this weekend!"

"Yeah. Yeah!"

"Wow! How have you been!?"

"I've been good – actually, *great* lately. How about you?"

"Can't complain." Maggie smiled and then playfully rolled her eyes, feigning annoyance. "But I basically have *no* free time now since I got my doctorate."

"Really?" Tom asked, impressed. "I knew you were in pre-med in college but I didn't know ..." Tom stopped himself from putting his foot in his mouth, but Maggie put it in there for him.

"... If I'd actually finish?" she continued.

Tom's face flushed, stuttering, "Well, no ... I knew ... I mean ... I knew you'd follow through! It's just that ... people change."

"Yeah," she nicely interrupted his awkward response. She looked at him with a flirting glare and repeated, "People *do* change."

"So what are you doing? I mean, what's your profession?" Tom realized how stupid he sounded. "You know what I mean."

Maggie couldn't help but giggle at his awkwardness and she answered, "I'm a cardiothoracic surgeon."

Tom tried not to show how impressed he was but he could tell from the look on her face that he had failed miserably. Just when he was out of words to say, Maggie opened the conversation back up for him.

"So what do you do now?"

"I'm in L.A. - working in reality television."

"Oooh! Anything I may have heard of?"

"Maybe," Tom said, his face slightly contorting. *"Fighting the Stars?"*

"Which one is that?"

"The one with the C-list actors boxing each other?"

Tom felt stupid hearing the words coming out of his mouth, and he could tell Maggie was desperately trying to recall the show but her face was a clear indication that she was clueless.

"I'm sorry," she said. "I don't think I've seen it."

Maggie could see the slight disappointment in Tom's eyes and felt sorry for him. She wanted him to know that she was still impressed and proud of him.

"But," she added. "I haven't really watched much TV the past six to nine years," Maggie said, then laughing.

Maggie's confession did make Tom feel better and he felt like their meeting was improving.

"I guess not with all that school!" Tom replied. "What made you go through with it? I mean, I knew you were interested in medicine back in college but you never told me why."

"I didn't?"

Tom shook his head and Maggie instantly knew that she never got around to telling him because their time together had abruptly ended when Tom saw her cuddling with Alex all those years ago. She still found it hard to believe that she never told him. She swallowed back the awkwardness that overcame her, as she tucked thin strands of her hair behind her ears.

"I ... uh ... I've always wanted to-," Maggie caught

herself and stopped. Something inside her wanted to tell the truth about wanting to attend med school. And she felt safe with Tom. "My mom has breast cancer."

Tom felt his face warp into that face that most would give when hearing of bad, unfortunate news or a horrible accident that befell a close friend.

"Oh, I'm sorry to hear that," he said.

"It's OK. I mean, she's just finishing up chemo now and the doctors are optimistic. My grandmother had it too. That's what started it." Maggie half rolled her eyes at the cliché speak that was coming out of her mouth. She opened her mouth to start speaking again, but nothing came out and she could feel a lump in her throat, causing her to abruptly stop talking.

Tom could see her eyes turning pink and tears welling in her eyes. He wanted to reach out right then and there and give her a big embrace, but time, memories and distance had quelled him. Instead, his face mirrored the pain that was in hers. Maggie took a chug of her beer, collecting herself long enough to speak again.

"Anyways, that's why I'm still into medicine," she said. She looked at Tom for any reaction, afraid of what he was thinking. Maggie figured that she was probably not Tom's favorite person since the time they last saw each other. And now she was almost afraid of what he would think and feel about her - if he ever thought about her at all.

"Well, I'm sure you're great at it," Tom said earnestly, then awkwardly fumbled back, "I mean, at the thardio – the heart–"

"Cardiothoracic," Maggie corrected him with a smile. Tom was still sweet after all these years.

"Yes!" Tom felt like a fool. He was thinking that Maggie probably thought he wasn't paying attention to her when he actually was just trying too hard. He could feel a spark with her that he hadn't felt for another woman since Jen.

"How's Jen? Are you two ...?"

"Oh. Jen! She's good ... I guess."

"You guess?"

"We broke up. Two years ago. We don't talk much anymore."

"I'm sorry to hear that." Maggie was not sorry to hear that.

"It's OK," Tom said. "We're still friends. Just different paths. She wanted a career in journalism, and I wanted to get into film production."

Maggie noticed Tom's empty glass and knew she wanted to keep the night going.

"You want another one?" she asked.

"Sure."

"Do you want another—?"

"Oh! A Manhattan? No. How about a Yuengling?"

"OK," Maggie said and she leaned toward the bar to get the bartender's attention.

Tom had always loved Maggie, and now that they were both here and reconnecting, he was hoping the night would go well and see where their relationship could go from here. She was still as beautiful as ever – in fact, even more so. The fact that she was ordering him another drink was a good sign that their night was getting off to a good start.

"So how long are you back in Delaware for?" Maggie asked, handing Tom his drink.

"Not long," Tom said, taking a sip of his drink. "To be

honest ... I can't wait to get back – and to get outta here."

"Back to L.A., eh?"

"Yeah. How about you? Where's home after this?"

"New York City."

"Wow!" Tom was impressed. He never would have guessed that Maggie would be a big-time doctor, let alone a city girl. "Impressive."

Maggie almost laughed out loud at Tom's compliment. She slightly rolled her eyes. "Yeah, right!"

"No! You should be proud of yourself. I mean, you set out to do something and you did it. Not many people succeed at that."

"I'll let you know once I make my first year."

"You gotta start somewhere," Tom said. Maggie liked his outlook on her and her future. She could tell Tom had matured more since they last saw each other in college, and the way he now carried himself looked good on him.

"Ya know ... I think we should do a shot. You wanna do a shot with me?"

"Sure," Tom was taken aback by her sudden idea. "What should we do?"

"Tequila."

"OK," Tom laughed out of surprise at Maggie's hard liquor suggestion. "But I'm getting this one!"

Maggie moved her hands toward the bar as if to say, "*Be my guest*," and the slight buzz from the alcohol almost made Tom laugh at her cute gesture.

"Two shots of Patrón," Tom said to the bartender.

Without even realizing, two shot glasses had been placed in front of them. Nearby was a salt shaker and small plate of lemon slices.

"OK," Tom said. "You ready for this?"

Maggie nodded, her movement a bit delayed from the drinks. The song had changed to David Bowie's "Modern Love."

"Let's do this!" she almost grunted, holding her fists up in excitement as if she were psyching herself up. Tom licked the section of the back of his left hand between his thumb and pointer finger, getting ready to tip the glass back, but Maggie grabbed his arm. "Wait, wait, wait!" Tom stopped and lowered his drink. "We should toast."

"What to?"

Maggie thought for a few seconds as she licked the section of the back of her hand between her thumb and pointer finger, then sprinkled salt on the area.

"Here's to ... to lying, cheating, stealing and drinking. If you're going to lie, lie for a friend. If you're going to cheat, cheat death. If you're going to steal, steal a heart. If you're going to drink, drink with me."

The two tapped glasses and sank the drinks down their throats, the tequila slightly burning down. Before the feeling could continue, they each licked the salt off their hands and popped a lemon wedge in their mouths, sucking on the sour juice, taking away from the strong liquor taste. Both fought the urge to squint over the liquor's strength even though neither was drunk yet.

"Whoa." Maggie's eyes quickly widened. "Haven't had one of those in a *long* time!"

"Me neither."

"Oh, I don't believe that. Out in L.A.? With all of those Hollywood types?"

Tom let out a small chuckle. "It may sound glamorous,

but, trust me, it's anything *but.*"

"Well, everyone's gotta put their time in. Whether you're destined to become a cardiothoracic surgeon or a Hollywood producer, right?"

Tom loved her outlook on life. Listening to her reminded him of why he loved her all those years ago and he was still in wonderment of her. She carried herself like a woman but had the air of an innocent optimism and wondrous curiosity. The two of them spent the remainder of the evening talking and laughing and sharing what they planned to do with their lives.

The talking had made the hours go by fast, and last call for drinks had crept up. The DJ played the last song of the night and the opening chords to Prince's "Purple Rain" blared through the speaker system. Tom looked to Maggie and saw her playfully nod her head back toward the stairwell leading upstairs to the dance floor.

Maggie was hoping Tom would get her message and want to dance with her. It had been years since they had seen each other and she hoped that bygones were bygones. Tom warily lifted himself from his barstool, somewhat in a drunken stupor, and followed her upstairs to the dance floor. The stairway was crowded, slowing down the traffic. Maggie reached her hand out to Tom and he smiled as he took her hand, and then looked up to her to see her beaming a smile too. As soon as they walked onto the small wooden dance floor, Maggie turned to face Tom and moved in closer to him. He took her small hand in his and gently placed his other hand on the small of her back, his thumb touching her exposed back. The touch sent goose-bumps along Maggie's skin. The liquor helped their bodies slacken just enough to sway in time with the music, and Maggie slowly raised her right hand to Tom's face, caressing his cheek then resting it on his right shoulder. She looked up to him, her eyes catching his, and all of the years they had been apart fell away. It felt good – for both of them. However, there was a pang of guilt that soon invaded Maggie's conscience. She knew Tom had seen her – all those years ago – out on the lawn with Alex, and even though they had not officially been dating, she still felt bad for giving Tom the wrong idea about their relationship. Tom was someone she could go to when she needed comfort – whether emotionally or physically. They never had sex, but she often liked cuddling close to him. And as much as she wanted to love him in a romantic way, she simply couldn't.

Tonight, though, after years of wanting and waiting to tell Tom, she had her chance. She opened her mouth to speak, but no words were coming out. She found herself stammering while Tom continued to gaze into her eyes. *Why can't I get the words out?!*, she wondered. She wanted to apologize for all those years ago in college when he had seen her and Alex together. Even though she never intended to lead Tom on, Maggie knew the attention she gave him didn't discourage him.

Maggie's anxiety was obvious to Tom but he wasn't sure what he had done wrong. He didn't want the night with her to end but he was tired of playing mind games or chasing after her. Tom decided if Maggie didn't want to stay with him than that would be it. He would chalk it up to simply a night of reminiscing and leave it at that. He was only hoping that they could—

"I'm sorry," Maggie blurted out. Tom looked at her,

wondering why she was apologizing. "I just ..." She looked down, ashamed to look in Tom's eyes. "... I just ... I've wanted to tell you I'm sorry for the way you found out about me and Alex." She looked back up into Tom's eyes, his face full of uncertainty. "I know you saw me and Alex lying together that day at Trabant. And I'm sorry ... if that hurt your feelings."

Tom had always wanted to hear that from Maggie - even though he never would have admitted it to anyone out loud. Tom looked into Maggie's stormy eyes and any trace of his unresolved contempt toward her disappeared. For the first time, Tom realized he had not thought about that moment in a very long time but it was no longer the open wound it had once been.

"You don't ... have to do that, Maggie."

"What?"

"You don't have to apologize."

"But I do. I'm not sorry that I didn't love you at the time." She looked into his eyes with earnestness. "I'm just sorry if I ... hurt your feelings. No matter how inadvertent it was. I just—"

Tom kissed her. He didn't need to hear anymore from her. Her apology was enough. It gave him all the incentive he needed. The fact that Maggie had thought about it enough to apologize was proof enough that maybe there was more to their potential relationship than merely friendship.

Maggie leaned into Tom, kissing him back, feeling something she had always known was there before, but never realized until now. She loved him. She loved Tom Frost. But she was still wary as to why he kissed her. She tasted of strawberries and honey and Tom couldn't help but hope that he didn't taste of beer and hard liquor – even though he probably did. He pulled back and she slowly opened her eyes.

"Wow," she breathed.

"Yeah." Tom wasn't sure what to say next, but he was happy he kissed her.

"I was hoping you'd do that."

"Me too."

Maggie laughed at his response and leaned in closer to him, continuing to sway to the song as Prince belted out his soulful *ooooo-hoooo-oooooos*. It was a good moment – and the beginning of a whirlwind romance for Tom and Maggie. Before they both knew it, Maggie was moving out to California to live with Tom. It took quite a bit of time, but she eventually found a residency with a nearby hospital, and Tom worked his way up in the reality show business.

* * *

Tom always thought of that reunion night he had kissed Maggie and all of the wonderful moments that followed. The past few weeks had been anything but wonderful. Tom felt Maggie emotionally slipping away from him, but he had no clue as to why. He worked hard, brought home great pay, and supported her in everything she did. Nevertheless, there was an awkward silence between them. They hardly talked. When they did, it was mostly about the TV show, and he was doing most of the talking.

"Hello!?" a voice snapped Tom out of his daydream.

"Yeah," Tom responded to Dylan.

"Tony needs your signature for the OK to go on this big

fiftieth episode. You know? The usual legal stuff."

"Yeah," Tom repeated, still breaking out of his daze as he looked up to Dylan and then over to their attorney, Tony. Even though Tony looked like a shyster lawyer you found in a seedy part of town, he was quite good at his job. His comb-over hairstyle and dwindling acne were the perfect complement to his chubby, sweaty face. Tony had once overheard one of his clients say that stripes made him look thinner, so, from that point on, Tony wore pinstriped, double-breasted suits, also believing the double-breasted style looked good on him. Tom grasped the fountain pen from Tony and signed on the bottom line of the contract. He wasn't quite sure but he swore he saw Dylan flash a smile, his lips curling back, reminding him of a classic Disney cartoon he watched when he was a kid – the one with those evil cats torturing Mickey Mouse's dog, Pluto.

Dylan and Tony stood up in unison and began walking out when Tom called out for Tony.

"Could you hang back for a second?"

"Sure," Tony said.

"Thanks, Dylan," Tom said. "Could you please shut the door on your way out?"

"Sure," Dylan said, a hint of wariness in his voice. He looked to Tony, who was looking at him, and Dylan retained his smile as he slowly shut the door.

When Tom heard the click of the latch, he started.

"Tony. I have to ask you for a big favor. I know this is Dylan's 'baby' and he has a hard-on for getting this thing on-air. But you've got to be straight with me. Is this viable? I mean, what if the shit hits the fan?"

Tony chortled, about to lose some imaginary food he

wasn't chewing.

"Tom! Isn't 'shit-hitting-the-fan' the entire drive behind the show?"

"Yeah! But this is the first time I've given Dylan the lead on this. And, add the fact that this will be live on TV. I'm just a little worried, s'all."

Tony placed his ham hock of a hand on Tom's shoulder, weighing Tom's shoulder down considerably. "Don't worry, Tommy. Dylan's got this. You'll do the show, it'll be a ratings hit, and we get showered with money!"

"Tony." Tom flashed a serious look and lowered his voice a bit to let his attorney know the seriousness of his words, and Tony's face turned serious. "I just feel ... like this all is – I don't know – going ... too fast or ... too easy."

Tony held onto his serious glare for as long as he could before his lips could no longer remain shut and he spit out into hysterical laughter.

"Tom. Do you realize how many producers and show creators dream of being where you are right now? I mean, damn. You've won an Emmy, for Christ's sake! Most reality shows are a joke! And yours is winnin' awards!" Tony took a deep breath and let out a long sigh, the stench of onions and coffee blasting Tom's senses. "Take this all as a blessing. Fast and easy isn't how show business always goes. But, when it does, you gotta take it all in for what it's worth. Ya even gotta appreciate the other thing that gets ya here."

"And what's that?"

"Luck."

5.

"Well, I know it wasn't you who held me down
Heaven knows it wasn't you who set me free
So often times it happens that we live our lives in chains
And we never even know we have the key"

--The Eagles
"Already Gone"

The house was vacant, cold and dark when Tom came home. The feel matched Tom's somber mood about his career and the thoughts of the poor young woman he saw in the video interview. There was no one in his group of friends he could talk honestly to about the feeling that struck him when he saw the tears running down her face. Dylan would only tell him he was being ridiculous. Tony had told him he was lucky to have what he did. And while Tom couldn't argue with that notion, he still could not help but feel as if he were doing the wrong thing with his career. He sat down on the couch, exhausted from his mind racing all afternoon, and turned on his iPod player, Titus Andronicus' "In a Big City" invaded the uncomfortable silence.

Tom knew he shouldn't be complaining or even overanalyzing what he did for a living. There were people in the world who would love to have his life - especially the opportunities which came with it. The entire reason Tom had decided to get involved with television production was so he could make a positive difference in other people's lives. When he caught Maggie out on the grass with Alex, he knew there were other people out there going through a similar situation just like him. Why not help them ... *and* make money doing it?

When Tom saw Amy's face in the video, for the first time, he felt like he wasn't helping her; he was exploiting her. Tom knew from experience that no matter what truth Amy discovered, her life would be changed forever. If her boyfriend was not cheating on her, she would have to live with the suspicion in her heart and the constant feeling as if she was not enough for him. On the other hand, if her boyfriend was cheating, then would come the ugly, sad confrontation, and, at minimum, three lives would be forever altered. Tom just hoped that neither side had any kids to further complicate matters.

The door lock clicked open and Maggie slowly walked inside.

"Tom?" she warily asked aloud.

"Yeah. I came home a little early."

"Oh," she sounded off, relieved. "This is a nice surprise."

She walked into the living room and saw Tom slumped down on the couch. The sight of him seemed off as Maggie could tell something was upsetting him.

"What's wrong?" she asked.

"I don't ... quite know." Tom went quiet, trying his best to think of a way to tell her what he was feeling. "I told you about the fiftieth episode, right?"

Maggie gave a slow, negative shake of her head.

"Well, Dylan wants us to feature this twenty-two-year-old on the show. She thinks her boyfriend's cheating and I know this is what the show is about. I know that! But ... there's something so ... so ... humbling and sad about this girl. She's different than the others we've featured. I don't know." Tom sighed out of frustration that he could not get the right words out. "Maybe things are different."

"Maybe *you're* different."

Tom flashed an inquisitive look.

"You obviously feel sorry for this girl," Maggie continued. "There's something to be said about taking an important emotional moment of someone's life and televising it. Especially a vulnerable moment."

"Never seemed to bother you before," Tom said with a bit of contempt.

"That's because it didn't ... back then." Maggie said, ignoring his tone. "Don't get me wrong, Tom. I appreciate what you do. I really do. I love that we live as comfortably as we do. But I think what you're feeling is what I've been feeling for some time."

"What's that?"

"Shame."

Tom let out a long, heavy sigh. He didn't know how to take what Maggie was telling him. Even though he was really pissed off, he couldn't help but be at least a little appreciative of her honesty. Tom's face betrayed what he was feeling at the moment, as if he were asking Maggie why she felt shame.

"Maybe it's not so great to be making money off exploiting other people's pain," she continued.

"I just ..." Tom paused, thinking how to precisely say what he wanted. "I just feel like I should be more ... devoted to the show. After all, I created the damn thing."

"There's nothing wrong with growing out of the show."

"Yeah, but if I drop out, what does that make me?" Maggie didn't know how to answer Tom but he didn't give her the time to speak. "It makes me a damn quitter!"

"No—"

"Yes, it does!" Tom slightly raised his voice. "And what happens if I leave the show!? Dylan takes over! I can't ... I don't know if I can stand for that. He'll make it trashier than it already is."

"Who cares? Let him. I think the reason you've been feeling so funky lately is because you're done with that show. You've gotten the Emmy. What more is left?"

"I feel like if I leave, I'm just giving up—"

"On what!? Giving up on what!?"

"My career! Us!"

"What? How could you quitting the show be giving up on us?"

Tom was surprised at his own admission; it just uncontrollably came out. He was not sure how to respond. He turned away, trying his best to examine and think of what he meant by his confession.

"I ..." He turned back to face her. "For as long as I can remember, I just wanted to become successful. I wanted to make something to be proud of. So when the network bought my show and it got popular and, now with the Emmy, I feel like it's something to be proud of. It's what I've been hoping for. Well, that and being with you. And I know you don't care about the money. But ... it's just ... if I'm not doing this – something I love – then what else will I do?"

Maggie could see the desperation in Tom's eyes, the feeling that he had put his all into this one career path and now he wasn't sure he wanted it anymore. Her first instinct was to try and fix the situation. She didn't believe in how most of her girlfriends acted. All of them mostly wanted to be heard with no real solution; Maggie, on the other hand, wanted a solution when she spoke of her problems.

"You've already got your Emmy – and a hit TV show. Your foot's in the door. I'm sure you can do pretty much anything you want."

"No," Tom said, shaking his head. "That's not how it works, Mags. In this business, it's unheard of to quit a successful show. And, if the show takes off even more after you're gone, then no production company wants to touch you. They think something must be wrong with you."

Maggie had to stifle a laugh at Tom's paranoia. He had done this many times before where he assumed what was going to happen, so she felt she wasn't being a jerk when she didn't take his supposition seriously. Still, no matter how many times she heard Tom's paranoia, she continued to humor him by listening and letting him air his thoughts. This time, she wouldn't stay quiet.

"You always say that, Tom," Maggie said. "How do you know?"

"I'm in the industry," Tom raised his voice. "I've seen it happen, Maggie, time and time again. Remember Danny? Danny Scott?"

Maggie nodded her head.

"He broke away from his directing blockbuster action films right in the middle of a shoot. Decided he wanted to direct his own original screenplays. So he quit and tried to start up his own production company only to fail – miserably. The company went under and he was left penniless. Tried to get back into directing those big moneymakers but no one wanted to hire him. They thought he was unreliable, too much of a risk. Now do you know where he's working?"

Maggie slowly shook her head.

"Oh, he's writing scripts, alright. I believe he's writing the *Transformers* at Universal Studios."

"So he's still in the business?"

"The *theme* park, Mags. He's writing the script for the *ride*. He's also bartending 'cause he doesn't make enough to live off."

"Well, who cares? I mean, damn, Tom! Take a risk!"

"There is no risk, Maggie! It's a guaranteed fail! Are you telling me that's what you want!? You want to lose everything we've worked for!? Everything I've worked for?"

There was a time when Maggie would have easily told Tom to quit, consequences be damned. But time had taken its toll on Maggie's fortitude of their relationship. She had now thought telling him to quit was useless – he would never quit. But not out of principle or his own moral beliefs. He was scared. And Maggie didn't have the stomach to see her husband continue with a life choice which made him unhappy, all because he was too scared to take a risk and try something new.

Tom gently placed his left hand down on the edge of the couch, still hoping for Maggie's right hand to reach down and caress the top of his hand. His view pointing downward, Tom saw her hand just a few inches from his, waiting for the slightest movement, but her hand dragged out of view as Maggie abruptly stood up and walked away. That was all Tom needed to believe his marriage was officially disintegrating. He didn't know what to do, what to say, and all he could wonder about now was why they couldn't simply talk things out, why the same mistakes kept being made. He let her leave the room.

Maggie closed the bathroom door behind her, locked it and sat down on the closed toilet seat. Her panicked heart fluttered like the wings of a hummingbird, her breath became shallow and she felt as if the walls were closing in on her. She tried to steady her breathing and her heart, closing her eyes tight and picturing her wedding day – the happiest day of her life. At the time, she and Tom were excelling in their careers, making enough money to afford the move to Los Angeles and their house. The location of their wedding was at a beautiful manor in upstate New York, with all of their friends and family in attendance. The ceremony was held at St. Mary's Church in Albany, New York – a small, quaint structure from the eighteenth century, with a French gothic style, making the inside feel like a trip back in time. When she and Tom exited that church through its wooden recessed-paneled doors, and Tom took her hand in his, flashing his smile, Maggie knew she would be his forever.

This realization jolted her back into the present as Maggie noticed she had been silently crying and she knew she couldn't abandon Tom. She made a vow and she was not a quitter. What they were going through now was just a blip in their lives together. They had been through moments like this before and Maggie knew they would get through this one.

A quiet knock on the bathroom door snapped her out of her thoughts. "Mags," Tom said. "I'm going to the office to get ready for the show. Wish me luck?"

Maggie wiped the tears from her eyes and gave a quick, short clearing of her throat so her words came out as just above a whimper. "Good luck."

"Maggie," Tom started. "Can we ... talk more when I'm done today?"

The hope in Tom's voice – as well as the idea that he was still willing to work things out with her – made Maggie's face crumple into a muted cry and the tears flowed again as she held her hand to her mouth to try to stifle her sad voice, so Tom wouldn't know she had been crying. "Sure," she quickly said, instantly covering her mouth with her hand.

Tom opened the door to his red 1994 Porsche 968 Turbo, slipped into the black leather driver's seat, turned on the engine as the radio instantly blared out Trampled by Turtles' cover of Bruce Springsteen's "I'm Goin' Down," and backed out of his two-car garage. As he sped away, Tom knew Maggie was right. She usually was. He would have to seriously reconsider his contract with the network and whether *Heartbrakers* had a place in his future.

6.

"And every time I've held a rose
It seems I only felt the thorns
And so it goes, and so it goes
And so will you soon, I suppose."

--Billy Joel
"And So it Goes"

Tom parked in his reserved spot in the vast parking lot of the studio offices. Beside his spot, Dylan's Cadillac was already parked. Tom let out a single, silent chuckle and laid his hand upon the hood of Dylan's car, checking to see if the engine was still warm, to gauge how long Dylan had been there. Cold. That meant Dylan had been there a long time, no doubt preparing for the long day. Many people didn't know the time it took to shoot just one segment of the show. The show's private investigators had already done the legwork by following the subject - in this case, Amy's boyfriend - for a week and recording who he was coming into contact with and what he was doing with them. The investigators were to always keep their distance from the subject and his potential lover, but just take video surveillance from afar. The video was edited by production staff and uploaded to Tom's iPad for the evening of live filming.

With the recent ratings boost of the show, the production company insisted on hiring more experienced investigators, ones who could also edit together the surveillance footage. As Tom entered the building, one of the investigators rushed up to walk alongside him.

"Hey, Mr. Frost." The man greeted. He was shorter than Tom, with curly, brown, scruffy hair and a permanent five o'clock shadow, which drew attention away from his wardrobe of T-shirts – which usually had some pop culture reference on them – and jeans.

"Hey, Joe. I told ya ... call me Tom."

"Um, actually, it's Andrew."

Tom stopped in mid-stride and winced. "Oh. Sorry, Andrew. I'm still trying to learn you guys' names around here. What's up?"

"I've got the entire surveillance feed queued up for tonight, and uploaded to your iPad."

"Thanks!" Tom said, looking down at his phone to see a message from Dylan. "Are you gonna be on-site tonight for the live feed?"

Andrew was a bit surprised at Tom's question. "I didn't know we were invited to take part. Mr. Vaughn said we weren't permitted to attend."

Tom stopped dead in his tracks, looked up from his phone and into Andrew's clueless face. "What? Since when?"

"I don't know, sir – I mean – Tom. I asked him this morning and that's what he told me."

Tom shrugged it off and flashed a smile. "Don't worry about Mr. Vaughn. If you run into any complaints, tell him I said it was OK."

"Thanks," Andrew said as Tom continued walking toward his office.

Tom walked into his office to find Dylan already waiting for him, sitting in his office chair.

"No matter how many times I see you in that chair, it still gives me the creeps," Tom said.

Dylan let out a single laugh. "C'mon! You know it wouldn't be so bad! To have another partner on this thing?"

"I thought we already *were* partners."

"Well, yeah, but – I mean – *complete* partners. Ya know? Fifty-fifty?"

Tom looked at Dylan, his feet still propped up on Tom's desk, reclining in Tom's leather office chair, not a care in the world. The truth was that Tom had always been jealous of Dylan. Ever since he had known him, Dylan always seemed to get what he wanted. Girls, cars, clothes, not to mention the latest in smartphones, music, computers, you name it. And while Tom didn't mind the material things, he was rather jealous – not of Dylan's sexual conquests, but rather the fact that he could get any woman to notice him. Dylan simply had no difficulty meeting women – and getting to know them – like Tom did. It was one of the many reasons Tom was thankful to have Maggie love him the way she did. He knew they had left things unresolved, but, after shooting this episode, he promised he would make it better. He already had it in his mind he would take an extended vacation – maybe to someplace like Hawaii, Barbados or Italy.

"Don't get too ahead of yourself," Tom said. For once, Tom was happy that he had something Dylan wanted and couldn't buy or charm his way into owning it. "Let's see how tonight goes and we'll go from there."

Dylan's smile grew wider, resembling that of the pesky trouble-making Cheshire Cat in Disney's *Alice in Wonderland*, and he stood up with a slow shake of his head. "I have a feeling this will be our best episode yet."

"Do we have a confirmation of when we're shooting this thing?"

"Yeah. Tonight. The dicks confirmed the boyfriend is," Dylan put his two hands in the air and made quotation marks with his fingers, "meeting up with friends tonight."

"They're investigators, Dylan. Not dicks. And they confirmed it?"

"Yeah." Dylan waited like a dog looking for the slightest movement of his owner to fetch after a stick.

"OK, then." Tom said.

Dylan jerked his head, whispering, "Yeah!"

"Get the camera crew prepped and, oh, I want you to go tell Andrew he can come to the shoot."

"Why? I already told him he couldn't."

"Yeah, I don't know why you would say that. The investigators are more than welcome to come see how everything plays out. Why did you say he couldn't?"

"I don't know. I just thought ... they shouldn't be there. Ya know? For their safety."

"What do you mean 'safety?'"

"Well, I didn't want to bring it up now, before our big night ... shooting live! But, *Jesus*, Tom, you know some of these cheaters we confront are not the friendliest, most appreciative people. I mean, it's bad enough we all have to worry about you and the camera crew getting hurt without having to worry about more people."

Tom knew Dylan was right but he figured if Andrew

really wanted to see an episode shot and see how his work paid off, then he should be allowed to watch.

"Well, I still want you to invite him."

"The dicks ... investigators have to be there anyway! They have to call and let us know when the guy's girlfriend is there. We don't need them rushing up and being on scene."

"By the time I go to confront the couple, we've already gotten the signal from them. Just please invite them. I don't want to talk about this anymore!"

Tom's decision annoyed Dylan and he didn't mind letting out a heavy sigh to show his frustration, but he forced a smile and gritted his teeth, saying, "Sure. I'll go tell him now."

"Thanks." Tom said as Dylan started going out the door. "Hey, Dylan! Make sure the other guy knows too."

"Will do." Dylan turned and left. He immediately marched to the shared office of Andrew and Paul – the other investigator.

"Hey, guys," Dylan smiled, immediately transforming the smile to a grimace. "I spoke with Tom about you being at the confrontation today, and reminded him about the insurance hazards, so, unfortunately, you both can't be there tonight. Maybe next time, though? When the insurance is cleared?" Dylan could see their deflated looks of disappointment and said, "But thanks for the great work! We couldn't have done this without you!"

Dylan turned around and left the office, closing the door behind him.

"Dick!" Andrew said.

"I *told* you," Paul said.

"So, are you gonna watch tonight?" Tom asked over the phone.

"I'll try, honey. I have to go to my parents to help my mom with some tax stuff, but we'll put it on," Maggie said from the other end of the phone.

Maggie still sounded distant to Tom, but he couldn't figure out how to ask her if anything was wrong. He knew he couldn't just come right out and ask because then that would bring up an entirely new issue he didn't feel like dealing with. So, he stayed quiet.

"OK." Tom said. "I'll see you later tonight. After the shoot. Love you."

"Love you too."

Tom hung up the phone, questions racing through his mind, wondering why Maggie had seemed so withdrawn lately. *Maybe she wasn't* completely *withdrawn,* he thought. She still went out to social functions with him and their friends, but there was somewhat of a sadness to her actions – as if she were trying to conceal something.

A knock sounded at his office door. Dylan peeked his head inside.

"Hey. I asked Andrew and Paul if they wanted to come onsite tonight and they said no." Dylan shrugged. "I don't know. Guess they changed their minds."

"OK. Well, at least we tried." Before Dylan closed the door, Tom called out. "Dylan."

"Yeah?"

Tom considered whether or not to let Dylan into the thoughts racing through his head. Dylan was his friend, but he wasn't exactly the type of friend Tom felt he could open up to. His worry for his marriage to Maggie trumped his worry over Dylan insulting him.

"Have you noticed anything weird about Maggie and me lately?"

"What do you mean?"

"It seems," Tom inhaled and threw caution to the wind. "There's something I can't put my finger on. I mean, she's been so supportive. But it feels like there's something she's not telling me."

Tom looked to Dylan, hoping for some inkling of support or an idea of what may be going on with Maggie. And, for a minute, Dylan looked as if he were about to say something profound and supportive.

"Hmm. Oh, well! Are you just about ready to meet with Amy?"

"Yeah." Tom should have known by now that Dylan was not concerned in the least about Tom's troubles with her. He knew Dylan didn't like her – ever since they were all in college. "Just give me a minute to get ready."

"OK." Dylan popped his head backwards and closed the door.

The framed photograph of Maggie caught his eye as he looked back toward his computer. The professional outside shot made him think more about her. His stomach felt queasy and a touch of vertigo ran around his head. Tom was making himself sick with worry and paranoia until it hit him. He remembered the fall after he and Jen broke up the first time.

* * *

Around the beginning of his senior year of college, when Tom had been working for the local channel eight news station, he went out to bars filled with walls of smoke, drinking all night and not getting to bed until three in the morning, even though he would only get two hours of sleep. He soon got a fever and his one-hundred-two-degree temperature wouldn't budge after two full weeks. Between the sharp shooting pain in his lower abdominal area and the persistent high fever, Tom couldn't take the pain anymore so he begrudgingly checked himself into an emergency room. According to the doctor, he caught pneumonia and a gastrointestinal infection. The doctor gave him a shot which quickly eliminated the abdominal pain, but his shortness of breath from the pneumonia persisted and he couldn't walk a few steps without feeling like he was going to crumble into a lifeless heap.

During his entire two-week stay in the hospital, out of all the friends Tom had, the only person to visit Tom every day was Maggie. She would bring him movies to watch, music to listen to and books to read while he was bedridden. One of the most memorable visits was sometime during the middle of his stay.

Tom himself didn't like hospitals - they were entirely too creepy. The sense of those who were there to die, or had died, was something he could never shake and that - along with the sickness - was enough to keep him from ever being comfortable in any hospital. But when he saw Maggie's beautiful, smiling face come through that door, he knew he would be OK. He knew there was someone out there who made him their priority. On this particular visit he remembered, Tom was feeling sorry for himself and wasn't in the best mood.

"Can I ask you something, Mags?"

"Sure."

"Why do you come here every day?"

"What do you mean? You're my friend."

"No," Tom said, slowly shaking his head. "No. I've got loads of friends and none of them have come to visit me every day."

"Well, if you don't want me here, I won't come."

Maggie began grabbing her coat and purse.

"No." Tom grabbed her wrist. "Please. It's not that I'm complaining. I just wanna know ... why are you here every day?"

"I told you. You're—"

"—a friend! *Really!?*"

"Yeah," Maggie said, her face almost breaking into a laugh. She looked more intently into his eyes, seeing that he was searching for some iota of confession that she liked him as more than just a friend. That look soon burned into her own thoughts, making her very uncomfortable as it was something she had not truly contemplated before that moment. She searched her feelings and sincerity soon beamed through her face.

"Look, Tom. You've ... been a great friend to me ever since we met. You've always been there for me. I can't tell you how ... important you are to me. That's why ... when I heard you were sick ..." She searched for the words to say but was at somewhat of a loss. "I wanted to be here for you."

Tom didn't want to force the issue anymore but he felt that if he didn't confront her on her feelings for him, he'd always wonder. Until today, he had always played it safe and not been too revealing about his feelings for her. Even though he had seen her out on the lawn with Alex years ago, and he had dated Jen for such a long time, his feelings for Maggie had not dissipated. He knew that now was the time to tell her. Tell her how he truly cared about her and loved her - and not in some friendly way but in a romantic way. He knew he should tell her and let the chips fall where they may.

"I care about you, Tom." She beat him to the punch. "You wanna know how I feel about you? I *care* about you ...," and she said the next words very slowly and intently, "very much." Maggie remembered that day when she saw Tom with Jen and how happy he was, as well as how much she yearned to be given the opportunity she now found herself in. "I love you. But I can't - I'm not ... ready to ... rush into anything. It wouldn't be fair for either one of us."

Tom's mind was racing as to what Maggie was thinking. With his way of thinking, it was simple. He was single, and she was single, and they both loved each other, so why couldn't they be together? Coming from Maggie, it sounded as though this was some issue as complex as trying to explain advanced trigonometry to a first-grader, and his puzzlement must have been plastered across his face because he could tell by the look on her face that she was trying to figure out what to say next.

He knew he could bring up how she had given him this same speech about needing to have her own space even though he had caught her - unbeknownst to her - cozying up to Alex that day after class. He wanted to shout about it. Insult and belittle her. But, he figured, what good would that really do?

Besides, as he peered into her face - full of sincerity and worry - he knew she was showing him, in her own way, that she cared about him. He honestly didn't care about Alex anymore. That was the past. It was time to leave it there. At least, he would try to let it go. The important thing was that she was here now - with him - and had been every day since he was first admitted to the hospital.

"You don't have to say anymore," Tom said. "I'm just ... really happy you're here."

"Do you still want me to come back tomorrow?"

Tom nodded his head.

"Good," Maggie said. "I like coming to see you."

"I like you visiting too. But I have to admit. I'd much rather it not be here."

Maggie cracked a smile at Tom's attempt to make light of the situation. "Couldn't agree more."

She couldn't help but think of Tom and how guilty she had felt when he first began complaining about his abdominal pain and fever. She felt he was just being a big baby, intolerant to a little stomach pain. Maybe if she had been more supportive or sensitive, he would've taken his illness more seriously and he would've gone to a doctor sooner. Visiting him every day was the least she could do for someone she cared about as much as she did for Tom. "I'm gonna go get something to eat from the cafeteria. You want something?"

Tom shook his head no. "Thanks, though."

"No problem."

Maggie left the room and Tom's stare stuck on the closed door. He wondered if there would ever be a time when that woman would love him the same way he loved her. From that moment, he made a pact with himself that he would remain friends with Maggie, and if something romantic were to happen between them, then it would happen. All he knew was: he couldn't lose her friendship.

* * *

For a southern California night, the air had gone cold and left a smattering of fog patches throughout the air. The sound and camera production crews sat huddled in the network's van as if they were some SWAT team, making preparations for a big drug raid. The space was cramped, hot and filled with the usual thick tension which always filled the air right before a production shoot. The entire experience almost made Tom vomit every time. The only time it was worse was on the rare occasion when Tom had to shoot a confrontation in another state. He was glad this one was in the same state, near his work, and he didn't recognize the neighborhood. By this point in the show's span, it was uncanny how many of the cheaters used the same hotels, motels and residential areas. Of all the seedy motels he had seen and visited due to the show, Tom could honestly not recall this one. It looked like something out of a classic 1970s B-movie horror film, with the doors to the rooms on the outside.

Tom looked over to Dylan and the rest of the production staff. They all appeared so self-assured and knowledgeable in what they were doing whereas Tom felt like a fraud. On the outside, he was cool and calm, but, on the inside, he was struggling to keep himself from crumbling into a pile of jittery nerves. Above all, he was afraid of being discovered as a fraud – because when the truth was all said, he had no idea what he was doing. He couldn't help but think of what would happen if this live shoot went wrong and the network wanted to ditch him.

"You ready for this?" Dylan asked, excitement in his voice and eyes.

Tom took a gulp, looked up at his friend and said, "As ready as I'm gonna be."

"You got this. Just remember to confront the boyfriend. And, when it's all over – if you can – get the clearances."

"I know," Tom said. He knew Dylan was referring to the clearances needed to be signed by the participants in order to have their faces shown during other broadcasts in future airings. He was tired of the way Dylan had been treating him like a little child lately. Dylan seemed to forget that Tom was the person who created the show and hosted it from the beginning; he knew what needed to be done.

"Do you want the vest?" Dylan asked, motioning to a black bulletproof vest on a folding chair.

Tom nodded his head, clamping his mouth shut as if he would vomit at any time. He hated the thought of having to wear it, but there were quite a few instances where the vest protected him – not just from bullets, but also knives. Dylan and the crew could see Tom's face turning a shade of pale green, making Dylan's mouth uncontrollably curl into a small grin. Dylan grabbed the vest and placed it over Tom's head, bringing it down around him like an actual vest. Tom immediately tightened the straps so the vest fit more snug against his body.

"Ya know," Tom started, lifting his head to look into Dylan's eyes, "when I started this, I didn't actually think it'd get this far." He let out a small, single chuckle. "I didn't think people would watch something like this." Dylan could tell he was struggling to get the words out, nervous at what lay ahead. "Guess it's a good thing I was wrong, huh?"

"Yeah," Dylan said. "Listen, you're gonna be OK. We go through this every time you go out there. And ninety-nine-point-nine percent of the time, things go off without a hitch. So you'll be fine."

"Yeah."

"And ... if there is trouble, our security guys are there. They'll have it broken up in seconds."

A crackling came to one of the walkie-talkies in the van and Dylan picked it up. "Yeah?"

"Amy is here," an assistant director said.

"OK. We're coming."

Tom took sharp breaths and exhaled slowly. He and Dylan exited the van and walked a few steps as the assistant director handed Tom an iPad. They soon came upon a cordoned-off area of a parking lot with big, bright lights and cameras set up and pointed on a particular spot. The young woman, Amy, was standing in the spot where the equipment was pointed. There were make-up artists surrounding her, using heavy amounts of concealer to cover pockmarks and premature wrinkles.

Dylan left Tom and Tom stepped off to the side, closed his eyes, and whispered a short prayer. When he was done, he shuddered off his negative feelings and stepped into the marked spot for him to stand.

"Hi," he greeted Amy.

"Hi," she said back, her voice timid and trembling, like the last leaf on a tree in the final throes of autumn.

"I'm sure you know how the show works, Amy. But I'll remind you. Our investigators have uploaded some footage to the iPad here that I'll go over with you. And, from there, we'll see where we go next."

"When will I know?"

"Well, if your boyfriend—"

"Nick!"

"Yes. If Nick is not cheating, then we can wrap it up. But, if he is, then it's up to you regarding what you wanna do next. I'll go over it again once the cameras are rolling."

He looked into Amy's eyes, welling up with tears, and he could only glare for a few seconds before having to look away. There was something about seeing the pain and sadness in his guest's eyes that was too much to bear. She nodded her head and they both looked away from each other.

"OK!" shouted the assistant director. "We're live in 5 ... 4 ... 3 ... 2 ..." The man pointed his finger and swiped it toward the camera.

Tom could see the camera light on, and he began his introduction.

"Good evening. And thank you for joining us tonight on this very special *live* episode of *Heartbrakers*.

"Tonight, we're here with Amy who believes her boyfriend, Nick, is being unfaithful to her." Tom turned to Amy. "Thanks for joining us tonight, Amy."

She gave a quick single nod to Tom.

"That's some winner you picked there, Dylan," the assistant director whispered to Dylan off camera, at the nearby video dock where the views from the multiple cameras could be viewed.

"Just wait. Once she sees that boyfriend, it's gonna be ratings gold. I bet you twenty bucks she cracks when that video comes up."

"You're on!" the assistant director said, not looking away from the video screen.

"OK, Amy," Tom said. "The show's investigators have downloaded some video surveillance to this iPad. So let's check out what they discovered."

Tom raised the iPad to his and Amy's view, while a cord linked it up to the live video feed so viewers watching the show could also see the footage.

An image of a young, tall man dressed in jeans, a black T-shirt, and a leather jacket quickly knocked on a motel door. A woman answered the door and he kissed her, sweeping her up in his arms and carrying her inside, closing the door behind them.

"Nick," Amy whimpered as tears rushed down her cheeks, making them glisten under the lights. Her voice squeaked out a pathetic, "Oh noooo."

The sound made Tom's heart break for her as the footage continued.

"So this is your boyfriend, Nick?"

Amy nodded her head.

The footage next showed the same man escorting the same woman into a different motel. They were holding hands and kissing repeatedly. "Here is from a different day, with Nick escorting the same woman into a different motel, and – as you can see – they are more than friends."

Amy looked at the video only long enough to see the first kiss and then sharply turned her head away, her eyes squeezed shut tight.

"I *told* you," Dylan said to the assistant director, almost teasingly, holding up his hand. The assistant director rolled his eyes and held out a twenty dollar bill. Dylan snatched it up, still not looking away from the video feed.

Tom looked at this damaged young woman in front of him. Her body slightly shook from her heavy sobs. Maybe it was her or maybe it was what had been bothering him leading up to this live shoot, but Tom felt much more sullen and empathy for this woman than he did for previous guests.

"Now, Amy," Tom solemnly said. "The next step taken all depends on you. Would you like to finish the interview now? Or ... would you like to confront Nick and see if you can put a stop to this affair?"

The young woman continued to tremble, her face red, the make-up running down her cheeks. There was a long silence on set while Amy continued to cry into her sleeve.

"It's like every second she cries, we earn another dozen ratings," Dylan whispered.

"I'm sorry, Amy," Tom gently said. "We can stop this if you'd like."

Dylan abruptly stood up. "What the hell is he doing!?"

The assistant director pulled Dylan by his shirt, back down into his seat. "Don't worry. He's got this."

Amy sniffled, wiped her red eyes and looked with desperation into Tom's eyes. It was at that moment that Tom truly felt that what he was doing was wrong. This poor woman was shattered, completely vulnerable and emotionally drained. This was a moment which should have been private. He knew that if it were him in her place, he wouldn't want this moment televised. In the past, he always justified the show by thinking that the subject agreed to have this personal part of their lives filmed and broadcast to millions of viewers. But now, he felt like the show was nothing but an intrusion.

"I want to confront him," Amy said.

"OK," Tom said. "We're just getting word from our investigators that Nick and the other woman have arrived at this motel here in the background. So we're now going to make our way to their room."

Tom guided Amy toward the motel until they approached a particular turquoise blue door.

"OK, Amy. Whenever you're ready."

Amy took in a deep breath, slowly released it and knocked on the door. She and Tom could hear movement inside and a man's voice. Footsteps sounded closer and closer to the door before giving way to silence.

"Open up, Nick," Amy said. "I know you're in there."

The door slowly swung open and a skinny man in his early thirties was standing in front of Amy, Tom, the cameraman, sound man, and two bodyguards. This was the man in question – Nick. He was about six feet tall (taller than Tom), had short brown hair, a pale complexion, wearing a New York Yankees T-shirt and blue jeans, which looked like they had just been thrown on. Regardless of his big blue bug-eyes and small mouth that made him look slightly like Gollum from *The Lord of the Rings* movies, he still seemed intimidating to Tom.

"What the hell is this?" Nick asked, kind of dazed.

"Hi, Nick. I'm Tom Frost from the show *Heartbrakers*. Amy contacted us becau–"

"What the *fuck* is going on here, Amy!?" Nick shouted.

"We just want to talk to you, Nick," Tom calmly said.

"Talk about what!?"

"Amy is worried you've been unfaithful in your relationship with her."

Nick coolly laughed. "Aw, man! This ain't any of your business."

"Where is she!?" Amy asked. "Where's the whore you're with!?"

"There ain't nobody here," Nick insisted.

Amy shoved past Nick and into the room. The bed linens were messed up and the room temperature was a bit high.

"Hello!?" Amy shouted. She moved toward the bathroom door – which was shut – and banged on it. "Get out here!"

"Nick," Tom said. "We know you've been seeing someone other than Amy. Our investigators have been following you and have seen you out with another woman."

"You have no fuckin' right to do that!" Nick shouted. "You have no fuckin' right to follow me!"

Amy's fist banged louder and louder on the bathroom door. "Come out!"

"If we could just have you talk to Amy," Tom said, "maybe we could rectify this situation."

"I told you!" Nick shouted, alternating between addressing Amy and Tom as he walked to Amy. "There's nobody else here!"

Amy could tell he was lying. The longer she had been with him, the more in tune she had become to detecting his lies.

"Don't you touch me," she warned as she turned away from him and continued beating on the bathroom door. "Come outta there, whore! We're not leaving 'til you do!"

"Babe! There's *no* one in there!"

The loud banging of Amy's fists suddenly gave way to silence as the door opened and her fist found nothing but air.

"Nobody in there, huh!?" Amy said.

Nick turned away from his girlfriend and squeezed his eyes shut, half out of annoyance, half out of agony, knowing he was now caught in a lie.

The woman stepped out of the bathroom as Amy backed away from her. Tom looked to see who the mystery woman was as the cameraman zoomed in to get a better look.

It was Maggie. She was facing Tom, tears streaking down her face, her hair and clothes disheveled. Tom's hand holding the iPad lost all function, sending the device to the ground and cracking the monitor.

Back at the video dock, Dylan saw the image of Maggie, stood up, and whispered, "Oh shit." He grabbed the microphone linked to the camera crew's headsets and carefully said, "Keep shooting this. No matter what Tom says, keep rolling!"

For the first time in Tom's life, his mouth hung agape in shock. All he could do was continue to stare at Maggie. Everyone else - Amy, Nick, the crew - seemed to not be there. For a few seconds, it was just him and her. Her mouth began to open but no words came out. Her eyes conveyed the pain and regret she was trying to put into words.

"I knew it!" Amy shouted.

Tom turned to the cameraman and whispered, "Let's cut it, please, Chuck."

But he could tell the cameraman was still recording. "Chuck?"

Tom turned to Chuck the cameraman. "I said let's cut it."

Chuck shook his head.

"He said to keep rolling," Chuck whispered.

"Who?"

"Mr. Vaughn."

Tom couldn't believe what he was hearing. Before he could get his walkie-talkie out to talk to Dylan, the shouting of Amy and Nick caught his attention.

"Go ahead!" Amy shouted. "Be with your *whore!*"

"No! No! No! No!" Nick shouted as his eyes welled up with tears. "You can't do this, Amy!"

"Tom, I—," Maggie started as she stepped away from Nick and Amy, toward Tom.

Nick reached out and grabbed Amy. He quickly reached into the back of the waistband of his jeans and whipped around a Glock 17 handgun, pointing it at Maggie and shooting her in the back. Maggie's crimson blood splattered onto Tom's shirt.

Tom's sight followed Maggie's fall forward. His knees buckled and he slowly sunk to the ground before coming to a rest on his knees. The bodyguards jumped through the doorway, around Tom, but Nick quickly placed the barrel against Amy's head, slightly burning a small circular barrel mark into her skin, stopping the bodyguards dead in their tracks.

"No, no, no, no, no, no, no!" Nick chanted. "*No!* No one's going anywhere!"

"Give it up, man," one of the bodyguards calmly said. "There's no way outta this. No one else wants to get hurt."

Nick still held firm to a weeping Amy, concentrating all of his strength on holding her, but he couldn't take his eyes off of Maggie. He ignored everything the bodyguards were saying, thinking of the beauty he had just destroyed. Then his gaze fixated on Tom, still staring at Maggie's lifeless body. He knew there was no way out of this. He had really screwed up this time. There was not going to be any reprieve from something like this. All he wanted to do was run away, but that was impossible now.

Nick uncontrollably began to chuckle at how screwed he was in all of this. The nearly-silent laugh got Tom's attention and he looked up to see Nick holding a gun to Amy's head.

Nick's gaze caught the sight of Tom, whose tears spread

beneath his eyes, and continued to stare as his laugh soon stalled to a stop.

"Ain't life a bitch?" Nick said. He squeezed the trigger, a bullet instantaneously exiting the other side of Amy's head. The bodyguards rushed toward the shooter, but he placed the smoldering hot gun in his mouth and squeezed the trigger, a round exiting the back of his head, his red and gray brain matter painting the wall and ceiling behind him.

The bodyguards' run halted to a stop, almost continuing to slide as if they were Wile E. Coyote chasing after the Road Runner, before their stride turned into a quick walk. His eyes wide – and having to suppress the vomit racing toward his mouth – Chuck the cameraman diverted his camera from the bodies of Amy and Nick to Tom, zooming in on his face.

Tom could see one of the bodyguards quickly approaching the bodies of Amy and Nick, checking their necks for a pulse. He saw one of the bodyguards race to the phone and calling 9-1-1 for medical help. He could hear the commotion over the walkie talkie, yelling at him that help was on the way.

"Hang in there, buddy!" Dylan's voice crackled through the walkie talkie. "Help's on the way! Help is on the way!"

Tom lowered his gaze back to Maggie. She was still alive, tears leaking from the corners of her eyes. He could see she was struggling to speak.

"Shhhhh," his voice broke. "It'll be OK."

"I ... I'm ... so ... sorry," she said.

"Shhhhh-hhh-hhh," the lump in his throat and tears running down his face made his gesture tremble and break up.

Out of his peripheral vision, Tom could see people and

shadows maniacally moving about, but his world was crashing down around him with every second that passed.

He was holding the woman he loved, a woman whom – he had only discovered a few minutes before – was cheating on him. All he cared about now was that Maggie lived. She opened her mouth to speak more and as much as Tom wanted her to save her strength, he also wanted to hear as much as she wanted to tell him.

"It ... was ..."

Tom waited for her to finish but she never did. Her eyes appeared as if they were looking beyond him – as if she were staring at something or someone other than him. He expected her to look back at him at any second but she was gone.

One of the bodyguards knelt down beside Tom and felt Maggie's neck for a pulse. He waited maybe ten seconds before he raised the walkie-talkie to his mouth and shouted into it. Even though the man was shouting, Tom couldn't hear him. He had heard of people getting hysterical blindness in moments of great stress but he had never heard of hysterical deafness.

Tom felt someone behind him grip his shoulders and tugging at him, to pull him away from Maggie. Tom fought to stay by Maggie's side, but the grip got tighter as the pull got stronger. The tugging made Tom look as if he were having an epileptic seizure as he fought to lower his face to her. His body jerked but his head remained still as he gently kissed Maggie's forehead. He knew it would be the last kiss he would most likely ever give her and he wanted it to last longer but, by this time, another set of hands grasped his arms. Tom gave up his stance and he was yanked away from her as her body slumped to the ground. He never lost eyesight of her as he was pulled through the motel room door and EMTs rushed in, starting to work on trying to revive her.

Tom was sat down in the back of an ambulance as an EMT checked his vitals. The EMT flashed a light in Tom's eyes, but Tom didn't blink – his stare remained on Maggie.

Dylan ran up to the scene and asked the EMT, "How is he!? Is he gonna be OK?"

"He's in shock," the EMT said. "Otherwise, he wasn't hit."

"Is he gonna be OK?"

"Yeah. But we need to get him to the hospital ... just to be safe," the EMT said as he laid Tom down on a stretcher and strapped him in. "Who are you?"

"I'm his friend. We're business partners."

"Do you wanna ride to the hospital with us?"

"No," Dylan said. "I'll meet you there."

The EMT laid Tom down on a stretcher, swung the ambulance doors closed, and the siren roared to life as the vehicle sped away to the hospital.

Dylan turned around and slowly walked toward the crime scene. By this time, police were there and starting to cordon off the room. Dylan noticed Chuck the cameraman, also looking like he was in shock, sitting on the hood of a car near the doorway. He was grasping the camera close to his chest, which was heaving, and his wild stare seemed to be looking at nothing.

"Chuck," Dylan quietly said. Chuck said nothing so Dylan spoke louder. "Chuck!" Chuck's attention snapped to and he turned to look at Dylan. "Are you OK?"

Chuck slowly nodded his head.

"Good. Tell me, did you get it all?"

Chuck just sat quietly, still looking at Dylan.

"The confrontation," Dylan confirmed. "Did you get the whole thing?"

Chuck slowly nodded his head again.

As upsetting as the entire event had been, Dylan was still shamefully happy it was all broadcast live. This would make the show into the big colossal hit he knew it could become – and he knew it would eventually benefit Tom's career.

7.

"I can't see my reflection in the waters
I can't speak the sounds that show no pain
I can't hear the echo of my footsteps
Or can't remember the sound of my own name
Yes, and only if my own true love was waitin'
Yes, and if I could hear her heart a-softly poundin'
Only if she was lyin' by me
Then I'd lie in my bed once again"

--Bob Dylan
"Tomorrow is a Long Time"

Tom could not remember being admitted to the hospital. He couldn't remember any of the next day. Nor could he remember the doctor checking him out. When he finally came to, he was in the hospital lobby, sitting in a wheelchair. He snapped out of what can only be described as a state of shock and saw the dozens of television reporters gathered outside of the hospital, through the glass sliding entry doors.

"Do you understand, Mr. Frost?"

"Huh?"

"Your doctor heavily advises you don't drive home," a nurse said. Tom turned around in the wheelchair and looked up to see a rather plain-looking nurse standing over him, her small hands still on the handles of the chair. She peered down at him almost as if she were disgusted with him. "Do you have a ride home?"

Tom turned forward and looked around but there wasn't anybody in the waiting room that he recognized. He faced toward the reporters – a smattering of cameras flashing and video cameras pointed toward him – and he solemnly shook his head.

"I'm here!" a familiar voice sounded from somewhere off to the side.

Tom turned his head and saw his agent, Sean Binder, emerging from the men's bathroom. Tom had known Sean since college, although they had been acquaintances during that time. When Tom's show was bought by the network, and he needed an agent, Sean showed up and Tom liked the idea of having someone he knew in such an important role. From what Tom knew of Sean, he had always been reliable and gave Tom the best advice he could. Plus, the fact that Sean had come along before Tom got famous was all Tom needed to think about when it came to keeping Sean as an agent.

"You OK, Tom?" Sean asked as he nearly pushed the nurse over to grab hold of the wheelchair handles.

"What the hell happened?" Tom quietly asked.

"Huh?" Sean leaned his ear down closer to Tom.

"What the hell happened?" Tom spoke up.

"You mean ... you don't remember what happened at the motel?"

"I do. But where is Maggie? They dragged me away before I could see her taken to the hospital. Is she still here? I'm not leaving without her."

Shit, Sean thought. He slowly came around and squatted down in front of Tom.

Through the front glass doors, the reporters could still see Tom in his wheelchair and watched as his agent squatted down in front of him. The reporters heard no sound – as if watching a silent movie – but they could see the agent telling Tom something, then Tom immediately lowered his head and his shoulders convulsed as his face wrinkled and he wept. The cameras lit up the night sky surrounding the hospital entrance, making a permanent light beam through the glass doors and windows. Every cameraman had their lenses zooming in and focusing on Tom, more particularly his face. Random passersby and onlookers were also amongst the crowd, recording what they could on their cell phones.

One of the microphone handlers – the boom operators – turned back and said with a suppressed smile, "I can't believe this is happening."

"Shut up," Jen Desmond said. She had pleaded with her producer to not be given the assignment but he gave her an ultimatum. She justified her covering the assignment by thinking if she didn't take it, someone else would be assigned and they would most likely ruin Tom's reputation. After hearing the boom guy's comment, she was almost sorry she agreed to take the assignment, but was also disgusted at how the media was covering this news. Jen already heard rumblings from some of the other reporters saying they were placing the blame for the tragedy on Tom.

As Jen stared at Tom crying one of the most hard, pathetic sobs she had ever seen from anyone, she couldn't separate her personal emotions from this story like she did with so many of the same kinds of tragedies on which she previously reported. Watching Tom emotionally crumble before her eyes sent a shockwave of grief over Jen. She knew she shouldn't give a damn about him or Maggie. She knew she had let go of the part of her life which had anything to do with Tom Frost a long time ago. But, for some unknown reason, she felt tears fill the corners of her eyes and the lump in her throat grew until she felt she couldn't breathe. She opened her mouth to take a breath and a muted whimper escaped, tears rolled out of the corners of her eyes.

* * *

Brenda and Eddie Russell sat in the waiting room of the hospital - waiting for a miracle that would never come. Their daughter was dead, killed on live television and all they could do was helplessly sit and watch her be taken out of the world. When the doctor delivered the news to the couple, Brenda had nearly fainted. It took all of her strength not to keel over, but she knew she had to be just as strong for Eddie as he was for her.

Brenda wanted to go home, but the doctor had told them to continue waiting as there was paperwork to sign and more news to come. She couldn't imagine what more there was to say, but she figured it was best to stay and get it over with now rather than have to come back. If it were up to her, Brenda would never again visit this hospital.

The doctor solemnly stepped into the waiting room, followed by the priest, Reverend Danny Taylor, from

Brenda's church. The first thing she thought was it would have been nice to have Reverend Taylor here when she and Eddie were first told the news of their daughter's passing. Then her thoughts quickly raced to worry and panic, as she wondered what kind of news could be so much worse that there needed to be a priest present.

"Reverend Taylor?" Brenda greeted. "What's going on!? Why did the doctor call you?"

"Brenda," Rev. Taylor gently grasped her hands. "The doctor called me because he felt I may be of help."

"Why?" Eddie asked.

The priest looked to the doctor, their stare the sad bridge of science and religion which so often exists when it comes to the dealings of mortality. The doctor stepped forward and placed a hand on Brenda's shoulder.

"Mr. and Mrs. Russell," the doctor let out a heavy sigh. "Your daughter was pregnant."

"What!?" Brenda's voice trembled and her knees uncontrollably shook.

"Are you sure?" Eddie breathlessly asked. The doctor nodded his head.

"From the looks of the tests we ran, it looks like she was three months along."

Brenda's head felt light and she remembered looking up toward the ceiling. The strength she had willed to support her husband as well as her consciousness failed her as she fell backward. The doctor called for a nurse and orderly, loaded her onto a stretcher and made sure she was fine. After determining there was no concussion or illness, Eddie called for the doctor.

"How can I help you, Mr. Russell?" the doctor asked.

"My daughter. I want to see her."

"Are you sure?"

"Yes. I *need* to see her."

"Follow me." The doctor led Eddie.

Eddie was not a man of emotions. He didn't cry. And he didn't talk about his emotions if he did have them. He had been raised that way. Now, he felt as if there were a stone in his throat – as if he were marching toward his own death. His palms and brow perspired; his heart beat faster and louder.

The doctor took Eddie to a room which was dark and the main display was a large window looking into a bigger room with a table in the middle. On the table laid a body with a white sheet over it. The doctor turned to Eddie and said, "Wait here."

The doctor stepped through a door into the next bigger room and drew in his breath as if he were about to go underwater for a deep-sea dive. After quickly releasing the breath, the doctor grabbed the top of the sheet and drew it back, exposing Maggie's head and shoulders.

Eddie drew in a sharp breath, covered his mouth with one hand and tears uncontrollably flooded his eyes. There was his daughter. She appeared as if she were sleeping – still beautiful and full of prospects. Eddie crossed through the doorway into the room with Maggie's body and stepped up to the table. He began to bend toward her body.

"Are you sure you want to?" the doctor asked.

Eddie stopped dead in his tracks and peered up at the doctor. "You can't stop me."

Eddie bent down and embraced her in an awkward hug, reaching his arms only around her head and the tops of her shoulders. She was cold and stiff. All of her warmth was gone. He knew the life he had helped bring into the world was gone.

"I'll always love you," he whispered into her ear, hoping there was still some way she could hear him. Then he let out a small wailing sob. With each intake of breath, the wail got louder and louder. Soon, Eddie was wailing as loud as his body would allow him.

"My daughter! Look at what he did to my daughter!" Eddie wailed. The doctor had to look away in order to keep his composure. "Oh, she's gone! She's *gone!*"

Eddie wailed until his voice gave out and cradled Maggie in his arms for two hours before he finally agreed to go back to his wife's room and stay with her overnight.

After his shift was over that night, the doctor got home and walked into his bedroom, seeing his wife in bed, asleep. He changed into his pajamas and left the room. He walked down the hallway, into another bedroom and crawled into bed with his six-year-old daughter. He slept there all night. He continued to do so for the next nine nights.

* * *

Inside the hospital, Tom tried to stop crying and was miserably failing. He sensed all of the camera flashes from outside, documenting what had happened to Maggie, and accepted at that moment that his life would never be the same.

"Sean," Tom controlled his sobbing so he could whimper. "I need to get outta here."

"I got a car coming, Tommy. Hold on."

The wait for the car may have only been two more minutes but Tom felt as if it had been an hour. He couldn't stand to watch upon the photographers and reporters taking his picture – wolves to the kill – but every time he closed his eyes, he could only see Maggie as she lay dying. When he was holding her, he didn't think it would be for the last time. He thought she would be rushed to the hospital and be saved. Tom hadn't thought of how she had been cheating on him. All he could think of was how much of a beautiful person she was and all the ways in which she had supported him. Yet, there were no *I-love-you*s and no profound discussions or words exchanged between them. She was just dead.

Tom felt his body moving forward as if he were trying to leave his thoughts behind. The movement was not of his own control; Sean was wheeling him toward the automatic sliding doors.

"Wait," Sean said. He stopped Tom's wheelchair and proceeded to take off his jacket. Sean handed the jacket to Tom. "Here. Don't let 'em see you cry."

Tom hesitantly grabbed the jacket and draped it over his head as if he were taking shelter from rain rather than camera flashes, microphones and pointed questions. Sean pushed Tom through the doors and into the media madness outside. Reporters and photographers swarmed around them both, with Sean trying his best to use one arm to push the chair and the other arm to keep the reporters at a respectable distance from Tom.

Tom could not make out any of the questions because all of the voices seemed to blend into one big cacophony. Even though he felt ridiculous wearing a jacket over his head, he was now thankful for it.

The wheelchair's footholds bumped into the rear tires of a limo Tom could only hope was his ride. He heard Sean open the rear door and shout, "Get back! Get back! We'll be issuing a statement as soon as possible."

Tom didn't know what to do – his fear and uncertainty left him incapacitated. A firm grip he could only hope was Sean grabbed a hold of his left arm and lifted him out of the chair. Tom stood up, still blind to where he was going, and the other hand guided him into the limo's back seat. As soon as he was in the vehicle, the door slammed shut and Tom pulled the jacket off his head. He stared out the tinted window and, through a small space between two reporters, in the distance, he could see Jen standing, staring. He knew the windows were too tinted for her to see him, but her stare made him feel as if she could see him, as if she were staring directly into his eyes. As the limo pulled away, and Tom got his last glimpse of Jen, he could see the tears in her eyes, which made the entire thing real. Maggie had been killed live on television, on his show.

* * *

It had taken the limo driver thirty minutes to drive from the hospital emergency entrance to Tom's mansion, but the street in front of his driveway was swarming with even more reporters and photographers than at the hospital.

"How the hell ...?" Tom whispered.

"Excuse me?" the limo driver asked.

"Oh. Nothing."

The limo stopped and reporters, photographers and bystanders – fans and haters – gathered around the vehicle. Tom was overwhelmed with the crowd; he didn't know how he was going to get to his house, let alone get through the inevitable mourning of his wife and publicity of what had happened. He let out a heavy, weary sigh, and slowly began opening the car door. Someone outside had grabbed a hold of the door and ripped it out of Tom's grasp, flinging the door wide open as a handful of people thrust their microphones and tape recorders in Tom's face.

"Mr. Frost!" a reporter shouted. "Do you think there is a future for your show in light of current events!?"

"We love you, Tom!" a bystander shouted.

"Did you know your wife was cheating on you!?"

"How do you feel knowing your show caught the entire thing for live broadcast?"

Tom walked as fast as he could toward his front door, his line of sight aimed directly on that wooden door. Each step closer to the door, the shouting voices around him softened and Tom focused his hearing on his heartbeat, thumping like some loud, distant war drum.

He didn't know if Jen was amongst the crowd and he didn't really care. His only goal now was to get to that door without shouting, screaming, punching, crying, fainting or vomiting in front of the cameras. When his first foot touched down on the welcome mat and his hand touched the doorknob, Tom instantly felt better. But just when he was opening the door and bolting through the doorway, he heard a voice to his left. It was a woman.

"*Murderer!*"

As Tom entered the house, he quickly turned his head to see who had yelled that word, and a nearby photographer snapped a photo of Tom's befuddled, alarmed face. That photo would be sold to, and published on the cover of, every major magazine and newspaper in the country.

* * *

The word still resonated through Tom's head as he closed the window blinds, shutting out the world around him and all of the nosy, prying eyes which may want to see what he was doing. Tom could not believe someone – anyone for that matter – would think of him as a murderer. He loved his wife. He still did.

Wait, he thought. *Is that what is being reported? Is that what people actually think!?*

Tom strode over to the minibar and grabbed a bottle of Lagavulin whiskey and poured the brown liquid into a tumbler glass. He took a long swig of the drink and sank down into his couch, closing his eyes and laying his head back.

Tom shot his head up after what only seemed a minute, opening his eyes, and noticed he must have fallen asleep because it was now dark outside. The digital clock on his cable box read 11:03 p.m. He could still see the lights from the reporters' spotlights and idling news vans, could still hear the blended talking of various reporters and onlookers. He needed something to drown out the noise, so he turned on the television. The TV screen lit to life and he saw some talking head on a cable news channel in the middle of a diatribe about violence and the media.

"—the tragic case of this poor woman – his own wife, Maggie Frost – and their unborn child on this reality show," the man said. He looked like a former high school or college quarterback – with slightly salt-and-peppered hair, wearing a suit and red tie, and sitting behind a news commentator desk with red, white and blue graphics wavering behind him. His voice contained a self-righteous cockiness and Tom noticed whenever he made an insult or judgment, he slightly cocked an eyebrow. When the talking head got heated, as he was now during this report, he often furrowed his brow and used his hands while speaking, making quick, sharp jabs. "And it was the victim's husband – Tom Frost – who is the host, creator and producer of this ... *reality* show, who is ... exploiting the unfortunate situations of these troubled individuals. Frost's show benefits off the shortcomings of others. And that is a form of entertainment of which no one should abide.

"Think about that poor woman tonight. Pray for her and her family and loved ones. Tom Frost should be ashamed of himself. He and his show, *Heartbrakers*, make my deadbeat pick of the day."

Tom turned off the television and leapt off the couch, striding toward the kitchen. The kitchen felt cold and it wasn't just the kitchen. The entire house felt cold – an unnatural occurrence in southern California. It reminded Tom of when he lived back east and he wouldn't turn on the heat for a day or two in the dead of winter. *What better way*, he thought, *to warm one's self than to have another drink?* Tom grabbed a regular drinking glass and returned to the minibar and the bottle of Lagavulin, but the drink had left a bad taste in his mouth and he searched for something different. His eyes fell on an unopened bottle of Patrón silver tequila. He poured himself the clear drink, filling up half of his glass, heading for a much-wanted vacation from reality. The telephone's mechanical ring broke the silence, making Tom slightly jump. When he walked up to the phone, the caller ID read "Private" and he instantly knew who it was on the other end: reporters. He raised the drink to his lips, awaiting the answering machine to pick up.

When the machine picked up the call, a woman's voice sounded off. "Hi, Mr. Frost. My name is Kimberly Carlton

..."

Tom stopped listening once she said which cable news channel she was from – the same one as the commentator he had just watched. Tom unplugged the phone and took a swig of the tequila. The first sting of the alcohol made him wince and he quickly took another drink. An insatiable urge to piss overtook him and he strode to the nearest bathroom, taking his drink with him.

Tom chugged his drink as he stood, relieving himself, and when he finished the drink, he looked to his side, peering at his reflection in one of the many mirrors. Being in the entertainment industry – as well as a huge movie fan – Tom could not help but recognize this would be the part in the movie where the conflicted, depressed protagonist feels sorry for himself and drinks himself into an oblivious stupor. *Screw that!* He finished his business and dumped the rest of his drink down the toilet before flushing. Tom looked to the clock. 11:30 p.m. He decided now was not the time to get drunk. Now was the time to get some sleep and get an early start to work in the morning.

An image of Maggie, staring up at him with pleading, teary eyes, lying on the floor at the motel, flashed through Tom's head. He winced as if he had received an electric shock. No matter how hard he tried, he couldn't get that image out of his head. A memory played through his mind again. Maggie dressed in a black Smiths T-shirt featuring a black-and-white photo of the band with the band's name in red letters above it, and a long, flowing Bohemian type of skirt, covering brown cowboy boots. It was sunset and she – laughing at him – was running away from him in the breaking waves at Rehoboth Beach. He next pictured them sitting together on that same day, he still in his red Funland shirt, tan shorts and black Chuck Taylors. She had brought peanut butter and jelly sandwiches to the beach. As the sun was setting, bringing a golden hue to the sky with streaks of pink and purple, he took a bite of his sandwich and looked over to her, her red hair cascading down her shoulders. He could tell by the look on her face that she was relishing the sandwich.

"Mmm," she exclaimed with a mouthful of sandwich before swallowing it down. "There's just something about the beach and peanut butter and jelly sandwiches. To me, they've always gone hand in hand." Maggie bit her lip as she talked and he marveled in her observation, thinking he was the only one who thought that.

"Yeah. Brings me back to when I was a kid and my folks would pack 'em for our beach trips."

"It's definitely one of the best simple pleasures in life."

She smiled at him and it was so damn cute, it tore him up inside, in a good way. He had spent time with her over the summer and what he once believed to be annoying traits of hers soon became endearing and attractive.

"All we need is some good music and we've got a perfect night," she smiled.

"What kind of music?"

Maggie shrugged and her closed smile revealed she was thinking about it.

"Who's your favorite singer?"

She thought for a moment and said, "Morrissey is a *god*. That's all I can say."

"Are you kidding me!?" Tom asked.

"*What!?*" her smile broadened and a laugh escaped.

Tom tried his hardest to not roll his eyes but he couldn't help it. "They're not bad, but they're not anywhere near great."

"C'mon! *Morrissey!?* Johnny *fuckin'* Marr!?!?"

Maggie didn't cuss so strongly very often, but when she did, he thought it was so damn cool.

"Amerdale says to never fall for a girl who likes The Smiths so ... passionately."

"Who?" she asked.

"That's right. You're still pretty new. He's our supervisor? The scrawny guy?"

"Oh!" Maggie remembered. "Well, maybe he doesn't know what he's talkin' about."

"I don't know. Maybe."

"Well, who do you like, then?"

"I don't know. I haven't really thought about it."

"*What!?* Are you *kidding* me!?" Maggie cocked her head back as she laughed hard. "You've gotta have *some* favorites."

"I like that Funland mix tape that's goin' around."

"Yeah, but those are famous songs. Everyone loves those. Don't you have a favorite band or musician?"

"I don't know ..." Tom searched his head for the first musician that came to mind. "Um ... Jimi Hendrix."

Maggie slowly nodded her head. "Yeah, he's great."

Tom remembered that day as perfect. He had just met Maggie at the beginning of that summer season, in May. Their days together were made up of moments like this which made him fall all the more in love with her.

Tom opened his eyes and he was back in the miserable present where she was gone. He had to think about it in order to believe it to be true. He hadn't felt it while the images played across his memory, but he discovered he was crying when the tears fell upon his hands. As soon as he realized it, Tom shook himself as if he was nodding off from falling asleep and he wiped his eyes dry.

He knew he wouldn't be getting any sleep for the rest of the night, so he slowly moved to his couch, turned the TV on, and – before the picture came on – changed the channel to the American Movie Classics channel. After a few minutes, he recognized the movie that was showing: the 1962 film *Days of Wine and Roses*, starring Jack Lemmon and Lee Remick.

Tom watched the entire movie, then the next – 1944's *Lifeboat* – and the next – 1950's *In a Lonely Place*. He must have fallen asleep some time during *In a Lonely Place*, because he didn't remember watching the ending (even though he knew what happened because he had seen it before). The next thing he knew, the sun was peeking through his window, shining directly onto his face. When he opened his eyes, the sun instantly stung them, temporarily blinding him.

His eyes adjusted to the light, he looked to a clock and saw the time. 10:23 a.m. He was late to work! His body jolted awake and he ran to the bathroom. There was no time to take a shower or shave so he wiped some deodorant under his arms, splashed some aftershave on his cheeks, brushed his hair and got dressed in different clothes. When he was done, he grabbed his car keys, about to go out to his car when he stopped short. He remembered there were reporters outside, waiting to get a statement from him.

Tom sauntered over to the window, then looking out toward the street. His car was there, along with at least ten different reporters and their respective camera crews, as well as a few paparazzi photographers. He knew he'd have to make his way through them sooner or later, but was hoping it would be much later. He dropped his head. "*Shit.*"

* * *

A knock on the van's window awoke Jen. She had fallen asleep in the network van outside of Tom's house, hoping for the first glimpse of him. The knock didn't come from Tom, though. It was her cameraman, Carl. He held up a Styrofoam cup of coffee and Jen couldn't think of anything better right now as she groggily stretched, yawned and opened the van door. She took the coffee and said thanks.

"Has he come out yet?" she asked.

"Not yet. Do you really think he's gonna come out—?"

The front door to Tom's house creaked open and Tom passed through the doorway, dressed in jeans, a button-up shirt, and a sports coat, and wearing Wayfarer sunglasses.

"Carl ...," Jen's voice grew tense. "Get the—"

"Got it!" Carl already had the camera on his shoulder and was recording. Jen grabbed her microphone and ran - along with the other reporters and cameramen - to the edge of Tom's property.

The closer Tom walked toward his car, the louder the reporters' voices got. Tom kept his head down, his view reduced to a small portion of what was in front of him - the tires of his car at the top of his sight with his feet popping into the bottom of his view like the moles out of a Whac-a-Mole game.

"Tom! Tom!" he heard Kimberly Carlton shout. There were several shouts of his name but he ignored them all, worried if he looked to any of them, they would rip away any strength he had left.

He collided with the side of his car, fished the keys out of his pocket, pressed the unlock button on his key fob and opened the door. As he got in and turned the key in the engine, the radio blared midway through Tony Lucca's cover of "Devil Town," and Tom's eyes connected with Jen's.

When Jen looked through the windshield and saw the look on Tom's face, she felt the pain and betrayal he felt. Tom had expected the media to exploit his pain. He had been in the media game for a long time and knew what drove a headline. Whether he liked it or not, Jen was a part of that world. But he was still hurt by her very presence there. The look he flashed her seemed to say, *How could you?* It was only then that he realized he had made the same living off of exploiting people's pain.

Jen felt awful for even being there. She couldn't help but feel as if she had let Tom down. She knew he wouldn't want to speak with any reporters, and now she clearly saw the pain in his eyes. It had been years since they last spoke, but it didn't make the betrayal of their friendship any less hurtful.

Tom's car sped off, leaving Jen and the other reporters behind. As the other reporters dispersed to their vans, Jen stood with tears in her eyes, wishing she were in that car with Tom. She wanted to be with him not to get the story or interview, but just to be there for him, to support him. The media reports she had watched so far told her that Tom's world was just beginning to be ripped apart.

* * *

The media and paparazzi swarmed around the television studio's entrance gate like wolves awaiting an injured animal. Tom's Porsche pulled up to the studio guard's booth and Tom instantly wanted to drive forward in order to avoid the press. The middle-aged guard at the gate couldn't believe what he was seeing. He had come to know Tom Frost as they greeted each other every work morning and said their farewells every work evening. They had a friendly rapport and the guard had felt Tom was good people with a solid head on his shoulders. Although, when he saw Tom pull up in his car, he was gobsmacked as to Tom being there now ... at this place ... after all that had just happened two days ago. For the first time since they met, the guard second-guessed Tom's common sense.

"Hey Scott," Tom greeted. The guard could tell Tom wanted to get moving through the gate as soon as possible, but, otherwise, he seemed normal.

"Hey ... Mr. Frost." It took the guard a few extra seconds to break out of his curiosity as to why someone who had just lost his wife and unborn child in such a violent, public way would be at work two days later. Tom's eyes broke away from Scott, prompting him to push the button to raise the gate.

Tom was happy to pass through the gate just as the reporters were starting to surround his car. He looked in the rearview and didn't see Jen. That made him happier than he thought. Her presence at his house was discomforting enough, almost a poison, and he didn't need any more salt rubbed in his wounds.

Tom was happy to pull into his reserved parking spot, and anxious to get back to work. As weird as it sounded, Tom felt working again was a nice distraction. He didn't want to sit. Sitting and staying at home meant he would have nothing to do but think about what had happened to Maggie. He practically jumped out from his car and strode into the office. The receptionist, Marcie, was on the phone when he glided by, quickly greeting her. Marcie was young and pretty and naïve, a recent college graduate who had just started three months ago to replace the receptionist who couldn't handle working with Dylan after they had slept together and he had started dating Lucia.

As soon as she was off the phone with the caller, Marcie pushed a button on her phone and spoke softly into the receiver, "He's *here*. He *just* walked in. I don't know. I think he's on his way to see you."

Marcie hung up the phone and, along with the rest of the office workers in their cubicles, watched Tom walk back to his office. When he reached his office door, he turned the handle and was surprised to find it was locked. He looked over his shoulder and could practically hear the turning of the heads of those sitting nearby.

Tom walked down the hall and entered into Dylan's office to see him sitting at his desk, watching Fox News on his big screen TV. The commentator was talking about Tom and the TV show, sounding just like the guy who Tom had watched the night before.

Dylan saw Tom standing in his doorway, but couldn't believe he was actually there.

"Hey ... buddy," Dylan said as he stood up and quickly walked to Tom. Tom could tell by Dylan's half-hearted hug that he was simply trying to feign sympathy. "Didn't think you were coming in today."

"I ... I needed something to distract me."

"You know you don't have to be here, though. I mean,

I'm happy to have ya here, but, if you need more time—"

"No," Tom's abrupt voice slammed down like a thick book in an empty library, and then softened with emotion. "I can't be there, Dylan."

Dylan had often been accused of being extremely dense in his thinking, but he immediately knew what Tom was talking about. Even though he had his qualms with Maggie – especially now after the world knew she was cheating on Tom – he knew his friend loved her. Dylan knew it must be a bitter pill for Tom to swallow but there it was.

"I need ... to keep busy," Tom said. "Or I'll go crazy."

"I'd like to have you here, Tom. But ..."

"'But' what?"

"I think the studio execs should talk with you about it."

"What is it, Dylan? What are you not telling me?"

Dylan looked away from his friend and out the large panoramic window. "It's Maggie's parents. They're suing the show."

"What!?"

"Yeah. They're claiming we were inadvertently responsible for Maggie's death. Involuntary manslaughter, I think."

"But I didn't know it was Maggie who was under surveillance. I didn't know she was involved at all. If I did, I sure as hell wouldn't televise it!"

"Your signature's on the consent form to move forward with the show."

"*What*!? Where?"

Dylan grabbed a paper off his desk and showed it to Tom, who snatched it away, reading as intently as possible. When Tom saw his signature, he knew it was his signature but he never saw a paper with Maggie's name on it like the one he was reading now.

"I never saw this paper."

"But that's your signature."

"Yeah! But I never saw a paper with Maggie's name on it." Tom delved into his memory, searching for what he did sign. "The only paper I signed was what you gave me about the Amy girl ... to move on with the show."

Tom's eyes caught Dylan looking away. Then he knew. He knew his best friend had tricked him. He couldn't believe it. He didn't want to believe it.

"That paper." Tom was slowly piecing the puzzle together. "You tricked me. That was *this* paper! That's why you didn't want the investigators on the scene when we recorded the show! Andrew *knew* it was Maggie. You didn't want him to give it away."

"Tom. I did it for your own good. For you and for the good of the show."

"She was my wife, Dylan!" Tom shouted so loud, the outside office workers and interns dialed security. "You had no right!"

Dylan held out his hands as if to keep Tom backed away.

"I don't know what to say, Tom," Dylan said slowly and softly. His eyes slowly filled with tears. "I was doing it for the show. For you. For ... my dad. It's like – the things I do for my old man. It's sick that I actually do the bad shit I do just to win his approval. Ya know? Just for him to think I'm cool? He's always saying, 'Dylan! You've got to be number one! I won't tolerate any losers in this family! Your intensity is for shit! *Win! Win! Win!!!*

"That son of a bitch." Dylan hung his head, placing his hand over his brow, hiding the tears, as his shoulders slightly convulsed as he wept.

"You ...," Tom said, his eyes in a thoughtful furrow. "... seriously think I don't know that's from *The Breakfast Club*?"

Dylan's head popped up with dry eyes and an almost cat-who-ate-the-canary look. "Tom—"

No words followed as Dylan's explanation was cut short by Tom's strong punch to the middle of Dylan's face, knocking him backward. Shattered glass shards exploded like fireworks throughout Tom's right knuckles as he immediately grabbed his hand to try and quell the pain.

"Ow!" Tom yelped. "Sonofabitch!"

Dylan regained his footing and lurched his head forward as blood gushed from his nose. He shot Tom a look of shock.

A burly security guard busted through Dylan's office door, saw Dylan bleeding and grabbed Tom to hold him back.

"What the *hell*, Tom!?" Dylan shouted.

"You asshole!" Tom tried to break away from the security guard's grasp, even though his knuckles were already swelling. "How could you do this to me!? How could you do this to *her*!?"

Dylan's secretary rushed into the office as the security guard hauled Tom out. She examined Dylan's handsome, bruised face while Dylan silently seethed, furious at his former best friend.

Tom heard the guard's heavy coffee-breath wheezing, his weight betraying his strength as he lugged the intruder down to the lobby. He knew he could easily break away from the guard if he wanted, but figured the damage had already been done. He had made his point and he didn't need to be there any longer. The guard hit the automatic door opener for handicapped convenience, lifted Tom by the back of his pants, lifting Tom's feet off the ground, and launched him into the outside light.

Tom didn't even try to catch his footing and fell face first onto the cold, hard pavement. He just lay there as passersby continued to walk around him without so much as a second glance. After a minute or two, Tom planted both hands on the ground and pushed himself up. He remembered the ironic sign-off he always ended his *Heartbraker* episodes with: "Remember! Life can put the brakes on love but never let love put the brakes on your life. Good night."

8.

"Sad deserted shore, your fickle friends are leaving
But then you know it's time for them to go
But I will still be here, I have no thought of leaving
I do not count the time
For who knows where the time goes?
Who knows where the time goes?"

--Nina Simone (written by Sandy Denny)
"Who Knows Where the Time Goes"

Tom awoke at the droning sound of his alarm. It had been going off for three hours before he turned it off. He rolled over and looked at the big red digital numbers staring back at him. 11:45 a.m. He remembered today wasn't the day after hitting his former best friend. That day, he turned off the alarm and rolled back over to go back to sleep. Today marked four days since the disaster at his job. Tom figured he would just get more sleep, but his cell phone rang and his mind played a quick game of tug-of-war, deciding whether he should answer it or not.

He got up and looked at who was calling. It was Lucia. He ignored the call and threw his phone down on his bed. Then he remembered what was happening today.

"Damn," he whispered.

Tom bolted up from his bed and almost ran to his bathroom, started his shower and jumped in before the water warmed up. Tom's brain went into automatic pilot, going through the motions of showering, brushing his hair, getting dressed in a suit, putting on his sunglasses, getting in his car and racing to his destination.

One of the things Tom hated about L.A. was how it was pretty much always sunny ... and smoggy. While the sunny weather sounds appealing to most everyone, he sometimes yearned for a few consecutive rainy days – especially today.

His car pulled into the church parking lot, the steeple's reflection looming in his car's front window. There were friends and family members he recognized and some he imagined he had only heard about from Maggie. Most of the bodies were dressed in blacks and dark blues to match their somber faces. If the collective mood could have wrought the weather, L.A. would now be subjected to its first monsoon.

Just beyond the entryway to the church were camera crews and TV news vans. Even on this sad day, the media still couldn't grant Maggie or her family any peace. Tom wondered if the media was expecting him to show up or if they were simply there to give the story more exposure. Either way, no matter what their reason, he felt they were wrong to be there. He, on the other hand, as her husband and best friend, had every right to be there.

He waited until everyone he could see was inside the church, then slowly got out of his car and inconspicuously walked toward it. Fortunately, the press was far away from the church entrance so he didn't have to worry about hearing any of their ridiculous questions or accusations.

Tom's hand reached out for the warm, metal handle, and pulled, making the door creak open and bright sunlight spill into the church. He ducked inside in case anyone was looking and his nerves got the best of him. He hadn't watched any television since the day he was released from the hospital, but he still received texts and updates on his phone. He saw proof that Dylan was telling the truth and Brenda and Eddie were suing the studio and production company for involuntary manslaughter in the death of Maggie. The news first came as a shock to him; although, after having given the matter some deep thought, he knew it was probably the sanest thing they could have done in their situation. He knew he'd be subpoenaed and the thought of going to court scared the shit out of him. Tom had never gotten in any major trouble before and never even went through the usual "rebellious teenager" phase, so dealing with authorities intimidated him.

He looked out at the sea of heads among the wooden pews, not sure where to sit or whether he should. Before he grew too self-conscious, he thought about Maggie. She had been his strength through a lot of tough times; his reason for going as far as he did in his job was because he knew it would make her happy. That's how he had been raised. A man provides for his family and if he can make them happy, that should make him happy. He didn't really care what anyone else thought and that feeling spurred him down the aisle.

Tom could feel most of the people's eyes on him as he walked by, and he knew the looks were anything but sympathetic. Their scornful stares burned into him, piercing like arrows. In the front pew, he saw Brenda and Eddie sitting as still as stones and he felt like a criminal caught in the act. He knew he couldn't sit next to them – or even in the same pew – but didn't know where to go next.

"Hm-hmm!" the familiar female voice of someone clearing their throat echoed through the church and Tom looked to the second row to see Lucia staring at him and nodding her head, motioning him to sit in the empty seat next to her. He was relieved to see Dylan was not with her – or there, at all.

He walked back to the second row and squeezed into the seat at the end. The eyes were still directed at him despite the priest's words and the coffin set front and center. Tom had made sure he missed the viewing of Maggie's body. He never minded funerals but he hated the viewing. It was a futile event which served the living more than the dead and he took no comfort in seeing someone's shell – which was once so bright and alive – in its dead, bleak stasis. What made the show so much worse was the process of painting the shell to make it look like its former alive self. Tom felt it all much too insincere and dishonest for a ceremony which was meant for celebration and honor.

Tom had to suppress a smile when he thought about Maggie and her true feelings about funerals.

* * *

"Ew! Gross!" Maggie exclaimed, her face clenching into a cute mix of fear and disgust. It had been two months since she and Tom reconnected at their college reunion. Maggie had gotten a residency at a hospital in L.A., and Tom's career with the television studio was rising. They mostly spent their nights just hanging out together in Tom's apartment.

Tom laughed at her reaction, not able to believe she felt so strongly about his admission. He watched her as she took a bite of her spoonful of chocolate ice cream and nearly lost it as a fit of laughter hit her again.

"What?" Tom asked through his laughter.

"I can't believe you *like* that song!"

"It's catchy!" Tom defended.

"That's *it*. You officially have horrible taste in music."

She looked upon Tom with wonderment and bit her lip without knowing she was doing it. Tom looked back to her and she swiftly looked away.

"I think you and my mom should hang out," she said.

"How's your mom been lately?" Tom asked.

Her face transitioned from jovial to serious. She took a gulp and steeled her voice. "She's ... OK. The chemo is going well. As well as it can go, anyways."

Tom knew this was a sore subject for Maggie and he had learned to just hear her out, to let her voice her apprehensions. He watched her, her eyes conveying her mind was somewhere else.

"Tom," she snapped out of her trance. "Lately, I've been thinking a lot about my mom not making it." Maggie took a deep gulp, trying to swallow down the tears. "I'm lucky that I haven't been to many funerals. But I remember the couple I've been to - my grandmother and my aunt. And I always thought the whole ceremony of it was so ... fake."

Tom had thought Maggie would say morbid or sad, but he didn't expect fake. He agreed with her one-hundred percent. He believed the way the mortician painted the faces up to look alive was morbid and more for show, but he didn't want to chime in with his opinion. Tom leaned into her as she continued, "Promise me. When I die, if you're still around, you won't hold some viewing of me. 'Cause ... that won't be me. That will be some painted-up puppet." She grew silent again, gears in her head turning. Tom could tell she was anxious to reveal what was truly on her mind. "Do you think there's a God?"

Tom's mouth practically hung open. He did not expect to be talking about such serious topics at this moment, but that was how these things often came up: suddenly and surprisingly.

"I guess the important thing is whether *you* believe in God," Tom said. "Do you?"

Maggie didn't like how Tom had sort of diverted the question back onto her, but she pondered the question.

"I ...," she paused, thinking more about the question. She had been raised Catholic since she was a kid and, when she reached high school and college, she questioned the validity of all she had been taught in Sunday school and church. She knew she could've just blindly believed what she had been raised to believe all her young life, but she wanted to seek out answers for herself. She had researched the church's stance as well as that of some of the pastors and priests she knew; and she had read texts by agnostics and atheists. By the time she had read all she did, she felt she had a mixed bag of beliefs. Ultimately, her belief was, "Yes. Yeah. I believe in God." She thought a moment and a small smile crept across her lips. "But I don't believe in painting yourself up after you're gone. Just seems more for the living than for the dead."

* * *

Tom sat in church as one of Maggie's friends spoke out a eulogy through her heavy sobs. He almost smiled at the warm memory, but stopped when he realized where he was and the thought entered his head about whether Maggie's belief in God had led her to heaven because of her belief, or hell because of her breaking a commandment. Tom forgot the thought as quickly as it had come into his mind, feeling bad about thinking it in the first place and thinking it ultimately didn't matter where she was now. She was gone. And she was never coming back.

The funeral ceremony soon ended and the organ played the hymn "Be Not Afraid" as the crowd slowly shuffled out of the pews and down the aisle. Tom remained until everyone was gone. He watched the pallbearers align themselves along both sides of the coffin. He thought about going up and taking a hold of one side, but both sides were already full to carry the casket. So he sat and watched as his wife's body was carried to the hearse waiting outside. When the church was empty and Tom heard no more echoes of movement, he bowed his head and cried for the first time since he was first told about Maggie's death at the hospital.

After the echoes of his sobs dissipated and he no longer heard his own childish blubbering, Tom wiped his face dry, stood up and calmly walked out of the church. By the time he arrived at the cemetery, he was met at the entrance gate by the appearance of Maggie's dad, Eddie, smoking a cigarette. He was a bit surprised and not sure what to expect. He parked his car and warily walked up to the man.

"Mr. Russell," Tom greeted solemnly.

"Tom," Eddie mumbled.

Tom abruptly stopped at the sound of his father-in-law's voice and peered into his bloodshot eyes. He could tell the man had been crying – most likely non-stop – for days.

"You're not welcome here," Eddie said.

"What?" Tom almost let out a laugh, thinking of the absurdity of Eddie's request. "But it's OK if I'm at the ceremony?"

"That was church. Everyone is welcome there. But not here. Not you."

"She's my wife, Ed."

"No, she's not. Not after what you did to her." He took one last puff of his cigarette and flicked it into the road.

"What *I* did to her!? What'ya mean!?"

"I know my Maggie wasn't perfect for you, but ... she didn't deserve what happened to her." Eddie's voice started cracking, sounding as if he were about to burst into tears at any moment. "And she damn well didn't deserve for the whole *damn* thing to be on *national* television!"

"Ed. I know. I'm sorry–"

"Don't you *dare!*" Eddie's voice growled in a way Tom had never heard from him before. "Don't you *talk* to me. She was *my baby*! My *daughter*! And thanks to your stupid show, she's dead! She was my *only* kid and she's *dead!*"

"Mr. Russell. You have to believe me–"

"Brenda and I are suing your trashy show," Eddie said in a whisper. "Stay the hell away from us."

"I–"

"Ya know. When you become a parent, you get your first glimpse of mortality and how much it truly sucks. I mean, when you're younger, you know you're gonna die. But you don't think about it because it's just you and it feels so far away. It's not until you become a parent that the idea of dying depresses the hell out of ya. 'Cause ... you know this tiny, amazing person you created is going to live on long after you're gone. And you wish you could be there for their entire life. Be there for every joy and every hurt. But you accept you won't and it slowly becomes OK. You're actually happy that they'll have an entire life ahead of them. A life hopefully with someone they love, maybe some kids of their own.

"So, when your child dies, you realize you still have a whole other life. A life *without* them. Ya see ... you continue to be a parent, but with no kid. And the life you hoped you would have is gone. The life you hoped your kid would have is gone. Your family ... is gone."

"Ed—"

Eddie punched Tom, landing a right hook over his left eye and pushing the younger man backward. The sting ripped through Tom's face and across his head, sending reverberations down his spine. Although the punch did not surprise Tom, his face relayed the opposite as tears welled in his eyes. Eddie's rage subsided and he felt ashamed at his outburst, looking away from Tom's wounded stare.

"No," Eddie's voice was not so much a demand as it was a pleading. "We don't want you here. Nobody does. Please ... respect our wishes. Go."

"She was my wife, Ed. I loved her." Tom was about to launch into how *he* had been the betrayed one here, how Maggie had lied and cheated on *him*, how Dylan had betrayed him and he didn't know anything about Maggie being on the show. However, when Eddie's eyes peered at Tom, the look in his father-in-law's eyes quelled his desire to speak his mind.

"One day ... you'll get to ... move on from all this, Tom," Eddie was close to sobs. "You'll most likely meet someone new and soon, while I know you'll think of Maggie, she'll just be some part of your former life. A distant memory of someone you may pray for ... until, one day, you've forgotten.

"But *me?* My *wife?*" Eddie continued. "We'll *always* have a piece of us missing. Our lives will never be whole again. And we'll never forget. *Ever.*" Tom no longer saw what he thought would have been Eddie's justified anger, but rather a man broken. "Please ... just go."

Edward Russell had been crying ever since he saw his daughter lying on that cold metal table; and since that day, his body had betrayed any strength he had tried to muster. He was weak. His voice trembled and his shoulders retained a slump as if oversized weights had been tied to his hands and worn away any remaining confidence and posture. His face had somehow acquired more lines and wrinkles as if an artist had drawn them on in the few days since Tom last saw him. Once Tom noticed the pain exuding from every look, every action from Eddie, he looked away in shame.

"OK," Tom mumbled as he lowered his head. By the time he looked up again, Eddie was already halfway back to the burial site.

Tom turned around and walked back to his red Porsche - the only splash of color in a sea of black, tan, white, and silver vehicles. When he got into the car and started the engine, a light drizzling had started and the radio played the slow tempo guitar riffs and echoes of Black Rebel Motorcycle Club's "Feel It Now." Tom sat and listened to the music while he watched the raindrops smear what portions of the funeral scene portrait he could see from his car. All he could do now was imagine the scene.

He thought of Maggie's inconsolable parents sitting in the front two chairs, their tears blended together with the raindrops. He thought of Maggie's girlfriends and their urge to stay strong while their faces betrayed them and their respective husbands placed a comforting arm around each of them. He thought about Lucia trying to be a good friend, feeling guilty from her association with Dylan and what the show had wrought.

A flash of red and blue lights and a knock at Tom's car window snapped him out of his thoughts. He looked outside to see two county police officers standing beside his car. Tom rolled down his window and the policeman standing closest to his car said, "Mr. Thomas Frost?"

"Yes?" Tom replied.

"Sir, could you please step out of the vehicle?"

Tom quietly got out of the car and he noticed both officers place a hand on each of their holstered guns.

"Mr. Frost, you are under arrest for the assault on Mr. Dylan Vaughn." The cop turned Tom around and placed both of Tom's arms behind his back, then placed the cold, hard handcuffs around each wrist as tight as possible. "You have the right to remain silent. Anything you say or do can and will be used against you in court. You have the right to an attorney. If you cannot afford an attorney, one will be appointed to you."

The cop continued to ramble out Tom's Miranda rights but Tom had stopped listening after the first sentence. He could not believe his best friend was pressing charges against him. His mind fought his mouth to speak but no words came out, making him appear as if he were a fish out of water, gasping for life. Both policemen escorted Tom to their nearby police car. One opened the door while the other guided him down into the backseat. The door slammed closed. Tom could still see the smallest sliver of the funeral scene. The car pulled away, making the scene disappear before his eyes, and that was how he said goodbye to his wife.

* * *

The idea of jail scared the hell out of Tom more than having to appear in court. The car ride to the troop station did not take long – maybe ten minutes. Tom wished it had taken longer so he would have more time to mentally prepare himself for what he knew lay ahead. The police car came to stop in front of the station and there were already reporters from every local and major news station standing around.

Tom was hoping the officers would pull the car around to another parking area, but the car pulled to a stop and the reporters swarmed the car akin to buzzards picking apart a dead carcass. The two police officers got out of the car, one shoving the reporters back while the other opened Tom's door, grabbed Tom's arm and lifted him out of the car. Tom lowered his head, not wanting to see who was there nor the looks on their faces. The walk from the car to the door was only maybe a few feet, but Tom felt as if each step had taken the time span of an hour. He heard the shouts of his name, the flashes from the cameras gave off a strobe light effect, and his heart beat so strongly it felt as if it were in his throat. He gasped for air and the reporters' voices became louder and their questions faster.

Tom watched the pavement under his feet but couldn't gauge whether he was close to the building or not. By this point, he had tried to single out Jen's voice among the crowd but he did not hear her. There was a slight rush of air and then silence.

"OK," one of the officers said. "You're clear."

Tom raised his head and saw he was in the precinct. The walk to the booking office was quick and uneventful. The motions of the officer booking him almost seemed robotic – an automated service from an automaton using monotonous, technical speak. *Stand there. Turn left. Turn right. Look straight. Right thumb here. Right index finger here.* And so on.

During his mug shot, he thought about how he certainly never believed he would be in a situation like this. Losing his wife. Losing his job. Losing his friends. Losing his freedom. The one thing he did not regret was *why* he lost his freedom. Dylan had deserved that punch; although, he had deserved more than just that. Tom hoped Eddie's lawsuit against the network and the show was successful, and, if there were any true justice, Dylan would lose his job.

Tom wasn't in the holding cell long before his lawyer, Robert McGuffin, stepped in front of him. Bob, as Tom called him, was an older gentleman of sixty-eight-years-old, although he looked ten years younger. His silver hair was brushed with a part on his left, his black eyebrows standing out, accentuating the eyes of a cowboy. His gray suit almost matched his hair but his red silk tie stuck out. His slight cockeyed smirk and classic movie star good looks made Tom think he was from the New England area and maybe he was an actor in his previous life, but the man was from Davenport, Iowa, and he was often soft-spoken and shied away from any limelight – his presence in the courtroom being the only exception.

"Mr. Frost," Robert greeted.

"Hey, Bob."

"You haven't said anything yet to anyone, have you?"

Tom shook his head no. The guard stepped away and Bob's demeanor somewhat relaxed. "Jesus *Christ*, Tom! What were you thinking!?"

There were no words Tom could muster. He stood still, his head slowly arching downward.

"Don't worry," Bob said. "The bail is only set at twenty-five thousand. We'll post and get you outta here." Bob turned to step toward the office, but a small voice stopped him in his tracks.

"No."

"What?" Bob turned back to Tom. "What was that?"

"No. I don't want to post bail."

"What!? Why not!?"

"'Cause I'm guilty."

Bob looked around, hoping no officer heard his client's confession. "You're *what*!?"

"Guilty," Tom said a little louder. "I'm in here for assault. I punched Dylan. And I meant to do it."

"You did it because of the stress—"

"I did it because I think he deserved it. Yes, I was under a bit of stress. But I knew what I was doing. And I meant to do it. So, I'm guilty. I deserve to be in here."

"Tom. I don't think you know what you're doing. This charge is bullshit. Dylan knows it. He just wants money."

"Well, he damn well won't get any! I'm not going into some big trial over this. I'm pleading guilty and I'll face whatever the judge gives me. Even if it's more jail time."

"Dylan will get money! Even if you plead guilty, the judge'll have you pay damages to him in the form of mental anguish. Dumbass!"

Tom would have laughed out at Bob's brief insult if it

weren't for the current surroundings in which he found himself.

"It doesn't matter," Tom said. "But I'm guilty. I'm staying here."

"Tom. Listen." Bob approached the cell and placed his hands on the bars. "I know you may be *feeling* guilty for what happened to Maggie. But this is not the time to take it out on yourself. Not here."

"You've been a great lawyer to me, Bob. But this is it. I've been fired from the show. The show and network are getting sued by Maggie's parents. I'm going to lose my money. So I won't be needing your services much longer. Then again, I won't even be able to afford your services.

"As one more favor to me. Please, let me do this. I'm guilty. I belong here."

During all of his twenty-five years as a lawyer, Bob had never heard such a request from a client. He thought Tom was stuck in his own self-pity, but, from the look on Tom's face, Bob knew Tom was sincere. And he couldn't help but feel sorry for the guy.

"Alright, Tom," Bob said. "If it's really what you want, we'll plead guilty. But I hope you know this charge will follow you all your life."

Tom's face cracked a smile, relieved at Bob's concession. "I understand."

"Well, you know who won't understand!? Your parents!"

"You called them?"

"Yeah! I told them you're in jail, and your mother's really upset."

"I know they'll be even more upset when they hear what I wanna do, but it's my choice. And I'll cross that bridge with them when the time comes."

"So what should I tell them?"

"Tell them ... tell 'em this is what I choose. I was charged with assault and I assaulted him. So I'm paying the price."

"OK," Bob sighed.

Tom did worry about what his parents would think of him, but he didn't care about the charge. Then he realized there was one more favor he wanted from Bob. "Bob. Before you go, I'll need your services for one more thing."

"What's that?"

* * *

The thirty-one days Tom spent in the holding cell (due to overcrowding in the nearest correctional facilities) were the most peaceful and welcome he had had since Maggie's death. There were no cameras, no reporters, no TV crews, no paparazzi, no bystanders shouting; and he relished the silence. So when the sheriff came in one morning and interrupted Tom's sleep, he was aggravated.

"Wake up, Frost," the sheriff growled. "Lawyer's here. Today's your hearing."

Tom looked up to see Bob - holding a clothes hanger with a suit on it - standing behind the sheriff.

"Did you do that thing I requested?" Tom asked.

"Yeah," Bob answered. The sheriff opened the cell door and Bob handed the clothes to Tom.

"My parents aren't here, are they?"

Bob's head gave a sharp, single shake no, and Tom's nerves settled. "Good."

Tom undressed right in front of Bob and the guard,

then quickly put on his suit. After he finished tying his blue necktie, he peered up at Bob, forced a smile and said, "Let's get this over with."

"Are you sure you want to do this, Tom?"

"Yeah."

When they left the police station, Tom was relieved to find the sheriff had taken him out a back entrance so there were no reporters, passersby or protesters to face. This was why Tom felt so disheartened when he, the sheriff and Bob pulled up in front of the courthouse and there was a massive gathering of local, cable and national news reporters gathered around the curb and steps leading to the entrance.

"Here we go," Bob sighed.

The sheriff threw open his car door and bolted out of his seat, with Bob following behind him. The sheriff drove himself through the crowds as if he were trying to walk in deep water against a strong current. The camera flashes were blinding and the shouts of both Tom's supporters and haters amongst the crowd were deafening. Among some of the shouts, Tom heard the words "murderer," "we love you," "guilty," and other words and phrases he didn't care to think about. Tom thought if this was the crowd for his small trial for assaulting Dylan, then imagine how big the turnout for Maggie's parents' trial against the show was going to be.

As he entered the courtroom, escorted by two bailiffs, Tom was relieved to not see Eddie or Brenda Russell in attendance. After ruling out their presence, he immediately looked toward the plaintiff's table and saw Dylan and his lawyers sitting there, not looking back toward him. Even when he and Bob sat at their table directly across from them, they still didn't manage to look over in his direction. From the looks of their smirks and laughs, whatever they were talking about, it seemed they were not concerned over Tom's show of violence toward Dylan or the possible harsh punishment that may lie ahead for Tom.

Tom leaned over to Bob's ear and whispered, "It doesn't look like Dylan is in too much distress over there, does it?"

Bob looked out of his peripheral vision toward Dylan, then gave another of his sharp head shakes to say no.

The judge came in the room, the people stood up; the lead bailiff announced the judge's name – Judge Anthony Stevens – and they were off to see where Tom would be living the next few months or years.

"In the charge of assault, how does the defendant plead?" the judge asked.

Bob stood up, cleared his throat and said, "Your honor, my client wishes to plead guilty."

"Mr. Frost," the judge said as Bob sat down. "Is there anything you wish to state before we proceed?"

Tom stood up and said, "Your honor. If the charge of assault entails the action of my punching Mr. Vaughn, then I am guilty. I fully admit to punching a man who deserved it." Tom looked over to Dylan, who was still looking straight ahead, noticing he smirked after the statement. "Also, it may help that today, my lawyer, Mr. McGuffin, filed a restraining order against Mr. Vaughn, so I can guarantee there will be no more harassment of Mr. Vaughn on my end."

Tom could hear Dylan and his lawyer turn in their seats. He looked over and saw that Dylan's smirk had turned into a shocked expression.

"Very well," the judge said as Tom sat down. "Does the plaintiff have anything to add?"

Dylan stood up and said with a sincere, hurt voice,

"Your honor. I understand that Mr. Frost is going through a difficult time right now, but that gives him no excuse to punch an innocent man, let alone a friend. I honestly hope he finds peace and eventually - maybe through God - happiness."

Dylan sat down and the judge looked to Dylan's lawyer - a young man of thirty-one-years-old - and said, "Mr. Gold. What are the damages the plaintiff requests?"

"Judge Stevens. If it pleases the court, the plaintiff, my client, Mr. Vaughn, is requesting the defendant pay damages in the sum of two-hundred-thousand dollars, for emotional distress."

Tom had to struggle to keep from laughing out loud. There was no emotional distress! Dylan's face was already healed, reshaped to the annoyingly perfect, handsome way it had been before Tom's fist met his face.

"Mr. Gold," the judge said. "You do realize that the maximum fine for assault is one thousand dollars?"

"Yes, your honor. But, Mr. Vaughn has had to endure extreme emotional distress over the betrayal of his once-best friend, as well as the physical damage to his face—"

"—which I see is completely healed, Mr. Gold," the judge said. "Let's not stretch this thing into anything more than it has to be." The judge perused a few papers on his stand. "Seeing how the defendant has pleaded guilty, the court is ready to hand down its sentence. Would the defendant please rise?"

Tom stood up and Bob stood with him.

"Mr. Frost," the judge stared straight into Tom's eyes. "I understand that your personal life has recently taken a tragic turn with the death of your wife, and, considering the circumstances of it being made so public, I can only imagine the anguish you must feel. However, regardless of Mr. Vaughn's actions, he did not deserve to be assaulted. Justice, Mr. Frost, is not the same as revenge. You cannot assault a person and not expect to face any consequences. You have no prior record and have taken responsibility by filing a restraining order, so I'm sure there won't be any more correspondence or interactions with Mr. Vaughn. Also, even though your thirty-one days in jail will be considered time served, you still have to pay damages.

"Therefore, it is my ruling that you pay the maximum fine of one thousand dollars to Mr. Vaughn, as well as his court fees. Court's adjourned."

The judge slammed his gavel on its block, making the sound reverberate throughout the courtroom. Tom's nerves fell into ease and he let out a long heavy breath. This time, it was Tom who didn't look over to the other table. The last thought running through his head before the bailiff led him out was if he didn't see Dylan ever again, it would be too soon.

9.

"Out of the blue and into the black
They give you this,
But you pay for that
And once you're gone,
You can never come back
When you're out of the blue and into the black"

--Neil Young
"My My, Hey Hey (Out of the Blue)"

It had been two months since Tom plead guilty to punching his best friend in the face. Most of the TV news vans, reporters and onlookers had disappeared from the street in front of his house. Since he had changed his phone number, the prank calls and interview queries had stopped. The media vultures seemed to have found some other unfortunate carrion of some poor soul's privacy of which to pick upon.

Every so often there were TV documentary specials or countdowns which listed the most shocking moments caught on video, where Maggie's death was replayed. Tom caught one such special and it made him race to the toilet and vomit. Social media was even worse, with hundreds of random people leaving comments on his and the *Heartbraker* web pages, saying everything from Tom being a murderer to how much of a lowlife whore Maggie had been and she deserved what she had got. Since that moment, he cancelled his cable subscription and deleted his social media accounts. Tom figured he'd catch up on his reading – some Hemingway, Dickens, Orwell, Fitzgerald, Flannery O'Connor, James Baldwin, Raymond Carver, Stephen King, and some random other books he had always had the intention of reading, but which had only collected dust until now. The new worlds he plunged into became a welcome distraction while the world outside moved on – one scandal at a time.

His stereo system was playing Amelia's "Better Than Sleeping Alone" and he was just under halfway into reading W. Somerset Maugham's *The Razor's Edge*, so Tom didn't hear the first few knocks at his door. When the casual knocks turned to a loud rapping, he took notice. This wasn't the first time someone had tried to lure him to the door, hoping to get an interview or catch a glimpse of the once-great reality-TV-producer-turned-recluse. He had learned to ignore the noise so the usual solicitors would eventually leave. However, this particular visitor's persistence was unlike the others. The banging continued until it became a steady, fast pounding that didn't seem to have any pause.

"Tom! Tom! I know you're in there!"

Tom recognized that voice. Lucia. He rolled his eyes out of annoyance, slammed his open book down on the couch, shot up and walked to the front door.

Lucia had been worried about Tom ever since she saw the live broadcast of Maggie's murder. She had tried to call him many times but got his voicemail message so much, she had it memorized.

Tom opened the door and he wasn't sure if it was the sunlight or Lucia herself, but a blaring light blasted him, making him squint as if he had just woken up. She looked as beautiful as ever – her raven black hair falling down over her exposed slender, tanned shoulders. Her dark eyes were covered by a pair of reflective aviator sunglasses but Tom could tell from her demeanor that she had been crying before knocking on his door.

"Where the *hell* have you been!?" she shouted, her voice full of equal parts tears and rage. "I've been calling and calling you!"

"I've been here. What time is it?"

Lucia looked over Tom's shoulder and could see a few small piles of random clothes along the floor.

"Have you been here the whole time I've been calling!?" Lucia asked. Tom's disaffected stare purveyed to her he didn't care what she was talking about. "Are you just gonna be some shut-in for the rest of your life!?"

"So?"

"*So?* It's time to stop feeling sorry for yourself! It's time to get out and *do something*! *Anything*!" She brushed past him and the smell of body odor and old food almost made her gasp out for breath. "It's 8:30, by the way."

Tom closed the door and went upstairs. Lucia followed him but stopped dead in her tracks at the sight of his bedroom. There were pizza boxes and empty heat-up meals peppered along the floor, caught in an endless wrestling match with shirts, socks and underwear. She noticed three stacks of books – hardcovers and paperbacks of all different sizes – piled up on Tom's nightstand. His side of the bed was unmade, a terrain of sheets and blankets pushed aside, collapsed and disheveled; while the other side of the bed was made, the comforter pulled tightly across, covering the crisp, unwrinkled pillow – a welcoming place of comfort – and the nightstand had only a clean surface.

"You're not drunk right now, are you?" Lucia asked.

Tom shook his head no as he walked past her and into the master bathroom. He didn't bother shutting the door; just walked up to the toilet, pulled himself out of his sweatpants and urinated, the long, steady stream echoing its impact on the water.

"Are you peeing?"

"Um-hmm."

Lucia reached for the bathroom door and slammed it shut, backing away from the door as if it were covered in filth.

"It's been a month since the Russell's trial, Tom. I know it's been rough for you. But you're not alone. You still have people who are here for you."

The urinating abruptly stopped, the door swung open and Tom popped through the doorway.

"My wife is dead, Lou." He sounded exasperated, as if it had taken all his strength to say that aloud. "She's gone." His voice cracked, on the edge of tears. The silence he needed to compose himself hung in the air and was awkward, but he didn't cry – especially in front of people. "Maggie's gone. And I'm responsible. It's my fault."

"No, you're not. Don't say that. It wasn't you. You were tricked. You didn't know." She grabbed his hands and he looked back toward her to see her dark eyes making direct contact with his tired eyes. "It's not your fault."

"My two best friends are gone! I don't even have a job."

"You'll get another job."

Tom dropped his hands, breaking her grip, and turned away from her. She didn't understand the way the business worked. He had been blacklisted – no studio or producer wanted to touch him, whether it be hiring him or taking on any of his ideas.

"Nobody wants to touch the asshole who got his wife killed. Besides, it doesn't matter."

Ever since Maggie's death, Lucia had always been afraid Tom would commit suicide; so when he made statements like the one he had just made, she tried to be reassuring and supportive.

"You didn't get your wife killed. And it does matter. It matters to me. I'm still your friend." She leaned toward Tom and their foreheads touched. "I know life sucks right now, but you've got to get up and get back out there."

"Have you heard from Dylan lately?"

The question caught Lucia off-guard. She backed away from Tom and the look on her face gave him the answer. Her eye contact broke away and she moved toward a pile of clothes on the floor.

"You really need to clean this place up," she said.

"Are you still seeing him?"

"Tom–"

"Are you?"

"It's ... complicated."

"You still love him, don't you? Even after what he did, you love him."

"He feels horrible about what happened."

"He's the one who *intentionally* set up the entire case! He knew it was Maggie!"

"Yes! But he didn't know she'd die!"

"Don't be naïve, Lou. Just ... just be honest." He could see her eyes well up with tears, her face contorting from fighting to breaking down in a sobbing mess. She placed her hands up over her mouth, turning away from him. "Tell me why you really stay with him."

"Don't turn this around on me. I'm just trying to help. I'm your friend."

Tom's laugh started off as a small puttering then got louder until he was practically hysterical.

"What?" she asked.

"It's," Tom began when his laughter dissipated until he could speak through his chuckling. "It's," his laughter had ceased but his smile stuck, "really OK. You don't have to explain."

"I wanted to talk to you about it. I just thought there'd be a better time for it."

"I don't think there'd ever be a *better* time to find out you're dating someone like that."

Tom moved away and sat down on the small couch, his head hanging low. Lucia knew Tom would have trouble accepting this bit of news, but she thought if Tom and Dylan could overcome this obstacle, they could all be friends again.

She sat down next to Tom and put her arm around him. Leaning closer to him, she said, "I know you're mad at him right now. I am too. But he truly didn't know Maggie was going to be killed much less be in any danger. It's not his fault and it's not your fault!"

For a minute, Lucia could see Tom perk his head up and take her words to heart. She knew if she continued to talk him through his anger and melancholy, there was a good chance to make everyone's friendship go back to the way it once was.

Tom remembered a year ago, at a party, when he and Lucia were both drunk and slow dancing together, and how she had confessed to him that she was attracted to him and if they were ever single, she'd love to be with him. The memory raced through his mind as he turned his head and passionately kissed her on the lips. She kissed him back for a moment before ripping away from his lips.

"What are you doing!?" she asked, incredulous he would attempt such a thing.

A devilish grin was Tom's only response to Lucia's question. She stood up, her thoughts and emotions in a frenzied fight for how to suss out the situation.

"I'm with Dylan," she said. "Maggie was my friend!"

"Well ... there you go," Tom said. He slapped both palms down on the couch cushions and pushed himself up off the couch.

"We can be friends again, Tom. We can go back to the way things were—"

"How can you *say* that!? My life will *never* go back to the way things were." Tom looked directly in her eyes and his voice grew cold. For the first time since Lucia had met Tom, she felt rage and contempt seething from his stare. The feel of the look made her back away from him. "Your boyfriend helped make sure of that."

"I know it's been hard for you—"

"You don't, Lou." His anger had turned to weariness and he sighed. "You really don't. Maggie is dead. She didn't love me! My career is ... over. I've been in jail. But, hey ... at least it was just a misdemeanor."

"You're not the only one who lost someone they cared about."

"You're right, Lou. I'm not. So I shouldn't be allowed to be pissed off that my best friend betrayed me! Or that my wife was killed on national television!" Tom's voice boomed louder and louder with every new sentence. "Or that my wife was cheating on me with some lowlife piece of shit! Or that everything I've worked for since college has gone down the drain! And I'm *not* allowed to be upset or emotional!"

"I didn't say that, Tom. I just," her voice broke with tears, "I came here looking for a friend. I just ... I just want our lives back."

Tom calmed down and saw the sadness in her face, but he knew what she was so desperately trying to avoid or ignore. "We can't. I ... I ... can't. Everything's changed."

Lucia moved closer to him and laid her hand on his shoulder.

"It really doesn't matter whether you see Dylan or not," he said. "Do what you want. But I can't be his friend anymore."

Seeing the determined but weary look in his eyes, Lucia knew she was fighting a lost cause. She could only take Tom at his word and respect that ... for now. She knew the only thing to do right now was to go. She gave a slow, sad nod to Tom and walked toward the door.

Tom looked away but heard the door open, saw the light from the outside filling his hallway, and heard her voice echo, "I loved her, y'know? She was a great friend to me."

The silence hung in the air as Lucia waited for some kind of response from Tom. But there was nothing. She knew she had lost him as a friend. The thought made a lump form in her throat as she choked back tears. She took in a deep breath, hoping to hear some kind of response from him, anything, but there was only the haunting silence. She solemnly turned, went downstairs, and pulled the front door shut as she left.

Tom thought about chasing after her. He thought about apologizing for the kiss, his attitude toward her, for shouting at her. However, his anger prevented him from doing any of those things. His thoughts were elsewhere, in the past.

* * *

"Do you swear to tell the truth, the whole truth and nothing but the truth, so help you, God?" the bailiff asked.

"I do," Tom said, his right hand raised while his other laid on a bible.

Tom sat down in the witness chair and tried not to look out into the court attendees. He tried to dodge making eye contact with Maggie's parents or with his former network associates – especially Dylan – or Jen, who was there reporting, notepad in hand. All he could do was look directly to the network's defense attorney, Rob. As the show and network's attorney, Tom knew Rob very well and the only time he played golf was when Rob dragged him out to the links. Rob was a cocky-yet-smart young guy who looked like he fit in more on an episode of Donald Trump's *The Apprentice* rather than in the courtroom. Rob usually had nothing but his pretty-boy smile and a kind word for Tom, but today it was all business.

"Please state your full name for the court," the defense attorney said.

"Thomas Robert Frost."

"Thank you, Mr. Frost," the defense attorney said. "Can you tell me how you came up with the idea for your television reality series, *Heartbrakers?*"

"Yes."

"How was that?"

"I had come up with the idea back in college."

"Please elaborate."

"When I was in college, reality TV was becoming popular, and I thought it would be a great idea to have a TV show where men or women could hire someone to see if their significant other was being ... unfaithful to them."

"What gave you the idea for such a concept?"

"I knew a lot of friends, acquaintances who were cheated on - or cheating on others - and that's where it basically came from."

"When did you first meet your wife, Miss Estella Margaret Russell?"

Tom was a bit shocked they wouldn't even use her married surname, his name. "We met the summer before I started college - in 1996 - working at Funland."

"Funland ... is an amusement park in Rehoboth Beach, Delaware? Correct?"

"Yes."

"How old were you at the time?"

"Seventeen."

"And Miss Russell was sixteen? Correct?"

"Yes."

"Did she graduate the same year of high school that you did?

"Yes. Because she was able to skip a grade."

"Did you continue to see each other at college?"

"Yes. We both attended the University of Delaware."

"Would you say your relationship during your shared attendance at the University of Delaware was strictly platonic?"

"Yes."

"Really?" the attorney asked, a curious scowl crossing his face. "One of you didn't have romantic feelings toward the other?"

"Well, I did. I mean, I had a crush on her."

"So your feelings went beyond platonic?"

"Yes."

"But her feelings were merely platonic?"

"As far as I know. Yes."

"Did you and Miss Russell ever date in college?"

"No."

"Was there an action or event which led you to think your relationship with Miss Russell was more than platonic?"

"Objection, your honor!" the Russell's attorney stood up. "Irrelevant."

"Overruled," the judge barked.

"We kissed a few times, on the lips," Tom answered. "And cuddled."

"Were these kisses just a peck on the lips like you would give a family member, or a romantic kiss?"

"Objection!" the prosecutor shouted louder.

"Overruled!"

Tom couldn't believe he actually had to answer such intimate questions. It was beginning to border on humorous. Like many in the courtroom, he wondered where this was coming from. He looked over to Maggie's parents, who sat rigid; Brenda's face tear-stained and Eddie's frown chiseled deep. Tom flashed them a pleading look as if to say, *I don't know what to do! I don't know why this needs to be said!*

"Mr. Frost," Rob said. "Could you please answer the question? Was it a romantic kiss or more of a platonic type of kiss?"

"It was romantic. At least, that's how I took it."

"So you thought your relationship either was – or was becoming – more than platonic?"

"Yes."

"Was there an incident between the two of you which may have contributed to your creation of *Heartbrakers*?"

"No."

"Are you sure? There was no incident where you felt cheated on by Miss Russell? A situation where you questioned her fidelity?"

"We weren't dating–"

"Objection, your honor!" the prosecutor shouted.

"Overruled! Mr. Richards, will you please get to the point here?"

"Your honor," Mr. Richards said. "I need to establish the relationship between Miss Russell and Mr. Frost in relation to the creation of the show in order to establish there was a conflict of interest when having Miss Russell appear on the show."

The judge looked over to Tom. "Answer the question, Mr. Frost."

For the first time since he took the witness stand, Tom looked out into the audience, first looking to Brenda and Eddie, then to Jen – a look of terror on his face. The last person he looked to was Dylan, a smirk skulking across his lips.

"There was one time," Tom reluctantly said.

"What time was that?" Mr. Richards asked. "And I want to remind you that you are under oath."

"One day, I was walking back to my dorm room from class. I was passing by the student center, Trabant, and I saw her lying on the grass with another guy."

"Was that Mr. Alex Silver?"

"Yes."

"Please. Continue. What were Miss Russell and Mr. Silver doing?"

"They were lying on a blanket, kissing. Making out."

"And that must've made you furious—"

"Objection!" the prosecutor shouted. "Leading the witness."

"Sustained," the judge said.

"I think it's already clear that Mr. Frost didn't just get the idea for his TV show from friends' relationships. Taking into account Mr. Frost's history with Miss Russell, it is easy to see why Mr. Vaughn would not disclose the news of Miss Russell being on the show. This Emmy-award-winning reality series is a business. And for the sake of keeping the logistics of the series from wading into a conflict of interest, one of the show's producers made an executive decision to keep production moving."

"He lied!" Tom shouted. The judge banged his wooden gavel on the block, the noise reverberating throughout the room as Tom continued, speaking louder, "He didn't tell me it was my wife! Now she's dead!"

"Order, Mr. Frost!" the judge shouted, still banging the gavel. "Order!"

"And now they're trying to say they have no responsibility, no negligence at all!"

The gavel nearly drowned out Tom's words, but it was the judge's booming voice which stopped him. "ORDER!!!"

When the courtroom had quieted down, the judge returned his tone to its usual decibel. "The jury will not take any of Mr. Frost's last statement into account." The judge turned to Tom. "Mr. Frost. One more outburst like that and I will hold you in contempt. Understood?"

"Yes, your honor."

"Continue, Mr. Richards."

Tom looked to Dylan and the other network and show bigwigs, and saw smirks on some of their faces, Dylan included. Rob Richards cleared his throat and Tom's attention was brought back to the lawyer in front of him.

"Mr. Frost. Is it true that you signed the legal authorization form so the show's production could carry forward with the episode featuring Miss Russell?"

"Yes, but—"

"That's all I need, Mr. Frost."

Tom looked to the judge, who gave him a stern look of warning. Tom considered making another outburst about how Dylan had tricked him into signing the authorization by making it out to be something else, but he knew it still would have been his own fault for not checking out what he was signing. And he didn't want to spend any more time in jail.

Rob looked at the judge and smiled. "I have no further questions, your honor."

The judge turned toward the Russell's attorney. "Your witness, Mr. Smith."

The attorney stood up and said, "Your honor, I have no further questions for Mr. Frost."

"The witness is excused," the judge said.

Tom felt his heart and stomach sink. He had let down Brenda and Eddie Russell for a second time and there was nothing more he could do to try and fix it.

The rest of the trial was a blur with Rob finding loophole after loophole to get Tom's and Dylan's production company, as well as the network, off the hook from taking the blame for Maggie's death. He made sure he was at the final day of trial when the verdict was read.

The jury had deliberated for three hours before they reached a verdict. Tom watched them all shuffle in - some with heads raised, unaffected, and others looking down, trying their best not to make eye contact with anyone. After they had all taken a seat, the judge's voice cut the silence.

"Has the jury reached a verdict?"

The jury foreman, a middle-aged woman, stood up and said, "We have, your honor."

"Would the foreman please give the verdict to the bailiff?"

The woman handed a piece of paper folded as if it were ready to be placed in a business envelope to the bailiff, who then gave it to the judge. The judge unfolded the paper and silently read the verdict. He held out the paper and the bailiff grabbed it and delivered it back to the jury foreman's hands.

"Would the defendants please rise?"

Rob, Dylan and the other remaining network executives stood up.

"Madam Foreman, please read the verdict."

"In the case of Russell versus Heartbraker Productions, et al, for the charge of second-degree murder of Estella Margaret Russell-Frost, we, the jury, find the defendant ... not guilty." There was a gasp throughout the courtroom – some in joy, some in disgust, all in shock. "For the charge of criminal negligence, we find the defendant not guilty. And, for the charge of involuntary manslaughter, we find the defendant not guilty."

The gasps and whispering became so loud, the judge had banged his gavel to order silence and the audience acquiesced. Tom's thoughts imploded. He couldn't believe this was happening. He looked over to Dylan, along with his former bosses and co-workers, and saw them give each other celebratory handshakes, pats on backs and shoulders, flashing smiles and talking about going hunting and golfing over the upcoming weekend. His heartbeat sped up as their actions moved in slow motion. He glanced over at Brenda and Eddie to see their entire world disintegrate as their tears destroyed any foundation left in their bodies and they both caved forward. Brenda's silent cry turned into a loud, continuous wail. Eddie – his eyes clinched tightly shut, the only thing escaping being tears – had both arms wrapped around Brenda, trying to prevent her – and himself – from fully falling to the floor.

Tom sat while Dylan and the execs left the courtroom, trailed close behind by the reporters in the audience. One of them had been Jen and she stared at Tom as her body carried her out the courtroom. The rest of the audience left, the judge retired to his office, and everyone filed past him as he continued to look to Maggie's parents. They remained on the same seats, their bodies slightly trembling. There were no words he could say to them. Nothing he could do. He figured he had done enough.

After about fifteen minutes since the last person left the courtroom, the couple stood up, shuffled toward the middle aisle and slowly walked toward the exit doors. Each slow, shaky step was carefully executed, the slightest misstep possibly sending them crashing to the floor. Tom watched them, hoping to make eye contact, but they never looked to him. Once they passed him, he looked forward to the judge's bench.

Brenda and Eddie Russell continued their sad walk, taking each moment to steel themselves and prepare for a media who were awaiting any shedding of a tear, any word of anger and outrage they could capture to feed to the devoted viewers of their respective news programs. From there, the Russell's words could be twisted in any way the media and consuming public wanted them to sound, furthering a particular agenda while the truth of the matter was lost on all who heard it.

The truth would continue to get lost on the public for the next two months. The truth was that a woman, a real woman was dead. And she wasn't some character in a fictional world. She had been born, was a baby with a mother and father who loved her more than life itself. They bathed her, took care of her when she was sick and relished watching her grow, guiding her and helping her to discover the world around her. Like all little kids, her cute, tiny voice made her parents' hearts melt with every word, and when she became a young woman, they cherished all she had accomplished. Now she was gone forever. Never coming back. Never smiling again. Never laughing again. Never getting to talk and share in moments again. All who knew her, loved her and met her would never see her again.

The double doors closed shut and Tom closed his eyes, wishing away the immense pain which made him feel as if there were a big hole in his chest and stomach. He thought about her and his body wanted to cry, but he couldn't. No matter how hard he tried, he couldn't cry.

10.

"I never will forget you, my American love
And I'll always remember you, wild as they come
And though if I saw you, I'd pretend not to know
The place where you were in my heart is now closed
I already live with too many ghosts"

--The Gaslight Anthem
"National Anthem"

The day after Lucia's failed intervention, Tom knew he had to make a new start. Staying in his large house was costing him, both economically and emotionally. His savings were running out and the once happy moments he had shared with Maggie in their home, their sanctuary, had turned into ghosts which haunted Tom's psyche and kept him in self-exile. He had ignored phone calls from any- and everyone, even his mother.

Without watching TV or reading the news, it had been easy to lose track of time. He didn't even know what day it was. Fortunately, he owned one of those fancy alarm clocks that tells the day of the week as well as the date. He glanced over to it and saw it was Wednesday. *Damn! Wednesday!* It was his self-appointed day to visit Maggie. He got dressed, got in his car and drove to the cemetery.

He had picked Wednesday because he realized after a few visits it was the day of the week with the least amount of visitors. The only time there were more than two visitors at a time was if there were a funeral or it was the anniversary of a particular loved one's birthday or death-day, and family had gathered to remember the deceased. Otherwise, it was him and maybe one or two others spread out wide.

As he entered the cemetery grounds, the satellite radio uncannily began playing A Great Big World's "Say Something" – the opening piano notes hitting at his heart, leaving a painful imprint. He parked along a tiny paved lane and looked to his right to see her gravestone. Even though it had a numerous variety of headstones around it, hers stuck out as if there were a light shining upon it alone. The lyrics continued to play after he had turned off the car engine and stepped out. He took a deep breath in and slowly let it out, starting to slowly walk toward the stark headstone, his heart beating faster and faster the closer he approached it.

The headstone was a dark charcoal, the words engraved on the stone came into focus and his breathing slowed. Her name was chiseled with light gray letters on the face of the polished front:

Estella Margaret Russell
Beloved daughter, sister & friend
Forever in our hearts
February 21, 1984 – October 29, 2014

Tom knew it shouldn't be any surprise that Brenda and Eddie didn't want his last name on the stone, but there was a sharp sting as to why. They didn't want her associated with him in any way, especially with all of the media coverage and controversy over Maggie's and his marriage. Looking at the gravestone, he could see why. There were several bouquets of flowers around the headstone, but Tom could vaguely see letters, which looked like they had been painted with spray paint or nail polish, across Maggie's name. He had to bend down to look closer to examine the faint traces of the letters. He could make out the curve of the "S" and the following "L" and made out the other two following letters. Slut. Whoever had scrubbed off the letters had done their very best to rid the stone of the word but the paint had still served its purpose. It made Tom's blood boil, his head feeling as if it were one of those cartoon characters whose anger transforms their head into a big thermometer with the bright red liquid bursting through the top. He stomped to his car, and tore away out of the cemetery and to the closest grocery store. He grabbed some heavy-duty cleaning spray and a steel wool scrubbing pad, bought them and raced back to the cemetery as if he wanted to beat anyone else there before they saw the word.

By the time he got back, the cemetery had a couple of new visitors but no one near Maggie's stone. He sprayed the spot with the letters, grabbed one of the pads out of the orange box and scrubbed as hard as he could. Tom scrubbed until he could feel the headstone slightly vibrate and thought it was going to move out of place. The scene reminded him of reading Shakespeare's *Macbeth*, when Lady Macbeth is trying to wash the blood off her hands and no matter how hard she tries, she can't seem to get her hands clean enough. Her words rang in his head: *Out, damn'd spot! Out, I say!*

He didn't know how long he was spraying and scrubbing that headstone, but that "Say Something" song and its melody stuck in his head the entire time he cleaned, leaving a residual guilt to wash through him. The feeling distracted him so much that he didn't notice the shadow rise over the headstone.

"Hm-hmm!"

Tom turned around at the noise and saw Jen standing there, a Canon camera hanging from around her neck, her left hand gripping a reporter's notepad and pen. Tom found it a little amusing how different Jen's personal life was in comparison to her professional life. He had gotten so used to seeing her in her professional role as a reporter, with her business dress and pantsuits, that he had forgotten her personal style. She was wearing brown knee-high boots with blue jeans, a brown halter top and a jean jacket.

"I never thought I'd see you here," Jen said. He turned back around and continued scrubbing the headstone.

"Sorry to disappoint you."

"What are you doing?"

"Just making sure everything's cleaned up. You'd think with a groundskeeper, there'd be better tending to the plots."

The truth was Jen knew why Tom was so vigorously cleaning the headstone; she had seen the lewd graffiti a few days before. She thought it was honorable that, even in Maggie's death, Tom was still trying to protect her.

"Haven't seen you in a while."

"Well, your ... *peers* haven't really let up on trying to get a picture or a quote from me the past few months. I've just been trying to lay low."

"I know," she said, a hint of sadness in her acknowledgement. "I told the station I wasn't reporting on you."

"I'm surprised they let you get away with that." Tom grabbed a bottle of water and poured it over the headstone, chasing the suds down toward Maggie's final resting ground. He stood up and wiped his hands together, then rubbing them on his jeans. "I'm sure they were just chomping at the bit to send you."

"I told them it was a conflict of interest."

Tom shot her a look as if to say, *Really!?* "I didn't know there was such a thing in journalism. I'd think you reporting on a former boyfriend would be a great advantage in getting the story."

Jen knew it was a great advantage but she wasn't sure she could do such a thing to Tom. They had moved on with their separate lives, but she still cared about him as a close friend. She easily picked up on his contemptible words but his stare was so cold it sent a shudder down her spine.

"It is an advantage. And my boss does want me to interview you – on camera. But I told him no."

"How can I trust you?"

Jen was hurt, not so much by the question itself but more in the way he said it.

"Tom. I can't begin to imagine what you're going through right now. But I'm trying to be your friend."

"My friend, huh? Where have you been these past few months?" He could see that she felt awkward at his question.

She opened her mouth to answer him but nothing came out. "Haven't seen you since the trial."

"I felt like ... you didn't need any more news cameras around."

"The news? I thought you said you were my friend."

"You know what I mean. I figured ... you didn't need any more media seeing a reporter coming to your house. I thought it would raise suspicions – especially given our ... personal history."

"I appreciate your thoughtfulness," Tom shot back with a biting attitude.

"C'mon, Tom," she sighed.

"I thought you didn't like Maggie."

"Of course I did. But I'm not here for her. I'm here for you." She changed her tone from sympathy to small anger. "But if you're going to be a jerk, I can leave right now."

Jen turned to leave and his voice sounded out, "Jen."

She stopped and slowly turned around to find Tom standing three feet in front of her.

"I can't sleep." He sounded as if he were admitting to having some major life-threatening disease. "It's been ..."

He considered telling her the truth, telling her how much he missed Maggie but how angry he was at her for cheating on him; how he sometimes wished he were dead; how he didn't really miss his job and felt it had become toxic to the public and he regretted ever creating the show; how he couldn't live in L.A. anymore because there were too many ghosts here and everywhere he looked, he saw Maggie; or how every day was a soul-crushing experience of which he couldn't escape. However, when he looked into her eyes, he saw in them a hint of desperation mixed with pity, and something inside him shut down wanting to tell her anything. No matter how much he wanted to, he couldn't trust her.

"Do you remember why we broke up?" he asked. "Why *you* broke up with me?"

Jen looked down and slowly, solemnly nodded her head.

"You said you wanted to focus more on your career; that I was putting too much time into us and not enough into my own career."

"And?" She looked up into his eyes. Tom realized that tearing her down wasn't going to accomplish anything.

"When you left me, it crushed me," he said. "I realized that I had put the girls I loved on a pedestal for too long. Don't get me wrong. I didn't become an asshole to women or anything. I still respected women. But I didn't go out of my way to be this supportive, nice gentleman.

"I just ... recognized what I should've known all along," Tom continued. "Women are just people. Just like me. They have faults and make lots of mistakes too. It's only when I stopped taking them so seriously that I think I finally started meeting women who saw me differently. They saw me as an actual romantic interest. And, as pathetic as it may sound, I could live a better life."

"Tom. I'm having a hard time following what you're saying."

"When I reconnected with Maggie at that stupid college reunion, I felt like life was ... rewarding me ... for doing something right with my life. Maggie was such a strong support system for me, and I was for her. At least, for a time, I was."

Tom fell silent, his words lost in emotion and memory. Jen thought he was going to cry but the truth was that all of his tears had left him months ago.

"Tom—"

"No, it's fine." He was silent, lost in deep thought, his eyes focusing on something else, somewhere else. Jen absorbed the silence by watching him. "Could you please go?"

"I'm here for you, Tom. We can work this out together."

"Maybe I don't wanna work this out."

"I'm your friend. We can—"

"I don't wanna work this out with *you*."

Tom could tell he hurt Jen, it was written in her expression. The truth was he felt too defensive around Jen, as if he couldn't open up. As long as he had known her, there was nothing Jen had intentionally done to make Tom feel that way about her. If he chalked it up to anything, the reason he felt so closed-off around her was because of her beauty. He had always felt she was much too attractive to be with the likes of him and one day, she would get wise to it and dump him. So, when she inevitably dumped Tom, it wasn't any surprise to him even though she didn't dump him for the reason he thought.

"Oh." Jen could feel a lump in her throat form but she looked away as if not looking at Tom would stop the sadness.

Tom instantly felt awful for saying what he had, in the tone he said it, but the truth was that Jen was a reporter. She was a part of the media that had made his life a living hell the past few months.

"It's just that," he said. "... I don't know if I want you here if ... anyone else is around. I mean ... what if there are other reporters around here?"

"I honestly wasn't thinking about any of that. I just wanted to come here and tell you I'm here for you."

"How did you know I was here? Today? At this time?"

"I'll admit it. One of our reporters has been tailing you recently. I heard the call at the studio."

Tom knew it wasn't merely that simple. He had worked in the business long enough to know how fast news crews were dispatched and he knew Jen's tricks of the trade too. There were no other reporters around, so the only reporter he figured who stepped up to the plate was the one he was currently staring down.

"I ... uh ... I beat the news van here," she continued. "But I don't know how much time we'll have left before it gets here."

"And you thought you'd beat them to the punch, eh?"

"Have you been watching the news lately, Tom? Have you heard what they're saying?" Tom remained stone-faced and gave a solemn shake of his head from one side to another. "It's bad. FOX, CNN, MSNBC. They're all railing against you but oddly sticking by the show."

"Doesn't surprise me," Tom said. "It doesn't matter, anyhow."

"What do you mean it doesn't matter!?"

"You've been in the game long enough, Jen. You know as well as I do that my career is over. It was over the minute that asshole pulled that gun."

Jen looked away, unable to look Tom in the eyes for fear she may burst into tears.

"Maggie's dead." The admission quieted him as the words washed over him and into his body, stinging every inch of him. He took a few deep breaths as if he'd just ran a sprint. "My life is over. Besides, I don't give a damn what those idiots say about me. Let them spit their poison and peddle it as truth. Let them have their ratings."

"Maybe you should go on record. Let them know your side."

"And you'd report it for me?"

Jen didn't know whether Tom was asking her a rhetorical question, poking an insult at her, or if he was serious. She mumbled out, "Ye-yeah. Yes. If you want me to."

Tom let out a silent chuckle. "Go home, Jen."

"I can tell your side. Give everyone the truth."

"You don't get it!" Tom shouted, his eyes wide with a touch of madness, the rest full of anger and frustration. "It doesn't matter that Maggie was killed right on live TV! Or that people saw the asshole who did it! And it doesn't matter that I'm not the one who pulled the trigger. You can't punish a dead man. So I'm the one the public wants to punish. I'm the one they need to punish. To feel like there was some kinda justice for Maggie. As far as the public is concerned, it's my fault she's dead.

"*Truth!?* The networks don't care about truth! None of them do. They just want what furthers their agendas. They don't care about Maggie! About me! They just care about ratings. And the public is no better. They eat it all up! Just so they can share some ignorant rant of a post on Facebook!" Tom calmed the storm thundering within him and he lowered his head as his demeanor lightened. "I thought you'd be different. I was *hoping* you'd be different."

"Don't say that, Tom. I'm still on your side. I'm your friend."

Tom looked back up at Jen. Tears welled along the bottoms of her eyes and he felt like a jerk for what he had said. "I'm sorry, Jen. I ... I know you mean well. I do. But ... I meant what I said about telling my story. Please ... just ... respect that."

She hesitantly nodded her head. "Are you staying? Here in L.A.? Doesn't sound like it."

"Not sure. But it really doesn't matter, does it?"

Jen stayed quiet. She remembered the exchange she had had with her boss that morning. How her boss had threatened her job if she didn't get some kind of sound bite or newsworthy quote from Tom. She argued that she wouldn't betray Tom's trust. Her boss appealed to her sense of wanting to protect Tom. He told her getting his side of the story was the best way to clear his name, otherwise the media would continue painting him as some callous television producer. Her boss told her she would be saving Tom, doing him a favor.

"It does to me," she said.

Tom stepped closer to her and slowly wrapped his arms around her in a loving embrace. She warily raised her arms and hugged him back. The hug stirred something in Tom he hadn't felt in a long time: honest compassion. The feeling spread a warm, comforting ease throughout his body until his right hand rubbed against something hooked to her back bra strap. He kept his hand moving so as not to alert her to his discovery. A wire.

"Will you promise me one thing?" Jen asked as she backed away.

"Yeah."

"When you *are* ready to talk, please say you'll come to me first."

"I promise you'll get the exclusive."

Tom thought about calling Jen out but he wondered what good it would do. It would just end in a shouting match, one person blaming the other for past hurts. In the end, she would still have the recording and there would be nothing but anger left between them. Besides, he figured he didn't give her anything worth broadcasting, and if he did, there was no guarantee she would actually use it. He had faith in Jen. He knew when it came down to it, he could trust her.

Jen smiled. "I'll give you some privacy. Sorry for interrupting."

"It's OK. See ya." Jen walked away, back to her car, and drove away.

Tom tried to shake the feeling of Jen's actions but he knew all he could do was wait and see what she did. He turned back to the headstone, the first thing catching his sight being Maggie's name.

"Hi." He released a heavy emotion-ridden sigh, as if saying that one word had taken all of the air and strength from him. If what Jen said was true, he didn't have much private time left before a news van came on the scene.

"I suddenly feel like this is some cheesy scene in a movie. Visiting your grave, having a heartfelt talk. As if you can hear me." Tom chuckled at himself and his expression slowly became serious. "I miss you."

Tom would give practically anything to hear her voice, to know she was still in the world. Her affair had hurt him but she didn't deserve this. The emotion arose in his throat until he swallowed it down.

"I'm ... sorry about what happened. I never thought ..." he suddenly shut up as if someone were watching him. He swallowed another lump and cleared his throat.

"I think about you all the time. I think I'll hear your laugh and I actually turn around, hoping to see you there. I thought," his voice wavered, "we would always be together.

"I often think back to when we worked at Funland. How you annoyed the hell outta me when we first met, how you loved to push my buttons. Mostly, I remember ... how much I loved those days.

"I know the last few days weren't the best, but I still felt like we were living some dream. Never thought you were doing ... what you were doing. Knowing you were sleeping with him, that it may have ... been his baby ..."

"The few people I know who still come around ask me about how I'm feeling. But I see that look in their eyes. They're just grateful it didn't happen to them. What do you say when your best friend is killed? How do I tell them that you made the world a better place by being in it? All they know - or can think of - is what they saw on that stupid show. They don't know about all of the time and money you donated to children's hospitals. They don't know about how you reached out to people and brought out the best in everyone you met.

"I don't know when ... I lost you. But ... I wish you were still here.

"Even if we weren't together, the world was a better place with you. I ... I ... I'm just ...

"I'm just ... so ... sorry."

* * *

Jen drove to the station and walked to her cubicle desk. She unstrapped the portable microphone off her back and connected a wire to it, then plugged it into the USB port on her computer. Her boss - a man about her age, with sandy blonde hair, who looked like he should be modeling for J. Crew magazines rather than be a news producer - popped his head over her partition.

"Did you get it?" he asked.

"Yeah, I got it," Jen said, guilt hanging heavily.

"*What?*"

"I don't feel right about this."

"But you did it. Besides, like I told you, this will help him. It's for his benefit! This way, the public will understand what he's going through."

"Yeah, well, I wouldn't expect too much from the recording. He didn't give up much."

"I'm sure it's fine. Cue it up."

Jen opened the recording on her computer and pressed play. They could both hear Tom's voice say, "I can't sleep. It's been ... Do you remember why we broke up? Why *you* broke up with me? You said you wanted to focus more on your career; that I was putting too much time into us and not enough into my own career."

"Please tell me you got more than some trip down brokenhearted lane!" the boss said.

She nodded her head and fast-forwarded the recording, then pressed play. Tom's voice returned over the speakers: "When I reconnected with Maggie at that stupid college reunion, I felt like life was ... rewarding me ... for doing something right with my life. Maggie was such a strong support system for me, and I was for her. At least, for a time, I was."

She paused the recording and looked to her producer, his eyes as wide as saucers.

"This is great!" he said. "Any more stuff like that?"

She nodded again. "Yeah. He goes on to admit his life is over, how it was over the minute that asshole pulled a gun."

The producer subtly calmed himself, cleared his throat, and said, "Great job, Jen. You think you can edit it together and have it ready for tonight's news?"

"Sure," she said. "But, Dennis, there's just one thing."

"What?"

"I don't want my name associated with it."

"What do you mean?"

"I don't want to be the person associated with getting the quote."

"No problem! We'll just say 'an anonymous source close to Mr. Frost.' Sound good?"

Jen lowered her head and nodded.

"Great!"

Dennis walked back to his office, leaving Jen still stewing in her guilt, regretful she had agreed to air the audio. She knew she had betrayed Tom, but she truly believed it would help air the truth about his situation and, ultimately, win the public's sympathy for his situation.

* * *

Tom stepped into his house, threw his keys on the closest table and walked over to his answering machine. He had grown uneasy at looking at his answering machine after returning from an errand because, after Maggie was killed, he had an overabundance of messages. Sometimes they would number in the triple digits! But now, most days, he was happy to see he often had none. Today, there was a blinking number one. He drew in a breath and pressed the play button.

"You have one message," the robotic voice sounded off, followed by a beep.

"Hi, Tom. It's Mom. I just wanted to call and see how you were holding up. I know you didn't want Dad and me there for the trial, but ... we worry about you. Please ... give us a call. We'd love to hear from you. Let us know you're alright. I'll talk to you soon. Love you."

Another beep sounded and Tom walked over to his couch and plopped himself down on it. He rubbed his eyes with the palms of his hands before moving them to rub his entire face, then looked at the time: 4:30 p.m. He grabbed Maugham's *The Razor's Edge*, opened to near the end and picked up reading where he had left off.

He was five pages away from the end of the book when a phone call interrupted him. He picked up the cordless phone.

"Hello?"

"Tom. This is Sean."

Great, Tom thought, *what the hell does my agent want?*

"Yeah? What's up?"

"Have you been watching WPNX? Channel six?"

"No. Why?"

"Have you been talking to Jen?"

"I just saw her this morning. Why?"

"Where did you see her? Did you talk to her?"

"I saw her at Maggie's grave. Yeah, I talked to her. Sean, what's this all about!?"

"You need to watch the news!"

"Can't. I don't have cable anymore."

"Damn! I forgot." Sean was silent for a few seconds. "Go to their web site."

Tom stood up and grabbed his laptop sitting on the kitchen island.

"What the hell is this all about, Sean!?"

"Just go to the web site and click on the video on the home page."

Tom logged on, opened his internet and typed in the news channel's web site. The first thing he noticed on the home page was a big video player with a reporter's smile frozen in the picture. Above the player was a headline reading *"Heartbraker* creator blames media coverage for recent misfortune."

"Sean! What the hell is this!?!?"

"Did you *only* talk to Jen?"

"Yes. But I certainly didn't blame the media for Maggie's death!"

"That's not what they mean. Watch the video."

Tom pressed play and the reporter's face became animated, transforming from the grin to a serious scowl.

"WPNX News has exclusive information regarding the story of reality TV show *Heartbraker* creator, producer and host, Tom Frost. According to a source close to Mr. Frost, it seems as if Mr. Frost blames the news media for his recent misfortunes such as the loss of his job and his financial problems.

"The source gave WPNX News exclusive access to an audio recording of Mr. Frost where he confesses his opinion. We will now play the audio clip in its entirety."

As the reporter's grim face stayed onscreen, the audio played and Tom heard his voice.

"I can't sleep. When I reconnected with Maggie at that stupid college reunion, I felt like life was ... rewarding me ... for doing something right with my life. Maggie was such a strong support system for me, and I was for her. At least, for a time, I was. You know as well as I do that my career is over. It was over the minute that *bleeeeep* pulled that gun. My life is over."

Jen's disguised digital voice came out, "Give everyone the truth."

"*Truth!?* The networks don't care about truth!" Tom's recorded voice shouted. "None of them do. They just want what furthers their agendas. They don't care about Maggie! About me! They just care about ratings. And the public is no better. They eat it all up! Just so they can share some ignorant rant of a post on Facebook!"

The reporter cleared his throat and solemnly said, "That was Tom Frost, former host of the Emmy Award-winning reality series *Heartbraker*, voicing his frustrations—"

Tom slammed his laptop shut, turning the video off. "What the hell, Sean!?!? Can they get away with this!?"

"Already called and talked to their attorney. He said you gave their source - *Jen* - permission."

"I didn't!"

"They played the tape for me. You said near the end that you would give Jen the scoop—"

"*Yeah*! When I was *ready*!"

"They also said you should know better - that by talking to a well-known reporter, if you didn't say you were off the record, you were otherwise on the record."

"Oh, this is horseshit! She's my friend! She knew I didn't want to go on record!"

"That's not what they're claiming."

"I wanna sue 'em!"

There was a long pause on the other end of the line. Tom wondered if Sean had hung up or not.

"Can't."

"*What!? Why!?*"

"First off, as a TV host, you're in the public eye. So there aren't the same privacy laws for you as there is for everyone else. Second, you said those words—"

"Yeah! But they were edited *way* outta context!"

"Doesn't matter! You said them! And as a TV personality in the public eye, you are quotable. And the last thing they claimed is that you *knew* Jen was recording you and you didn't say anything. Now, *that*, I think, is nonsense."

Tom's rage subsided as he did know he was being recorded. He had felt the mic on Jen's back.

"That *is* nonsense? Right, Tom? You didn't know Jen was recording you, right?"

Tom thought about lying, taking this to court, going before a judge again, for the third time in a row in the past three months, and having to perjure himself. But for what? The damage had already been done. His recording was on the internet and TV for all to hear. No sum of money would take it all back. Besides, he did know Jen had the mic. He had just given her the benefit of the doubt and hoped she wouldn't have used the recording. She was his friend and he bet on that. Unfortunately, he lost.

"I ... I ... I did know, Sean."

"You *what*!?!? You *knew*!?"

"Yeah."

"Tom, man ... If you knew, and didn't say anything, there's not much of a case here. I don't know how to spin this."

"Then don't."

"Don't what?"

"Spin it."

"Tom ..."

"Sean. You've been a good agent. And I thank you for everything. But it's clear that ... my career ... it's over."

"What?"

"You're fired, Sean."

"Tom. Don't do this. You can still make a comeback!"

"I can't, Sean."

"Yes, you can. We just have to get you—"

"I don't want to," Tom lied. The words made Sean stop in his tracks, shutting him up. Tom continued, "I don't want to ... make a comeback."

"Don't say that. We can fight this together, Tom. I can get you booked on a media tour, strike back at Jen and WPNX!"

"You know what they've been saying about me in the news, Sean. You think parading me from network to network is gonna change their minds!? You think I won't get blasted by every news host on every network? They'd take sound bites of my interviews and pick them apart until it was whittled away to what they wanted."

For once, Sean couldn't lie about the situation. His silence told Tom all he needed to know.

"What are you gonna do, Tom? You're losin' money. You're gonna lose your house."

"Honestly? I don't know. But ... I'll think of something."

II.

"This town is a workshop
For wordsmiths and grifters
And misters and misses
And cheeks full of kisses
And all of you bidders
Can't wait 'til I'm bitter"

--Joe Firstman
"After Los Angeles"

The phone had been ringing nonstop after Tom hung up with Sean. The first message came from a producer with the same cable news network which featured Tom's most harsh critics - including the commentator Tom referred to as "The Douche" (the guy with the eyebrows and the star-spangled background), and the Carlton woman. As soon as Tom heard the producer enunciate the first syllable of the network, he hit the delete button, immediately silencing the producer's voice. The next message was from his mother.

"Tom. It's Mom." He could tell she had been crying. Even now, the cry was stuck in her throat, cracking her voice. "I ... I just wanted to hear your voice. I hope ... uh-hmm. I hope you're doing fine. I worry about you. Please give me a call."

The following message was from another news network's producer and Tom knew that news channels were all he would hear. He grabbed the cord to his answering machine and yanked the plug from the electrical socket.

Within an hour, the news trucks started showing up and parking along the front of his property. Tom looked through one of his blinds to see the media run amok. The camera operators, reporters and sound technicians exited their vehicles and set up cameras, lights, and shading screens. Tom let out a weary sigh as his eyes sunk below the crack of the blinds.

He didn't know if he could go through another media circus. The thought of it all drained him of any energy he had and he felt like he was under house arrest. He couldn't even leave to go to the grocery store without a mob of reporters surrounding him or his car.

To pass the time, he popped in a DVD of the 1976 film *Network*. There was a part in the film which ironically correlated with what Tom was experiencing. In the film, the scene when news anchor-turned-madman Howard Beale (played by the late Peter Finch) hosts his own variety show and he rants a fundamental truth about the television news to his viewer audience as told through writer Paddy Chayefsky's script:

"... *And when the twelfth largest company in the world controls the most awesome God-damned propaganda force in the whole godless world, who knows what shit will be peddled for truth on this network?*"

Tom stood up and walked over to his front window

again. He stuck a finger between the blinds and opened one of the horizontal blinds, peeking out at the news crews as Finch's Beale rallied on about television not being the truth and how the public will never get any truth from it.

Tom thought about all of the extremely asinine reality shows and cable news stories he had seen in his time on the network or from sitting at home during the primetime hours, and he was disgusted he had been a part of it. Now he was the one in the crosshairs of the media and they spun his story how they wanted to further their own ratings and agendas. He watched the on-air personality reporters straightening their clothes and practicing their vocal exercises as if they were about to belt out a big showtune. Tom heard Finch chuckling to himself during his monologue, as if he were laughing at Tom's own situation.

Tom could not take his eyes off the reporters outside, scrambling to get a prime spot in front of his house so they could get the better shot. Hell, for all he knew, his single eye peering out from the blinds was being filmed right now. He thought he even saw some reporters nudging each other for a better patch of space to get the best shooting angle. He saw their fake smiles to other competing reporters followed by annoyed eye-rolling. Their venomous comments spoke through clinched teeth and plastered smiles, coifing their own hair, the applying of make-up – he had seen it all before but never thought they would be there for him. The field producers all started turning on the set lights to rid any pesky shadows from spoiling their reporters' looks.

Tom's sixty-inch flatscreen TV showed Finch's Beale collapse to the floor and his live audience erupting into applause as Tom kept his eyes on the news cameras, watching as they began filming. He snatched his finger out of the blinds, closing them shut, and moved away from the windows. All he could do now was wait until the movie was over, hoping some of the news crews would retreat back to their stations.

As entertaining as the film was, time dragged until the movie ended around 10:45 p.m. There was only one way he could think of to escape by this point: leave now under the cover of night, hope any leftover reporters or paparazzi would be too busy concentrating on him leaving out the front door or garage, and walk a few blocks, then call a taxi to pick him up. Tom had dressed himself all in black – t-shirt, slacks, socks and a pair of black, casual slip-on shoes he had bought at Wal-Mart but never worn. Looking as if he were some generic bank robber in a B-movie, he slipped out the back door like a thief who had just pulled a big score.

The idea of besting the press amused Tom. It was the only small victory he could claim in his otherwise downward spiral of a life. He went through a mental Rolodex of contacts he could turn to so he could lay low for a while; get out of his place and away from the media. Despite all of the Hollywood contacts Tom had, all the random people who had inserted themselves into his social circle since winning the Emmy, he had lost all of them. There were only two people nearby he could think to go see and he made his way toward one.

Tom slipped out the back and crept a through the cover of darkness until he tried to remember how long he had been walking, realizing he must be at least five blocks away from his home. He grabbed his cell phone and called a cab. The cab driver didn't make it to him until 11:45 p.m., but he was happy nevertheless. He told the cabbie his destination address and nerves poked in his stomach the entire trip, making him nauseous. Tom believed the person he was going to see would either help him or leave him out for the night, but, no matter what the outcome, he had to try.

Tom's palms sweated profusely as he neared the apartment building front doors. There was no doorman at this hour and the only presence seemed to be the night front deskman. He hesitated before buzzing the apartment, the nerves getting the better of him, making his hands tremor as though he suffered from Parkinson's. His shaky finger jammed down on one of the rusty buttons and the butterflies turned into ravenous mosquitoes, jabbing at his stomach, making him feel as if he would vomit at any moment. A chill ran up his spine as the repeated buzzing sounded like a telephone call. The buzzer picked up.

"He—?" the voice sounded, muffled by faulty wiring.

"Hello?" Tom said. "It's me ... it's ... it's Tom. Can I come up?"

A different, longer buzz sounded and the door lock clicked open. The outside of the building carried plenty of cracks and dilapidated fronting after years of neglect, but the inside of the building was very upscale and its décor looked like something brand new from the 1940s, a very art deco style with a few modern-day amenities scattered around – a fifty-inch flatscreen TV here, a wi-fi computer over there. The scarlet red and gold coloring of the trim and curtains reminded Tom of one of the old, single screen cinema houses he used to go to as a kid. For an instance, the memory soothed him, taking him back to those carefree days when he saw four funny guys trap ghosts or a comedic spoof of *Star Wars* with characters called Dark Helmet and Lone Starr; but when he saw the elevator, his nerves woke up and started kicking his insides again. He hoped to avoid the deskman's attention and stood with his back to the front desk as he pressed the button for the ninth floor. The doors dinged open and he practically fell inside the empty car. He jabbed the "elevator close" button repeatedly until the doors obeyed. By this point, he couldn't tell if the nauseous pit in his stomach was from the elevator ride or his nerves.

The doors opened and he walked slowly down the hall toward the third door on the right. His feet - as if they had a mind of their own, knowing something he didn't know and screaming for him to stop - got heavier with every step. He stood in front of the brownish-red door for a minute or two before he lifted his hand to knock, but his fist hung in midair. He gulped down his nerves - along with a bit of vomit - and pushed his fist forward, knocking twice. The door swiftly opened and Tom's face froze in a panic as if he were expecting to be hit with a splash of freezing water.

"Yeah?" Lucia asked. "What do you want, Tom?"

"Thanks for seeing me this late." His face and body relaxed when he realized she wasn't going to hit him. "Can I come in?"

She was dressed in a ratty pair of pajamas, the kind Tom guessed she didn't wear to impress guys. She sidestepped and waved her arm as if to say, *Be my guest.* "What's going on?"

"The reporters are back at my place."

"What about?"

"The recording the news is playing on repeat every fifteen minutes!"

"Jen," Lucia said with a tone that was not so much a question as it was a bold declaration.

"I expected to be screwed over by any of those bloodsuckers out there, but Jen ..."

"But you *did* say those things, Tom."

"They edited them outta context! Wait. You don't believe me?"

Lucia had to actually think about her answer for a moment and she could see the shock in Tom's expression.

She let out a heavy sigh and rolled her eyes. "Of course I believe you." She waited for him to say something, but he just sat on one of her chairs, looking up at her with desperate eyes. "How do you want me to help?"

"I just ...," he fought to get the words out. "I just ... I need some place to sleep – just for a night."

Lucia shook her head. "Not after what happened the other day." She looked at Tom and saw him lowering his head like some pathetic puppy dog being scolded by its master. She calmed her tone. "I tried to be your friend, Tom. But you made it very clear that you're too busy feeling sorry for yourself. I have to admit that ... I'm a little pissed off at you ... for what you did. Kissing me? I thought we were friends. I thought you were my friend."

"I am. And I'm sorry if I upset you." Tom wondered why *he* was apologizing to *her*. Sure, he had tried to kiss her. But he clearly wasn't in a good place – emotionally or mentally – right now. He felt a little pissed off at her for turning this around on him. Then again, if there was one thing Tom remembered Dylan telling him about Lucia, it was that she was the deflecting queen in an argument. She could turn anything around and make the other person wind up being the one to apologize. "I just need one night."

She stood with arms crossed, pondering Tom's plight. She wanted to be there for him, but felt he was blowing this media coverage out of proportion, and she was too tired to deal with him tonight.

"Tom ... I can't," she pretended as if it were a tough decision. "You ... you need to face the world. I know you miss Maggie. But, like I told you, it's time to get back out into the world."

"And this is how you're going to force me?"

"I'm not forcing you, Tom. I'm just not *enabling* you."

"What kind of pretentious bullshit is that!?"

Lucia was surprised by his outburst.

"You're not going to *enable* me!? When have you been enabling me since Mags died!? I mean, you come over to my house and tell me you're still dating the jerk-off who tricked me into permitting my wife onto the show, which ultimately got her killed. I make one little move on you and that's *enabling!?* I think you need a dictionary."

He could tell she was fuming but he didn't care anymore. He felt as if he had kowtowed to her and everybody else for far too long and now he had had enough. So, consequences be damned, he was going to speak his mind.

She stepped over to him with a look as if she were about to burst into tears and looked at him for what seemed like an eternity, the silence flooding the room. He opened his mouth, getting ready to ask, *What?*, but she slapped him as hard as she could, sending him back a few steps.

"Screw you, Tom," she said. She marched to her door, opened it, and said, "Get out!"

He looked at her and saw a mix of rage and hurt. His anger transformed to guilt and sympathy. "Aw, I'm sorry, Lou—"

"*Get! Out!*"

Tom knew if she were to get any louder, the cops would be called and all he needed was some trashy tabloid getting shots of him being hauled away by the cops to add to his downward spiral in the press. So, he left.

As soon as he crossed the door frame, the door slammed shut, almost hitting him in the ass.

* * *

An hour later, Tom stood in front of another brownish-red door for a minute or two before he lifted his hand to knock. The door slowly opened and the disheveled appearance of his lawyer, Bob McGuffin, stood before him. Bob side-stepped, like Lucia had done, and tiringly waved Tom inside.

"Thanks, Bob," Tom said as if he were some teenager looking for a place to crash.

Bob invited him into the kitchen for some chamomile tea and, due to his nerves, Tom was all too eager to take him up on the offer.

The tea kettle whistled, the pitch getting higher and higher, until Bob moved it from the hot oven range. Tom looked around Bob's house. It was a simple-looking, one-story single family home, like something from the late 1970s or early 1980s, with a simple floorplan. There were no pricey electronic items or expensive works of art. The wallpaper was old and slightly yellowed after years of being exposed to the elements. Sitting in Bob's simple breakfast nook, Tom could tell there was more to Bob than he had ever let on to him.

Tom looked around for any kinds of personal pictures while Bob poured the tea. All he could see on the shelves were books. Tom checked the walls and he saw an 8x10 studio photo, but all he could see was the left side of the photo, which showed Bob standing in front of a fake autumn scene backdrop, stuck in a permanent smile, his right hand on someone's shoulder. Tom leaned forward to catch a glimpse of who was next to Bob. He saw an older, thin woman, who looked to be close in age to Bob, sitting, with her hands folded in her lap, in front of and to the side of Bob. A warm smile graced her face, the top portion of which was covered by eyeglasses and she was dressed in a rose-colored sweater, with a white collar sticking out the neck. She had a classic grandma look to her and the photo was comforting yet a bit sad. Tom couldn't figure out why, but, even though Bob and the woman were wearing genuine smiles, something felt very off about the photo.

"Oh," Bob interrupted Tom's train of thought. "That ol' picture."

"Who is that?"

"That's my wife, Gilda."

"Like the movie?"

"Heh," Bob let out a chuckle. "Yeah. Like the movie." Bob handed Tom a teacup on a saucer. "I'm surprised you know about that movie."

"I've been watching a lot of classics lately."

Bob sat down with a heavy sigh and peered up at the photo. "Yeah, Gilda was no Rita Hayworth, but she was a beautiful person all around. A warm soul."

"How come I've never met her?"

"Oh, she passed."

"I'm sorry."

"No. It's OK. It's been, hell, eight years. Breast cancer." A memory raced through his head of him and her in the midst of an uncontrollable laughing fit over their shared twisted humor. The memory chiseled a small smile onto his face.

"I'm sorry." That had taken the steam out of Tom's desire to rant about his own problems. He sipped the hot tea, the heat spreading throughout his body, comforting his nerves so he no longer felt like he was riding a rollercoaster.

"What's going on, Tom?"

"I'm sure you saw that story on the news. The leaked audio of how I'm bashing the press?"

Bob gave a single nod as he sipped his tea.

"I'm thinking I need to leave."

Bob placed his teacup back on the saucer. "Leave?"

"Yeah. Leave L.A."

"And do what?"

Tom took a long sip of his tea and shrugged.

"What does Sean have to say about this?"

"He doesn't know," Tom said. "I fired him."

"Fired him?" Bob couldn't believe what he was hearing. He thought Tom didn't have a clue as to what he was doing. "But how are you going to get any work?"

"I'm not. I've been thinking a lot lately about the business and it disgusts me. I don't wanna be a part of it anymore. I *can't* be a part of it anymore."

"Then, where are you going to go? You can't just live here without a job."

"I'm not planning ... on ... living ... here."

Tom saw Bob's head stop moving, his eyes slightly widen. He knew what Bob must be thinking. "I'm not ... I'm not going to kill myself, if that's what you're thinking."

"I'm not thinking that." Bob was thinking that.

"I mean ... I'm moving outta state."

"You're not going to escape it, y'know?"

"Escape what?"

"Whatever it is you're feeling. Guilt. Anger. Sadness. All of the above. They'll follow you wherever you go."

"Then I'll deal with them when I get there. But I can't do it here, Bob. I came to you tonight 'cause I wanted you to do a big favor for me."

"What's that?"

"Since I'm leaving, I wanted to make sure all of my ... stuff ... here was in order. Could you help me with that?"

"Sure. Like what?"

"My house, my car. Big things like that."

"So just those two things?"

"Well, my furniture too. Can you sell it, get rid of it, for me? I'll give you fifteen percent."

"I can draw up some paperwork, sure. But what are you going to do? Where are you going to go?"

"I'd rather not say. Just please ... help me. You've always treated me with respect and been very discreet ... and I appreciate that. It's definitely what I need right now."

"OK. But I'll need to know how to get you the money from the sales."

"I'll send you an address."

Bob nodded his head and the emotion dawned on him that he was actually going to miss Tom. "Just let me know when you've landed on your feet."

Tom nodded in agreement and the two finished their tea. Tom faded into one of the best sleeps he had had since Maggie's death. Bob's home was a welcomed comfort zone, away from the media and paparazzi blitzkrieg.

The next morning, Tom woke up around five o'clock. He quietly got dressed, and studied more of Bob's life, looking at diplomas, pictures, books, movies, and other random knick-knacks around the living room. He thought he heard Bob stirring in his bedroom, so Tom eased out of the house and called a taxi on his cell phone. Just to be sure Bob didn't come outside and find him there, Tom walked a few blocks out of sight.

By the time Bob did come out of his bedroom, all he found remaining of Tom was his cell phone and a small handwritten note which said: *Sell everything except my books. Please send. Thanks.*

Tom walked out in the slight cool of the morning, nervous about his next move. There was the tinge of excitement about starting over, but there was also that sadness mixed in, knowing that what he had set out to do so long ago was over. He began thinking of that 1970s Gordon Lightfoot song, "If You Could Read My Mind," one of the most depressing songs he'd ever heard. The music was the first thing that invaded his brain before he started humming the melody. He didn't know all of the lyrics but he remembered reading how Gordon had written it during the aftermath of a failed marriage. It seemed appropriate to Tom that he was singing it to himself now.

The taxi pulled up to the curb, and Tom opened the door and hopped in to discover the taxi's speakers were belting out the same damn song. He slumped back into the seat and the cab driver asked, "Where you headed?"

"LAX."

Before going to the airport, Tom had asked the cabbie to stop at an ATM. He took out some spending money to get him by until Bob wired more money into his account. At the airport, he had bought a seat in first class to avoid as many people as he could. The only things he had were his iPod with headphones and *The Razor's Edge*, which he read in the airport waiting area and when he was first seated.

When the book was done, Tom put a pair of small, white ear buds in his ears. With a quick rotation through the menu of his iPod, he accessed his song playlist and found one of his favorite songs. He pressed play and Bruce Springsteen's 1975 live recording of "Thunder Road" from his *Live 1975-1985* album began with the announcer saying, "Ladies and gentlemen, Bruce Springsteen and the E Street Band." The applause soon gave way to a solo piano, followed by a lonely harmonica rift, sounding like an old dirge, like something out of an old Wild West film. Bruce's deep, soulful sandpaper voice, singing of outcasts and romance, drifted into his ears and Tom feigned falling asleep – to avoid anybody near him recognizing him or wanting to make small talk.

He tried to think about what he would do when he got to the east coast but came up with nothing. He knew he would contact Bob and have him forward the cash from selling his house and car, have him send some essentials and donate the rest. Tom was scared. He didn't have a job or friends, but he knew he could no longer stay where he was, and anywhere was better than L.A. He thought about Maggie and how he couldn't save their marriage, and then, her life. The pit in his stomach crawled from his gut to his chest and he thought the feeling would never go away.

The plane vibrated from the starting up of the plane's engines and Tom turned his head to peek out the nearest window and see the plane taxiing down the runway. He closed his eyes again, the sound of the engine grew louder and the plane picked up speed. Most people would be awake for the takeoff but Tom was too tired to worry. Bruce's weary, lonely voice belted out the closing line of the song:

It's a town full of losers and I'm pullin' outta here to win.

The piano and glockenspiel danced in time with each other, sounding almost like the tiny tinkling of a small music box, as Bruce's soulful wails sporadically joined in. The harmonica and piano duet ended on an epic note as the plane rose above the permanent haze of Los Angeles. Bruce's final words stuck in Tom's head as sleep soon overtook him and all he could think was that he couldn't have agreed more.

SIDE **B**

"... before I can live with other folks,
I've got to live with myself. The one
thing that doesn't abide by majority rule
is a person's conscience."

--Harper Lee, *To Kill A Mockingbird*

12.

"Every time I hear another story
The poor boy lost his head
Everybody feels a little crazy
But we go on living with it"

--The Head and the Heart
"Another Story"

The muted sound of the distant waves crashing upon the sandy shore was the paramount reason she had decided to live at the beach. Every morning she woke up, whether it was sunny or rainy outside, she was thankful she had made the move to Rehoboth Beach, a small resort town in Delaware that proclaimed itself the "nation's summer capital." It definitely wasn't an easy move. She had taken a huge pay cut from her job as a financial lawyer to live here, but she was happy. It was a drastic change from New York City. Downtown Rehoboth consisted of small side streets labeled as avenues, and, in the center of town, the boardwalk was littered with arcades, an amusement park, a mix of pizza joints, soft serve ice cream shops, and a couple of small five-and-dime stores. The busy season was the summer when the tourists and part-time residents visited from May to

September; the rest of the year, known as the "off-season," belonged to the true locals. Down the center of town was the main strip referred to as "the avenue," which housed a broader mix of retail stores – everything from clothing to books to beach-going essentials – and restaurants. Every summer season tourists repeatedly drove back and forth from one end of town to the other in their constant struggle to search for an empty parking spot. During the off-season, places closed down relatively early each night compared to the twenty-four-hour business hours of New York, and the only thing heard throughout the night were the same waves she heard now.

Jade Saha already felt it was going to be a good day. It was sunny and the nice weather was starting to finally creep into the area three weeks after the first official day of spring. She stretched as far as her limbs could reach; her eyes shut tight, taking in a deep breath and releasing it with a smile on her face. The sun shone through the windows, slicing through the dark space of the room, and caressed her caramel skin. Her smile widened, revealing her dimples, as she opened her dark brown eyes and looked at her clock. 7:01 a.m.

She sat up; her raven black hair cascaded down over her slender shoulders as she looked out onto the rest of her room. She had made enough money while practicing law to buy a small car, a beach cruiser bicycle, and rent a nice, cozy two-story apartment, which used to be a detached garage, behind someone's house. The location was perfect for her: stuck amongst houses, so she was surrounded by people – albeit some were just seasonal residents – and two blocks from the beach, two blocks from the avenue, so she could walk or bike to either place whenever she wanted.

Jade walked up to what looked like a classic 1940s radio, which actually was a record player, radio, CD and iPod player deck all in one. Her iPod was plugged into the radio and she pressed the "RANDOM" button, then the "PLAY" button. The opening strings to Lauryn Hill's "Everything is Everything" played and the upbeat tempo helped Jade to shake out any stubborn, remaining sleep. She went through her usual routine of brushing her teeth, taking a shower, getting dressed and eating oatmeal and a fruit-and-vegetable smoothie.

The only connection Jade had to the area with which she now lived was that she had visited Rehoboth for a two-week vacation one summer, back when she was sixteen-years-old. The memory of walking the boardwalk with her friend, Aishwarya, riding the rides at Funland, and wading the cool waters of the Atlantic Ocean were some of her favorite in a vast sea of adolescent memories. If all it took were happy places and times she had had in her childhood, Jade could have picked any place along the Mid-Atlantic States – Maryland, New Jersey, Pennsylvania, or Virginia – with which to move. She picked Rehoboth because it was just close enough to her parents in Washington, D.C. (about two hours away), but just far enough to give her the space she needed from them.

Ever since she left New York, her parents had never failed to bring up in conversation how she should get back into law and find a good man to marry. She didn't have the heart to tell them she didn't have even the slightest interest in any of those things. Being so studious and alienated in high school and most of college, she didn't get to have as much fun like the other kids had during that time. Those adolescent high school days were so full of put-downs or flat-out being ignored that she still felt the reverberations in her confidence to this day. So now was all about making up for lost time. After all, she had been a good girl, a good student, and done what was required of her. She had gotten great grades, graduated summa cum laude, and made class valedictorian. Her time of being the proper, by-the-book girl was over. She wasn't looking for trouble or making mistakes, but if she did, so be it.

Today was too nice of a day to drive. She wanted to take her time and enjoy the weather. Jade put her wavy hair up into a loose bun, grabbed her iPod, messenger bag, and what was left of her smoothie, and walked out the door. She passed through the small screened porch where she grabbed her sky blue beach cruiser and made her way between the two houses which fronted her apartment. Small streams of sunlight shone through the canopy of the trees and speckled her face. The smell of the ocean air mixed with the smells of a new spring: gasoline from lawn mowers, fresh cut grass and freshly unearthed dirt. It only took a few steps to reach the sidewalk and she hopped on her bike and headed away from the beach. The sidewalk led her to the next road where the sun completely bathed her. Despite the beach town, her way to work reminded her of a suburban neighborhood one might find in Pennsylvania: tree-lined roads with sidewalks and houses just close enough to keep neighbors from becoming strangers, and to keep strangers from bringing crime into their lives.

Continuing to follow her route to work, Jade couldn't help but think what crossed her mind on a daily basis: she was so happy to be here, in this place. Pedaling out of the neighborhood and onto the backstreets of Rehoboth, she saw the sign for Rehoboth Elementary School. An uncontrollable smile spread across her face, thinking of those kids. They had good days and bad days but, overall, they were great. Jade realized it was a cliché response when people asked her what she did and she told them the kids taught her more than she probably taught them – but it was true.

When she got the call to substitute at the elementary schools, there usually weren't a variety of subjects to teach; it was either first grade, third grade and so on. Fortunately, there was a separate music class at Rehoboth Elementary so it gave her a chance to teach what she loved talking most about. She had made it a rule never to teach at any of the high schools because teenagers were still as cruel as when she went to school with them, but that wasn't completely what kept her from working there. The fact that teens were much too curious and had the means to search her name on the internet meant they could easily find out particular truths about Jade's past which she didn't want to surface.

She pulled up to the school and checked in to the office to get her assignment for the day. A smile spread across her face when she saw she had her favorite subject: music class. Jade's smile continued to beam as she got to the classroom, the little fourth grade kids poured in and she began her lesson.

The rest of the day had been a blur, but it was fun. Jade almost forgot that she still had another job to go to for the night. She looked at her watch. 3:45 p.m. She figured she might as well bike straight to the restaurant. Bartending part-time at the Shorebreak Lodge was the best kind of job for her: her co-workers were really cool, and the customers were mostly friendly. She always imagined herself as some wise, philosophical bartender in some small dive bar, doting out advice to poor schlubs, who were getting drunk off cheap booze. But she quickly found out that was not the case when it came to working in Rehoboth – especially in the summer season.

Between talking to customers and making drinks, working the bar on weekend nights was fast-paced, almost to the point of dizzying. There were slower nights when she occasionally worked during the week, and she had a lot of laughs with the restaurant's co-owner, Matt Sprenkle (who some referred to just by his last name), the wait staff, and the regulars who came in. Today would be a little more crowded than usual for the off season since the weather was beautiful, it was Friday and the part-time residents were coming in to open their beach houses for the upcoming summer.

The commute from the school to the Shorebreak took about fifteen minutes. It beat any traffic in New York or D.C., and getting to see the sights of the local businesses – and those who worked in them – made the ride all the more enjoyable. She cut through the same suburban-looking neighborhood she had used to get to the school, and careened through side streets until she reached the horizontal roadway of King Charles Avenue, where she cut a left and biked two blocks over until seeing the small green street sign reading Wilmington Avenue. She made a right-hand turn and relished the ocean breeze washing over her face and through her hair.

The place didn't open to the public for about another hour but, looking through the glass windows, she could see Sprenkle already standing behind the bar, getting ready for another night of business. He was only a few years older than Jade and he looked somewhat like a professional surfer. His curly, dirty blonde-mostly-brown hair and suntanned skin were a nice compliment to his blue eyes, which, throughout his nights at work, were often covered by a pair of black, rectangular horn-rimmed reading glasses. He was dressed in a pair of jeans and an O'Neill t-shirt, a true reflection of his laidback, likable personality, which made nearly everyone who met him feel comfortable around him.

Jade walked up a few wooden steps next to the outside patio, up to the side entrance door, tapped on the window and waved. Sprenkle smiled, walked over to the door, unlocked it and let her in. The restaurant's colors where white and a blue color which Jade could only describe to anyone as "TARDIS blue," although she knew she was one of a few *Doctor Who* fans who lived around here who would get her reference. In the forefront of the restaurant was a grand dining area with tables and chairs, the centerpiece of the restaurant being a big table with two white couches on both sides; and all customers in this area were able to turn their heads and look out the grand window overlooking the sidewalk and street. Around the left side of the restaurant was the walkway to the kitchen behind the bar, as well as more seating to the left, with the restrooms in the rear. The bar was U-shaped with the bottom part seating the most patrons and the right side devoted to bar order/pick-up and an entrance/exit to the kitchen. It was the kind of restaurant which was a nice mix of something you might find in the city but with the feel of hanging out at someone's house for the night.

"Hey, Jade," Sprenkle said. "Thanks for comin' in tonight."

"No problem," she smiled. "So am I serving tonight or at the bar?"

"At the bar."

Jade was happy to hear that. She didn't mind waiting tables too much but she preferred bartending a lot more. A waitress walked by and greeted Jade as she took her place behind the bar.

"Anything I need to get ready?" Jade asked Sprenkle.

"We need more of the wine on tonight's menu. Could you go look in the back for more?"

"Sure. But I get to play my music!"

"OK."

Jade plugged her iPod into the restaurant sound system and played Mary Wells' "Bye Bye Baby."

Five o'clock came and went. A few of the regulars came in and sat at the bar, a mix of locals and seasonal visitors had dinner. Around nine o'clock was when the bar seating filled up. It didn't take long before most of the customers on the barstools had a nice buzz going, laughter and conversation hanging in the air. Jade didn't pay too much mind to the crowd sitting in front of her ... unless they spoke up first. She was friendly but somewhat shy when it came to starting conversation. She honestly didn't know how Sprenkle did it. The man could talk to pretty much anyone and, if tempers ever flared, he could diffuse the situation and calm down the most pissed-off person. It's what made him a good bouncer all those years ago when he worked at a bar called Summer House. She knew she could do the same in some situations because she was a woman, and most men thought she was pretty, which her self-deprecating manner would prevent her from believing, but she didn't have what Sprenkle had. In the work setting, he could connect with people and make them open up to him in a way she could not.

"Hey," a voice at the corner of the bar said above the music of She & Him's "Sweet Darlin.'" "Can I get a beer?"

"Sure," Jade smiled and walked down to the guy leaning forward. He was in his early fifties, dressed in the usual vacationer garb, but he inexplicably looked at least ten years younger. "Which kind can I get ya?"

"What kind ya got?"

"Bud Light, Miller Light, Corona—"

"Actually, I'll take a vodka martini."

"OK." Jade retained her smile as she went to work, bringing out the chilled martini glass.

"You look familiar," the man said. "Have we met before?"

"You live around here?"

"No. Down for the weekend. I live around D.C."

"Oh yeah?" Jade turned around and her smile faded as she grabbed a bottle of vodka and dry vermouth. Her heart beat faster and she kept her breathing from getting out of control.

"Yeah. Have you ever lived around there? Did you go to school around there?"

"No. I went to college in New York." She hoped to change the subject. "Why? What do you do?"

"I'm actually a reporter, a journalist. I write for a newspaper."

"Oh yeah? Which one?"

"The *Washington Post.*"

"Wow."

"I know this sounds crazy but I remember faces really well. And I *know* I've seen you before."

"Well, I've lived here for a long time. So maybe you've seen me when you've visited the beach."

"No. That's not it." The man searched his mind for any clue that would tip him off to how he recognized her. He figured the best way was to get a name first. He stuck out his hand. "My name's Peter. And you are ...?"

"Jade." She stuck out her hand and shook his. "Nice to meet you."

"You too." Peter ran the name through the Rolodex in his head. There weren't many people named Jade, especially ones he had met, but where he knew this girl from confounded him. He shook it off and chalked it up to age. "Well, I guess maybe I was mistaken. Can I see a menu?"

"Sure," she smiled. She handed him a menu and walked to the other end of the bar, letting out a small sigh of relief. The last thing she wanted was to have someone remind her of the past she was trying so hard to move on from.

* * *

For the first time since he had gained his celebrity status, Tom was happy to arrive at an airport and not be recognized. There were no press, no autograph seekers, and no paparazzi. He passed through the arrivals gate at Baltimore-Washington International airport, and the only sight he saw which stoked envy were some of his fellow passengers arriving to families: wives, husbands, kids. It only reminded him of Maggie. Then his thoughts turned to his parents. His stomach turned at how they might treat him, what they must think.

His mom had tried calling him a few times since the incident, but Tom ignored all the phone calls that came in. Besides, the sound of her voice only made him feel more ashamed. He hadn't been home in about ten years nor had he thought of that place since he last visited. Delaware had been the furthest thing from his mind in the time since Maggie and he had moved to L.A. The last time he had seen his parents in person was at his and Maggie's wedding. He paid to fly them over to California, and they visited most of the tourist traps. The wedding itself was magnificent and everyone seemed to have a fun time, but his parents' departure was somewhat cold. Every time Tom came face to face with his father, there was some unspoken dissidence between them. It had been boiling under the surface for quite some time but Tom refused to blow up over what he believed to be petty differences. Nevertheless, he felt as if his father didn't fully accept him for who he was or what he believed in, and, because of that, he felt he couldn't talk to his father, he couldn't open up. It was that same dissidence which currently turned Tom's stomach in knots.

"Sir? Excuse me, sir?"

"Wha—?" Tom asked, breaking out of his thoughts. He looked behind him to see an older woman speaking to him.

"You're next."

That's right, he thought. *The rental car place.* Tom looked forward to see the rental agent waiting for him. He stepped forward and the rental agent forced a smile.

"Good afternoon, sir," the man greeted. "What can I do for you today?"

"I'd like to rent a car."

"Which kind? An economy, compact, luxury sedan?"

Tom thought for a moment. He didn't want some small piece of crap compact, but didn't want a car that would call any unwanted attention to him. His mind raced trying to think of the perfect vehicle for where he was headed: the beach. He remembered a lot of people drove Jeeps around that area. Hell, it seemed as if there was some state law that required a resident or property owner to own a Jeep in order to live there. So, by his reasoning, he would blend in with *a lot* of people.

"Do you have any Jeep Wranglers?"

"Let me check that for you." The sales agent's smile remained plastered on his face as if he were some creepy automaton painted with an immovable expression.

"We have one available. It's a 2003 Wrangler. It has—"

"Fine. That's great," Tom cut him off. He now wanted to get out of the airport before anyone might notice him. He forced a smile. "Sounds good."

"OK. If you'll let me see your driver's license, I'll get started on the invoice."

Tom handed the license to the sales agent and the man went to work on entering Tom's information.

"Oh. Can you tell me if the Wrangler is for sale too?"

The man gave a single nod and continued to clack away on his keyboard.

"Actually, yes, it is. We don't get many of those for sale."

"How much is it?"

"Thirteen thousand even. That's with ninety-five thousand miles on it."

"I'll take it," Tom said, throwing his credit card on the counter, catching the agent by surprise.

"It'll take some time to run through the process, sir."

"I'm kinda in a hurry."

"I need to run your credit history, there are forms you need to sign ..."

"Is there any way I can buy it at the rental place at my destination?"

"Sure."

"OK. I'll just do it there. For now, I'll just take the rental."

"OK."

The man went back to typing away at his keyboard before he finally had Tom sign a receipt and handed him the keys.

The agent walked Tom out to the rental lot to see a midnight blue Jeep Wrangler – the only Jeep in the lot.

"Just make sure if you return the rental that you fill up the gas to where it was."

"Thanks."

Tom stepped up onto the running board of the Jeep and hoisted himself in. He was so used to a luxury car that sat close to the ground that he wasn't used to the feel of the 4x4. The inside of the vehicle was pretty basic – no fancy bells or whistles and the transmission was a stick shift. He waited for the sales agent to leave, but the man constantly looked over his shoulder as if he was studying Tom's face in case he might be a criminal. Or maybe the man simply recognized Tom's now infamous face. Either way, Tom couldn't get out of there fast enough. He turned the key, rolled down his window and continued his journey, leaving Baltimore in his wake.

After a few minutes, the silence was too much for him and he needed a pleasant distraction from his thoughts and memories. He turned on the radio. Nothing but static and crappy music. The pollen tickled the inside of his nose and he let out a violent sneeze. He quickly shot his hand to his nose and caught the snot but he didn't want to take the hand away and get the ooze all over his clothes. With his other hand, he opened the glove compartment, searching for a napkin or some kind of paper towel. He found an old brown napkin and wiped away the thick snot. When he went to shut the small compartment, he wasn't sure but he saw what looked like an audio cassette tape case sitting atop a CD and a few random papers. He almost couldn't believe it because he hadn't seen an audio tape in years. Luckily, the Jeep had a factory cassette player and CD player. Tom thought the rental places cleaned out any stuff previous renters left behind, but maybe whatever was on the tape was better than anything he was finding on the radio. He grabbed the small case and looked on the front. It was a Maxell blank audio cassette tape. A smile broke out when he realized it was a mix tape.

Tom looked on the front of the cover and saw two handwritten book quotes – one on side A and one on side B.

Under the left-hand "Side A" heading, the handwriting read:

"Our lives are not our own. We are bound to others, past and present, and by each crime and every kindness, we birth our future. "

--David Mitchell, *Cloud Atlas*

Under the right-hand "Side B" heading, the handwriting read:

"Before I can live with other folks, I've got to live with myself. The one thing that doesn't abide by majority rule is a person's conscience."

--Harper Lee, *To Kill a Mockingbird*

He looked to the side of the sleeve and saw the handwritten title:

Forgotten Mile Mix

Tom didn't study anymore of the cover and just popped in the cassette on side A. The speakers went silent for a moment before the sound of a hi-hat cymbal and single guitar strumming took over the quiet. A piano soon ran onto the scene and Bruce Springsteen sang "It's Hard to be a Saint in the City." He turned up the volume so loud, he drowned out any other white noise he heard. It was a good song for Tom to drive to, and he was happy to have any noise in his head other than the ghosts which had come to haunt him in recent months.

Each song on the first side of the tape was a classic - songs from the 1970s and 1980s - until the last two songs, both by some guys he didn't know, but the last song was ironically titled "After Los Angeles." He looked at the case and while it didn't look that new, Tom knew it couldn't be that old with those last two songs on the mix. When the last song ended, the tape seemed to stop but he kept waiting for it to automatically turn over. A muffled screeching erupted from the player and he instantly knew something wasn't right. He hit the eject button and the cassette popped out halfway. Tom grabbed the cassette and pulled it out to see a long stream of thin brown tape flowing behind it.

"*Shit!*"

Tom began to gently pull the tape itself out of the player, hoping it wouldn't break. After a slight tug, the tape yanked free of the player, unbroken. He didn't want to risk playing side B and it getting stuck again, so he went back to try and find a station with some decent music. It wasn't long before he remembered there was a CD in the glove compartment too. He opened it up, pulled out the CD case and looked at the cover with four guys on it, the band's name in white letters, and the album title in blue: The Gaslight Anthem "The '59 Sound."

The disc slid in with ease and the speakers came alive with the sound of an old scratchy record rotating with a guitar melody repeating three times before the powerhouse rock of a full band and the lead singer's vocals blasted through. Tom listened to the lyrics of the title track, "Great Expectations," and found he could relate to a lot of it:

> *I saw tail lights last night in a dream about my first wife*
> *Everybody leaves and I'd expect as much from you*
> *I saw tail lights last night in a dream about my old life*
> *Everybody leaves, so why, why wouldn't you?*

The Jeep drove a bit rougher than his Porsche but he liked it. It made him feel more connected to the road while clips of memories played on cue. Music hadn't affected him like this since ... he couldn't remember when. His eyes locked on the road ahead as he soon came to the Chesapeake Bay Bridge; long, perforated lines of chrome and steel stretched from the many toll booths back for at least a mile. Why the hell was it so damn busy when it was still the off season!? The answer came as quickly as his annoyed question. It was after Easter. All of the tourists and seasonal residents started making their annual pilgrimage to the beach to open their beach houses and take advantage of the first nice days of the season. *Damn.* All he could do now was wait out the line as each vehicle played its own game of "Red Light, Green Light." While he waited, he grabbed the cassette tape and poked his pinky finger in one of its spokes, meticulously winding the tape back into the cassette. When it was all back in, he put the tape back into the cassette player, but let the CD play.

Fifteen minutes passed and Tom made it to the booth only to pay six bucks to make his way over to the peninsula. The price had increased since he was last here, but he figured he shouldn't be surprised. If six dollars was all he needed to pay to get further away from his troubles, then so be it. Along his trip, in Denton, Maryland, Tom noticed an auto body shop called the Wayside Body Shop. Its marquee sign always had a different fortune cookie-like aphorism posted every week. The business – and its sign – had been there as far back as Tom could remember and a small part of him always looked forward to seeing what words of wisdom the sign had to offer the travelers who passed by. He looked up and saw this week's saying:

Despair makes victims sometimes victors.

Tom wondered if anyone else who saw the quote knew who said it: Edward Bulwer-Lytton, the English author who also coined the famous phrases "The pen is mightier than the sword," and "It was a dark and stormy night." The

Gaslight Anthem album played on and as it ended, he pulled into the town limits of Lewes – pronounced "Lewis" and not "Lews," like the tourists often called it – with its small-town feel. Tom passed by his alma mater, Cape Henlopen High School, which had gotten a major facelift since he attended. After a mile or so, he drove to the main street in the town, Second Street, which was lined with quaint shops, cafés, restaurants and a few bars. By the time he arrived, it was around dinner time and the nice weather had lured the locals and tourists out, taking their families to the variety of restaurants.

Tom's Jeep sputtered for a moment before he shifted to first and turned into a small neighborhood in Lewes – a fisherman's type of haven with docks for fishing boats scattered along the canal, which cut through the town. Houses of all kinds lined the streets as well as small neighborhood communities sprinkled throughout.

The next right turn was Tom's destination but when he turned the corner, he pulled the Jeep over and focused on the house where he had spent his early life. He thought about going inside to see his mom and dad, and face the music. His head got the spins as if he had drank himself into an alcoholic stupor and he felt light-headed. Saliva built up in his mouth and he felt the instant urge to swallow. It happened again. And again. And again. Then, nothing. Tom swallowed down another mouthful of saliva, his head sweaty and skin looking peaked. He raised his head to glare at his parents' home.

* * *

"Why don't you just listen to me!?" Tom shouted.

"You're being stupid!" Mr. Frost shouted back. "What you're talking about is asinine!"

"Why!? Because you disagree!?"

"Because it's *wrong!*"

"I'm not getting into this with you anymore."

"You're the one who brought it up."

"I thought you'd listen to me. Not just attack me. Then again, I guess I shouldn't be surprised."

"What are you talking about, Tom? This doesn't sound like you."

"Nevermind." An eighteen-year-old Tom turned away and stormed out of the room, leaving his father as fast as he could. He found himself in his grandmother's sitting room. He was so angry that he didn't even notice his grandma sitting in her chair, watching the small TV.

Tom had never exploded like that at his father before, but, this time, he couldn't contain his emotion. He had become lost in his thoughts, wondering if his father would ever take him seriously enough to hear him out without insulting him.

"What's wrong, Tom?" the elderly female voice asked.

Tom looked to the small, plush rocker in the corner and saw his grandma sitting there, staring at him with big pleading brown eyes. As long as he could remember, his grandma had white hair, a thin face, and she smelled of a blend of menthol cigarettes and Chanel perfume. She was one of the first single mothers in a time when being a single mother wasn't applauded or praised but rather frowned upon. Raising seven children had made her will strong and her body thin and somewhat weary at times. For her grandchildren, she was a loving pillar of support who would watch over them any time she could. Tom had spent most of his youth around her as she watched him while his parents were at work. Now that he was older, he didn't get to spend as much time with her, but he still relished every moment with her.

"Sometimes I wonder if I'm meant to be here," Tom said.

"What do you mean?"

"It's as if ... everyone around me - my friends, my parents - has different ... views than me. I'm not mad they have different opinions. I'm mad they treat me like I'm some idiot just 'cause I don't agree with them."

"Tom. You're going to experience that all your life, no matter where you go. What's this really about?"

"It's Dad. He said I was being stupid 'cause I didn't agree with some politician. I told him the guy was wrong. Even pointed out some facts from the news, but he just dismissed it as liberal media." Tom took a few breaths to calm his nerves. "It's not just him. I also hear from a lot of my friends on things I just don't agree with, or I know is wrong. But ... if I ever say anything, they get ... so ... disrespectful. I don't care if they disagree with me. I just know I wouldn't be that way with them."

"Tom." His grandma knew what this was all about. "Your father loves you. And I'm sure your friends like you. But people are people. They get defensive and cruel when anything they take as truth is questioned. Most of 'em - like your father - let their pride get the best of 'em. They think they're doing you a service by 'educating' you to their truth. But all they end up doing is raising their voice, saying offensive things, and riling up themselves and everyone who disagrees. Wars have been started over such behavior."

"Sometimes I think it'd just be easy if I ... changed. Maybe be ... more like them."

"Don't you ever be like them, Tom, just 'cause you think it'll make 'em happy. It's important that you're different. Different is what makes all of us grow for the better. Different is what helps us see something in a new light. Listen, I know most of the people you know are ... conservative and you're not. I know there are many things that people your age are and you aren't. And that seems important 'cause everyone makes it seem that way.

"I also know you don't let some other person's opinion sway your thinking just 'cause everybody else believes it. Places that tend to have one kind of person need people like you -- people who think and feel differently - to keep a balance to things. Of course, those people in the majority don't like it, and they show it! But it doesn't make you - or what you think - any less important. If anything, it makes you more important. If it weren't for people who thought differently, we wouldn't have most of what we have now. Most scientists, artists, musicians, scholars and other people who've made a change in this world wouldn't have done so.

"You've always been an inquisitive child," his grandma continued. "You've never assumed to know the absolute truth until you get definitive proof. And people who do agree with something just 'cause it backs up their belief don't like that. They don't like people who can't be easily swayed with a few fancy words and flashy images.

"I know it's not easy, but, trust me, don't ever change for them. Be you. 'Cause it's more important to them than they, or you, think."

"You know what, Grandma? I think you're a great woman."

His grandma let out a short, single laugh at him, as if what he said were a joke - even though, she knew he was being serious.

"I love you, Tom. Don't *ever* change - unless you know it's what's best for *you*."

Tom stood up, knelt down and embraced his grandma in a loving hug. "I love you," he said.

"I love you too."

Two months later, the cancer in her lungs had taken over and that was the last conversation he had had with her. Tom had been working at Funland when he got the call, telling him she was gone.

* * *

Screw this!, Tom thought, then grabbing the door, slamming it shut and driving down the street, past his parents' house. He returned to Second Street, past the boutique shops, the cafes and restaurants, until he saw what he needed. He parked, then walked toward a small restaurant: Gilligan's Restaurant and Bar. When he came through the door, there was a nice open room the size of a family room, with tables and chairs filling up most of the hardwood floor space. Tom walked straight toward the rear of the room and through a door, taking him out to the bar area which was converted from an old charter boat, which looked like the S.S. *Minnow* from the TV show with which the establishment derived its name, *Gilligan's Island*.

The L-shaped bar had a few open seats but most were occupied by what Tom would only guess to be locals. There was a small television broadcasting a baseball game but the music from the radio dominated the sound system. The bartender looked around the same age as Tom and had a familiar face - like someone he had gone to high school with - but he couldn't remember the guy's name. He was hoping the guy wouldn't recognize him.

"What can I get ya?" the bartender asked.

"Something strong. What do you recommend?"

"Well," the bartender said, grabbing a bottle from behind the bar and showing it to Tom. "This one will get ya shitty." Then he grabbed a different one and held it up. "But this one can get ya obliterated."

"Obliterated."

The bartender gave a single, confirmatory nod and poured two shots worth of the brown drink into a highball glass. Tom grabbed it up and took in all of the drink in one gulp. For the first millisecond, the liquid had no taste, but the remaining time was all his taste buds needed to catch up. The fire in his throat gave way to the stomach-wrenching effect of the heavy alcohol as Tom imagined the bartender had played a cruel prank on him by giving him the stuff they used to scrape off paint. In Tom's mind, he had taken the drink with an unaffected reaction, but, in reality, his face contorted every which way; his mouth opened repeatedly and his tongue pushed out of his mouth as if it was desperately doing anything it could to get away from the drink.

"Ya here for the weekend?" the bartender asked.

Tom shook his head, still trying to shake the taste of the liquor. "Indefinitely." He tapped his finger, pointing toward the empty glass. "I'll have one more of those."

"You sure?"

"Yeah."

The bartender poured another double and Tom swallowed it down again. This time, the aftertaste wasn't as biting. His stomach warmed, spreading to his chest, and he felt slightly numb.

"I'll see ya, Drew!" a vaguely familiar voice sounded from behind Tom, who turned around to see the source of the voice. The quickest glimpse was all Tom needed to recognize Rich Feltz.

Feltz was a few years older than Tom, someone he knew from his days working at Funland. His presence in the local bar scene made him a bit of a celebrity in that nearly every local resident knew him and he was a friend to nearly all of them. When he smiled, his brown eyes conveyed the friendly, jovial personality which he was mostly known for in the area. But if some idiot had the mistaken sense to get on his bad side, those brown eyes could practically burn a hole through anything. His faded goatee matched his short brown, spiky hair, and he was wearing a black button-up shirt with tan slacks and black shoes. They both had gained a little extra weight since they both attended Cape – Tom was a sophomore when Feltz was a senior. Feltz had to have known what Tom had been going through the past months and the last thing he needed was to have someone he knew judging him. Tom turned away, hoping Feltz didn't see him.

"Frost?" Feltz said.

Damn.

"Tom Frost? That you?"

Tom slowly turned to face Feltz, already sitting beside him.

"Hey ... Feltz."

Feltz knew of Tom's troubles. Hell, everyone who followed pop culture, or had a television, knew. He knew

Tom must be hurting and he wasn't going to add to it. Besides, Tom was a friend. Always had been ever since they worked at Funland together. It was just a part of the inexplicable bond they and everyone who worked there during that time shared.

"I didn't know you were in town," Feltz said.

"Just got in today."

"So how's everything going?"

Tom wondered if Feltz honestly didn't know what was going on with him lately or if he was just being nice.

"*Faaan*tastic," Tom said with a hint of sarcasm. "How 'bout you? God, I haven't seen you in ages. What have you been up to?"

"Oh, same ol' shit. Workin' at the outlets. I'm the manager at Columbia."

Tom nodded his head. "Cool."

"You stayin' here a while or ... are you on vacation?"

"I'm staying ... indefinitely."

"Cool." Feltz took a swig of his beer. "You plannin' on visiting anybody while you're here?"

"Just family, I guess. Why? Anyone I know around?"

"Yeah. Sprenkle's got a restaurant and bar in Rehoboth. Shorebreak Lodge. It's a really cool place. Most of us go there when they're in town."

Feltz delved into the latest goings-on of former co-workers. Tom had almost forgotten about the Funlanders' names Feltz was mentioning, it had been so long since he had seen or talked to any of them. Flashback clips played in his mind of the laughs they had all shared, the late nights, the parties, and the hot, sunny days lifting kids into rides.

"I was gonna go over there now. Wanna come?"

"Sure."

"How about a shot first? Wanna shot?"

"Sure."

"Drew! Two Fireballs."

The bartender strode over and poured the amber drink into three shot glasses: one for Feltz, one for Tom and the other for the bartender himself. Feltz raised his glass and the other two followed suit.

With that, the men lightly clanked the small glasses together and downed the liquor in a swift jerk of their heads. The alcohol wasn't as prevalent to Tom as the taste of the red hots candies.

"OK. Let's roll," Feltz said.

Feltz had offered to drive them both to Shorebreak, but Tom politely declined. Seeing a familiar face again was both comforting and uneasy all in one. He hadn't seen Feltz in a little under twenty years but seeing him again reminded Tom of a more carefree time. The buzz from the whiskey gave him as good of a second wind as any energy drink or cup of coffee. He only hoped the crowd at the next bar wasn't patronized by anyone he knew or ... recognized him from the show. It had become a recurring theme these days.

Tom turned on the radio to help calm his worry and Edward Sharpe and the Magnetic Zero's "Better Days" was playing. The ride down Route One went fast as the towns were back-to-back, the downtown areas only fifteen minutes apart. The entry to Rehoboth had changed in the twenty years since he had last seen it. What had once been a normal two-way road into the town now had a roundabout to help the flow of traffic. All Tom could think of was the scene in *National Lampoon's European Vacation* where Chevy Chase's character couldn't turn off of the Lambeth Bridge roundabout and kept driving around it all night.

The avenue was still not awake to its full capacity as tourists had not yet transitioned to summer mode yet, but he did notice slightly more businesses than when he had last been here. The change of restaurants and shops was staggering. The avenue had gone from somewhat flashy to complete flash and traded some of its quaintness for contemporary style. The overall layout was still the same and he could almost see the ghosts of his times long gone on those dark side streets.

Feltz's car made a slight right turn and Tom felt déjà vu as this was often his route to Funland when he worked there. Tom followed Feltz to the ocean block until he pulled in front of a small restaurant with a side patio and an upstairs vacant apartment. Tom pulled into a spot next to Feltz and turned off his engine. *OK, here we go*, he thought, taking a deep breath and slowly releasing it. He flung his Jeep door open, throwing caution to the wind, and popped out to find Feltz already beside him.

"So you really just got in today?"

"Yeah."

"Your parents still live 'round here?"

"Yeah." As they approached the steps ascending to the door, Tom's nerves rumbled in his stomach and saliva flooded his mouth. He felt he was going to puke at any moment. "Maybe this isn't a good idea, Feltz. Besides, I don't have much cash on me."

"Don't worry. I'll buy ya a few. You can't visit without seeing Sprenkle's place."

Tom figured there was no use in going to his parents' house yet, he had hours to kill, so ... why not?

"OK."

The two of them walked through the door to see Sprenkle and a woman, who looked Middle Eastern or Indian, standing behind the bar. The place had a few random couples sitting, eating dinner. Sprenkle looked almost the same as he did when they worked at Funland together.

"Sprenkle!" Feltz greeted.

"Tricky! What's up?"

"Nothin'." Sprenkle took a cold Miller Lite out of the cooler and Feltz grabbed it. "Hey. You remember Tom Frost? Used to work with us at Funland?"

Sprenkle looked at Tom, his eyes making a connection but not so much because of their shared employment history. "I thought you looked familiar."

"He's visiting from California."

Tom wondered how Feltz knew that unless Feltz already knew about the show, about his wife, all of it. The nerves kicked up his throat, but, thankfully, a silent burp came out rather than vomit.

"One coast to another, eh?" Sprenkle said.

"Yeah." Tom pushed out a small smile and Sprenkle could tell Tom didn't really want to talk too much.

"What ya havin'?"

"I'll have a shot."

"Which kind?"

"Your choice."

Sprenkle took down a shot glass and filled it with Patron Silver tequila.

"Hey, Sprenkle. Get a glass for us too."

Sprenkle didn't drink as much behind the bar nowadays, but he figured he'd make a special exception tonight. The glasses were filled and there was no special cheers, no salutation, just a clank of the glasses and the disappearing act of the clear liquid.

"Can I get you something else?" Sprenkle asked.

"I'll have a Narragansett," Tom said. Sprenkle grabbed a can of the New England beer, opened it and handed it to Tom, who immediately took a drink.

"Feltz. You know Jade." Sprenkle nodded toward the Indian woman, who flashed a warm smile their way. "You guys need anything, let her know."

"Thanks, Sprenkle." Feltz turned to Tom. "So ... I saw the show."

"Yeah? Well ... who didn't?"

"I'm sorry about Maggie. How ya been?"

"Shitty." There was an uncomfortable silence and Tom waved toward the woman. "Can I get another shot?"

Jade walked over with another shot of Patron. She walked away as Tom downed the shot.

"Look, Feltz. I ... I'd really appreciate it if you didn't tell anyone ... that I'm here. I'm tryin' to get away from all that."

"Hey, no problem." Feltz took a swig of his beer. "But you're gonna have a hard time tryin' to find someplace where no one knows about what happened to ya. We *do* get cable and internet around here, ya know?"

Tom could feel the buzz transform into a fully-fledged drunkenness. "I just thought ... I would come back ..."

Feltz waited for Tom to finish his sentence but there was nothing. "Come back for *what*?"

Tom had been asking himself that same question since he crossed the state line. The only answer he kept coming back to in his head was the answer he gave Feltz. "To get away.

13.

"Everybody's tellin' me what to do, and I can't choose.
And everybody wants control, to hang me up by their noose.
But if they only knew, they'd laugh and dance like fools.
If they only knew, souls cannot be fooled."

--The Apache Relay
"Power Hungry Animals"

Tom jumped out of his deep sleep as if he were startled by some loud horn or siren. His arms and feet slammed against the sides of something he couldn't quite make out. The last thing he remembered was drinking at the Shorebreak with Feltz. After that, it got hazy. The first thing he recognized was a soft-top roof and all he could muster was that he must have passed out in his Jeep. It only took two seconds for his headache to hit - a hammer slamming right between his eyes - and he winced in pain. His neck, back and sides ached from the crammed position in which he had slept in the compact 4x4. The worst part, though, was the nausea. If he had puked, he wouldn't be feeling the way he was now. His stomach tangled in knots, saliva consistently filled his mouth no matter how much he swallowed as if there were an unfixable leaky pipe filling a room. He knew it was coming. Tom jumped over the center console and pitched himself toward the driver's side door, throwing the door open with enough force that it swung all the way until it hit the side of the vehicle. He popped his head outside as vomit gushed out of his mouth like wastewater from a drainage pipe. The fast food he had had for last night's dinner came up, as did his soda and a Snickers bar. He puked until there was nothing left, and then he puked up bile. He thought he even felt some in his nose, and the smell overtook his senses, making him retch again.

Tom spit out the remaining mucus and his head drooped, feeling so heavy, as if it were that lone, red Christmas ornament on the Charlie Brown Christmas tree. Green garage doors with white trim came into focus and he knew exactly where he was. He was just happy it was still April and Funland didn't open until Mother's Day weekend. There wouldn't be any crowds waiting anxiously for the rattling of the chains connected to those green doors to crank open, sounding like the lift of a roller coaster before the big drop. Thinking about the noise made his head pound even more.

Each pounding made him wince in pain, shutting his eyes tight, and seeing a flash of Polaroid pictures of the prior night. He and Feltz taking shots. Laughing over old Funland stories. Chugging down a beer shooter with Sprenkle. Leaving Shorebreak and walking across the street to another bar called Zogg's, where he nursed some beers. Talking to a few of Feltz's friends. Buying a T-shirt off someone he didn't know and stripping off the shirt he was wearing to put the new shirt on in the middle of the bar. Leaving the bar and stumbling one block over to Funland. Trying to climb the twelve-foot employee chain-link fence entrance only to fall off, waving his arms and legs helplessly about, looking like a turtle turned over on its back. Attempting to get into the former upstairs Funland dorm stairway entrance only to see it boarded up. The last flash was him climbing into his Jeep, and curling up before passing out. It was all he needed to remember.

Tom pushed himself upright into the seat and stared long at the place he used to work, where he had met Maggie. He looked at the yellow shirt with a black silhouette of the state of Delaware on the front; it must have been the shirt he drunkenly bought the night before, although he didn't know what he had found so special about a shirt with just the state of Delaware on it. His watch said 8:07 a.m., but it felt earlier. The need for fresh air willed him out of the Jeep, making sure not to step in his sick, and into the cool shade found against Funland's closed doors. Tom followed the sidewalk until the pavement met the boards and the sun completely enveloped him. The salty ocean air was especially potent as seagulls' faraway cries, sounding almost like laughter, perforated the sound of the crashing waves. Joggers, bicyclists, dog walkers and power walkers were already taking advantage of the nice weather and the pre-tourist population. Some passersby rapidly turned their heads when they saw the back of his shirt, while some silently chuckled, and Tom had no idea why they were doing this. He failed to remember the small, centered letters located on the back of the shirt, near the top, which read "Delaware, Motherfucker."

Seeing the beach at this time of day took him back to the mornings he would work one of the Funland boardwalk games, yearning to be out on that sand, in those waves, soaking up that sun, rather than stuck working. Despite his love for the beach and living near one for so long, he didn't take the time to enjoy it. It was the same for Maggie. He had loved her but he was sure she hadn't fully believed it. None of it mattered, though, because she was gone and there was nothing he could do to fix that.

Tom's head had subsided from a heavy pounding to steady throbbing. He may not have been able to do anything about Maggie, but there was something he could do about the pull he now felt.

* * *

"What do you mean you're afraid of the water!?"

"I didn't say I was afraid," a teenage Tom said. "Would you watch the ride please?"

Tom stood in his tan shorts, Nike running shoes, and Funland shirt - a bright red polo with a small white carousel horse printed on the left breast, the word "Funland" above it and "Rehoboth Beach" below. He was holding a clipboard with a checklist attached, standing beside a red-haired girl about his age, suppressing a laugh. She turned her head back to the kid's ride she was operating: fire engines as red as the shirts they were wearing. He glanced at the paper and saw her name: Maggie.

"You said you didn't like swimming in the ocean," Maggie said. "The only time people say that is when they're *afraid* to swim in it."

Tom looked to the ride's timer and saw that the two minutes were nearly up. He was relieved because this girl was starting to seriously annoy him.

"I mean ... what is it? Drowning?"

"No. It's shaurrr...," his explanation turned to a mumble.

"It's what?"

"Sharks! OK? It's sharks."

Maggie laughed as she pressed the stop button on the ride, slowing it so the kids stopped right in front of their respective parents.

"Not bad," Tom said, noticing how quickly Maggie picked up stopping the ride where it had started – an aspect most couldn't do or didn't try. He watched her go around and unbuckle some of the little kids, helping them out of their seats or handing them to their doting parents. By the time she made it around the circle and back to him, a wicked smile was still on her face.

"Sharks!?"

"Yeah! Haven't you ever seen *Jaws*!?"

"That's just a movie, isn't it?" Maggie laughed.

"Ye ... Well, yeah. But ... you never know what's out there! I mean, I'm not gonna be some*thing*'s lunch just because I wanted to go swimming. That's why we have swimming pools now!"

Maggie laughed louder at the absurdity of Tom's reasoning, even though she could see where he was coming from.

"That's not how I see it," she said.

"Please. Enlighten me."

"I love swimming in the ocean." She thought about what she was about to say and bit her lip, thinking it sounded like the cheesiest thing she'd ever said, but it was how she honestly felt. "To me ... it's ..." Embarrassment caught her again and she turned her head away.

"What?"

"It's being a part of something bigger. The ocean relaxes me. And not just the sound of it, but ... this sounds cheesy. I feel rejuvenated. The cold, salty water on my hot skin, the movement of the water and waves, the smell. It's enough to make you feel connected to the planet.

"And I don't mean in some hokey tree-hugging way. I mean ... I feel ... closer to life. It makes me appreciate it and love it even more."

She indeterminately looked at Tom, his face frozen with awe at her description. It was that moment that Tom started to have romantic feelings for Maggie. She took his silence as a sign he thought she was dense so she started collecting the green ride tickets from parents, buckling in the next bunch of kiddie riders.

Girls had always had crushes on Tom. He was a good-looking guy but his modesty instilled in him by his parents prevented him from knowing or thinking this truth. His parents, and the movies and television shows he watched constantly, instilled within him the belief that your looks shouldn't be the only thing to define you ... and, if you get a lot of attention because of your looks, you should never think you're better than anyone else.

Halfway around the circular ride, Maggie looked up to Tom, her look had turned from being unsure to a growing smile that wasn't so much timid as it was the kind of smile a young girl flashed in the movies. Tom called it the "happy ending smile." It was the smile that resulted after the guy and girl in movies looked across a room at each other and the girl often smiled as hope twinkled in her eyes. Tom swore it was *that* kind of smile!

When Maggie saw he was looking at her – not the kids, the parents or anyone else – just her, her smile grew bigger and she looked down to help a kid get buckled in. He had never had a girl look at him that way. It left him speechless and nervous. For the rest of their time together, every time

Maggie would flash that smile at him, he felt just as enamored with her as he did that day.

* * *

Tom opened his eyes and saw he was standing on the sand, the sound of the ocean waves louder, bringing his senses to attention. There was no better place than the beach for him at this moment. Something in his brain took over. He didn't care about any beachgoers or passersby. He just started taking off his shoes, his socks. Each movement grew faster and more furious as if his life depended on stripping down as quickly as possible. His Delaware shirt, his jeans. The only article of clothing on his body was his black boxer briefs, which kind of looked like tight swim trunks. The dry, hot sand had invaded the tiny crevices between his toes. He wriggled them to plant his feet deeper as the warmth shot up from his feet and into his legs.

Breathing had become easier, as if the mix of the smell of the ocean air, the noise of the crashing waves, and the shedding of his clothes had freed him and made it easier for his body to take in air. Tom enjoyed one deep breath and slowly released it as he ran toward the ocean. Without hesitation he ran as far as he could in the water before his feet became cumbersome and he dove in like some bad *Baywatch* lifeguard impression. The water was near freezing and he thought maybe this wasn't the right time of year to be taking a swim. He made sure to dive under the breaking line of the waves, feeling the water getting colder and colder. The water cooled his sun-touched skin and the taste of salt licked the insides of his mouth as some water found its way in.

Tom swam just under the surface until his lungs felt as if they may explode. Within seconds, his head erupted from the ocean's surface and he looked back to the beach to see he had swum further than he thought. He pushed his wet hair back and thought about a shark cruising by, just looking for its breakfast. *No*, he thought, *I'm not gonna think about that. I'm going to be in the moment.* He focused on the beach, a sparse population of sunbathers and toddlers spread across the strip of golden brown. Beyond them was Funland and he remembered a lot of the great times he had had working there. Some of the best moments of his teenage years happened at that place. But he couldn't go back to that time. He wasn't that guy anymore. He didn't know what kind of man he was now.

His legs began to burn after treading the water for so long and he realized that maybe he had come back to Delaware for more than just seeking anonymity. He was here to see his parents too. As much as it pained Tom Frost, he had to admit that, at thirty-two, he was afraid of seeing them. He didn't know why. They had been good parents ... as far as parents go. Their personalities, the things they believed in, were drastically different from what he believed in. Sure, they hadn't been perfect. The psychological scars were there even though Tom didn't know they had been left since childhood. It was no different than any kid who grows up to realize the world doesn't fit into the package their parents brought them up within. But he couldn't be mad at them. After all, he knew parenting didn't come with an instruction manual and all of that other cliché crap those self-help books spouted. They had only done what they thought was right.

Tom closed his eyes and tilted his head back, taking in the sun as it evaporated the beads of ocean water on his exposed skin. He did feel something. Something different. Something visceral and calming. All the years he had lived here before he went away to college, he had never felt this before. It rejuvenated him, just like Maggie had said. He thrust his legs forward, bringing them to the surface, so that he laid on top of the water. His body urged him to return to its vertical position but he soon relaxed and let the water bob him up and down. He floated for what only seemed seconds, but when Tom finally righted himself up and looked toward land, he saw he had floated a few yards down north from where he had started. Tom took a deep breath and swam to shore. The water almost felt as if it were pushing against him, trying to prevent him from going back to shore. It reminded him of the last lines of *The Great Gatsby*.

Maybe the past was a dangerous place to revisit, but it was all he knew. Tom thought it inevitable to confront one's past in order to be able to move forward. He just hoped his jaunt down memory lane didn't leave him so lost that he didn't know how to get his life back on track. The first thing he knew he had to do was see his parents.

Despite his slightly muscular tone, his arms and legs began to tire, burning as he neared the shore. He was determined and the few people on shore watched him as he strained in his movements. He emerged from the water feeling both rejuvenated and weary. Tom moved past the wandering eyes and swiped up his clothes and shoes as he continued to walk off the beach and toward his Jeep. A quick turn of the key and he was off to Lewes, to the home in which he grew up.

The fifteen-minute drive went faster than he would've liked and before he knew it, Tom pulled up to the curb alongside the front of a small one-story ranch-style house, wedged in a row of other similar-looking houses. The house had partially exposed brick and long, sky blue siding board, with a freshly cut, green front lawn. The neighborhood block still looked the same since he was a kid, which shouldn't have been a surprise to him. Here, in Sussex County's small, long-established neighborhoods, things stayed the same.

Tom took in a deep breath and slowly released it. *Do I really want to do this?*

The loud, constant whirring of the vacuum cleaner helped Judy Frost focus on the task at hand. Saturdays were her marathon cleaning days. She got up early and worked straight through until the early afternoon hours to make sure every bed was made, all the clothes were washed, dishes cleaned and put away, floors cleaned, glass surfaces cleaned, furniture dusted, and any other items lying about were put away.

Judy's short, blonde hair was beginning to show random streaks of gray. She stood at five-feet, five-inches and had a slightly plump figure. She wasn't a flashy woman and there was little she wouldn't do for her family. Tom's friends had always thought her a quaint, soft-spoken woman, and her reserved nature only reinforced that claim.

The vacuum drowned out the sound of Tom pulling up to the curb outside, and when he rang the doorbell. The storm door was open and he could see her, but she, with her back turned to him, had no clue he was there. Tom banged on the door with loud, heavy knocks until she turned around and saw him framed in the glass of the door, a heavy sigh coming out of him, forcing his shoulders to slump down further.

Judy turned the vacuum off, keeping eye contact with Tom. Her eyes brimmed with tears and she put her hands over her mouth as if she were seeing something horrifying unfold right in front of her. The sentiment was not out of horror but rather a mix of joy and sadness; joy that her son was home, and sadness that Maggie was dead and a majority of the country blamed him for her death.

"T-Tom!" she called for her husband. "Tom! It's Tommy! He's home! My boy's home! My boy's home! My boy's home!" The more she repeated the phrase, the more her voice got excited and cracked with emotion. "Oh, my boy!"

Judy opened the storm door and latched onto Tom, her embrace tightening like a Boa constrictor. Despite the pinching feeling of his arms, followed by numbness, Tom was happy to feel the embrace of someone who he knew truly cared for him. He couldn't tell whether she was happy or sad because her giddy laughter mixed with sobs.

"Hi, Mom," he said.

Judy let out a single laugh, happy to hear his voice. She hadn't talked to him since he won his Emmy. She had tried calling and calling but he never answered or returned her calls. Despite hearing nothing but the digitized automatic voice of his voice mail, she never gave up.

"Let me look at you," she said. She backed up and her eyes drank in his face, noticing the beard stubble, the bags under his eyes, his skin slightly red and the salt water fragrance from his swim earlier in the day.

"Tom*my*. You should shave."

Tom ignored her disguised reprimand and looked past her to see his dad round the corner from the hallway. Since Tom was a teenager and broadened his musical interests, he thought his father looked like Tom Waits – dark, curly hair, slightly pockmarked skin, and a voice sounding as if his vocal chords had been dragged for miles through a mix of gravel and glass shards. As opposed to his mother, Tom's dad looked unaffected by his return.

Tom had always thought his dad was the biggest, tallest, strongest man on the planet, but, looking at him now, he wasn't so tall and his movement had slowed. The man gave him a nod and said, "Hey, son. When'd you get in?"

"This morning. Went into Rehoboth first. How are you?"

"Good," his dad said as the two lightly hugged. "I'm sorry about Maggie."

Tom Sr. opened his mouth to say more but no words came out. Tom wondered, *Is my dad about to cry?* The only time he had seen his father cry was twice, both times a long time ago – once, when his dad's mom died; and the other time, when he watched *Brian's Song*. According to his dad, the only times it was acceptable for a man to cry were at funerals and when watching *Brian's Song*.

"Thanks." Tom wanted to erase the uncomfortable silence.

"I've been watching the news," his dad said. Tom knew what his dad considered "news" was the cable news channel that was home to "The Douche" and that Carlton woman. He could only imagine what they were saying about him since he last watched. His dad's appearance may have changed but his preference for news had remained the same, no matter how perverse it had been. "The latest says you're blaming the media for her death."

"Dad—"

"It's that damn liberal company you worked for! Country's gone to hell because of them damn liberals."

"Dad," Tom spoke up. "They're just assholes. It doesn't have anything to do with politics."

"Oh, c'mon," his dad chuckled. "*Everything* is politics, son."

Tom had to suppress the urge to roll his eyes or say anything. He had gotten used to it since he was about nineteen and started becoming more aware of politics and the repugnant behavior it stoked in people. Tom didn't agree with his dad on a lot, and when it came to such issues, he found it near impossible to talk with his dad. He didn't care that his dad didn't agree with him, he didn't even care about most political issues. What he found so offensive was how disrespectful his father's behavior was whenever Tom believed in anything different from him. Tom knew his dad meant well, his dad had once said he didn't want Tom to make any of the wrong choices in life; but the behavior had caused a rift between them of which only Tom knew.

"How long are you staying for?" his mom asked with hope in her voice.

"I'm ... I'm not sure."

"You stay as long as you need."

"Thanks, Mom." Tom smiled. "I just needed to ... get away. I ..."

Judy laid a gentle hand on his shoulder and peered up at Tom with teary eyes. "You don't have to say anything, Tom."

Tom nearly burst into tears at his mom's kindness. She had always been a sweet-natured woman who knew just the right way to teach him right from wrong. While Tom's father had been outspoken, boisterous and a bit of an extrovert, his mom was at the other end of the spectrum. The two complete opposites had caused a major conflict in Tom's thinking all his life. Until recently, he believed it to be a curse, but he soon realized it was more of a benefit.

"You can stay in your old room," his mom offered. His parents guided him down the hall, to the first room on the left, as if he might have been away so long that he had forgotten the way.

Tom walked into his small room and found it had been completely changed. The walls which had once been dark blue were now taupe, the new carpet had a lighter, sandy color of which the blackout curtains were an exact match, and any trace of his having once inhabited the room was now gone. He didn't think he'd care if his parents had changed his room – after all, it had been so long since he last lived there – but there was an inexplicable melancholy within Tom. His face must have conveyed his slight shock because his mom spoke up.

"With you living in California, we decided to turn it into a guest room. Don't worry. All of your stuff is in the attic." His expression eased and she asked, "Do you like it?"

Tom slowly nodded his head. "It's very ... tan."

"Where's your stuff?" his dad asked.

"This is it."

"You didn't bring any clothes with you?" his mom asked.

"I honestly wasn't thinking about that, Mom."

"What about your house? Your car? How are you gonna pay your bills? Did you—"

"There were reporters everywhere." She could hear his frustration and dismay beginning to mount. After the incident, she had rehearsed how she would act around him when she eventually did see him. She didn't want to dwell on the incident and thought if she didn't bring it up, then life would soon right itself and Tom could move on. Although, seeing him now, and hearing his wavering voice, she realized she was saying the wrong things. He continued, "I just wanted to get outta my house! I had to leave there."

"You can't just leave all that stuff behind, Tom," his dad said.

"I know, Dad."

"Well ... what are you gonna do!?"

Tom felt like exploding at his father with a barrage of unfriendly cuss words. Or even something like, "I don't know, asshole! Why don't you piss off!?"

Instead, he did what he had done his entire life. He kept quiet.

"Now, Tom," his dad continued. "You know we love you. We just want you to ... I just want you ... to ..."

"To what, Dad!?" Tom's anger boiled but it soon subsided back to calm. "What do you want me to do? Tell me. 'Cause I don't know what I'm doing. I have no big plan. I'm just ... trying to ... make it one moment to the next."

His dad looked away and his mom stepped forward.

"You've still got some clothes here," his mom gently said. "I packed them away in the attic. Why don't you go up there and get them. The box is marked with your name. You'll see it."

"Let's give him some privacy, Judy," his dad said. "We'll be down the hall when you wanna come out."

His father left, with his mom hesitantly following behind, staring back at Tom with a big smile, as if he were some magical anomaly she would never see again if she took her eyes off him. She kept her head in the doorway, watching him, as long as she could before there was no more space and she closed the door all the way.

Tom honestly wasn't sure he wanted to leave the confines of those four walls. He could understand why some college graduates reveled in returning home. He slumped down onto the queen-sized bed, covered with a white cotton blanket with a waffle-looking weave – the same kind used in hospitals and hotels. His eyes surveyed the room, searching for any trace of his former residence there.

Framed pictures lay here and there on various bookshelves and a dresser, one of them was Tom's high school graduation photo. He got up and peered at the image of a younger, skinnier version of himself, dressed in a powder blue graduation gown and cap, looking back at him. The reflection of his present self with beard stubble, messy hair, tanned skin, tired eyes and a little extra weight almost laid perfectly over his younger image. He hadn't been that kid for a very long time; and not just the physical one, but the optimistic-yet-sarcastic kid with a quick wit.

Seeing the graduation photo made him remember his final days of high school and how he couldn't wait to get out of there. He let out a single, silent chortle and set the photo back on the shelf. The rest of the photos were of cousins, aunts, uncles and long-dead relatives, and his thoughts of them spun through a revolving door in his memory, questions about them going out of his mind as quickly as they had entered.

Tom sat back down on the bed and a sudden vertigo struck his sight, his mind still feeling the effects of his hangover. He kicked off his shoes and laid down on the bed, a short, sharp moan escaping from him every other second, compliments from the uncomfortable accommodations his Jeep had provided the previous night. His head carefully rested onto the soft pillow with its newly washed pillowcase and exhaustion weighed down his eyelids. He didn't put up any fight and let sleep overtake him.

Tom's body jolted out of sleep the way someone uncontrollably jumps when dreaming about falling. His body was covered in a layer of sweat and he was surprised to see nothing but darkness. He could feel that he was in his king-size bed at home in L.A. Maggie stirred in the bed next to him, and touched his shoulder.

"Tom?" she said, her voice somewhere between asleep and awake. "You OK?"

"Yeah." He sounded relieved. "I had this ... horrible nightmare."

She turned on her side to face him and propped herself up on her elbow, her tired head resting on her slender shoulder. "What about?"

"You. It was you. I ... I lost you. You were killed."

"It was just a dream—"

Tom reached over and kissed her. He passionately kissed her so hard until he had to stop to gasp for air. He had never been so happy to wake up from a dream as he was now. Maggie had to keep from laughing so she returned his kiss. They kissed long and hard until the kiss turned into short pecks, feeling like tiny bubbles popping over his skin.

Tom's feeling of dread evaporated and had been replaced with resplendent joy. As he saw Maggie smile, his face lit with a smile. He gave her a quick flash of a kiss and hugged her. It was really her. He almost didn't believe it, but her warm skin and perfume were evidence enough.

"It felt so real. It was during the taping of the show."

"Speaking of that, how did the fiftieth episode go?"

"The what?"

"The girl." Maggie's face kept her smile plastered across her face, almost as if she were a mannequin. "Oh, what was her name? Amy? Did things work out for her?"

Tom's stomach dropped.

She laid her head down and snuggled in closer to him. "Are you still having second thoughts about the show? I've been thinking it over and I support you, no matter what decision you make."

The joyous look on Tom's face slowly shifted toward terror, tears lining the bottom of his eyes. It felt as if a cruel trick had been played on him. He was in a dream. Part of him wanted to relish the moment and take in every second he could with her, but he could feel himself about to wake up. Maggie's expression turned from her gorgeous smile to troubled puzzlement. He could only imagine she was wondering why he looked so spooked.

Neither of them said a word, just stared at each other, two people knowing the moment they were in was a lie. Tom knew it was a dream, but his heartbeat quickened so much, the feeling as though it was going to burst out of his chest felt very real. He was soon gasping for breath, his eyes widened with fear, his skin immediately drenched with sweat. Within seconds, each inhale of breath was long and labored, making Tom sound like a swimmer coming up for a desperate gasp of air.

Tom's body collapsed onto the bed, staring up at the ceiling, as he heard a faint, consistent flatline from a heart monitor, just like in the movies and TV when someone on the hospital operating table dies. Only he was still alive. He couldn't move, but he was still alive. Maggie came into view, looking down on him with a curious look. She almost looked as if she were smiling.

Tom blinked and it was still night, but the ceiling had changed. It no longer was a smooth surface but a popcorn ceiling, making it almost look like satellite images of the moon's surface, save for the ceiling fan. Delaware. He was in Delaware. He turned his head to see a small plate with a sandwich and potato chips, next to a bottle of water, on his nightstand.

He got up, opened the door and poked his head out to see if his parents were still awake or not. The house was dark so he crept out into the hallway and found the string to the attic door hanging from the ceiling. He turned on the light switch for the attic light, and pulled the folded attic stairway down with it screaming a loud creak all the way down. Tom mouthed a few cuss words, hoping not to wake his parents, looked behind himself to see if the coast was clear, then unfolded the second set of steps down.

The attic was a long strip running the length of the house with boxes, plastic containers and various holiday decorations populating most of the distance. Tom stepped up into the space, his eyes still adjusted to the light as he perused the area, looking for any box with his name on it.

It didn't take long to spot a big, brown cardboard box with his name written in big capital letters with black permanent marker. He hunched down so as not to hit his head and walked to the box. Tom didn't know what he was expecting – or hoping – to find, but this was a welcome distraction after his sudden bout of insomnia.

He flung open the cardboard flaps and dove right into his pool of reminiscence. There were random pictures of friends, some from high school, others from his summers at Funland, parties, road trips. There were too many to look through. He dropped them back in the box and noticed a few various-sized frames. He picked up two and saw the photos had Maggie in them. Judy had done the best she could to eradicate the house of any memory of her son's murdered, adulterous wife. The permanent smile on Maggie's face reminded him of the nightmare he had just had so he put them back in the box, on their sides so the images faced away.

There were a few random CDs of bands popular throughout the early 1990s. One of them was a DVD of his and Maggie's wedding. His mom really went out of her way to clear the house of everything Maggie! He dropped it back in the box and rifled through miscellaneous mix tapes made by friends. One of them he remembered fondly. The title on the side read "The Trilogy Mix" and he knew it was the mix about Funland that a co-worker had made many years ago. He slipped the tape in his back pocket and continued digging through random letters and scraps of paper. They had been letters from Funland friends, most of them girls long since forgotten. Below them were two pristine Cape Henlopen High School yearbooks (one from his junior year, one from his senior year) which looked like they had never been opened. Tom pushed those aside and saw the last item before he saw the neatly folded clothes his mother had mentioned. It was a faded, tattered-cornered Snoopy folder. The famous white-and-black beagle stood with his profile, walking along a sunny day with all of the colors of the rainbow surrounding him as the little yellow bird, Woodstock, flittered about his head. Tom opened the folder and saw report cards, drawings, various homework and book reports dating all the way back to kindergarten. His mom had saved everything she could for what reason Tom didn't know. Just like the reason she never stopped calling him, no matter how many times he didn't answer. He guessed moms were just that way. It didn't occur to him that there were a lot of mothers in the world who wouldn't be so loving, so sentimental or so caring as his mother.

He looked at his report cards and read his teachers' comments. Most of them said things like, "Is very smart but needs to participate more," or, "Needs to be more social in class," or, "Happy to have Tom in class but needs to apply himself more." Tom was noticing a pattern here. Most of his grades were excellent until he reached high school, then they dropped to the average range. Even his college grades were in there. Mostly "A"s, a few "B"s and one or two "C"s. The folder was the place where his mother had kept all of his accomplishments that made her proud of him, mixed amongst reminders of his marriage to Maggie, a definite blemish in his mom's eyes. He put the papers back in the pocket and closed the folder. He grabbed all of the clothes out of the box and placed the folder back in, then closed it up.

Tom got back to his room and noticed the time was about quarter to three in the morning. He slapped the mix tape on his dresser and figured he'd look through his clothes when he woke up. It was time to try and get some more sleep, except now, despite his dragging feeling, images of happier times invaded his mind and prevented him from closing his eyes. Hours later, the sun began to hit his blinds as he finally fell asleep.

14.

"Everybody knows
It sucks to grow up
And everybody does
It's so weird to be back here.
Let me tell you what:
The years go on and we're still fighting it,
We're still fighting it"

--Ben Folds
"Still Fighting It"

Jade had grown up an awkward, gangly kid with big rectangular glasses. Her ethnicity had not been a blessing, growing up in a predominately white-then-black school system. Although, the color of her skin was not so much the issue as it was her simply being Indian. Most kids seemed to either be so cautious around her or would flat out ignore her. Even when she moved to D.C., she thought going to a public school in a big city would increase her chances of meeting at least a few like-minded kids she could be friends with, kids with the same interests as her who were more accepting than those at her previous school. With her big eyes, thick eyebrows, brown skin and short, bowl haircut which made her look like a boy, paired with her quiet, shy, introverted nature, Jade's adolescence was a trial by fire when it came to making true friends who were accepting of the true her. The drawback to her situation was that she didn't really have any close friends, but the ultimate advantage, as difficult as it was to see, was that those who were her friends, were true friends. When her best friend died back in college, Jade reevaluated her path in life. She continued to go for her law degree and pass the bar exam – even though her career would only last two years – but her concept of how to live a truly good life was shaken. Her faith in life itself was shaken. The unpredictability of life scared the hell out of her more than anything.

She grew into her looks, like a predictable plot to some cheesy high school "ugly duckling-turns-beautiful" movie. She replaced her glasses with contacts, grew her beautiful, black hair longer, and, as her personality blossomed, so did her physical features. Nowadays, her looks, combined with her caramel skin, seemed to be more of an attractor rather than a hindrance – except on the very rare occasion that someone mistook her for some nationality such as Iranian, Pakistani, Iraqi, or any Middle Eastern country which was considered to be on America's terror watchlist. There had been several instances where, simply based on her looks, she had been called, both to her face and behind her back, a terrorist. Nevertheless, she still believed that people were inherently good and, above all, that people wanted to help one another. Once things like politics, religion, beliefs, and other dividing factors were taken away, people were people – they all breathed, slept, bled, loved, and died. Jade believed we are all in this life, at this moment, together. And we could either waste our energy with hate and self-exile, or we could be helpful to one another with every chance that comes our way. Stereotyping sadly still existed in this country, but if it ever reared its ugly head at Jade, she chose to face it head-on and prove it wrong. Her upbeat disposition may lead most to think she had never experienced any wrongs in her life or was extremely naïve, but it was the wrongs which helped make her stronger.

She awoke to another sunny day in Rehoboth and her Sunday morning was off to a relaxing start. She walked down the narrow stairway which came down into the kitchen, and opened her cabinet to a numerous variety of different teabag boxes. Her mouth pushed her lips to the side, wondering which to choose, before she grabbed the Constant Comment. While the water was heating in her small, green teapot, she picked up her paperback copy of Ernest Cline's *Ready Player One* and started reading where she had last left off. The book was just one of many she had bought used from yard sales, an old book store in Lewes, or at the library. Her small bookshelf was littered with many of them, featuring tattered copies of *The Upanishads*, *The Complete Stories of Flannery O'Connor*, Sheila Weller's *Girls Like Us*, Malala Yousafzai's *I Am Malala*, Harper Lee's *To Kill A Mockingbird*, and Maria Semple's *Where'd You Go, Bernadette?* She had gotten far in Cline's tome when the teapot blew out its high whistle. Jade drank her two cups of tea while reading, then took a quick shower, put on what looked like a 1940s swing dress, put her iPod on shuffle – with Postmodern Jukebox's adaptation of Ellie Goulding's "Burn" filling her ears – and walked to a nearby sandwich place called Dave & Skippy's.

Most every day, Jade was thankful she had moved to Rehoboth. The people of the area were so much more relaxed and there was a big sense of community throughout the county. She lived in the beach community where commerce and tourist dollars brought the residents' livelihood, but there were more little towns where agriculture was still a major part of life. Taking in the sights of the town, awakening from its winter-long nap, Jade gained an extra spring in her step, smiling at the few people she saw during her walk. The Postmodern Jukebox song ended and the iPod shuffled to the next song, Kate Nash's "Do-Wah-Doo." She only got half-way through the song before she reached Dave & Skippy's front door.

"Hey, Jade," a familiar guy's voice said. The guy behind the counter greeted her with a smile. Jimmy had gotten to know Jade ever since she started coming to the store a year ago.

"Hi, Jimmy," she smiled. "I was hoping you guys would be open today. How's your morning so far?"

"Really good. I was at the inlet this morning. Caught some pretty decent surf. Well, decent for here, anyways."

Jade had once had a crush on Jimmy but his reputation as a ladies man put somewhat of a damper on his good looks. Most women would classify him as "hot," and Jade was included in that statistic, but she was still wary of being just another notch in his bedpost. He didn't act like a womanizer but Jade knew those were exactly the types of men to watch out for because they usually were. Still, he was a nice enough guy, and a little mutual flirting never hurt anyone.

Jimmy subtly glanced Jade up and down, taking note of how the dress she was wearing showed off her legs and almost form-fitted her body.

"You look great!" he continued.

"So do you," she said. After all, he did look good, the perfect picture of what most women would want in a man.

One of her friends even told Jade that she was crazy not to pursue a relationship with him. But Jade couldn't satisfactorily convince her that she honestly wasn't looking for any romantic entanglements at the moment.

"Where are you off to today?" Jimmy asked. "And ... can I come too?"

Jade giggled at his small attempt at flirting. "I'm just gonna go to the library in a little bit. Then I'm headed to lunch."

"Hey. Were you workin' at Shorebreak Friday night?"

"Yeah. Why?"

"I heard Tom Frost was there!"

"Who?"

"Tom Frost. He's the guy who used to host that cheating reality show." Jimmy could tell by the look on Jade's face that she didn't know what he was talking about. "You know? The show did a live episode where the guy found out his wife was cheating on him, *and* she was killed on TV!"

"Oh! I've heard of that but I haven't seen the show. Was *that* the guy who was there last night?"

"Yeah!"

"Wait. How do you know that was him?"

"Ran into Feltz last night. He told me."

"Yeah. I noticed Feltz was with him. How does he know him?"

"They used to work at Funland together and he said Frost went to Cape too. I'm surprised you didn't hear."

Jade knew better than to take some random gossip as gospel but she figured this Tom guy probably didn't want his story spreading around. And if he didn't, then he came to the wrong place. Even though the population swelled in the summer months, the overall, year-round community was small and it wasn't hard to play a game of "six degrees of separation" around here; most everyone knew each other, whether directly through a friend or relative.

"I bet he came here to get away from the press," Jimmy said.

"You think?"

"Have you *seen* the news? He's been their whipping boy lately."

Jade honestly had not watched the news in a long time. If she did, it tended to be on the local television station or, very rarely, the news hour on PBS. She had come to the conclusion years ago that news – particularly cable news – didn't care about giving objectified reporting so much as spouting out whatever opinion their CEOs believed in.

"Well, I don't think he'd be advertising something like that," Jade said.

"Who knows?" Jimmy shifted gears and Jade could tell what was coming next. "Hey, you wanna go out tonight? Dinner? Maybe a movie?"

"Oh, I'd like to, Jimmy, but I've got work tonight."

Jimmy served up her usual bagel with cream cheese. "No problem. How about tomorrow?"

"I'm sorry. I can't," Jade said with an embarrassing smile and nervous laugh, feeling sorry for the guy. "I've got plans."

"That's cool," Jimmy's bruised ego did its best to shake off its wounded pride. "I'm sure I'll see you soon, though."

"Sure. See ya!" Jade left, just barely hearing him say goodbye.

She realized she would eventually have to be more honest with Jimmy, and, to most who probably watched the situation, she probably seemed as if she enjoyed the attention and was maybe unintentionally leading him on, but those observers would be wrong. The truth was that, for a long time, Jade had not been honest with everyone she met nor with herself.

The truth was that despite her altruistic, idealistic way of life, she had secrets. Secret thoughts and secret fears. Her optimism was no illusion, but her life wasn't as simple as she made it appear to others. Jade knew anybody could claim the same about their life, which is what made her not feel sorry for herself, but she often wondered if anyone around her knew when she was being genuine and when she was lying. Beneath her calm, devil-may-care demeanor, there was a raging storm of sadness, anger, and mostly fear stirring within.

Thinking about her predicament made her mind turn to the guy she had seen drinking with Feltz at the bar on Friday night: Tom Frost. She hadn't seen any news reports on his situation, had only heard the basics of the tragedy, but while she didn't know the exact reason as to his need for escape, she knew that was why he was here. It was the reason *she* had first come here, but it wasn't the reason she stayed. She genuinely loved the place and the people. Her first instinct was to look him up on the internet, maybe see any video clips or news reports on him, but her empathy defeated her curiosity on the matter and she stopped herself from grabbing her smartphone.

A picture of him – exhausted, sad eyes, a permanent beard stubble coating and disheveled clothes – from the Shorebreak that night flashed in her mind. She figured that whatever he was escaping, it must have been catastrophic. Jade also figured it was only a matter of time before news of his arrival had spread in the area, and then she most likely wouldn't see him ever again. That thought made it easier not to let her curiosity get the best of her. *In the grand scheme of things*, she thought, *it doesn't matter what his story is 'cause he'll be gone real soon.*

* * *

"I know you don't approve, Papa," Jade said, pain cracking her voice. "But this is where I need to be right now."

Jade had just left New York and relocated to Rehoboth, where the three of them stood on the tree-lined sidewalk outside of her rented apartment on Laurel Street. To say her parents didn't approve was an understatement. Her mother was slightly understanding of Jade, but her father was beyond livid.

"Jade," her mother's soft voice escaped. "Your father and I just don't know why you have to move here."

"The city is suffocating, Mama. Besides, this is a great town! Don't you want me to be happy?"

"Of course I do. And this area is a beautiful place, but your career—"

"I can do the same thing here."

"Once you pass the bar in Delaware," her mom said with doubt.

"I can do that."

"I know you can do it, honey. But I'm wondering if it's truly what you *want* to do."

"Mama ..."

Jade could tell her mom was getting upset. She looked to her father, his face superglued in a scowl.

"Papa ...," her voice pleaded. "You told me that I should do what's right for me. Well ... *this* is what's right for me right now. I need to be happy."

His perpetual scowl set on the distance. He was the disapproving father and although he didn't like the role, he couldn't help but feel like some one-dimensional cliché. Dr. Sawa couldn't help the way he felt. Like any parent, he just wanted what was best for his child ... especially when she was making what he perceived to be the biggest mistake of her life.

"Papa ... please talk to me."

He turned his cold stare toward her and said, "I'm just ... disappointed ... that you would make such a reckless decision. Your mother and I taught you better than that. At least ... I thought we did."

The words had pierced Jade's heart because, although most people in their late twenties would probably tell their own relative – even a parent – to piss off for making such a statement, Jade cared about what her parents thought about her. Her entire life, she had never had a rebellious streak and always wanted to make her parents proud. Until this moment, she had succeeded in her task. Now she was everything she had strived not to become: a disappointment. Most kids knew the sting of hearing that word from their parents but Jade felt the sting all the more than most and it was enough to bring tears to her eyes.

Jade felt the only way she could get through to her dad was to speak their native language, so she did – the Hindi which translated to this tearful plea. "<Papa. All my life, I have only wanted to make you and Mama happy. To make you proud of me. And, by doing so, it made me happy.>" She had to stop speaking for a moment so the sobs would not make her voice or strength falter. She continued in Hindi:

"<But, now that I have grown up, what I thought would make me happy, it does not. And that makes me sad because I know it would make you and Mama happy and proud.>"

Jade could see her father's eyes rapidly blinking in short spurts. The tears were building.

"<I feel like I need to do this right now. I need to do what I know will make me happy. I am sorry if you are disappointed because it is not what you wanted for me. But I am not sorry for doing what you always taught me: to do something meaningful with my life, which will help others and make me happy.>"

Deep in his heart, Dr. Saha knew what his daughter was saying was true. However, his pride in thinking he knew better than her made his eyes dry and his heart harden.

"<I ...>," he also spoke Hindi, "<respect your intentions, but I cannot ... respect your choices.>"

With those words, Jade knew she wasn't going to win this battle with her father. If there was one thing she knew about people, it was that there was nothing more difficult to revolutionize than when a man's pride stood in the way. The epiphany had made Jade's emotions go on lockdown and she steeled herself to the truth of the matter. She took in a deep breath, wiped away her tears and spoke calmly, steadily and returned to English.

"I understand, Papa." She turned to her mother. "Is this how you feel too, Mama?"

Mrs. Saha looked like she had more to say, like she yearned to say something different. She even opened her mouth but no words came out, as if the weight of her husband's dissidence had stolen her voice.

Jade willed for her mom to say something, for the words to come out. Just when she thought her mother would say nothing, Mrs. Saha spoke.

"I think you should not be disrespecting your father's wishes."

The sting ripped through Jade's body and it was at that moment that she knew there was no way of educating her parents on what made her – not them – happy.

"I'm sorry to be a disappointment, Papa." Jade's tone was cold and distant. "Thank you for helping me with my move."

Jade had hoped that her tone and demeanor might evoke some kind of regret or shame within her parents, a last-ditch effort to change their minds. However, her father remained stoic, her mother quiet, and Jade knew from that moment on that she was, for all intents and purposes, alone.

That was when her reliability on others – even those she felt were close – had pretty much evaporated. It was a sad, unfortunate truth that Jade figured she would just have to face. This lesson had not made her a hardened individual the way it would most people. If anything, she felt greater empathy towards others for learning such a lesson because, the way she saw it, if everyone acted the way her parents had toward her, there would be no one to turn to when life – as it so often does – went askew. She wanted to be someone her parents were not, someone who would be mostly considered an endangered species in today's world: a support system for people facing difficult life choices, an optimist and an educator.

Jade turned her back on her parents, picked up her bags and carried them around back to the small above-garage apartment. To this day, she had not called or written them.

* * *

Tom emerged from his bedroom, into the kitchen to see his mom, who had just gotten back from church. She was cooking breakfast while his dad sat in front of a small television set in the breakfast nook area, watching the same conservative news channel that had been running Tom's name through the mud the past few months. Before the incident, Tom had always wondered how his father could watch such one-sided nonsense, but still let it go because that was his father's choice to watch such propaganda. Now, though, after the way the cable news channels' talking heads had talked about and judged Tom, he perceived his father's viewing of that channel as an insult.

He hoped to sneak by without his father noticing, but that scratchy voice called, "Tom."

Tom's faced bunched up as if he were still a teenager getting caught breaking his curfew. "Yeah?"

"What've you got goin' on today, son?"

Tom came into the breakfast nook area, making himself visible to his father. He wore an old black t-shirt with a faded picture of Jimi Hendrix kneeling before his guitar, alit in a sacrificial fire, summoning the flames to rise higher; a pair of faded blue jeans which looked a size too small for him; and a pair of brown flip flops. His father, dressed in pressed, tan shorts, white tennis shoes, socks and a dark blue t-shirt which read "Freedom Is Not Free," appeared quite the opposite.

"I think I'm going to Rehoboth to get some Louie's for lunch. It's been ages since I've had a chicken cheesesteak."

His father looked perplexed for a moment then shot out, "What are you *doing?*"

"I told you—"

"No. I mean ... what are you going to do now? With your life?"

Tom knew this was coming but his father had still caught him off-guard. He searched his mind as quickly as he could for any reasonable-sounding answer, but the closest he got was: "I ... I just ... need ... some time to figure things out."

"Figure what out?" His father was relentless. "It's been months, son. Now, don't get me wrong. Maggie was ..." Again, his father looked as if he were about to burst into tears at any moment just at the mention of her name. He sniffed, let out a fake cough or clearing of the throat (Tom couldn't tell), and continued. "Maggie was a fine woman. I know it hasn't been easy for you. But it's time to start getting back to life."

Tom waited for his mom to chime in with any of her own opinions but she remained quiet, keeping herself piddling about in the kitchen.

"You can get back to work if you just ... apply yourself. There are still plenty of opportunities for a guy like you."

"Like what!?" Tom's voice had burst out, surprising all three of them. Tom thought of running out and not saying anymore, but his emotions got the best of him and he continued. "I mean ... *really*, Dad!? Like what? Honestly."

For the first time in his life, Tom could tell his dad was at a loss for words. His father's eyes still pierced through Tom's soul, not with hatred but rather with an intense mix of curiosity and perplexity. Tom's voice slowed to an exasperated crawl.

"Because I've been through it all in my head a million times already. And I'm tired. I'm tired of thinking about it. About Maggie. About what the news thinks I should do. About what some dipshit commentator or randomly-interviewed citizen thinks I should do. About what my lawyer thinks I should do. About what few friends I have left think I should do. About what internet polls think I should do. And about what you and Mom think I should do."

Tom felt on the verge of tears so he stopped himself and took in some deep breaths.

"Maggie loved you, son. And your mom and I—"

"That's bullshit and you know it!" Tom erupted again. "She didn't love me. Someone who truly loves someone wouldn't sneak around behind their back like that."

Mr. and Mrs. Frost couldn't remember if they had ever heard their son get so angry. Mr. Frost had to stifle a small fit of nervous laughter.

"She *did* love you, Tommy," his mom said.

Tom could be more reserved when it was his mother speaking, but something about his father's tone made his blood boil.

"Mom," Tom's voice stiffened. "I just wish you both would acknowledge the truth of my situation right now. I'm not this successful television host anymore. That Emmy I won? It's useless. May as well be a huge piece of tin. And she didn't love me!"

"That's not the way I raised you, Tom," his father said.

"Will you both just *STOP!?!?*" Tom's shout caught them off guard again. He took a few exasperated breaths and calmed himself. "I need to leave. I can't stay here."

"Where are you gonna go?" Mr. Frost asked.

"Not sure. But I can't stay here. It's only been two days and I feel suffocated here."

"Please don't leave, Tom," his mother pleaded.

Tom moved to his mother to give her a hug, but his father's words cut him off.

"Doesn't surprise me." He turned to his son. "It's like the news says. Your generation is so damned lazy. Want everything given to you."

Tom knew where this was all coming from and he told his father so. "You really gotta stop watchin' that channel, Dad. It's brainwashing you!"

"It's more like the truth!"

"The truth, huh?" Tom almost laughed but his fury was overpowering. "So you think they're telling the truth when they say I'm responsible for Maggie's death!? Do you think they're telling the truth when they show just what you want to see, making it look like I blame the media and the public for her death!?"

"Well, it's a recording of you, son!"

"I was talking to Jen! You know? My old girlfriend?"

"She's a reporter now for the local channel out there. She wanted an exclusive interview with me and I told her no. She tried to convince me and I said what I said. Then I said I thought she'd be different than the other media who've been hounding me since day one of Maggie's murder."

Tom looked at his parents – his mother with tears in her eyes, his father with that same intense look of mixed curiosity and perplexity.

286

"But, you're right, Dad. I said what I said. The news picked it apart and now I have to live with it."

His voice cracked as if someone had slammed a tuning fork against his vocal pipes. "I just thought ... you and mom would be a little more understanding than a bunch of strangers on TV."

Tom's anger had overtaken any remnant sadness and he waited for either of them to speak, to say anything. He looked to them for any kind of reaction but his mother stood still, tears running down her cheeks as she silently wept until she took in a deep breath. The muffled noise was the only reaction Mr. Frost needed to hear to prompt a response.

"What is this about, Tom?"

"What!?"

"What is this *really* about? Because you seem to be lashing out at me, the media, the public, Maggie, Dylan, this Jen girl, everyone but yourself."

"Are you kidding me!? Didn't you hear the part about how Dylan tricked me into signing those waiver forms? Or did your 'fair and balanced news' conveniently not cover that!?"

"I never heard anything about that, but I'm not talking about—"

"Of course you haven't! You—"

"That's *enough!*" his father shouted. Tom quieted and his father's voice immediately transformed back to its normal tone. "I'm not talking about *how* Maggie and your private affairs ended up on the show. I'm talking about what happened to cause your wife to stray."

Tom couldn't believe the audacity of his father ... or the nerve of his mother for not protesting such a statement.

Throughout his entire life, since he figured out that parents were just people like everyone else – and prone to make mistakes – Tom still had a particular respect for his parents. He knew, deep down, that his father meant well, even when he was spouting off some nonsense or seemingly insulting remarks. This time, though, had been the limit, the last straw to break the camel's back.

"Ya know," Tom spoke with his normal, calm tone, "I've always known you've wanted what's best for me. And I'm thankful for that. But I've also always felt that you both – especially you, Dad – don't take me seriously. You act as if I don't know anything. I'm thirty-two-years-old! There are *some* things I know by now!"

His dad turned around, looking drained, then sharply said, "There are things you *don't* know, son." Mr. Frost raised his voice more. "If you ever have kids, you'll understand."

That was all it took. Tom had had enough. He knew there was a really good chance his dad didn't know about Maggie's pregnancy, or maybe his dad did but just didn't care and made that remark regardless. Either way, this topic was off limits. The world turned to slow motion. Tom could feel his right arm reflexively wind back, his mind forming his right hand into a fist and his mind throwing the punch. It was as close to what he imagined a paranormal possession than anything else of which he could compare. Tom's fist connected with his dad's warm, hard face, which felt solid like a brick wall against the bones in his hand. The world returned to its normal, fierce speed and his dad fell back onto the ground as Tom's mom let out a scream.

Tom's knuckles on his right hand were bloody and throbbing like hell but he couldn't feel any of it. Tom pictured that scene from *Back to the Future* where the geeky George McFly finally punches out his bully, Biff, and thought this adrenaline rush of satisfaction is how he probably felt, but the rush only lasted a minute or two before it gave way to guilt. Tom looked down at his father sprawled out on the floor, struggling to get back up, and couldn't believe he would ever do something so visceral. His father had different opinions than him, and could be insensitive to those with different opinions other than his, but he wasn't exactly a bully. His father was simply a man like most in the world: his beliefs were so uncompromising that they acted as blinders, making him unaware or uninterested in anything around him which was different. The sight of his father in pain and struggling to get back up were almost too much to bear as the guilt spread throughout his entire body, leaving a pit in his stomach.

When his gaze turned up from the ground, he saw his dad, unharmed, still standing in front of him. He had imagined the entire thing but the guilt still lingered.

"We love you, Tom," his mom finally broke the silence. "We just want ... life to ... work out for you."

Tom's spirit drained out of him. He was lucky to know that, in their own way, his parents loved him; but he couldn't talk to his father and he couldn't live there in that house with them. His parents had done a lot for him throughout his life. They were good parents in that they did the best they could. That's why Tom felt so distressed when he realized he could no longer stay there. He knew most people in his type of situation would like nothing better than to stay enveloped where they were taken care of and with people who love them. But it had become clear to Tom in that moment that his parents had always been who they were. It was he who was now different. Maggie's death and its aftermath had drastically changed him – even when it came to his relationship with his parents – without him fully recognizing it until this moment.

"I gotta go," Tom said. He sped past them and out the door.

"Tom, don't go, honey," he heard his mom plead as he slammed the door. He drove toward Rehoboth, hoping to find a realtor who was open on a Sunday.

15.

"She's his yellow brick road
Leading him on
And letting him go as far
as she lets him go:
Going down to nowhere"

--Michelle Branch
"Something to Sleep To"

Jade walked out of the Rehoboth Beach Library and into the midday sun. Tucked in her arm was a copy of Dennis Lehane's *Shutter Island*. The vibrancy of the day gave her spirit a lift and she was content to have such a lovely day. One of the best things Jade enjoyed about downtown Rehoboth was having the ability to walk practically everywhere. Some places she could bike to and for others – like out on Route One – she had her car. But if she could get some place by walking, she did it. The only errand she had to run today was paying her monthly rent at the realtor's office, so she turned left out of the library and headed down the avenue. The realtor's office was near the exit/entrance to Rehoboth, past the small drawbridge which served as the official entrance to the beach town, so it was quite a hike and she would usually ride her bike, but Jade wasn't bothered on a day such as this.

Jade preferred going on Sundays to turn in her payment because there were usually less people there that day. When she reached the office, there was little activity going on, a few random people here and there. One guy sitting in one of the reception area chairs looked vaguely familiar, as if she had seen him recently. The scowl across his face made him appear as if he were pondering something life-threatening while his slouch, matched with this clumped, messy attempt of a hair style and five o'clock shadow, made him seem as if he had just crawled out of bed.

Tom Frost recognized the woman looking at him, attempting to appear inconspicuous. It was the bartender from Shorebreak. She looked like she was getting ready to go swing dancing or to some big, themed dance event. He was never a big fan of small-talk so he looked away with the hopes she would ignore him.

The minute the man turned his head, Jade recognized it was the guy from Shorebreak a couple nights ago, Sprenkle's and Feltz's friend. She struggled to recall his name. Jade had always been great with faces but terrible with names, she considered it one of her major flaws. *John? Ben? Aaron? Ron? Bob? Tom! That was it! Tom.*

By the looks of him, he didn't seem to want to be bothered so she pretended not to see him and walked to the receptionist's desk.

Tom was relieved she didn't recognize him. She probably knew about the incident by now, probably wondering why he was here or what he did to wreck his marriage. Tom had to forcibly stop his mind from going to those dark, paranoid places it naturally wanted to go. His memory loosely recalled camera phones taking pictures the night of him putting on his new shirt in the middle of Zogg's, so he had worried about people posting them on social media, soon followed by reporters tracking him down. His fears of this had abated when he turned on one of the cable news channels and saw no mention of him or the incident. It appeared as if the tragedy had been replaced by news of Middle Eastern terrorists, Iran's nuclear deal, and NCAA basketball national champs. Maggie's life had quickly been forgotten by the same networks, producers, reporters, entertainers and writers who used her death to twist the story (if necessary) and push forward whatever political agenda in which they believed. For Tom, he would always carry her with him. No matter how much time passed or whether Tom ever remarried, while the rest of the world might forget Maggie or push her into a particular list of tragic statistics, she would always be in the back of his head, holding a piece of his heart. At least, that's how it felt to Tom.

Jade paid her rent to the receptionist and thought about the man sitting there. She didn't watch much reality television, much less television, at all, but she could tell he was going through something very emotional and traumatic. It was the way he carried himself. She had no desire to be thrown into his personal drama but she couldn't ignore someone she had just met a couple of nights ago, especially if he knew her boss. Jade turned around to leave, took a deep breath and approached him.

"Hi." Tom had his head pointed down when he heard the woman's voice. He saw the navy blue, low-top Chuck Taylors, and moved up to see her brown legs, dress, then meet the face of the woman he had been trying to avoid.

"Hey," he said.

"Weren't you at Shorebreak on Friday?"

"Yup, that was me. Why? I didn't embarrass you or anything, did I?"

"No," she started to laugh and caught herself. "It wasn't *me* you embarrassed."

Great, he thought, *must've been embarrassing myself.*

"It's not as bad as you think." Jade could tell he was getting self-conscious and decided to break the ice more. "How has it been?"

"What?" Tom's paranoia screamed within him. This was what he had been waiting for. This was when she asked about the incident.

"Your visit? I'm guessing you don't live around here."

"Oh." His inner self let out a big sigh of relief. "I'm actually from around here."

"So that's how you know Feltz and Sprenkle."

"Oh, no. We worked together at Funland."

"Oh, I've heard stories. Not about you specifically, but, I guess you'd say general stories."

"About parties, I'm sure."

"Among other things."

Curiosity nipped at Tom's brain and he fought the urge to ask her what exact stories she was talking about as he could only imagine some of the humiliating stories Feltz had told her.

"Are you staying for a while?" Jade asked, referring to the obvious fact they were in a realtor's office.

"Um, yeah. No. I ... um ... I don't ... know, to tell you the truth. But I need someplace to stay and I don't feel like going to a hotel."

"You don't have anyone to stay with?"

"Not really."

Jade could tell she was beginning to be too inquisitive. She had always had a very curious nature and it had always been more detrimental to her rather than advantageous. "Sorry. I don't mean to pry."

Tom laughed at her quick switch from prying to immediate apologies. He actually laughed. It was the first genuine laugh he had had since the incident and he relished it for the few seconds it had happened. His smile melted to a solemn, empty glare, looking to nowhere in particular, as he suddenly felt as if he had no right to be laughing, as if he should be in some constant state of mourning.

"It's OK," he said. "My parents live around here, but ... I can't live there. My dad ... he's a good man. But ... he's very different from me. And there's nothing wrong with that. I'm used to it by now. At least, I *should* be used to it."

Jade knew what Tom was talking about, no matter how muddled his words. She had felt it herself with her own father.

Tom grew self-conscious and changed the subject. "*Shutter Island*, huh? Have you seen the movie?"

"Oh," Jade's thoughts of her father vanished. "No, I haven't. I wanted to read the book first. All I know about the movie is Leonardo DiCaprio is in it. Have you seen it?"

"Yeah." Tom modestly said. "I actually ... went to the premiere."

"Seriously!?"

"Yeah. A buddy of mine got tickets."

Tom waited for the usual reply he got when he said he went to the premiere: Do you know Leo? How is he in real life? Did you meet any other famous people?

"Was the movie any good?" she asked.

Tom was caught a little off-guard by her non-celebrity question. "Um, uh, yeah. I liked it. But the ending's seriously messed up."

"Oh, no." She almost put her hands to her ears. "Don't tell me. I want to read it first."

"Do you like thrillers?"

"It's not my usual go-to genre but I've nearly finished the current book I'm reading and a friend said this one was good, so I'm gonna try it. I like to try and read all different kinds of stories. You never know which may surprise you and affect you in all the right ways."

"I just started reading more recently."

"Have you read this?" she asked, referring to *Shutter Island*.

"No. Just saw the movie."

"What was the last book you read?"

"Maugham's *The Razor's Edge*. It's my favorite."

"Oh, *really* good book!"

"What about you? What's your favorite book?"

"Definitely *To Kill A Mockingbird!* There are so many great lines and words of wisdom in that book. I read it once every year."

"I've never read it."

" *What!?* Seriously?"

"Yeah. I mean, I know what it's basically about, but I've never read it."

"Have you seen the movie?"

"Nope."

" *What!?* You definitely need to add that to your reading list. It's such a great story."

"So when did you start working for Sprenkle?"

Jade opened her mouth but another voice sounded out. "Mr. Frost?"

It was one of the rental agents. Tom was disappointed to be called away from the first real-yet-trivial conversation he had had since he couldn't remember when.

"That's me," he mumbled.

"Oh, OK," Jade said. "It was nice meeting you and good luck finding a place. Maybe I'll see you sometime at Shorebreak."

"Yeah." Tom stood up and walked back toward the rental agent's office as she turned and walked toward the exit.

Some kind of inexplicable feeling made Jade turn around to watch Tom, traipsing toward the woman standing at her office door as if she were the school principal and he were some student about to face his punishment. Jade knew this was no fairy tale. No matter his aspirations or potential at greatness or how cute he was, Tom Frost clearly had personal issues and she couldn't be some kind of savior for him. She had already spent too much of her life living out one man's particular expectations that, since moving here, she unequivocally decided now was her time to do what she wanted for herself. Nevertheless, she hoped Tom found happiness; and if he just so happened to stop by the bar from time to time, she wouldn't mind some more friendly conversation. After all, she had plenty of acquaintances but she hadn't had any true, deep friendships since college. She turned and walked out the exit.

Tom had felt what seemed like a genuine connection with this woman. She had to have known his story. This may have been Delaware but it wasn't the sleepy little state most people made it out to be and Tom figured most people he came into contact with in the area knew what had happened with Maggie - especially since they both were from Delaware. Regardless of what Jade knew, Tom was grateful for the brief moment he was able to take his mind off of that which had been his main focus for the past five months. Romance was the farthest thing from his mind but, to him, in his current situation, there was a lot to be said about making a friend.

He turned around to look and see if she was still there, but she was gone. He turned back and continued into the rental agent's office.

"I'm Michelle," she said, and they shook hands. She was tall, dressed in a long, professional skirt, armless blouse, and looked young and Italian, with dark brown hair, brown eyes. He swore she had gone to his high school, but he hoped not. If she knew about his infamous celebrity, she never showed it. She asked him how much he was looking to spend and in which neighborhoods he might be interested in searching. Tom told her money was not an issue, but, when it came to location, he wanted to be someplace that was close to town but not so close that there was constant activity. The agent asked him about downtown Rehoboth and he shot that suggestion down. Too busy - even in the off season. Tom said he wanted something a bit more private.

"I think I have just what you're looking for," she said.

The agent proceeded to grab a set of keys, made a phone call and asked Tom if he would like to see the property right now. Tom agreed and followed her out to Route One - called Coastal Highway by locals. They turned left, heading southbound, and Tom feared she was taking him to Dewey Beach. To him, Dewey was a party town - a place for locals and tourists alike to go for a night out dancing, drinking and seeing a mix of local and famous bands. While there was nothing wrong with the town, he wasn't much in the mood to have easy access to the numerous bars which aligned the main highway, as well as no desire to risk having drunk tourists accidentally walking through his yard.

He followed Michelle over a small bridge, but before Dewey, he watched as she headed toward a salon alongside the left side of the highway, made a U-turn and made a right turn down a side road called William F Street. She turned left to the first house on the block. It was a typical quarter acre lot, much different from the mansion he used to live in. The driveway started off as gravel but quickly turned into broken cement. The house was a small, one-story single family home with dark blue paint (it didn't look like there was any siding whatsoever) and crimson red shutters. There was a small, straight paved walking path which led from a makeshift additional parking space at the edge of the front yard, between two trees, directly to the front door. The tree foliage covered the two windows along the front of the house, not that it would matter much because the neighborhood block looked somewhat vacant. Houses stood with empty driveways and the only noise filling his ears were the sounds of the speeding vehicles swooshing past on the highway.

"Do you like it?" Michelle asked, then before he could answer. "Three bedrooms, central A/C, one-and-a-half bath. The owner doesn't live here. Just rents it out. So if you're looking for an indefinite amount of time to stay, that would certainly be an option."

* * *

"So what do ya think?" Tom asked.

The house was a bit run down, but for the area, the asking price was a steal.

"It's OK," Maggie said, standing next to Tom, in front of a small mansion in the Hollywood hills. "But, Tom ... don't you think it's ... a lot of work? I mean, why do you wanna buy a house that needs work when we can buy a new one?"

"It's got promise. Besides, I'm making more money now. I think we can afford to have some renovations done."

"You think we can afford that on just your salary!?"

Money had been a touchy subject for both of them since Maggie moved out to L.A. two years prior. She had not been able to find a job at a hospital as quickly as she thought and she was starting to grow anxious.

"I'm not worried. Why? Are you?"

"It's just ..." Maggie didn't know how to say this to Tom without sounding like a brat. "It's just ... this place ... wasn't what I expected."

"I know it doesn't seem like much, but we can design it ourselves." Tom became a bit excited at the potential. "We can put in a lot of upgrades as we go." Tom stopped and saw the look she was giving him. He realized Maggie's previous reference to "this place" wasn't the house; rather she was talking about L.A. and their life together so far. Tom immediately grew quiet as if someone had flipped a switch, and his previous excitement disappeared.

Maggie looked away from him, toward the house. He couldn't tell whether she was crying or not, but he had a pretty good idea. She sniffed and quietly cleared her throat.

"I know you're excited about us finding a real house together, but I can't get excited about this when I don't even have a job yet."

Tom could tell Maggie was honestly frustrated and scared. The best thing he could do was reassure her everything would work out fine. She was just overthinking the situation. She'd get a job soon and be so immersed, she'd be grateful to have a place to call home. Still, he didn't want to rush her into anything for which she wasn't ready.

"We don't have to do this now, Mags, if you're not ready. We can wait some more and come back to it later."

Maggie felt bad for Tom. He was trying to make the best of the situation but, despite his tender understanding, she could feel she still wasn't being straightforward enough with him. She turned back to him and grasped his hands as tightly as she could. The cold, hard grip surprised him.

"Tom. What I'm trying to say is ... I feel like things are moving too fast for me. I don't even have a job yet. You're so focused on us and *me* ... and I feel like I have to focus a lot on you." Maggie struggled to put the words as delicately as possible so Tom wouldn't get offended. "I need more time ... for me."

"Maggie, if you want to hold out until you find a job, I completely understand. We can do that. I can give you some time to devote to applying to jobs, and—"

Tom stopped himself. The epiphany had struck him and shut him up as if he had just been shot dead in the middle of talking. He knew where she was going with this. It was the break-up, the "let's-call-it-quits-before-things-get-too-serious" chat, as if her moving out to L.A. and living together in a small apartment wasn't serious enough already.

Whatever it was, he wanted to hear it from her lips so he waited.

"This thing ... we have ... it's just ... it's not working." Maggie let the last word just hang there, out in the open, with no further explanation.

Tom had noticed Maggie's enthusiasm waning over the past couple of weeks. He knew it hadn't been as easy for Maggie to find a job as they both initially thought, and he believed it was that frustration which was the source of her recent sadness. So this had to be a mistake, some kind of preemptive break-up (like in that *Seinfeld* TV episode) in order for her to spare his feelings.

"No, no, no. You don't have to do this, Mags. I can give you some space to do what you gotta do. And ... as far as the place goes, we can hold off on it."

"It just takes too much effort."

Maggie's tone was a bit cold, standoffish. It wasn't much but it was enough to tear down all of Tom's optimistic delusions; and he hung his head in despair for having to accept this for what it really was: a break-up. He didn't think about what he said next, he simply said what he felt.

"Maybe it shouldn't take so much *damn* effort."

When Tom looked up to face her, Maggie's expression had answered all of the questions running through his head. Shock would have been the simplest term to diagnose, but, to Maggie, the bottomless pit punched into her stomach felt less like shock and more like a damn horror show. She choked back the tears flooding her eyes and swallowed down the sob racing up her throat. What she couldn't shake was the repetitious feeling as if she were sitting in the front car of a roller coaster, overlooking the first steep drop.

Tom realized her cold tone had only driven his anger out, but his careless statement had ripped up her entire insides. He lowered his head like some old dog that was being shamed by its owner for ripping up the furniture. He awaited his verbal punishment but there was nothing. Silence.

Maggie didn't recoil but stood rather stoic - except for one small detail. Her eyelids continually struggled to not collapse and push out the tears as the corners of her eyes trembled. She had never heard Tom speak that way to her ... or anyone. He was always so affable, making his reaction unexpected. Everyone had a limit - a particular point that people reached before someone would lash out - and Maggie had inadvertently found Tom's limit. She knew this wasn't easy for him to hear and it wasn't the worst reaction she had ever gotten from a guy when she told him disappointing news regarding their relationship. Yet, her hurt feelings and pride overrode any consideration to his feelings, so she did what anyone would most likely do in the situation: she turned the tables on him and used his reaction to her benefit.

"Why would you say something like that?" her tearful voice asked. "I'm just being honest with you."

"Maggie. This is the first time I'm hearing anything like this from you."

"You know I've been upset for a while."

"Sure. Maybe. But I'm not a mind-reader."

"Do you really have to read my mind if you see me being upset!?"

"And you can't come to me when something about our life together is upsetting you?"

"Just do what you want," Maggie's tone had grown bitter. "You always do. Just like with this dump."

She pointed to the mansion and turned away, letting out a heavy sigh. Tom had no idea where any of this was coming from. When she moved out to L.A. to be with him, she insisted it was what she wanted to do, and never said any different. She insisted he focus on his job while they spend as much time together as possible. Her entire face now contorted, her eyes leaking tears, as she said, "I don't know why you always get so angry when I talk to you. It makes me afraid to open up to you."

Maggie hurriedly walked away from Tom and her manipulation left him befuddled. He had no idea what she was talking about as he had never raised his voice to her before. The sight of her crying left him sympathetic and feeling somewhat guilty for her fake-yet-believable tears, making him fall victim to her ruse.

"Maggie ... I," he approached her. "I know we can work this out. I love you. I'm sorry if I lost my temper. Please ... just talk to me."

Maggie's demeanor changed – albeit not immediately so she didn't seem too obvious – but she still felt a little sorry for him for being so clueless as to her true motivation. "I can't talk about it anymore. Why don't we forget this place and let me find us a place instead."

"If that's what you want."

She perked up even more. "That's great, Tom! I promise I'll find us a great place." She was thinking it would be a much better place than the dump he had picked out.

* * *

304

"Would you like to take a look inside?" Michelle asked.

Tom blinked and saw the small, dark blue one-story house in front of him. He wished he could shake these memories of Maggie, but they persisted, leaving a lot of sleepless or interrupted nights. He looked over to the rental agent to get his bearings again and said, "Yes, please."

The walkthrough of the house was quick and everything was pretty much how the agent had described it to Tom. There were no big screen TVs, no hot tubs, no eternity pools, no two-car garage, nor a large, open kitchen. The house was practical and simple, and it worked for Tom. By the time, they reached back to the entrance, before the agent could ask his opinion, Tom said, "I'll take it."

Michelle seemed calm and demure on the outside but, on the inside, she was freaking out. This property had been listed and been on the market for almost a year. Michelle knew the winter would be slow, but thought the summer would bring someone looking to rent – whether it be a tourist family, graduating seniors, or some low-income single person searching for someplace near the beach. Tom was the taker she had been awaiting.

"On one condition."

Damn, she thought, *here comes the rub.* "What?"

"I want you to be one-hundred percent honest with me. If you are, you have a better chance of closing this deal with me."

"Sure."

"Do you know who I am?"

Of course she did! He was the host of that screwed-up reality TV show, the one where his wife was killed. "Yes."

"OK. Now here's my condition." Tom took in a deep breath, looked her in the eyes with a serious glare and said,

"You cannot tell anyone that I'm renting this place. I don't want any reporters coming here. And I don't need people dropping by to catch a glimpse at the poor bastard whose wife was killed on live TV. I'm not some zoo animal on display."

"Of course not."

"'Cause if that happens, I'll know it was you, Michelle, who ratted me out. No one else knows I'm here, at this address, so I'll know it was you for sure. And then, our contract is done and I'll sue for breach of contract." Tom knew he sounded a bit like a jerk but he had to be sure he got his point across. He had already been screwed over because he tread lightly when it came to people's feelings, and he didn't want his plan of staying here to blow up in his face. The threat of suing was nonsense, but he figured he'd bluff and see if it scared the realtor into submission to his agreement. He added a meek afterthought, "I just wanted you to know where we stand."

Michelle wondered who the hell this guy thought he was and started losing the smallest inkling of sympathy she had had for him before he said that. Of course, she absolutely had every intention of telling her co-workers, but now she couldn't even tell *them*. The nerve of this guy!

"I promise you, sir. I'll be very discreet."

"Thanks," he smiled. "When can I move in?"

"Let's go back to the office, we'll get started on the paperwork and you can get in there today."

"Thanks."

They both returned to Michelle's office and after an hour or so, Tom left with a set of keys and nothing to move in with but the clothes he was wearing, an iPod, his worn copy of *The Razor's Edge*, and the Delaware shirt he had gotten at the bar. As he stepped into his Jeep and plunked into the seat, catching a quick look at his barren vehicle, he was thankful the house came furnished. One less thing to worry about. He turned the key and the Jeep rumbled to life. Tom looked in the rear view mirror to see if anyone was behind him. In the small rectangular mirror, his eyes were met by Maggie's smiling face peering back at him. She didn't look like a ghost or anything, but rather with makeup and her hair made up as if she had just come out of the salon up the road. The fright had sent an uncontrollable spasm through Tom's body, his heart going from zero to ninety in one palpitation. It had only taken one second to look back into the mirror and see she was gone. He turned around just to make sure and there was still no sign of her. Tom didn't believe in ghosts – at least, not the kind that takes physical, visible shape – but he did believe that the mind can play tricks on you.

He looked in the rear view mirror again, put on his Wayfarer sunglasses and left the office parking lot. He went to the closest grocery store, then to the house. As Tom pushed the door open, there was an eerie silence that hadn't been there when he went through it with the agent. He stood with a few grocery bags hanging from each hand, closed his eyes and stood still, taking in the silence. The absence of noise was actually a welcome comfort to him and as long as he kept a low profile, he could continue to have the peace and quiet he had craved since getting out of jail.

Tom put away his groceries then proceeded to place his single book on the big book shelf in the living room, making it the only book on all five shelves. He folded his Delaware shirt and placed it in the empty top drawer of the dresser in his bedroom, plugged in his iPod charger and laid it on the nightstand next to his bed, then sat down on the living room couch. *Maybe quiet was overrated*, he thought. He jolted off the couch, grabbed a copy of the rental agreement, left the house without locking the door, got in his Jeep and drove back to the rental office.

When Tom stepped back through the entrance, the receptionist recognized him and he asked to see the agent who had just helped him. When Michelle emerged from her office, a look of suspicion was painted across her face but she forced some of it away with an awkward smile.

"Hi, Mr. Frost. Is everything OK with the house?"

"Ah, yes. I was actually just wondering if I could use your phone to make a call." Tom could tell Michelle was annoyed – her face conveyed as much. "I don't have a cell phone and I would've gone to a payphone, but I haven't seen any."

Michelle thought for a second, although her actual thought was why most of her customers were such pains-in-the-ass. "Sure."

She showed him to her office and gave him some privacy. Tom struggled to remember the phone number. Most of the numbers he used were saved in his cell phone, but, fortunately, the number he needed was one of the first ones he memorized. He dialed the number and his breathing grew shallower with each ring.

"Hello?" the old man's voice answered.

"Hi, Bob? It's Tom. Frost."

"Hi, Tom. How are you?"

"I'm good. How're things back there?"

"Good. Things are fine."

"Listen, Bob. I'm sorry about the way I left outta there. I just ... I had to get away."

"No need for apologies. I get it."

"Thanks for wiring the money. It was quicker than I thought."

"You're welcome. How're your folks?"

Tom let out an exhausting sigh just thinking of having to explain it all. "Same as ever. I thought I might be at least a little more welcome. Ya know, after everything that's happened?"

"Yeah. I know."

"My dad's just being ... a complete ..." Tom wanted to call the man worse but all he could get out was, "... jerk."

"Your parents love you," Bob reminded him. "And your father is just doing the best he can with what he knows and what he thinks is best."

"I know, Bob. I feel bad even saying all this out loud. I feel bad for even *thinking* it. But he just ... It's how I feel." Tom took a deep breath and changed the subject quick. "I just hoped ... when I moved over here I'd get away from all the ..." Tom lowered his voice to a barely audible whisper, "... bullshit."

Tom always felt guilty for cussing around Bob because he had always considered Bob a surrogate father; it's why he didn't cuss all that often. So when he did do it, he couldn't help but pause before saying it and then whisper said cuss word.

"It doesn't matter how many miles you put between yourself and your problems. They'll follow you wherever you go."

Tom grew quiet and Bob worried that maybe he had overstepped his bounds, maybe Tom thought he was defending Tom's parents but disregarding Tom's feelings. Before he could say anything, the younger man replied.

"*Now* you tell me."

Bob had to stifle a laugh. "Listen, Tom. I get it. I know what you were trying to get away from. But before you deal with others or live a life away in peace, you have to deal with your own problems first."

"Well, I'm hoping I made the first step in that direction today."

"Why's that?"

"I found a place to rent." Bob's silence was too much for Tom to tolerate so he rambled on. "I couldn't stay in my parents' house anymore. And you're right. If I have any chance of getting myself together, I need some time to work on myself. I need ... to ... go it alone."

"That sounds good, kid. But the only problem with that is life isn't going to go on hiatus while you straighten out your issues."

"I know." Tom didn't want this talk to be all about him. "How've you been, Bob?"

"Me? I'm good. I'm taking on fewer cases."

"I didn't call any media on you, did I?"

"No. I'm just getting tired. Although, that friend of yours came by here a few days ago - the lady reporter. What's her name? Um ... Jennifer?"

"Jen? Jen Desmond?

"Yes."

"What did she want?"

"She wanted to know how you were doing after the newscast."

"You didn't tell her where I was, did you?"

"No."

"Good." Tom's heart calmed and he caught a breath. "Good. She just wants to find out where I am so she can report on it."

"She sounded naturally concerned to me."

"Ya know, Bob? For a lawyer, you're awfully damn naïve."

"I don't see how trusting people and trying to be positive has hurt me or my career after all these years."

"You *are* a lawyer, right?"

"How would you rather I be?"

Even though Bob didn't sound it, Tom could still tell he had hurt his feelings and it made him readjust his attitude. After all, Bob's optimism was one of the main reasons Tom hired him in the first place. "Just ... trust me. After what she did, her intentions are far from anything remotely good. Just please ... don't tell her."

"I won't. I promise."

"Listen ... how's the sale of my house going? Any bites yet?"

"I have a few interested buyers. I'll email you the offers when they come in."

"Just take in the first offer that comes in at one-point-five or two. And when you sell the house, could you please wire me the money as soon as possible? The funds in my main account are dwindling now that I bought a Jeep and made the down payment for the place."

"Sounds like you're well on your way over there."

"How are Maggie's parents? Have you heard anything from 'em? I haven't watched any TV so I haven't heard anything."

"It's the same old story. After it happened, they were being interviewed by every media outlet you could think of, but now ... nothing. No matter how many times I see it, I never get used to it – all that attention then they're dropped, forgotten. And now, Maggie's all but forgotten. Just another name."

For the first time since the incident, Tom had found someone he genuinely wanted to talk to about Maggie, about that night, but something within him prevented him. Despite his sadness and the pit it carved within his stomach, Tom felt like if he allowed his melancholy to overtake him, it was just another cause for him to feel sorry for himself; and he had spent enough time feeling sorry for himself.

"Bob. I gotta go. But you can email me. I'll be able to check it now."

"Sure. Listen. Can I ask you one question before you go?"

"Yeah."

"Did you move back there for any specific reason?"

Tom had asked himself that same question every day since his plane touched down in Baltimore. He wasn't even sure he had a definitive answer. He searched his mind for the most honest answer he could give. "Yeah. My family's here. Plus ... I have a lotta good memories here."

"I know. But ... I mean ... what's your plan?"

"Honestly? I'm thinkin' I lie low here for a while until the media feeding frenzy dies down. Then I can maybe break into some network's production staff. Hell, I'll even take MTV at this point. Whatever it takes to get my foot in the door. I'm still fairly young. I can—"

"Do you honestly believe that, Tom?" Bob only gave about two seconds for Tom to say anything before he elaborated. "Don't get me wrong. I want you to do what makes you happy. But ... the jail time alone ..."

"Bob. Do you realize how many producers have a record!?"

"Yes, but, Tom ... what happened on air ..."

Tom looked up and through the door window to see Michelle staring at him as if she were about to bust down the door.

"Bob. I gotta go. My rental agent is staring at me as if she's about to kick down the door. I'm sure she's not gonna be too happy when she finds out I called California."

A small laugh escaped Bob. He had always liked Tom, thought of him like the son he never had. He only regretted that he didn't hear from him more. "You take care of yourself, Tom. Remember, no matter what, life is only going to give you what you put into it."

Tom said goodbye, hung up and took a moment to dwell on what Bob had said. He always said that somewhat vague cliché; in fact, he had the phrase framed, hanging up in his house. Then Tom thought about what Bob had said about him getting back into the television production business. For once in his life, he hoped Bob was wrong.

16.

"I look around for the friends that I used to turn to,
to pull me through
Looking into their eyes, I see them running too."

--Jackson Browne
"Running on Empty"

Jade had good days and bad days. Today was a bad day. It hit her without any internal warning nor a set schedule – sometimes going months without it, sometimes just hours. Her knees uncontrollably shook, appearing like thin stilts bending from the strain of a heavy object, then buckled. She reached out for the closest thing to grab onto in order to balance herself but her vision and head spun as if she had just ran in circles for a half hour and were now trying to stand still. Her brain and vision continued the spin of the stationary objects with which she focused, and the feeling overwhelmed her as the strength in her legs slowly melted her down onto the floor. Ice water ran through her veins and her breathing became very shallow, making her short breaths come out more like a dying animal gasping for air. Before long, she could barely breathe. Her heart rate rose to marathon-like numbers as pins and needles pricked at her face before it went numb, making her think every time, no matter how many times she'd experienced it, that she was having a stroke. This was Jade's panic attack.

She knew she was in the thick of it and learned about a year-and-a-half ago not to try and fight it. Fighting it only made the whole thing worse. She knew in order to get her breathing under control, she was going to have to take a more controlled breath from her belly so she could stop hyperventilating. The only bad part was doing what she needed to do wouldn't feel good.

Jade placed one hand on her chest and the other on her stomach so she could feel which muscles her body was using. By her own control, she breathed shallower for a few gasps, making her symptoms' effects enhance – this was the part that sucked – then let out a gentle sigh as if someone had just told her something annoying. With her sigh, she let her slender shoulders and the muscles of her upper body relax with the exhale. She closed her mouth and could already feel her body relaxing as she inhaled slowly through her nose, pushing her stomach out. When she inhaled as much as she could without straining, she held her breath for a little under a minute, then opened her mouth and exhaled the breath, pulling her belly inward as her captured breath escaped. With her breathing under control, the spins were dissipating and her blood pumped through her veins once again. It didn't matter that Jade knew what she was experiencing was a panic attack, it didn't make the fear it produced any less real, but she considered herself lucky that most times she could come out of it fairly easy. What sucked the most about her attacks – more than the tinge of pain she felt in her remedy – was the not knowing when it would strike. It didn't matter whether she was in the privacy of her home or out at a restaurant or walking amidst the crowded boardwalk. When it struck her, the best she could do was walk as far as she could away from people, which was never usually that far, and ride it out like she had just done. The only aspect to her attacks that she had figured out since she started having them was she seemed more susceptible to them when she was in crowded places and her anxiety got the best of her.

Today she had just finished doing some grocery shopping. She had just paid for her items while the cashier placed what few bags she had in her cart, and **WHAM!** It hit. She smiled through the first bout of panic and thanked the cashier than located a small sitting bench in the store – an oasis in the desert – set between the men's and women's bathroom entrances. She quickly strode to it as the strength in her legs eroding with each step. At the same time that she had begun to master her panic attack survival technique, she had also lost her ability to care what the strangers around her were thinking while seeing a young woman reacting to such a horrific, indescribable malady. Besides, most people ignored her anyway. And those with whom she tried to explain her attacks, while they could sympathize, they had no way of fully comprehending or imagining what the feeling was like – only those who had experienced an attack firsthand could imagine the feeling. This aspect highlighted one of the worst tenets of the rest of the population not suffering from panic attacks: the belief that those suffering from attacks could simply be cured if they just "snapped out of it," or "sucked it up and pushed through it," making sufferers feel as if panic attacks were some shameful taboo they couldn't talk about.

After a few more of her exercises, her breathing had returned to normal and the anxiety had subsided. She sat for a minute or two more just to get her head wrapped around the fact that everything was fine and she could function without any danger of losing control of her body. Jade stood up, took another deep breath, released it, and walked out of the store. She tried not to think about it the rest of the day, it was just something she got from time to time and she felt fortunate that the numbers of these attacks were diminishing more and more as she got older. She never got her head shrunk to see what was the ultimate cause of the attacks - if there *was* one "ultimate cause" - but thought maybe it had to do with the untimely death of her best friend and roommate, Vanessa, back during freshman year of college.

As much as hearing of Vanessa's tragic death had made Jade's world, and all the safety she felt within it, crumble, she couldn't help but admit to herself that she was glad she hadn't been with her friend that sunny, fall day when Vanessa's drunken, abusive father confronted his only daughter with a gun. She had mourned for a long time. Not just for Vanessa, but also for her own loss of the youthful innocence of the importance in friendship and the bond it constructs. Jade had friends - more like acquaintances - but she never had another friend like Vanessa, no one with which she could open up to or build that kind of bond. She figured maybe friendship was that way. The friendships we make when we're older can never compare to those we made when we were young and full of ideals and wonder.

Despite her quantity of friends, Jade was happy ... overall ... which was why it still pained her to try and figure out what was causing such debilitating panic attacks. If it wasn't Vanessa, Jade figured they had come on strong around the time she moved to Delaware and she chalked up their intensity to the stress and uncertainty of the move and the life she would have in a new place. After she settled in and found work she enjoyed, she figured the attacks would stop fairly quickly. There was even a long period of time when she didn't have one and she believed they were gone. It nearly broke her heart when about a month to the day of her last attack, she had another one. But it wasn't her way to mope about such things. She had always tried her best to meet adversity with a stiff upper lip - that is to say, she didn't completely bury her negative feelings away. She let herself feel sadness or anger, but she didn't dwell in those emotions - it often led nowhere but to a dead end.

Jade came out of the store and loaded the groceries into her powder blue 1982 Volkswagen Rabbit convertible peppered with a few small rust spots here and there. Today was a nice enough day to have the black top down. The car would've been considered a classic if it weren't in such poor condition, but that didn't bother Jade. She had always wanted one and it got her from point A to point B, which wasn't very far since she pretty much stayed within a thirty-mile radius of the Rehoboth community. The only addition to the car was located between the license plate and the right-hand taillight - a round bullseye-like bumper sticker with the white, lowercase words "life is good" in the middle of the red center.

She got home and was halfway through putting away the groceries when her cell phone started ringing. She looked at the caller ID and saw it was her mother. Since the fallout with her father, Jade's mom had only called her on special occasions - specifically Jade's birthday, Christmas, and Diwali, even though Jade didn't celebrate the Indian festival anymore.

"Hello?" she answered.

"Hello, Jade. It's your mother." Jade was never sure if her mother knew that the decades-old technology of her cell phone's caller ID would already give Jade such information. Regardless, her mom always answered the same way. "How are you doing?"

"Hi, Mom. I'm good. I just got back from the grocery store. I have to work tonight so I'm just having some quiet time. How are you?"

"Very well. Speaking of jobs, I heard there are a few practices looking for attorneys in your area. Would you like me to forward the announcements?" Jade wasn't surprised by her mother's overzealousness to have her daughter enter the world of law again. Mrs. Saha had always marveled at her daughter's intelligence and passion for wanting to help people – and if she just so happened to make a great salary and obtain wonderful health benefits from it in the process, then that was a much-welcome bonus!

"Mama. I don't know how many times we have to go through this. I'm happy where I am right now."

"Yes, Jade, but you are twenty-eight-years-old. You are not getting any younger and, with all due respect, what you do now is not a career."

"Have we traveled back in time? Is this 2010? Or maybe it is 2012. Wait, I'm noticing a pattern. This happens about every two years. Although it's been – what? – three years now since we last had this talk? So, let's get this out of the way now and I won't have to worry for at least another two years. But I'll tell you, my answer now is the same one I have given you during all those past times. And it will be the same answer I will give you in two more years. I have to do what makes me happy. If I don't, I'm no good to anyone. If my heart is not in it, I'm certainly no good to my co-workers or the people I'm working for."

Mrs. Saha had never known the true reason for her daughter's decision to study law. Jade's parents had always assumed their daughter chose her career path because it was one of the two careers they had chosen for her and she was respecting their wishes. When she was in elementary school and junior high, she was following the proverbial path they had laid out before her. That all changed when she entered her freshman year of high school. She had been assigned to read Harper Lee's *To Kill a Mockingbird*, and it changed her entire concept of life, people and law. Like with most readers, the character of Atticus Finch had opened her eyes to being a truly good person. She allowed her parents to continue to believe that her becoming a lawyer was solely because she knew they would be proud, but it was Atticus who had become the main inspiration for her choosing to pursue a law degree. When she got into financial law rather than criminal, she quickly saw what it was all about: money, greed, pettiness. She wasn't helping the disenfranchised and she certainly wasn't making a difference in anyone's life. Corporations, yes. But the people who actually needed help? They did not exist in the world of financial law.

"Happy?" her mother said. "Do you think everyone in every field of work is happy? Do you think the trash man is happy? Do you think a single mother working at McDonald's is happy?"

"OK, Mama. I get it."

"Do you? Because your father and I only want what is best for you, but you appear to be driving further and further from that life. And from us."

"Mama. I am not pushing myself away from you and Papa. It's just ... you don't know what it was like to work in that environment, to see the things I saw every single day, to be treated the way I was treated."

"What do you mean the way you were treated?"

"They ..."

"If they treated you unfairly, you could have found a job elsewhere."

"They treated me unfairly because I wasn't, according to them, performing to their standards."

"So you get in there and do better. You're a bright, young woman, Jade. There is no reason you should—"

"I do not want to be better at *that* kind of work, Mama. I felt like I was losing my soul at that place."

"Oh, Jade. Do not be dramatic."

Jade rolled her eyes at her mother's discountenance of her phrasing.

"Mama. I have to go. I have a friend coming in to visit and she'll be here soon."

"Who?"

"Katie."

"The one who lives in New York?"

"Yes."

"What does she do again?"

"She works for a P.R. firm in Manhattan."

"Public relations?"

"Yeah."

"Ah, yes. I remember. The one who gets paid to party. Well, at least she is making good money."

"Yes, Mama. And her parents do not mind visiting her or supporting her choices."

A knock came to Jade's door and her eyes widened at the relief of being saved from any further conversation with her mom. "Mom, listen, she's here. I have to go."

"Then go, Jade. Do what you want."

Her mom hung up before Jade could get out an "I love you" or "goodbye." For now, she had to throw that conversation out of her mind. Jade wanted to be in a good mood for her best friend's visit. She hung up the phone and strode to the door as fast as she could without running.

Jade swung open the door and saw an attractive woman her age, holding one medium-sized piece of luggage, standing in front of her on the small, screened porch. Katie had long, curly light brown hair, blue eyes covered by reflective aviator sunglasses, and all the looks of a white-bred New Englander, having been born and raised in upstate New York. She was dressed in a form-fitting jean jacket, white tank top, and a long, brown cotton skirt which stretched down to just above her ankles. They had met soon after Jade was hired at her firm in Manhattan. It was a gala for each of their respective employers' clients and the two of them immediately hit it off. Whereas Jade was the quiet one, Katie was very much gregarious. Sure, the term "opposites attract" seemed every bit the cliché – even in plain friendships – but sometimes clichés were nevertheless true.

Katie let out a squeal of joy at the sight of her best friend and Jade returned the same sound, their tones combining to such a high pitch they were in danger of shattering glass. Jade knew during this brief time that she turned into one of those girls she despised, making that annoying squeal, but she just couldn't help herself. Katie put the luggage down and the two embraced. Jade invited her in to the small kitchenette, which took up the entire downstairs.

In front of the doorway was a staircase leading up. The style of the kitchen, with its slight low ceiling and layout gave away that the structure was quite old. The kitchen appliances further proved that this quaint little garage-turned-apartment had not been altered since the structure was first built. The women sat down at a small, dark green table which resembled a picnic table that had been cut in half, with the cut half built into the wall.

"Looks like I picked the right time of year to come visit," Katie said. "Is this always how it is this time of year?"

"Pretty much. Although you did get here before the weekender rush."

"I don't have to worry about a permit, do I?"

"No. You're good."

"What kind of people do you get this time of year?"

"Right now, there's a bunch of snowbirds about to come in to start opening up their seasonal homes."

"So it's gonna be us and the old people tonight?" Katie asked with an animated air of part sarcasm and part true enthusiasm, a goofy look stretched across her face.

Jade had to suppress a laugh for what reason she couldn't tell. It was their dynamic – always had been since they met. "Not likely. There may be a few of the locals there."

"Ooh. Can we go out to dinner tonight?" Katie didn't know why but she felt most times as if she always had to explain herself. Now was no exception. "It's been so long since I've last been here, I'm sure there's plenty of new places to check out."

"Sure. We've got all kinds of places to eat around here. I don't know how much I can afford, though."

"I'm paying. Don't worry about it."

"So I take it the job is still going well?"

"*Hell* yeah! Just got a promotion. I'm the new communications director at Edelman."

"Wow! Congratulations!"

"Thanks. I wanted to get away before the craziness. I've got a bunch of new potential clients lined up me for when I come back."

"Well then ... the sky is the limit, I guess. What are you in the mood for tonight?"

"We should go to that place – Shorebreak. I've never been there and I'd like to finally see where you work."

"Sure. But, next time you come with Bryan, I want to make sure we take him there so he can see it too."

"Yeah. Maybe next time," Katie said, suddenly sounding vacant. The shift at mentioning Katie's fiancé was noticeable to Jade but before she could ask, Katie perked up and changed the subject. "So! I've been in the car for too long, I need to freshen up. Mind if I take a shower?"

"No. Go ahead. I'll get ready while you're in there."

"You look beautiful, J. You don't need to change."

"Hey. I gotta keep up appearances to hang with you."

Katie smiled, grabbed her bag and Jade told her to follow her. They walked up the stairs, into the open living room with a couch on the right-hand wall, a coffee table in front of it and a small television tucked into the corner of the opposite wall. To the right of the room was a bathroom and beside the bathroom was a regular bedroom which was obviously Jade's. Katie noticed the 1940s radio with an iPod plugged in, and the sight piqued her interest.

"Ooh. Can I play some music?"

"Sure." Jade pressed the random button and play. The guitar strumming beginning of Avicii's "Wake Me Up" burst through the speaker.

Katie looked upon her friend with a sentimental graciousness. "Thanks, Jade ... for letting me come visit this week. I really needed it."

Jade saw the shimmer of sadness in her expression, but carried on like nothing was wrong. "Are you kidding? It is no problem. I'm so happy you came!" Katie went into the bathroom. "There are already towels in there."

"Thanks," Katie flashed a small smile and closed the door. The song kicked in with more electronic beats and chords as Jade wondered what Katie was trying to avoid. She pushed the thought to the back of her mind, thinking if Katie wanted to share what was going on with her, she'd have done it by now.

It had taken Katie an hour to get ready and Jade waited by reading some of her library book, while the Avicii song finished and the playlist ran on. They both agreed to walk since the restaurant was only a few blocks from Jade's place. They stepped into the slightly chilled early evening air, the Avicii song stuck in both their heads. The sun had not set yet and the unseen feel of spring, with all of the promises it brought, touched every space and aspect of the beach town. Walking up Wilmington Avenue toward their destination, there were a mix of restaurants and hotels which aligned both sides of the two-way street, most of which were just re-opening for the new summer season.

The two ladies arrived at the restaurant about a half hour or so after it had unlocked its doors for the day's business. The two shared a bottle of Pinot Grigio over dinner and didn't speak much as their appetites – and the good food – kept them from any serious conversing but rather just occasional small talk. However, the silence didn't linger too long. The clanking of their forks upon their empty dinner plates became an unorthodox start bell to carry on conversation.

"So, what did you think?" Jade asked.

"Ohmygod! *Soooo* good! And you *work* here!? Man, I'd get fat."

"I highly doubt that. If I can do it, you could do it."

"I don't know. I've been so stressed lately, my appetite rages on me every day and I just wanna pig out."

"Well, the big day will be here before you know it. Then you can relax and pig out all you want."

Katie took a big swig of her wine, gulping down the last of it.

"By the way," Jade continued, "how is the wedding planning going? Is Bryan helping you or is he trying to stay as far away as possible?"

The exuberance in Katie's face rapidly deteriorated as if there were an open drain at the bottom of her chin and all trace of happiness had just ran down through it. Sadness now crinkled her nose, drew the corners of her eyes tight with tears coming out, and made her lip quiver. She tried her best to remain stoic but the mix of alcohol and the mere mention of her fiancé's name betrayed her fortitude. Katie looked out the side window as if there were some strengthening distraction to keep her from breaking down any further.

"Katie," Jade's voice grew concerned. "What's wrong?"

Katie tried to talk but talking would only cause her voice to crack and the foundation would burst into a blubbery, teary mess. "Is it Bryan?"

Katie nodded, her lips sucked in as if it were the final method to keep the words and tears from exploding out. Jade reached out and grabbed her friend's hand, holding it steady but gently, and that was all it took to tear down Katie's faltering strength. A short, silent cry escaped and her face caved in, tears streaming down her cheeks.

"What happened?" Jade asked.

"Jade," her voice escaped as a cry more than a normal tone of voice, but it was not so high-pitched that others in the restaurant could hear. "I don't know what I'm gonna do."

"What's wrong?"

"Bryan," Katie caught a breathy sob. "He's," another breathy sob, "cheating on me."

Katie remembered where they were and wrangled in her hysterics so people wouldn't stare. She drew in a deep breath and slowly, evenly released it, then placed her palms to her cheeks and wiped away the tears.

"Oh, Katie." Jade fretted, genuinely not believing this was happening to Katie ... of all people. Jade looked at her friend as one of the kindest, funniest, most generous people she knew and Katie certainly didn't deserve what Bryan had done to her. Then again, Jade knew more than most that very bad things happened to very good people more times in this world than what would be deemed as fair.

Katie decided she had cried enough on the drive down so she took a deep breath, pushed out the air in her lungs as if she were evicting any remnants of sadness within her entire body, and ran a slim finger over each eye to dry away the tears. Her once smooth, young face looked as if she had abruptly aged ten years as her skin stretched tighter at the corner of her red eyes, causing deep lines, which looked just this moment as if they had sunken in a bit. The skin on her hands had contracted just enough so anyone who noticed could see veins and bone, and Jade noticed the missing engagement ring – its only trace of having existed a thin tan line stretching around the base of its former home. Katie began moving her thumb and pointer finger over where the ring had once rested and Jade didn't know if she were doing it from habit or if her friend had seen her staring.

"He," Katie cut herself off, afraid she may burst out crying again at any second. She looked down at the tabletop and blew out more sadness in one continuous exhalation. "He ... came home one night and ... I was planning the seating arrangement and ... he just sat down and told me."

"What did he say?"

"He told me he was sleeping with someone else, some girl from his work." Thinking about it made her shudder in disgust as she continued to look downward as if she were some small child trying to explain away being caught doing something they knew was wrong. "The way he talked. He was just so damn blasé about the whole thing. He told me he had been sleeping with her since before we were engaged. I asked him why he proposed to me if he was cheating on me and he said he thought us being engaged would make him stop." A single sob escaped her lips. "But it didn't.

"I asked him if he loved her and he said no. He said he loved me. I asked him how many times he slept with her and he couldn't even look me in the eyes." Katie's anger had overpowered her sadness as her voice seethed, "He couldn't even *tell* me, Jade, 'cause they had done it *so* many times."

Katie raised her head and made eye contact with Jade. Jade hoped her friend wasn't looking to her for advise as

Jade hadn't had to worry about serious guy problems in a long time. She searched Katie's eyes and the only thing she could see was desperation. Eyes pleading, *What am I gonna do?*

"I came here to tell you personally that the wedding is off."

"I am *so* sorry, Katie." Jade took a hold of both her friend's hands and tightened her grip. "If there's anything I can do, I'm here for you."

"Actually ... there is something you can do."

"Name it."

"I need a few days to lay low. Stay away from him and New York. The city has become full of ghosts, apparitions of the two of us appear everywhere I go. I can't deal with it."

Katie's explanation made Jade take notice as she knew a thing or two about ghosts, memories too painful to endure. All Jade had wanted during her tough times was a shelter from the storm too.

"You can stay with me," Jade said.

The downturned corners of Katie's mouth gradually turned upward into a relieved smile. "Really?"

"Of course. The couch is a pull-out bed. Stay as long as you need."

"I promise it'll only be about a week or so."

"Don't worry about it, you goof." Jade smiled to assure her friend she was sincere with her decision. She wanted to be there for Katie, and having some company for a while may be nice; she could show her around.

"I think I need another drink," Katie smirked, noticing her glass – and their bottle – was empty. She looked to Jade's glass and it was half full. "I'm gonna order something a little stronger, if you don't mind."

"Go for it," Jade said, a smile cracking wider across her face.

Katie waited for their server to get closer to their table and she ordered a cosmopolitan – a holdover from her enduring obsession with *Sex and the City*. The two had bonded over their mutual love for the HBO series; however, whereas Jade somewhat moved on after the series finale and the films, Katie still watched at least one episode every other day. Jade believed Katie was almost trying to assimilate her life to that of the show's protagonist, Carrie Bradshaw.

"I thought ... life with Bryan would not only be this great adventure but that it'd be a nice way of settling down. With the man I love. I felt comfortable with him. My life felt stable ... in a good way. I felt safe.

"But that's all bullshit. His commitment was bullshit." Katie took both of Jade's hands again and looked straight into her eyes to convey her sincerity. "Don't ever just settle for *any*thing, Jade."

Jade felt that her friend was usually joking when she did and said things like this, but this time was different. This time, Katie was anything but joking. Her eyes burned with an intensity of which Jade had never seen before. "Find something that keeps you excited and is mutually beneficial to you and the world, and do it as much as you can."

"I think you've had too much to drink," Jade joked.

"I'm serious! I know you of all people understands what I'm saying. I mean, you left your job in the city and moved here. Now you're doin' what makes you happy."

Jade smiled but her silence alerted Katie.

"You *are* happy, aren't you?" Katie asked.

"Sure, but ... I'm not exactly sure what I want to do. I love teaching. Working here is fun too. But I really have been getting into something lately that I love to do. The only thing is ..." Jade silenced herself and waved off her thought in embarrassment.

"What?"

"Well ... it's just ... I've really been getting into photography lately."

"*Whaaat?*" Katie's voice jokingly raised an octave. "I didn't know you were into anything creative like that. When did you start getting into photography?"

The truth was that since she had moved to Delaware, Jade had not just taken a liking to and practiced photography, she also taught herself how to play the guitar, started painting and dabbled in pottery when she could get behind a potter's wheel at the Rehoboth Art League.

"I actually got into it back in New York, while I was still working for the firm. I had just lost my eighth case, I think, and I decided to walk home." Jade could vividly picture that day in her mind as she reminisced about it with Katie. "I was told to leave early ... I guess because the higher-ups didn't want to see my face around the office for the rest of the day. On the way home, I decided to take a stroll through Central Park. The sun was starting to set and I saw this section of sky just above the tree line. It looked beautiful. I didn't have a professional camera." Jade laughed at the thought of it. "All I had was the camera on my phone. I knew it had different styles and ... I figured it was better than nothing, so I took a picture. It wasn't much, it certainly didn't look very special ... but ... it was enough to get me hooked. The next day, I went out and bought myself a Canon and I've been hooked ever since. It's hard to explain but ... I felt this tremendous ... satisfaction?" Jade said as if she wasn't sure satisfaction was the right word. "I had never felt that before, not even in practicing law. It was like some wonderful, euphoric drug I couldn't get enough of. I don't know if the picture was any good – or what people would think of as good – but it made me feel ... happy. Fulfilled. It gave me bliss.

"I went home and found some photos of this guy's art. His name is Andy Goldsworthy. Have you seen any of his stuff?"

Katie shook her head.

"Oh, he's so great! He only uses items found in nature to build these pieces of art, then takes pictures of them. It's amazing." Simply describing Goldsworthy's art and thinking about it got Jade excited, but she quickly calmed again. "I'll have to show you some of his stuff. He's what cemented my interest in wanting to get better at photography."

Katie was sipping on her Cosmo, half in a daze, because she had never felt what Jade was trying to explain. "OK, so, how come you never told me before ... or never showed me your stuff!?"

"I don't know." Jade's bashfulness bunched in her shoulders and arms. "I'm still just starting out. I just haven't thought to show anyone yet. It's not like I'm intending to do it for a living. Right now, it just makes me happy."

"I wanna see some of your pictures. Show me when we get home! Please!"

Jade was unsure as to whether she honestly wanted to show Katie her work or not, but, for the sake of argument, she acquiesced. "Sure."

"I don't think I've ever felt that way ... about anything."

"You are a really good writer. You mean to tell me you don't feel that way about writing?"

"No. Yes. I don't know," Katie flinched from her own confusion. "What's so great about writing anyway? It's not like some talent you can show off."

"A writer is a powerful thing to be."

"How's that?"

"Ever heard the expression 'the pen is mightier than the sword?' Think about it. Words leave a much deeper scar than any bruise or cut ever could. I mean, cuts heal. But a really well-written reply can scar for life. Or, if it's inspiring, can instill a priceless amount of hope in someone's life."

Jade's interpretation surprised Katie. She had never felt that way about writing before. It came easy to her all her life, and the only time she thought about becoming an actual writer, a novelist, was when she first entered high school. However, when her parents told her to pick something more practical and a job which would make more guaranteed income, she quickly dismissed the idea. Katie thought that maybe there was something when it came to trying to turn her silver-tongued publicity blurbs into an actual story. It was too much to think about now, and she couldn't be bothered to make room for it with all her thoughts about Bryan and that mess. She shrugged it off and continued to work on her food.

Soon after finishing their dinner, Katie paid the bill and they decided to move up to some seats at the bar. They hadn't noticed how busy the place had gotten and were lucky to find two empty stools down near the end, next to one of the kitchen entrances.

"Hey, ladies," Sprenkle's voice greeted them, followed by a black cocktail napkin sliding down on the bar in front of each of them. "How's it goin'? Jade, it's your night off and you're here? We can't get rid of ya."

"Guess you can't," Jade smiled, going along with his joke. "Matt, this is my best friend, Katie. Katie, this is my boss, Matt."

"Nice to meet ya, Katie," Sprenkle reached out his hand.

"You too." She shook his hand.

"What can I get you two?"

"I'll have another Cosmo," Katie said.

"You know me," Jade smiled.

Sprenkle brought out the bottle of Pinot Grigio and was about to pour it when Jade noticed the epiphany strike his brain. Sprenkle put the wine bottle away without explanation and placed three highball glasses on the bar.

"You want one, Frost?" Sprenkle asked as if he were questioning the air.

"No, thanks," Tom said. He was sitting a few seats down the bar from them, nursing a dark amber drink which looked like a Manhattan. Jade was surprised at herself for having walked by him and not noticing him, although they weren't exactly what would be considered as friends.

She leaned forward into the bar and raised her voice just enough to be heard among the growing background chatter coming from the full tables. "Hi, Tom."

He looked toward her and she noticed for the first time how sad he looked. It wasn't a conspicuous sadness but subdued. Nevertheless, Jade noticed it. Maybe that was some weird special talent of hers: to pick up on when someone was upset.

One by one, Matt grabbed a glass and filled each one half full of draft beer.

"Tom, this is my friend, Katie," Jade said. She waited for Katie to say hello back but she was busying watching

Sprenkle, who soon slid one to Jade, another to Katie and held the last one for himself.

"First, before any more drinks, let's take care of this," he said, holding up his glass. "Cheers."

The ladies clanked their glasses against Sprenkle's. "Cheers," they both said. The three of them downed their beer shooters, with Jade taking the most gulps to get all of it down. Sprenkle collected the glasses and went to work on their drinks. By this point, Katie had a heavy buzz going on and her expression revealed it.

"Oh, Jade," Katie turned to her in excitement. "We should go out tonight! I mean, out bar-hopping."

"What are we? Twenty-two?"

"Let's go to that town you told me about. What is it? Dewey?"

"Yes. Dewey Beach." The last thing Jade wanted to do was go to Dewey. It just wasn't her scene. "I don't know, Katie. That place gets too crowded for my liking."

"Aw, c'mon!"

"Trust me, it's just one big party without the payoff of actual fun."

"Don't be such a stick-in-the-mud!" Katie's expression turned to resemble a hurt puppy dog, looking into its master's eyes with a sad, "please love me" look. "*Pleeeeaaase!*" She then stuck out her lower lip to add some extra pout.

Jade had to laugh at the melodramatic, pathetic pleading. She opened her mouth to answer when a familiar voice interrupted.

"Hey, Jade," the man's voice said.

She turned around and saw Jimmy, the guy from Dave & Skippy's, standing behind her. He looked especially attractive tonight; she could tell Katie was burning holes in him from staring at his tanned muscles, straight dirty blonde hair, and piercing blue eyes.

"Oh, hey, Jimmy," Jade said. "What are you up to tonight?"

"Not much. Just about to go out with some buddies of mine. Thought we'd stop by here and pre-game it."

Despite her current attractive looks, Jade's experiences when she was younger humbled her and prevented her from currently thinking too highly of herself. She had endured insults, alienation, and being ignored for so long she sometimes wondered whether she was exactly what they called her. Although she was still humble, she had come a long way since high school and college; she knew she wasn't the worse of what her peers had called her – from terrorist to dyke to slut. She did, however, currently take pride in identifying herself as some of the names which once seemed embarrassing but were so true: dork, geek, nerd. Nowadays, most people gladly carried those same monikers, but there weren't many of them in her age range in this part of Delaware.

"Where are you heading out to tonight?"

"Probably Starboard. Do you ...," he looked around her to see Katie sitting beside her, "and your friend want to come along? Hi, I'm Jimmy."

Katie shook his hand. "Hi! Katie."

"Oh, Jimmy," Jade said. "I don't know. I think Katie and I ..." A swift, subtle kick to the back of Jade's calf cut her short, letting her know Katie's stance on the matter. "... Sure. Why not?"

Then she remembered Tom still sitting down the bar, looking lonely. She leaned forward again and called out,

"Hey, Tom. Would you like to come out with us to Dewey?"

Tom turned their way and flashed a sad smile, said, "No, thanks," and turned back toward the bar.

"Great!" Jimmy said. "Mind if we join you until we all leave?"

"Sure," Katie answered for her.

"Awesome," Jimmy said. He ordered some drinks from Sprenkle, introduced his two guy friends to Katie, and when he got his beer, he turned to Jade. "Damn. Is that him? Is that the guy whose wife was killed on TV? It looks like him."

"What do you mean it looks like him?" Jade asked. "Have you seen the video?"

"Yeah! You haven't?"

"No. If it is what you say it is, I can't watch that."

"The guy didn't do *anything*. Just stood there ... frozen. I just wonder why none of those security guards were armed. I mean, how do—"

Jade blocked out what Jimmy was saying as she worried that she was having another panic attack. In reality, she just didn't want to hear what he was saying anymore. The thought of driving into Dewey and hanging out in some crowded bar with these guys made her nervous and not anticipating the night whatsoever.

"I'm sorry, Jimmy," Jade interrupted. "I have to use the restroom. Please excuse me."

"Sure."

Jade got up out of the seat and tugged on Katie's shirt to get her attention.

"Excuse me," Katie told one of the guys and she followed Jade back to the bathroom. They both stepped inside the single restroom and closed the door.

"I don't know if I wanna go out anymore tonight, Katie."

"Aw, c'mon. It'll be fun!"

"It's just ... I've got a bad feeling about this."

"What? *Why?*"

There was no easy answer for Jade to give Katie with which she would understand. It was just a feeling, as noticeable as a splinter sticking out of her palm.

"Isn't that Jimmy your friend?" Katie asked. "I think he likes you."

"Yes, I know him. But ... it's just ... I didn't really ... want to be in a crowd tonight. I mean, I didn't really want to hang out with those guys tonight."

"Oh, I'm sorry!" Katie's buzz made her gush with extra sympathy. "I thought you'd want to hang out with him. I just didn't want you to say no on my account."

"It's OK."

"Do you, though?"

"Do I what?"

"Like him? I mean, you either like him or don't like him."

"Jimmy is just a friend. To be honest, I haven't thought about it."

"There's not much thought to it. You just know whether you do or not."

"If you're asking how I feel at this exact moment, then he's just a friend."

"Fair enough. We don't have to go."

Jade felt bad that she was keeping her best friend from going out and needing a much-needed fun night out. She figured she could go outside of her comfort zone for one night – especially since Starboard wasn't too crowded this time of year.

"No. I want you to have a good time. Let's go."

"Really!?"

"Sure."

"Thank you!" Katie's beautiful smile beamed. She gave Jade a quick squeeze and the two stepped out.

When they returned, Jimmy and his friends were still talking. Jade noticed Jimmy pointing out an unaware Tom to his buddies, most likely telling them all about the tragedy and going on the same diatribe she had just avoided.

Jade stopped at where Tom was sitting as Katie continued back to the trio.

"Hey," Jade greeted.

"Hey," he said. "So ... headed to Dewey?"

"Yeah."

"Sorry. I overheard."

"No worries. I'm not exactly thrilled but Katie needs a night out." Jade was trying to stretch out the conversation – if anything, just to prolong her time away from Jimmy and his friends. "So did you find a place around here?"

"Yeah. Down near Made Ya Look."

"Oh, you're in the Forgotten Mile."

"The *what?*"

"Forgotten Mile. It's what the locals call the one-mile stretch of Route One between the bridge and the entrance to Dewey."

Tom had grown up, and lived, in the area for quite a long time but he had never before heard of that stretch of land referred to that name by anyone. Maybe she was screwing around with him, but, for now, he'd take her word as gospel.

"Wonder why they call it that?" Tom asked to nobody in particular.

"It's because—"

"Hey, Jade," Jimmy called out. "You ready?"

"Yeah," she sighed, a hint of exhaustion. "Well, if you change your mind, we'll be at the Starboard. Good luck with the place."

"Thanks. Good luck with ... tonight."

Jade stifled a laugh, threw up a hand in a still wave. "See ya, Tom."

"See ya."

"Frost," Sprenkle said. "You need another drink?"

"No. Think I better call it a night."

"You sure?"

Tom didn't know whether Sprenkle's tone regarded having another drink or passing up on Jade's invitation.

"Sprenkle?"

"Yeah?"

"You think I should meet up with 'em?"

"What's that saying? 'You miss a hundred percent of the shots you don't take.'"

"Yeah. I'll see ya."

"See ya!"

Tom got Sprenkle's answer, but he was still unsure. He looked at his watch, it was nearly midnight. His stomach decided he was hungry so he drove out of downtown Rehoboth and headed north on Route One until he reached a Wawa quick stop. The place had become a refuge for those seeking late-night munchies, smokes or whatever else one needs before the long trek home.

He was especially hungry so he ordered a turkey club and he swore the lone girl making the sandwiches rolled her eyes as soon as she saw the request come across the order screen. He was lucky there weren't too many people in the place yet. It was still about an hour until last call at the bars, which is when the flood of people would come spilling through the doors, looking to absorb the alcohol filling their bellies.

Tom realized he was happy being out for the first time in a long time. Maybe it was the slight buzz he had going, but he felt free. He felt so free that he decided, against his better judgment, to go to Dewey and see if he could catch up with Jade and her friends. His former self – the young guy he was before Maggie – would have been too unsure of the situation, and himself, to make such a bold leap as to meet up with people he hardly knew. Now he was a new man. Maggie's death had baptized his new life. He hadn't asked for it but there it was. And he was going to make the best of where life had taken him. He got in his Jeep, turned up the volume on Alice in Chains' "I Stay Away," and headed to Dewey.

By the time he reached the town limits of Dewey Beach, Tom was beginning to think this was a bad idea. The speed limit of the highway drastically slowed to thirty miles per hour upon entering the small town that was only about a mile long, making it a formidable speed trap for locals and tourists alike. He noticed a couple of town police cars stationed on each side of the highway and a paddy wagon parked just outside of the very bar he was going into: the Starboard. The first thing he saw was the big sign with a cartoonish great white shark jumping above the bar's name in yellow letters, and below was an electronic board to announce daily bar specials and the upcoming musical acts.

The one-story bar, which also functioned as a restaurant, was situated on the corner of Route One and a small side street, with a small parking lot in the front just big enough to fit maybe five or six vehicles. The right side of the establishment looked like a normal eatery, long plywood boards painted blue with single, white-framed windows lining the front and around the side, while above the windows hung a banner announcing the bar's famous breakfast specials – the only standout was the giant great white shark's head crashing out of the space above the sign and windows. To the left side of this was a deck covered with a long blue-and-white-striped awning, which connected to the main part of the establishment where the bands also set up to perform for the nights, as well as a separate little area for official merchandise. The place had slightly grown since Tom last visited it, with a smaller bar entrance on the far left end. While the place was busy, it was nowhere near the capacity it would reach in summer once the tourists and college seniors returned to mix upon the locals. Because there weren't too many people in Dewey for the season, and some had not moved into their summer houses yet, he knew he could drive down one of the small side streets and find a parking spot.

Tom pushed himself with every step he took. As he got to the end of the street, he could hear the muffled music emitting from his destination. Then he heard a few young guys shouting, *Yeah!* This sound made him immediately turn on his heel and head back to his Jeep. He had made a terrible mistake coming here. He thought, *What was I thinking!?* Jade was just being nice by inviting him, but he doubted she or her friends actually wanted him there. For him, a practical stranger, to just show up? And what if someone recognized him? No. He was better off going back home. He reached his driver's side door and heard a faint voice calling out.

"Tom!"

He figured it was just some drunk young woman calling out for her boyfriend up on the sidewalk which fronted the highway. He opened the door and heard it again.

"Tom!"

Tom turned and saw two people at the end of the street. The two were holding up another person in-between them and Tom wasn't quite sure who would be calling out his name.

"Tom!" the female voice came again. This time, Tom recognized Jade's voice.

He locked his door, closed it, walked up to meet the group, and saw Jade and Jimmy holding up Katie. The scene reminded him of that late 80's comedy movie *Weekend at Bernie's*, where Jonathan Silverman and Andrew McCarthy have to hold up their deceased boss and pretend he's still alive. Tom would have laughed had the faces of Jade and Jimmy not looked so serious.

"Hey," he called out. "What happened?"

"We got kicked out," Jade said. "Katie's had too much to drink."

Tom looked to the girl hanging between them and saw a smile grace her face. Katie slurred as if someone were holding her tongue in place while she tried to talk, "Those guys were just a bunch of party poopers."

"We're lucky those cops back there didn't take us in," Jade said.

"Oh, Jade," Katie pouted as she perked up, planting her feet solid on the ground to stand on her own, then looking from Jimmy to Jade. "I ruined your date. I'm sorry."

Jimmy just smiled at the notion while Jade's face reddened a bit from embarrassment, knowing full well this was anything but.

"You didn't ruin anything," Jade said. "Let's just get you home."

"Always taking care of me," Katie said. "This girl is a keeper."

Jade turned to Jimmy. "Could you please give us a ride home?"

"No problem."

"What about your friends?"

"It's cool. They'll be fine."

"Tom. Could you please help us walk Katie to Jimmy's car?"

"Sure."

"It's right up this way," Jimmy said, pointing to the other end of the street.

The two men lumbered forward with Katie held up between them, an arm over each of their necks, looking like some old snapshot Tom had seen of Army guys in World War II helping a wounded buddy off the battlefield.

Jade walked alongside Jimmy, who seemed more interested in conversation with her than holding up his half of Katie's weight.

"So, Jade," he said. "I was thinking maybe we could go out to dinner sometime this week."

"I don't know, Jimmy. My schedule is kinda hectic now ... especially with Katie staying with me."

"You don't have to entertain me," Katie chimed in.

"Which one is your car?" Tom interrupted.

"Oh, the black Ford F-250." Jimmy nodded his head toward the end of the street and Tom saw the long, extended flatbed truck with a cab in the back for passengers.

"Here. Let me," Tom said, then arching to the side, stiffening his back and scooping Katie off her feet to hold her like a prince carrying his princess to "happily ever after."

"See, Jade!" Katie shouted as Tom quickly walked ahead of them. "I told you I'd get a ride!"

Katie's cackling laughter could still be heard as it got further and further. Jade was pleasantly surprised to see this man they just met genuinely taking care of Katie. Seeing Tom carry her best friend made him OK in Jade's book. Jimmy lifted his key fob and pressed the unlock button twice, flashing the lights on the truck.

"So, how about it?" Jimmy turned to Jade as they continued to walk toward the truck. "You? Me? Tomorrow night?"

"I can't tomorrow. How about next Monday?"

"Sure. Sounds good."

"Good."

When they reached the truck, they saw Tom was still holding Katie. Jimmy jogged over to the truck and opened the doors for them.

"OK," Tom said. "Here we go." He carefully lowered Katie's legs to the ground, still holding her under her arms. Her head swung around and when her neck connected with his shoulder, her chin leaning over it, she vomited all over his shoulder, with puke cascading down his back.

"Ohmygod!" Katie said. "I'm so sorry!"

Jade and Jimmy stood in shock, until Jimmy broke out a laugh. Jade smacked him in the stomach and whispered, "It's not funny."

"It's OK," Tom said. He looked Katie in the eyes to convey his sincerity. "It's OK."

He saw her mouth gasping for small bits of air and he knew she wasn't finished yet. He grabbed her side, held her hair back and she puked again, this time with the sick painting the road.

"Sorry, everyone," Katie said, her voice weary.

Tom looked at her and could see some vomit on the corner of her mouth. He grabbed the bottom of his shirt and proceeded to wipe the mess away.

"I'm sorry about your wife," Katie's weary, drunk voice blurted out with genuineness. Tom stopped wiping, and Jimmy and Jade could hardly breathe.

Tom looked at Katie and even though he had only met her a few hours ago, he could tell she was being honestly sympathetic. Only Katie could see that Tom's eyes briefly became covered with a thin layer of tears before they quickly dried up again. It seemed like everyone was waiting to see what Tom would do next.

Tom thought it very much ironic that this woman's drunken apology was the first sincere-sounding apology he had received since Maggie's death. Everyone back home and in public seemed to only want to assign blame to someone for her death. He didn't think it would make a difference but it did. It was a touching moment and Tom took it in.

"It's ... OK," he said, then releasing a flash of a small smile. "Thanks." Her words touched him more than he thought or could show. "Let's, uh ... let's get you home, OK?"

Tom helped Katie into the back cab of the truck and made sure she buckled her seatbelt before closing the door. He turned to Jimmy. "Are you OK to drive?"

"Yeah."

"Thanks, Tom," Jade said. "I'm really sorry about ... the ... puke."

"Believe it or not, not the worst night I've ever had."

Although Tom wasn't referencing what had happened to his wife, that was where Jade's mind wandered to and her sympathy transformed her smile into a sullen glare, with her not being able to make eye contact with him.

"Well, thank you."

"Get home safe," Tom said, raising for a frozen wave goodbye as he turned around and walked back to his Jeep.

He couldn't believe he had said that and expected anything *but* the way she reacted. By the time he reached his vehicle, the smell of the puke on his shoulder and down his back was beginning to turn his stomach so he took it off and dropped it on the ground. He felt stupid and awkward for saying such a thing, and was happy to be calling it a night. He sat himself in the driver's seat and looked into the rearview mirror at himself.

"Idiot."

17.

"And in my heart there are these waters
Where I put you down to lay
While I can learn to live with it,
Until I'm free"

--The Gaslight Anthem
"Keepsake"

Tom had soon grown to despise his new residence.
Wait. No. That was wrong. It wasn't the house he despised.
It was being cooped up inside all day that he despised. Up
until this point, Tom had felt quite comfortable with staying
indoors, away from anyone in the area who may notice him
and call the media. It had been almost a month since he
returned to Delaware and, as far as he knew, none of the few
people he had come into contact with had given him away.
Sitting on his couch, his knee repeatedly jittered up and
down and there was no doubt he'd go crazy if he didn't get
out of that house and do *something*. After his little adventure
last night, he figured it was time to start wandering into the
land of the living. The first step was to get a phone. He had
left his cell phone back in L.A., and had no way of
contacting his parents (unless he went to visit them) or Bob
or anyone. Tom had tried his best to go as long as possible

without such a device; not because he wanted the internet or the bells and whistles which were attached to it, but more because he was afraid the media would somehow get a location on him and make another circus around his new home. He balanced the idea of the media tracking him versus being able to call on family and friends. It only took about two minutes to decide that family and friends had won. He grabbed his car keys, took the top off his Jeep, and drove north for the first phone store he could find.

He found one not far, in-between the main entrance road to Rehoboth and Route One, across from a huge water slide park called Jungle Jim's, which looked a lot different from his youth when the place was simply called the Sports Complex. The six tube water slides were an improvement over the former three. Since he moved away, he almost missed seeing the water park come alive on Memorial Day weekend, finding kids and adults of all ages trouncing up the hill to go down the many slides, and families playing the gratuitous vacation round of mini-golf. Across the highway were a variety of stores, one of which was the phone store he was looking for. When he came out with his new smartphone, he looked across a side distance to the side of a coffee shop called The Point and saw Jade coming out of the main door. He was surprised for having noticed her as she looked almost unrecognizable, wearing a pair of round, tortoise-shell glasses resembling the ones Gregory Peck's Atticus Finch wore in the film version of *To Kill a Mockingbird*; her dark hair was put up into a ponytail with a charcoal newsboy cap covering most of the top of her head; a pair of brown corduroys; and a dark blue t-shirt with a distressed Superman symbol on the chest. He was a little surprised to see her out and about after last night.

Tom continued to his Jeep, not thinking she would see him, but as he opened the door, he faintly heard his name being called out. He turned and saw Jade walking toward him, a smile on her face.

"Tom!" She caught up to him. "How's it going?"

"Good. Just figured it was time to finally get a new phone. Connect to the world. I haven't had one since I got here. What are you up to?"

"Picking up some coffee for Katie. She's a little hungover this morning."

"Oh, yeah," Tom let out a small laugh. "I figured. But, hey, we all have those nights at some point."

"Yeah." Jade's smile faded to a serious expression. "Listen, Tom. I ... I wanted to thank you for last night."

"For what?"

"For helping with Katie. I'm glad you showed up when you did."

"It's no problem."

"Did your shirt make it?"

"No. Sadly, it was a casualty," Tom joked.

"Oh, no," Jade spluttered out a laugh. "I'm sorry."

"No. You kidding me? Don't worry about it. It's just good to hear your friend's OK."

"She's been having a rough time lately. I don't want to give away any of her personal business, but just trust me when I say she needed to blow off some steam."

Jade was worried she was sounding melodramatic but she didn't feel it was right to tell a practical stranger her friend's business, and Tom respected her loyalty and conviction.

"No worries," Tom said.

Jade still felt a tad bit of sympathy for him, but, more than that, she felt gratitude for how he helped her and her friend. She thought about how he seemed like a good guy. If things with his wife went down the way people were saying they did, and she was pregnant at the time, he must be facing down some unfathomable life questions.

"Well, thanks," Jade said. "I guess I'll see you around."

"Jade. Could you do me a favor?"

She nodded her head.

"I could use some kind of work. If you hear of any job openings – I mean, *anything* – could you let me know?"

"Sure," she turned to go then turned back. "Wait. How do I get in touch with you?"

"Oh, right." Tom walked over to her. "Let me give you my phone number."

He had to look at the provided phone number as it was still new to him. He quickly thought twice about giving her his number because he wondered if she might tip off any inquisitive media as to his whereabouts. But, ultimately, he thought, *What the hell? She seems like a trustworthy person. If I can't learn to trust* some *one, how can I expect to share a life with* any *one?* Tom told her his new cell phone number and she entered it into her phone.

"OK," he said. "I'll see ya around."

"See ya," she smiled as she watched him turn to go. He seemed to live an awfully lonely life and she couldn't help but think of how it must feel to be new in town and not have anyone to talk to. She thought about when she first moved to Rehoboth and all those times back in school when people ignored her, how she felt so alone and hoped someone would reach out to her. She opened her mouth to say something but no words came out. Her face made a pained expression as if she were agonizing over whether to speak up or not.

"Listen," she said. "I'm getting hungry, and it doesn't look like Katie will be up and moving any time soon, so I was going to go grab some lunch or something. Wanna come along? I mean, after I drop this off to Katie."

Tom wasn't sure if she was feeling sorry for him or simply attempting to thank him for helping last night, but either way, he was lonely and any kind of human interaction was welcome.

"Sure."

"Good. There's this place a little south of here called Hammerheads. But it's not the one in Dewey. It's called Dockside, right at the inlet."

"The inlet?"

"Yeah. Do you know where the Indian River Bridge is?"

"Oh, yeah. Where exactly is Hammerheads?"

"If you take the last right turn before the bridge, you'll wind around and soon see it straight ahead. It's where the docks are."

If this were Manhattan, Jade would have avoided this man she had met just a week earlier; but in Rehoboth, the game *Six Degrees of Separation* was an easy one to play – nearly everyone was connected in some way or another. She knew Tom was friends with Sprenkle and Feltz, and after his helping her and Katie last night – despite their being strangers to him – she figured he was probably a good guy. Besides, they were going to go to a public restaurant in the daytime. Unlike a majority of her peers, Jade was careful to be too curious as to Tom's past and the tragedy which seemed to be a part of nearly everyone's conversation. She had picked up bits and pieces of what happened to Tom's wife on his reality show, and it was enough to piece together a full picture. What Jade knew above all was that one should not judge others or assume they know the entire story based on word of mouth because facts often had a way of kowtowing to popular opinion. All that interested her were facts and the only place anyone could get Tom's full story was from Tom himself.

"When should I meet you there?"

"If you can, you can head there now and I'll meet you there."

"OK. Thanks, Jade. This means a lot."

"You helped me last night. I at least owe you this."

Tom didn't think she owed him anything. He was just doing the decent thing.

"So I'll see you in a bit," Tom said.

"Sounds good."

Tom got in his Jeep, started up the engine and the middle of My Chemical Romance's song "Fake Your Death" blasted out of the speakers. He pulled away and noticed Jade watching him so he gave her a wave. He took the highway through the busy town of Dewey before it quickly became a long stretch of highway and tall grass with water on both sides. It was a beautiful sunny day and the straight road was open with hardly a driver upon it. With the top of his Jeep off, he enjoyed the wind whipping through his hair, the sound of the seagull cries and the smell of the salty ocean air, which was probably his favorite smell as it had a strange way of rejuvenating him. He filled his lungs with as much of it as he could take in and, for the first time in a long time, relished his life. He had happiness for a few seconds before hearing the next song playing on the radio – "Glycerine" by Bush.

He remembered Maggie. It had only been six months but he was already feeling happiness. Tom felt as if he were betraying the memory of his dead wife simply for feeling something other than misery.

* * *

"You're probably loving this, aren't you?" Maggie asked, reaching to Tom's car radio and turning down the volume on the same song. Tom could still faintly hear the music but Maggie's tone drowned out any enjoyment he was just feeling.

"Why would I not be? The network picked up my show!"

"I'm happy for you, Tom," she said in a tone which in no way matched her sentiment. "But, the type of show you're planning on doing? Don't you think it's kind of ... I don't know ...," she thought of the best way to phrase it without offending him, "low-brow?"

Tom's jovial mood turned solemn and Maggie could tell her attempt had failed. She waited for him to say something, anything. Gavin Rossdale sang with an accompaniment of a lone electric guitar, violins and a cello:

> *Could have been easier on you*
> *I couldn't change, though I wanted to*
> *Should have been easier by three:*
> *Our old friend fear, and you and me*

When Tom's silence had gotten to be too much, she spoke up. "*Great.* Just don't talk - like you usually do!"

"What do you want me to say? I thought this'd be a great night for us." Tom's tone grew tight and more serious. He clenched a fist as if he were about to slam it down on his steering wheel but instead unclenched it and very slowly slapped it on the wheel. "I *really* wanted it to be a great night. Why can't you just be happy?"

"About what!?"

"I'm finally making it. We're making it. You've got that job at the hospital. Everything's falling into place the way we planned."

"I wasn't even really talking about that, Tom."

"Then what were you talking about!? 'Cause I'll be honest, Mags. This back-and-forth shit is really getting on my nerves."

"What do you mean 'back-and-forth?'"

"First, you tell me you want to be here just for me and support me in my career. Then you talk about wanting your career too and I say go for it. Then you tell me the house I pick isn't good enough and you'll take care of it, and I say go for it."

"You're going to bring that up *now!?*"

"Then, after the house, you tell me you need something more," Tom continued his rant. "When I ask you what, you tell me you don't know and leave it at that. And now, I've finally landed what I've been trying so hard to accomplish these past few years and you think it's ...," Tom tried to get the words out of his mouth, as if speaking them would cause an immeasurable amount of pain throughout his body, "... low-brow?

"I mean ... is that what you think of my work?"

Maggie rolled her eyes and released a heavy sigh. "I don't mean it like that."

"Then how *do* you mean it?"

"I want ... I want .... I want to be a part of something special. And I want that for you too. I want you to do something ... truly remarkable."

"And this isn't *special!?* Creating, hosting and producing a show *isn't* special!? That's not *remarkable!?*"

"You wanna know the truth? No! It's *not.* It's *not* special. It's *not* remarkable. What you're doing is ... it's ... insignificant."

The word hit him a lot harder than "low-brow" and left a hole in his chest. Maggie could tell she had seriously wounded him. The song was the only noise to cut the awkward silence.

Tom could not think of another time when he had been angrier with Maggie. He knew he wasn't saving lives in the same physical sense she was with her career, but that gave her no right to disrespect him for the choices he was making to give them a better life. For once, he just wanted an apology from Maggie. He wanted to hear an "I'm sorry." It was a sentiment he found that he had said a lot, but he had only heard her say it to him maybe once or twice since they had first known each other. The most notable was when she drunkenly apologized about Tom seeing her with Alex back in college.

Tom knew he wasn't perfect, but he also knew she wasn't either and there were plenty of times she could have apologized to him. But it never happened. It was as if Maggie was completely oblivious to, and incapable of, uttering anything resembling an apology – and it hurt their relationship. He often found that women in his love life who did or said things which often gave cause for an apology were the ones to least likely do so.

Tom thought giving the silent treatment would convey to her just how angry he was with her, but he had learned early that giving a woman the silent treatment was either a surefire way to backfire on you as she would play the same game, often going the distance with silence; or would just give her more ammunition to ultimately turn it back around on you.

"That's a really shitty thing to say to me," Tom spoke up as he turned off the radio.

"It's no less shitty than jumping down my throat just 'cause I'm being honest."

"You were the one who told me to go for it when it came to my career. And, now, what? You don't approve of the show!?"

Maggie sat silent, the sound of the speeding tires providing white noise, as the car sped smoothly along the highway as if it were on a monorail. Tom looked to the road ahead then back to Maggie and noticed she had started to silently cry, a single stream of tears running out of the corners of her eyes.

"What's wrong?" Tom was concerned.

"I need more, Tom."

Tom's mind panicked and his body wasn't far behind. He thought she must want a better life – something more than he could give her – and it was very likely that she wanted a divorce. He opened his mouth to speak but couldn't find the words. Then she spoke for him.

"I ... I've been asked by the hospital administration to be one of three doctors to lead up an on-site drug abuse rehab clinic. I've been having a tough time making the decision 'cause I know it would drastically cut my hours I get with you at home. But I think it's for the best.

"I've already looked over the files," she said, drying her eyes. "The first patient is this heroin addict, Nick. I feel like these people could really use my help."

Tom's anger took a backseat to his concern. "Wait. Drug rehab? What do they want with a cardiothoracic surgeon when it comes to helping some drug addicts?"

"The administration feels I'd be a good reference to the effects drugs have on someone's heart. These are people that need help, Tom. Just like you described to me about the people you'll have on your show. I know I can do good with this."

"Well, are you gonna be safe? I mean ... you're not gonna be dealing with any violent people, are you?"

Maggie could tell Tom's concern for her was genuine and she couldn't help but crack a small, sideways smile at the thought of it.

"Some of them, maybe," Maggie said. "But they're not gonna have guns or knives or anything on them. We'll be seeing them during their stay in rehab. The entire thing is safe, overall. I looked into it already."

With that, there wasn't much more to say. Tom could've come up with all kinds of concerns or petty comebacks, but he figured he would be the better person here. If Maggie wanted to do this rehab clinic, then who was he to stand in her way? If she needed more in her life to make her feel accomplished, then he would be there for her by supporting her.

"If it's truly what you want to do, then you should do it."

"Really?" Maggie was stunned but there was a tinge of hope in her tone. "You're OK with it?"

"It's what you want, isn't it?"

Maggie slowly nodded her head as if she were afraid he would lash out in a rage if she gave the wrong answer. "Yes."

"Then it's what I want too. For you."

Tom looked forward to the road, and could see out of his peripheral vision that she had cracked a hopeful smile and looked forward too. They were on a road home and hopefully into a better future for them both. Tom felt her warm hand slide over his hand on the stick shift and he couldn't help but smile just the same as his wife.

* * *

Tom pulled into the big parking lot shared by Hammerheads and the marina. There were boats of all sizes lining the docks, most of them placed in a seasonal timeout until a few weeks from now when they would be let loose to play in the nearby waters. He parked as close as he could to the restaurant and smelled the blend of salt water and fresh-caught fish which often accompanied docks. A mid-sized tabby cat poked its head out from behind a dock post, spying in search of any leftover fish scraps lying around which would make up its next meal.

Most of the small establishment was made up of the outside seating area. Beyond the entrance was a seating area to the right with about four to five picnic tables under a big pergola; and to the left was a medium-sized pergola with regular small tables and chairs set underneath. An inlaid brick walkway separated the two sides which were covered with sand, leading to the stormy blue restaurant building, where the left side was cordoned off with a guard rail for outdoor seating under its tiny overhang and the right side had a small outside bar. Music speakers set up around the outside of the restaurant were blasting a quarter of the way through Trampled by Turtles' fast-tempo alternative rock, bluegrass song "Wait So Long."

There were already a few people along the outside L-shaped bar as the aroma filling Tom's nose changed from salty fish to grilled meat and spices. Tom decided to stay at the outside bar until Jade arrived, so he pulled up a bar stool and ordered an iced tea. The bartender asked to see if he wanted a menu and Tom said sure. His thinking about Maggie had made him feel uncomfortable and wanting to speed back to his place and hide the rest of the day. He asked himself, *What's the point? You're not ready for this. Not ready to move on with other people.* He already had enough issues – not just from Maggie, but also his supposed friends back in L.A.: Dylan, Lucia, Jen. He had trust issues with all of them and he wasn't sure opening himself up to Jade or anyone here was the right move.

Tom took out his new smartphone and sent a text to Bob, giving him his new phone number in case Bob had to talk to him about the sale of his stuff or any other issues. He thought about asking his attorney for any updates on Maggie's parents, but decided against it and hit the send button.

"Is this your first time here?" a man's voice asked.

The bartender put the iced tea in front of Tom, who looked to his right and saw a guy, slightly older than him, sitting a couple of seats down. The guy had short, dark brown hair, a heavy five o'clock shadow and bright, light blue eyes which looked like small swimming pools. He wore dark grey shorts which came down to his knobby knees and covered his thick, pasty white thighs, a pair of black flip flops which looked like they had seen their end a year ago, and a dark blue t-shirt with big block print words "Big Damn Heroes" made out of light blue spacey sky, forming a picture within the letters. In the "B" was the titular spaceship from the cult TV series *Firefly*, and in the bottom right-hand corner of the words were silhouettes of three characters from the show striking a *Charlie's Angels*-type pose. He was slightly rotund although not noticeably yet, and looked to be alone.

In Tom's business on the show, there were two types of people: the "mark," who was the person his investigators were tailing as well as the person who was believed to be the cheater; and the "vic," short for victim – because the crew couldn't very well call a person a victim to their face or within hearing distance – who was the person being cheated on. These vics were usually nice people who didn't deserve what had happened to them (if their significant other *was* indeed cheating on them) and their harmony with the workings of people was often viewed as naïve or fiercely affable to a fault. That was what this guy seemed like: fiercely affable to a fault.

"Ye-yeah," Tom said, flashing a short smile to the man and turning back to the menu.

"*Every*thing is great here."

"Thanks."

"If you like seafood, you *gotta* try the fish tacos! I cannot recommend them enough! So damn good."

The bartender came up to Tom to ask him if he had decided yet. Tom told him he'd have the fish tacos and the bartender approved his selection with, "Good choice."

"Trust me, you won't be sorry," the vic said. Tom gave a single nod of thanks. "My name's Will." The man held out his palm and Tom was hesitant to grab it. He didn't know this guy from anyone and no one had ever approached him so blithely. Tom felt like this guy was trying too hard to befriend him. Maybe he was a reporter or some kind of investigator. Either way, Tom wasn't sure if he wanted to open himself up to such a risk, and there was no polite way to tell a nice person to get lost.

Tom grabbed the man's hand and shook, quickly considering giving the guy a fake name but deciding against it. "I'm Tom."

"Hey, Tom. You live around here?"

"No."

"Yeah, didn't think you looked familiar. Just visiting?"

"I actually just moved back."

"Oh, you lived here before."

"Lewes, actually, yeah."

"Oh ... well, welcome back! What brings you back?"

"Just visiting family for a while." Tom tried to keep his answers as short and non-descript as possible, just in case this guy was a reporter.

"Well, welcome back!" Will took a swig of his Leinenkugel's Summer Shandy beer. The spastic charge of guitars and fiddles gave way to Bradley Nowell's booming voice starting out Sublime's "Same in the End." "Are you staying in Lewes?"

Tom was becoming more and more convinced that Will was a reporter. If not, he was the most inquisitive person Tom had ever met. He considered getting up and moving to the inside but it was a beautiful day and he didn't want Jade to think he stood her up. He kept his seat and threw caution to the wind.

"No. I'm actually living near Made Ya Look."

"Oh. You're in the Forgotten Mile."

"Yeah. Someone just told me that last night. What's with that name?"

"It's called that 'cause it's where a lot of people come to forget."

"Forget what?" Tom asked, his voice full of curiosity.

Will spit out a single laugh. "I'm just screwin' with ya! I thought you said you were from around here? Locals know about the Mile. Well, most of 'em, anyway."

"Honestly, I've lived here most of my life, but I swear I've never heard of it."

"It's just called that 'cause it's the last mile of Rehoboth that most people tend to forget about. As you're driving south, it's right after you come over the bridge, so nobody really notices that stretch of road."

"That's *it*?"

"Well ... yeah. Some locals have their own reasons for why they think it's called that, but that's the truth. It's actually quite nice. Sure, the highway has its usual traffic, but, during the summer, when the area is usually jammed full and crazy with tourists and part-timers, the neighborhoods there are pretty ... serene."

Before he hosted his TV show, Tom had always been cautious of people who were so eager or open and willing to speak to strangers. When it eventually became necessary to be open and inquisitive with the vics featured on his show, Tom had to force himself to be loquacious and open with his guests.

"So you live around here?" Tom asked.

"Yeah! I rent a place in Rehoboth, but I work down in Bethany. At the comic book shop."

"From around here?"

"Nah. Moved here from New Jersey about ... thirteen years ago. Haven't looked back since."

"Hey, Tom," Jade's familiar voice sounded behind him.

Tom twisted around his upper body to see Jade coming towards him. She still had on the same hat from earlier, but this time, her hair was cascading down, and her glasses had been switched to contacts. She had also changed her outfit into a denim skirt and a heather grey t-shirt with the distressed graphic of the official NASA logo on it.

"Hey," Tom smiled back.

"Hey, Jade!" Will said.

"Oh! Hi, Will!" Jade said as she gave him a hug in the form of a brief squeeze. "Good to see you! What are you up to today?"

"Day off. Just figured I'd have an early lunch." He held up his beer.

"OK." An endearing giggle escaped her. "Will, this is Tom. Tom, this is Will."

"Oh, we've already met," Will said. Jade looked to Tom, who gave an assuring nod. "I've been telling Tom about the Forgotten Mile."

"You didn't tell him that lame explanation about it being where people want to move to forget, did you? It's not Neverland, Will."

Will smiled wide and Jade had her answer. She had to look away and shake her head at Will's insistence at continuing to tell that unfunny anecdote.

"There's no truth to that," Jade told Tom.

"I told him the true reason! But I wouldn't discount my explanation so easily," Will said. "I bet some people are there for that very reason."

"If you say so," Jade patronizingly said. She turned to Tom. "Did you order yet?"

"Yeah. Fish tacos per Will's recommendation."

"Ah, they're *so* good!" she said. "That's definitely what I'm getting!"

The bartender came, took Jade's order and went back to put it into the kitchen. Will looked at his watch and said, "I gotta go. It was good seeing ya, Jade. Tom, nice to meet ya! Let me know how those tacos work out for ya!"

"See ya, Will," they said in succession as he did a little jog to the parking lot.

"Sorry it took me so long," Jade said. "I had to tend to a sick friend and change."

"No problem," Tom said. "I've never been to this place. It's great back here."

Jade felt as if she couldn't admit the other reason she was late. She really did have to change clothes and help Katie, but she also had a panic attack when she got into her car to come here. Usually she would just cancel her plans and go back into her house for a few hours until she felt comfortable again; but this time something was different. She didn't want to stand Tom up.

"Yeah. One of my favorite places," Jade smiled. "You really haven't been here in a long time, have you?"

"Never really had a reason to come back."

"I doubt that. Didn't you say your parents live here?"

"Yeah," Tom's tone was solemn and Jade knew, from the way he said it, what he was trying to get across to her. She remembered back at the rental office what he had said about his dad. She could see his relationship with his dad was broken. After the conversation she had with her mother yesterday, it was a feeling with which she could relate and sympathize.

"Listen, I really am sorry about your shirt—"

"Don't worry about it. Besides, that Jimmy guy looked like he could've done what I did."

"Well, it was nice of you to help out a practical stranger. I just wanted to say thanks. And I brought this for you to borrow." Jade reached into her small purse, pulled out a tattered paperback copy of *To Kill a Mockingbird*, and handed it to Tom.

Tom took the book, his fingers slightly touching hers. "Thanks."

"I think you'll really like it. It's such great writing and it's helped me more than once when it came to figuring things out about life."

"That's ... kinda ironic you're giving me this 'cause I could really use some of that right now."

"Well, there you go. I hope you enjoy it." She smiled and Tom noticed how pure her expression was, how simple this woman made being kind seem.

The song over the speakers changed to Blue October's "Bleed Out," but neither of them noticed. The bartender brought out Tom's fish tacos and they looked exquisite, but he didn't want to just pig out in front of her.

"Man ... those *do* look good," Tom said.

Jade let out a giggle and said, "You don't have to wait for me if you're hungry."

"Thanks." He took a bite and he couldn't control the satisfying groan that came from deep within him, through his closed, food-filled mouth. Jade laughed more but Tom didn't care. During their conversation, he would steal away as many bites as he could.

Once he swallowed, Tom said, "Will was right. They *are* damn good."

"Yeah, they're one of my favorites."

"I have to admit. I'm a little surprised you wanted to meet up."

"Why?"

"Well ... I don't know. You don't know me very well. I guess not many people would be so ..." Tom tried to think of a word that wouldn't insult her but would rather sound more complimentary without sounding tacky. The best he could come up with was, "... nice."

He could tell she was trying to think of something to say and he was afraid it wouldn't be good so he quickly added, "I really appreciate it. Thanks."

"You can't be that bad if you're a friend of Sprenkle and Feltz. After all, I was gonna eat anyway. Might as well have some company."

Jade's attempt at being nonchalant made Tom smile just as much as her generosity did. Then the thought hit him that this was the first time in a long time that he had genuinely smiled.

More than the tragic accident with his wife, Jade wondered what issue Tom had with his parents. She could always google the accident to view many different opinions and explanations - as well as actual video - of the event if she wanted; but she had no way of knowing what was going on with his parents. However, she dismissed the curiosity as it wasn't any of her business and admitted to herself that the only reason she was curious in the first place was because of her own issues with her parents.

"Did you see that the sequel to *Mockingbird* is coming out this summer?" Tom broke the silence.

"Yeah! But she wrote it the same time she wrote *Mockingbird*. I cannot *wait* to read it!"

"That good, eh?"

"Are you kidding? It is one of the best books ever written." Jade thought a second about what she was saying and backtracked a bit. "Well, maybe I'm overhyping it, but *I* think it's one of the best ever written."

"How's that *Shutter Island* working out for ya?"

"Like I said, I don't usually like those kinds of books, but I have to admit it's really drawn me in. I'm always looking for something new to read so Browseabout is one of my favorite shops around here. Oh, and if you're in Lewes, there's the cutest little shop called Biblion. Definitely check it out if you get a chance!"

Every local person who grew up in Sussex County, Delaware, knew about Browseabout Books. The independent book store had once been small but expanded over the years, taking up two stores worth of space. Tom knew both Browseabout and the other local book store, Bethany Beach Books, were two of the most beloved stores in the area by locals and tourists alike. But he didn't know about Biblion, so he made a mental note of taking her advice.

The bartender brought out Jade's food and she had no qualms about taking that first bite, joining Tom with his meal. She swallowed her first bite and asked, "So ... have you talked to your parents lately?"

"Not yet. Now that I've got my phone, though, I'm going to. Just not sure I want to."

"I hear ya."

"So I'm not the *only* adult with parent issues?" Tom sarcastically asked.

"No!" Jade feigned shock, then she got serious. "They thought it was a mistake for me to move here."

Jade realized she had not had this conversation with a lot of people - let alone someone she had only seen a few times. Whether there was something about Tom or she was simply growing more comfortable and confident with her own situation, she didn't know the reason; but she was going to just go with it.

"Why'd they think that? If you don't mind me asking."

"I was a lawyer - a financial lawyer - before I moved here."

"Really!? Where?"

"New York City. And trust me when I say the city was *not* for me."

"I know exactly what you mean."

"Yeah ... well ... my parent's didn't. They still don't." Jade felt she was saying too much. The scared, insecure teenage girl she had once been possessed her and made her grab her glass to take a long drink from her water.

"So how long have they been ... that way?"

"Since I moved here ... two years ago. They wanted me to stay in New York and keep practicing law."

"What made you want to stop?" The second Tom had asked the question, he regretted it. He worried he was overstepping his bounds with someone he had just met. He intently watched her, trying to get a read on what she was thinking.

"I think the best way to try and describe it is that old Maslow quote. What is it? 'What one can be, one must be.' Don't get me wrong. The world needs financial lawyers. Being a financial lawyer is great ... *if* that's what you truly want to be. I realized it wasn't what I wanted to be. I wanted to make a different kind of impact on people." She let out an afterthought of a laugh at herself. "My parents called it a crisis of conscience ... as if having that was some kind of bad thing. Maybe that *is* what happened to me ... but I'm happy it did."

There was something so enchanting about Jade; listening to her talk and watching her mannerisms, Tom knew she was the kind of woman who men just fell in love with just by talking to her. Love, or any kind of romance, was the furthest thing from Tom's thoughts, but he felt a connection with her. Listening to her thoughts on her former job was as if she were speaking how he had felt about the TV show shortly before the incident with Maggie. Despite his simpatico feeling, Tom wasn't feeling the urge to share in his experiences. It was one thing to commiserate over a career, but to admit to a stranger that you helped get your wife killed was another.

"Well," Tom said, "... you're not the only one who's had that kind of crisis."

Jade knew Tom was talking about his wife and the TV show, and she was just as curious as anyone would be when it came to what was now going on in his life, what he was thinking. Jade knew finding a countless variety of opinions, suppositions, and commentaries on both sides of the spectrum of Tom's tragedy was just a click of the mouse away, but personal experience had taught her firsthand that those opinionated voices from overpaid talking heads were mere dreck and the only voice – the only opinion – that mattered was from the person directly affected. She didn't know that Tom was interested in hearing about her issues; it kept him from focusing too much on his own problems.

"I love my parents. But I'm almost thirty and it's as if my father still doesn't respect or trust my choices."

"I think your dad and my dad should go bowling," Tom said. "My dad thinks if I don't believe in what he believes in, I'm wrong, I'm naïve. I have to admit ... I'm just happy to hear I'm not the only one who still deals with this kind of bullshit."

Jade couldn't help but chuckle at Tom's honesty, putting him more at ease and feeling like he could open up more to her.

"You know what I find most aggravating?" Jade asked. Tom shook his head. "The fact that from the time we're kids, first going into school, we're told we can be anything we want to be. The sky's the limit. Anything is possible.

"But when we get older and choose what we'd like to do, if it's not what lives up to certain people's standards, particularly our parents', we're told to be more realistic, pick something more practical, something that pays better. And if we don't, we're labeled as immature or extremely naïve or stupid."

"Yeah," Tom agreed. "It's the same hypocrisy that comes when you're raised with all these books, movies, music, and even lessons from our own parents, family, and teachers constantly drilling into our heads that we need to be kind to others, apply the 'golden rule,' don't fight, don't hit, clean up after ourselves, be accountable, apologize for our mistakes, and to share and not be greedy. But the minute you become an adult, those rules seem to go out the window. Everyone thinks their way is the better way, the only way, and if you don't believe what they believe in or act how they would act, you're wrong. A lot of people call you something they think of as degrading just for trying to do what was drilled into your head when you were a kid.

"But those people don't really matter in the long run. It's inexplicable, but, in the long run, it's how your *parents* view you as what becomes your main concern."

"Yeah. Why *is* that?"

Tom looked her in the eyes and shrugged his shoulders. "Don't know. All I know is I'd probably die of shock if my old man honestly admitted to me that I was right about something and he was wrong."

"Aren't we a bit old to be talking like this?"

"Definitely."

"I look at my friends and most of them seem to get along great with their parents. I know everyone has their own issues, not all of them get along with their parents, but they seem to be ... satisfied with what they do, who they are. And so are their parents."

"Yeah, but don't you think that's just an act? I mean, deep down, I think most people have that one thing that makes them feel like they're not living to their full potential."

"Sure, they do," Jade said. "That's not what I'm getting at. I guess what I'm trying to say is that, for me, I feel like there's some kind of crucial life experience most people my age go through that I didn't. Or maybe I forgot to." She looked to Tom and noticed he was trying to figure out what she was saying. "I mean, I had a normal childhood. I wasn't spoiled but I also wasn't deprived of anything either. I know my parents love me ... overall. It's just that they have a twisted way of showing it. I guess I don't know what is missing. All I know is that something is."

"I know what it is for me."

"What's that?"

"Respect." Tom cracked a small vacant smile after hearing himself. "Not to sound like Rodney Dangerfield or anything." Jade laughed under her breath at his reference. Then his serious look and tone reemerged. "Here I've graduated college, bought a huge house, a nice car, got a great job that I had to work my way up to get, gotten married ...," Tom stopped dead in his tracks, trying to decide whether he should, or could, finish the sentence. *Too soon*, he thought. He sniffed and took a gulp of pain, forcing it back down into the pit of his stomach where it continued to churn as it had been ever since Maggie's death. Jade wanted to look away at the awkwardness of the situation but her eyes remained steadily fixed on his. "There are times they say things that make it sound like they respect me. But I can tell when I'm around them, it's just not there. The way they act around me. I've carried on with my life ... with this adult life ... and my parents still can't find a way to show they respect me in *any* way."

Tom's mention of his failed marriage – and what happened to his wife – was what Jade couldn't get out of her head. It was difficult to focus on anything else. She could tell he was hurting and she wanted to hear his thoughts about it all, but she wasn't going to force him to talk about it. She also didn't want to be some hero who swooped in to try and change him or fix him.

"Well, that's one sure way to kill a good time," Tom said. "Let's talk about our deep-seated issues."

"There's nothing wrong with some meaningful conversation. It's a breath of fresh air compared to some of the conversations I've been having lately."

"Yeah, but how do you recover from that? I mean, it's not like I can immediately transition into 'what are your top five favorite movies of all time?'"

"*Amélie*, the original *Parent Trap*, *The Shawshank Redemption*, *Groundhog Day*, and *The Mirror Has Two Faces*." She spouted the titles out in one long breath as if she had had them memorized for years, having to give no thought whatsoever. She examined Tom's expression, a steady mix of awe and puzzlement. Then she added, "In no particular order."

"Wow. That was fast."

"I just know what I like. What about you? Favorite movies – c'mon, let's hear 'em."

"That's a tough one. I guess ... in no particular order ...," Tom thought about all the titles he could, looking up to the sky as if the list for his top five were up there. "... I'd have to say ... *Miller's Crossing* ... um ... *Tombstone* ... *Airplane* ... *Braveheart*, and ..." Tom thought and remembered the movie he had seen right before he left L.A. "... *Network*."

"See. The transition wasn't all that hard, was it?"

"Guess not. I have to say, you're movie selection is ... interesting."

Jade picked up on Tom's playful tone of thinking her picks were weird; it was a form of sarcasm she had utilized herself many times.

"*The Parent Trap* is a *very* underrated film," she said in all seriousness until a smile cracked her veneer.

"Hey, I'm not judging." Tom's smile grew as he held up both of his hands like a suspect at the scene of a crime.

"Yeah, I didn't think so."

Tom's cell phone rang, taking them both by surprise.

"Wow," Tom said. "Someone's already calling."

He excused himself from Jade as he got off the stool and took a few steps away from her earshot.

"Hello," Tom said into the phone.

"Tom?" He recognized Bob's voice right away. He remembered he had texted Bob his number right before leaving the phone store.

"Yeah. Hi, Bob."

"Tom, have you seen the news yet?" Bob sounded almost out of breath and Tom had learned that when he was asked if he had seen the news lately, it was not good news for him. His stress spiked and his pulse quickened.

"What news?"

"There was a report last night on one of those news channel's shows about you."

"Which show? The Douche?"

Bob automatically knew who Tom was talking about and corrected him. "No, the other man. The older, taller one. Jim O'Leary."

Tom knew him as one of his father's favorite commentators on that channel. "So what's he saying?"

"During his 'straight talk' segment on his show last night, he brought up your testimony in the case against the network and the show – how you said Dylan tricked you into signing the permission to move forward with production on ... that episode."

"Dylan *did* trick me, Bob. You know that."

"I know that, Tom. But O'Leary is basically saying that you're just shamefully trying to ... oh, I forget. Hold on. I printed out a part of the transcript." Tom could hear Bob shuffle around through some papers. "OK. Here's what he said. 'Mr. Frost is trying to pin his blatant, destructive negligence, which led to his wife's death, on the network, the show's producers – even Mr. Vaughn – and anyone else but himself, who is the only person truly to blame in the tragic incident.' I can't read anymore," Bob's disgust was recognizable in his tone. "He goes on and on. I think the only reason the man hasn't been sued for slander yet is because he's so crazy that he believes his own lies are truth. Unfortunately, it's not just that one news channel. All of them are picking up on the story and spinning it the same way. But O'Leary's was the worst."

Tom wanted to see the clip. He had gone without any media for a long time and hoped his story would've died by now, stored away in the annals of tragic TV history. For some reason, however, his story was still in the news ... as hard to get rid of as a case of head lice.

Jade had switched between eating her tacos and looking back to Tom to make sure everything was fine, even though all she could see was his back. He didn't seem to be talking now but trapped in thought.

"Tom?" Bob asked after a minute or so of silence.

"Yeah. Yeah. Thanks, Bob. Thanks for the heads-up."

"You hang in there, kid," Bob said with all the warm affection of a grandfather. "Give me a call if you need anything."

"Thanks. I will." Tom hung up and had forgotten where he was. All he could focus on now was seeing that video clip.

"Is everything OK, Tom?" Jade's voice was closer behind him.

He turned and saw her standing near. "Oh, yeah. I just ... I got some news from a friend of mine."

"Is your friend OK?"

"Oh, yeah! Yeah. Actually, I forgot my wallet in my car. Mind if I go grab it real quick?"

"Go for it. But don't dine and ditch. I know how to find you."

Tom smiled and went to his Jeep. He got into the driver's seat and did an internet search on his smartphone of the O'Leary video clip. He pulled it up and pressed play.

"On tonight's straight talk, I'd like to talk about the tragic incident involving the reality TV series *Heartbrakers*. In recently released testimony from the court case involving Mr. and Mrs. Russell - the parents of the victim Maggie Russell Frost - versus the network and series, producer, creator and former host, Tom Frost, testified that he was tricked by co-producer Dylan Vaughn, also his best friend, into signing a waiver, giving permission to have his own wife on the show.

"It has become obvious that Mr. *Frost* has joined the ranks of these Hollywood *lowlifes* who profit off tragedy but quickly shift the blame when their feet are held to the fire. Their absence of morality is leading to the decline of morality in the masses who watch their TV shows. We here at the show have discovered that Mr. Frost is no longer living at his current address and has moved out of state, so he has decided to slink away, shirking any responsibility for his actions." Tom was soon listening to the part Bob had read to him.

"Mr. Frost is trying to pin his blatant, destructive negligence, which led to his wife's death, on the network, the show's producers - even Mr. Vaughn - and anyone else but himself, who is the only person truly to blame in the tragic incident. Frost and others of his ilk are given a free pass by the elite liberal media and progressive movement when it comes to any crimes because they are a part of the progressive ideological machine to deliver the message that the country is in a decline. He and his Hollywood constituents help sell the image that America is morally corrupt." O'Leary's intimidating, stern voice matched his personality. "What Mr. Frost needs to do is to *shut up*," his voice boomed then lowered back to sternness, "stop telling lies which take aim at corporate business and capitalism, and take accountability for what *he* has inadvertently caused. And *that's* the straight talk."

The clip ended and Tom's stomach tightened into a knot. He didn't know anything about a progressive movement or elite media or an agenda; he was just doing a TV show. Tom closed the internet and put the phone in his center console lockbox, as if hiding away the phone would make the entire segment blink out of existence.

He looked out the window and saw Jade still sitting at the bar, eating her meal, and was unsure he could continue to act as if he hadn't just seen his name get eviscerated on national television and across the internet. He took some deep breaths then pushed himself out of his Jeep and toward the restaurant.

As he neared the entrance, the bartender came out and turned the channel on the big flat-screen television hanging over the back of the bar. The Jim O'Leary clip Tom had just watched took over the previous broadcast of a baseball game, and it stopped him dead in his tracks. The bartender turned up the volume as he, Jade and the other few patrons watched the segment. Tom wanted to turn around and get the hell out of there, but he couldn't leave Jade with his bill. So he quickened his pace, grabbed a twenty-dollar bill out of his wallet and continued to the bar.

Jade turned her head from looking at the TV to watching Tom, his expression full of shock and embarrassment. She felt as if she had been caught talking badly about someone behind their back and all she could do was keep looking back and forth between the TV and an approaching Tom. As soon as Tom got within earshot, Jade said, "Tom—"

"Hey, Jade," Tom plastered a fake smile as they could obviously hear O'Leary ranting about him. "I hate to eat and run but something just came up. I really gotta go. But I had a great time."

"You don't have to go."

Tom looked at the other bar patrons, who all looked at him without trying to be noticed. Their expressions were a mix of disdain and judgement which could not be fully described or noticeable unless you have experienced such looks before.

"Yes. I do." He put his twenty down on the bar and grabbed Jade's copy of *To Kill a Mockingbird.* "Thanks again for this and for inviting me out. I'll see ya soon."

The entire moment only took about a minute and it was a minute too long for Tom. He couldn't get out of there fast enough.

18.

"... All the memories of the days you lost
You add them up and then you count the cost
You're just a shadow of a man undone,
Another life that has just begun"

--Neulore
"Shadow of a Man"

Since O'Leary's segment, Tom became a recluse for the next two weeks, only leaving his house to make quick trips to the closest grocery store – and even then, he shopped as fast as he could, wearing a Bethany Beach baseball cap and sunglasses to minimize his chances at getting recognized. His phone had been busy, receiving text messages and voicemails from Feltz, Jade, Bob, his mother and even one message from his father, who was calling more to chew Tom out over worrying his mother more than for any personal concern for Tom.

As much as he wanted to avoid any further judgement, Tom's guilt at keeping his mother worrying outweighed any morality lectures Tom may receive from his father. He drove to their house and hadn't even made it to the front door before his mother opened it. She pushed open the screen door and held out her other arm to receive him with a hug.

"Tom! Where have you been!?"

"Rehoboth," Tom said, his voice without emotion, as if he were in shock. "I found a place to rent there."

"I've been calling your phone. It is your new phone, right?"

"Yeah. I'm sorry, Mom. I just ..." He looked up into her eyes and saw she was sad for him, but she was trying her best to hold back tears. He wanted to tell her about that day of the incident, about his jail time, about the media and public scrutiny, about Maggie, about how he felt when he heard she had been pregnant. Most of all, Tom wanted to tell his mother about how alone he had been and how he truly didn't feel he could come to his own parents when it came to anything. "I ..."

The doorbell rang and the two of them turned to see the next-door neighbor's little girl at the door, adorned in her Girl Scout uniform and holding a clipboard.

Judy smiled at the little girl and said, "Hold on, Tom. I'll be right back."

Judy's smile beamed as she opened the screen door and greeted, "Hello, Kara!"

"Would you like to buy some Girl Scout cookies, Mrs. Frost?" the little girl asked, using an extra sweet tone to coax her customers into buying her product.

Tom walked out of the living room and into the kitchen. There was no sign of his father, which made him calm. Tom could only imagine what they were thinking of him now with this latest row in the media. They had never been fully supportive of his career, and they both had loved Maggie, but he knew his mother would be more supportive than his father. He knew his journey here today was going to end in heartbreak for someone, possibly everyone. But it had to be done.

He knew before he could move on with his life, he had to confront what most young men confronted and rebelled to establish when they are in their late teens or early twenties: independence. Tom's issue had been infecting him and gestating within him for the past twenty years and he had to confront his parents now before it killed any relationship he – or they – hoped to have.

Tom noticed the red, digital number on the answering machine. There were seventeen messages on the machine. Tom's curiosity overtook him and he pressed the play button. The first message was from a week ago, from Jen Desmond, and her message was cut short when Mrs. Frost picked up the phone, abruptly cutting off their conversation. The second message was from a producer for Jim O'Leary's talk show; the very prick who had called Tom a lowlife was now calling Tom's parents to get them to do *what*!? Get them to come on O'Leary's show!? The producer's voice on the message was not the booming thunder most heard from O'Leary himself, but rather a soft-spoken man who sounded like some distant uncle who was calling to caringly check in to see how the family was doing. "Hello, this is Adam Fisher, from the Jim O'Leary show. I was calling because Mr. O'Leary was hoping to interview you both on his show. Mr. O'Leary–" Tom hit the next button, which lead to another cable news show, and another, and another, and so on.

Around the fourteenth or fifteenth message, after the introduction of some producer for a tabloid news TV show, Mr. Frost's voice came on the recording and said with an agitated tone, "I wish you people would stop calling here!

How many times do I have to tell you all that we're *not* interested!?"

"Mr. Frost. We would like to hear your side of the story. And your son's."

"So you can attack him on your show!? I know how this all works! What is wrong with you damn people!?"

"Mr. Frost. We—"

"No. We are *not* interested. And I won't tell you how to get in touch with my son. Ya ask me, all of you have been beating a dead horse. Please just leave us the hell alone."

The call clicked off, leaving a few seconds of the persistent dial tone before the machine went quiet.

Tom was shocked at his father's words. He had never heard him speak that way before – especially in his defense. Then a thought struck him like a rat trap. Maybe his parents were going through just as much a tough time since the incident as he was. Their pain was silent but just as agonizing. Tom had thought about what Maggie's parents must be going through, and he realized he had only experienced the judgement and scrutiny in the tragedy's wake from his own perspective; he honestly never thought about what his parents must be going through when it came to the media coverage. Nevertheless, his parents never communicated with him. In fact, all they – particularly his father – seemed to expound was their disapproval of his career choice and the way he chose to live.

* * *

"Visual communications!?" Mr. Frost asked with a bit of a puzzled laugh, as if his son had just told him a joke he didn't understand. "That's your ... *major*? What do you use it for?"

"What do you mean?" Tom asked. He was seventeen and had just gotten his acceptance letter from the University of Delaware. "I told you. I want to go into media production."

Tom noticed his father's expression melt from excitement to despondence. His father found the strength to ask, "What are you gonna do with that?"

"I want to produce a show someday. Maybe develop a series."

"You're gonna do that in Delaware?"

"No," Tom was annoyed. He knew he hadn't discussed his plans with his dad too many times, but he knew he mentioned it at least once. "But there's plenty of opportunity in L.A."

"Tom. Do you know how much it costs to get a start out there?"

"Yes."

"I don't think you do."

"Tom," his mother chimed in. "You really should think of getting something more ... practical." Tom was fuming mad inside, but he wouldn't dare erupt at his own parents; he had been that way since he was a child. She continued, "There are plenty of good-paying jobs around here with health benefits."

"I'll truly miss these inspirational talks when I move to Newark this fall," Tom said.

"Tom," his mom scolded. "We're serious. Your dad and I want you to really start thinking about your future."

"I have."

"You need to be more realistic," his father's rigid voice struck.

"What's so unrealistic about me wanting to get into TV production?"

"It's not – if you follow through with it."

"So you're saying I won't follow through?"

"Son, honestly, I'm just going off how you've been your whole life. You get interested in things and just when any effort has to be put forth, you still enjoy what you do, but you don't ... *go* anywhere with it."

"I've been a *kid* up to this point," Tom's aggravation and frustration was growing, and his tone revealed it. "Isn't that kinda the experience of being a kid!? To try and find what you wanna do, who you wanna be!?"

"Look," his father's voice became sterner. "If you want to do this, that's fine. But this is not some piddly little activity you can quit. This is college. It's expensive and I want you to be absolutely sure this is what you want to do. Don't screw it up."

Tom wanted to confront his father, to ask him if he screwed up, would they still be supportive and understanding. But, deep down, Tom knew the answer. He recalled from all the prior years when his father proved that failure was frowned upon, and how not being in agreement with his father's beliefs or knowledge was a complete transgression worthy of his father's ridicule and scolding.

For once, Tom didn't want to do what he had done since he was old enough to learn how to handle situations like this – which was to remain quiet. He wanted to say something. His brain shouted his thoughts to his vocal cords, and the noise unexpectedly came out.

"And what if I *did* screw up? Drop out? What if I changed my mind on my major and had to completely make up a lot of courses? Would you still be so proud of me? Would you still be supportive?"

"Oh, Tom," his father practically laughed. "Of course I would. Your mother and I are always there for you."

"*Really*!? What if I became someone you don't agree with? What if I believe in things you don't? Would you be so welcoming then?"

"You're being ridiculous."

Tom wanted to put his foot down and call out his father on the man's quickness to dismiss any serious thought or opinion Tom had as ridiculous. But he knew it would be pointless and this confrontation was only going to go around in circles. He looked to his mother and she sat in silent resignation.

"And you're being an asshole."

Tom hadn't said that out loud, but his mind, driven by emotion, was screaming it. All he could do was take himself out of the situation before he did say something he might regret, so he left.

The rest of the school year and the summer working at Funland raced by without either of them mentioning their quarrel. Before any of them knew it, Tom was packed and on his way to college. He may have left behind his parents, but his unresolved issues with them followed him there and had remained with him ever since.

* * *

"You didn't think he'd tell them where you were, did you?" his mother's soft voice broke him from his memory. She stood, leaning against the door frame to the kitchen.

Tom kept his back to her. "Honestly ... maybe. Yeah. I don't know what he's thinking."

"Then talk to him."

"Yeah. 'Cause *that* always ends *so* well!"

"You never talk to him."

"I tried, Mom. Remember? When we talked about my major after I got accepted to U of D?"

"You're still fuming about that?"

"Why wouldn't I!? We never resolved anything!"

"Judy!" Mr. Frost's voice broke up the moment, making Tom's body go rigid. "Is Tom here?"

"Yes, Tom," she called back.

His father slowly walked into the room. "Where've you been, Tom? You had your mother worried sick."

"I found a place in Rehoboth," Tom said.

Mr. Frost could tell by the uncomfortable silence that his son and wife were in the middle of something. "What's going on? What're you two talking about?"

"He heard the messages, Tom," she said.

"Hell," Mr. Frost mumbled.

"You asked me where I've been," Tom said. "Where have *you* been?"

"What are you talkin' about?"

"Back in L.A., I was alone. Maggie was dead. I lost everything. And where were you?"

"Your mother tried to call you—"

"But what about you, Dad!?"

"When she told me you weren't picking up, I figured you were too busy feeling sorry for yourself and wanted to be left alone. So that's what I did. I just thought you wanted some time alone."

"Well ... maybe I did need you. Maybe I needed you both real bad. I could've gone anywhere when I left L.A. I should've gone somewhere no one knows me. But I didn't. So why do you think I came here?" Tom grew silent for a few seconds as if his anger were running out of steam. His parents both contemplated the last question, and they knew the answer. They knew he was looking for support. Tom's anger exploded again as he thought of more to say. "Ya know, you've always been so quick to dismiss me whenever I don't agree with you, whenever I say something you think is ludicrous. In fact, if I don't agree with your opinions, your feelings, your outlook on anything – politics, media, religion, *any*thing – you think I'm some dumb kid!"

"That's because you're being dumb!"

"I'm thirty-two years old, for Chrissakes! Can't you respect me as a man!? The man *you* raised!?"

"I'm just trying to teach you the right way of things, son! Parenting doesn't come with a manual, ya know? And it certainly doesn't ever end. Even when your child is an adult."

"This is different. This goes beyond just being a parent." Tom thought for a couple of seconds, and his voice grew solemn. "It feels like you're trying to turn me into someone *you* want me to be. Not who *I* want to be. Or who I am."

"Tom, I—"

"No! Do you know how it feels when I just *try* to speak my mind about ... anything ... and you *berate* me!?"

"I don't *berate* you."

"It feels like you don't respect me."

"I *do* respect you."

"No, you *don't!* You don't. You should hear yourself when I say something you think is wrong. You laugh at me like I'm so naïve. I mean ... did you ever think that maybe I'm right? Or maybe, even if you think I'm wrong, I'll discover my own way?"

"You shouldn't have to discover your own way. That's why I'm here. To tell you. Especially when you're wrong. Besides, part of being an adult, being a man, is knowing that people are going to disagree with you."

Tom was beginning to understand that, in his father's own twisted way, he meant well. When it came to topics and know-how Mr. Frost thought Tom should know, he wanted to guide him through life without the hardships of having to find his own way. However, to Tom, that had done him nothing but a disservice when he was younger and now, at his age, his father's method was backfiring. Tom didn't feel like his father was lovingly guiding him, accepting of him or respectful towards him.

"I know you think you're doing me a favor by trying to teach me your way. By pointing out when you think I'm wrong. But the way you do it ... it's degrading ... and ... it's disrespectful." Tom's drive was waning as his father stared him down and he looked away to gain more strength, taking it in like a deep breath before going underwater. "Maybe I should have been more vocal about our differences when I was younger, in the moment. And maybe I'm being this way now 'cause I didn't when I was younger, when most kids do it. Either way, I'm saying it now. I'm a grown man now. And it doesn't matter if I agree with you on politics or sports or any damn thing. I'm a good person.

"When I instinctively give my seat up to a woman on a bus who's struggling with her baby and stroller, it's not because of who I voted for in some stupid election, or who I pray to - or if I believe in anything to pray to at all. It's because I'm a *good person*.

"And, to me, that's a hell of a lot more important thing to be in this world than any of your beliefs."

"You still don't understand," Mr. Frost said. "It's different when you're a parent."

Tom looked down and shook his head, almost laughing at his father's incredulous behavior. His father acted as if he hadn't heard him just pour out his heart.

"Did you know she was pregnant?" Tom broke the silence. "Maggie. She was pregnant."

"Oh ... Tom," his mother's breathy voice sounded.

"I don't even know if the baby was mine or if it was ..." Tom couldn't finish the sentence because the thought of the baby being that murderer's was too much for him to bear. "But she's gone now. And so is ..."

"Tom," his father sounded as if he were trying to get his attention, get him to stop.

"I think I would've been a good dad. I just ... I wanted to wait and have a baby until after I had finished the current season of the show. Knowing now that Mags knew she was pregnant. How she must've felt when I acted the way I did ..." Tom sniffed as a thought crossed his mind. "I should've been more present ... instead of just ... being on autopilot."

"You had no way of knowing," Mr. Frost said.

"Well, that's easy to say and I can think that over and over ... but it doesn't make it anymore easy to actually believe. What has been racking my brain is trying to figure out why something like this would happen to her ... and to me. I wondered if it was the way I lived. I mean, I'm not some bad person or anything, but I wondered if it was because what I did in my work. Exploiting others' pain. Or maybe I wasn't being a good enough person ... in general, I mean.

"But these past few months, I think I've discovered why. It has nothing to do with any of those things. It's not just my fault. It's hers too. What happened is on both of us.

"I can easily say, *oh, this is my fault, I drove her to that asshole's arms*. But the truth is ... I tried to be the best husband I could be. I really did try. I never hit her or yelled at her. I did things around the house, I cooked. But I'm sure I still *did* drive her away. I didn't exactly share myself with her. I may have provided financially for her, but emotionally ... I never shared what I was feeling or thinking 'cause I was too damn worried that if I pissed her off enough, she'd get fed up with me ... with who I was, and leave me. Stupid, huh? Still ... what you fear, you create.

"I may have driven her away, but her sleeping with that asshole? That was her choice. Sometimes I get so angry, so full of rage, I wish she were still alive just so I could scream and yell at her." For the first time in his life, Tom wished he could cry. Maybe then some of the pent-up sadness, which had stuck to his insides like freshly spit chewing gum on hot pavement, would be expunged. The pit in his stomach maybe could be filled again. But the tears had dried out long ago, so the pit remained agape and bottomless. "We were like a perfect storm ... which is a pretty shitty way to describe a marriage."

Tom's rant had left his parents speechless. Outside their windows, the world carried on with lawnmowers buzzing, birds chirping, kids trying their best to win at their bicycle races, and local mariners breaking in the new season by taking their boats out of the nearby docks and into the canal. Seeing his father quiet and his mother with a river flowing out of each eye was what he had tried to avoid his entire life. Tom always figured that if he caused them any pain, worry or sadness, he was not a good son. It wasn't something that they had ingrained into him; he honestly didn't know where he had gotten the idea from and had just chalked it up to some expectation he had put on himself growing up.

"I ...," Tom tried to search for the truth. He wanted to get everything off his chest. He wanted to come clean – not so much for his parents' sake but for his own sake. "I did everything I thought was right. But Maggie's dead. My career is over. I've got to ... find some way to ..." His words failed him and all he could do was use his hand in a sweeping motion as if it would help him get the correct term out. "... get through this." He looked to his mother then into his father's eyes and his voice strengthened. "But I'm trying. I haven't given up."

"What do you need from us, Tom?" Mrs. Frost asked. "How can we help ... make things better for you?" Tom turned to face her.

"I just need you ... to be patient with me." Then he turned to his father.

"And I need you to be more understanding."

"What do you mean understanding?"

"I mean ... be a little more accepting of our differences."

"I'm accepting."

"Haven't you been listening? You think I'm some naïve dimwit just 'cause I don't agree with you on something. I may or may not believe what you believe in. I may not have the same viewpoints as you on certain things. And I may not know what you know. But I *do* know *some* things – like truth and loyalty and tolerance and empathy. You both taught me those things. And I'm thankful for that.

"I know I'm gonna make mistakes, and there's no way you can prevent that. You may think you're helping me by trying to press onto me your knowledge and what you think is the best way to live life. But it's not helping. The way *you* do it? It only makes me feel like I'm not living right and I don't live up to your standards. What you do only pushes me away. It has been for years.

"So you're gonna have to trust me to be the man I want to be. I'm your son. I'm a *good* person. But the way you react to me when I oppose anything you believe in, it makes me feel like I'm not."

"Why haven't you come to me like this before?" Mr. Frost asked.

"I've tried, Dad. But whenever I've spoken out on something you don't agree with, you chastise me and talk to me like I'm some stupid kid."

"I don't chastise you!"

"You do! And I know it's not just me. You do it to a lot of people. To you, anyone who doesn't agree with you is wrong. And you laugh at that and take pride in it. But it's not funny to those who feel their opinion or belief is just as important as yours. It's not funny to me.

"When you're offended, everyone should take you seriously because you think your way is the right way. But when others are offended, you say they're wrong and laugh them off as if they don't know what they're talking about."

"Since when did you get so indignant?" Mr. Frost asked.

"*Me?* Indignant? Maybe it's been from all the years I've kept quiet ... or maybe I got a little of it from you. I don't know." Tom took in a deep breath. "And I should have said all this to you years ago. I just ... didn't ... I couldn't."

"What can I do?"

"I'm not expecting you to completely change. Just ... treat me with some respect."

"I do respect you, son. And you're right. You *are* a good man." Mr. Frost walked closer to Tom, then put his heavy hand on Tom's shoulder. "And I love you."

Tom slowly nodded his head, taking comfort in his father's reaction.

"I was just doing what I thought was right for you," Mr. Frost said.

"I know. And maybe that's why I never spoke up before now."

His father grabbed him and slowly pulled him toward him, giving him a tight, awkward hug.

The two of them pulled away and Mrs. Frost moved closer to her son and gave him a hug and kiss on the cheek. "I love you, son."

Tom gave her a bigger hug and held on as if his life depended on it.

"What are you going to do now?" Mr. Frost asked.

"I've been thinking about that a lot lately," Tom said, delicately backing away from his mother's embrace. "I actually thought I could get my foot back in the door at some production company. A network. Something.

"But, talking just now, admitting out loud that my career is over ... I think I've just been fooling myself. Hell, I don't know if it's what I *want* to do anymore."

"Who says it's over?" Mr. Frost asked defiantly.

"The news, the public, and basically all of the networks."

"Screw 'em! You'll find something. After all, don't people like a good comeback story?"

Tom smiled and shook his head at his father's meager attempt to inspire him, then earnestly said, "I just hope I didn't let you down."

"Of course you didn't," Mr. Frost said. "You never have."

19.

"In just a glance
Down here on Magic Street
Love's a fool's dance
I ain't got much sense but I still got my feet"

--Bruce Springsteen
"Girls in Their Summer Clothes"

Three weeks had passed since Tom spoke with his parents and in that time, he had heard from Bob, who told him he had sold Tom's house, his car and all of his stuff back in L.A. Now that Tom had money, he knew he could rely on the money for a little while before he needed to start seriously contemplating a job. A few days before his conversation with Bob, he had sat down and brainstormed about what kind of potential jobs might be a good match for him. Being in Delaware left no televised media choices save local news, and L.A. was a definite no-go; Tom had no desire to move back west. Having felt more of a bond with his parents after his cathartic confrontation, he asked them if they had any career ideas. His father asked if he wanted to stay in the area or move away. Tom was open to both ideas, but neither of his parents had any viable options.

Now it was already Memorial Day weekend. Tourists and part-time residents had begun to swarm the area, sending Tom into even more of a reclusive way of living. Most of the people he had met or reconnected with had stayed silent and kept their distance from Tom since O'Leary's broadcast, and Tom was happy for it. Then the phone rang. Tom looked at the caller ID. Feltz. He pressed the "accept" button.

"Feltz. How's it goin'?"

"Frost! What's up, buddy? What are ya doin' today?"

Tom looked at the yellow steno pad, a few lines with his handwriting of career suggestions all scratched out. "Nothing. Why?"

"Good. You're comin' out!"

"Comin' out where?"

"It's Sunday Funday, man. We're goin' to a few bars!"

"Whoa! I don't think so, Feltz. I just can't be going out all over the place—"

"Why not?"

Tom found it hard to believe that Feltz didn't know of his predicament by now, but, if he didn't, Tom didn't want to have to say it to him. "I ... I ... just can't."

"I know, Tom."

"Know what?"

"I may live in Delaware ... and this may be 'slower lower,' but I'm not *completely* out of the loop."

"Then you know I can't just go out bar-hopping."

"Why not?"

"Feltz, the last thing I need is some random stranger taking a picture of me at some bar, posting it and having a media circus set up shop around here! I moved here so I could get *away* from all that."

"You worry too much. Besides, we can go somewhere low-key. Maybe Shorebreak?"

Tom thought of Jade and how she had seen O'Leary's segment, right there in front of him. For some inexplicable reason, her seeing the segment, more than anyone else, was completely embarrassing to Tom. He didn't want to see her. Not yet, anyway.

"No. How 'bout someplace else?"

"We could go see Love Seed. They're playin' at Paradise Grill."

Tom knew the band Love Seed Mama Jump. They were a six-man rock band from the area that Tom had first seen when he was a senior at University of Delaware. He had used a fake ID to get into a show at the Stone Balloon bar one Thursday night, and from that point, he had become a part of the huge fan following. The last time he had seen them was in Dewey Beach, the summer after he graduated college, and he got to get up on stage with them and sing background vocals to their cover of The Rolling Stones' "Sympathy for the Devil." As much as he would like to see them now, he wasn't in the mood to go to a party-like atmosphere and he was still too worried about being recognized by someone. He could mentally picture the headlines now: *TV Reality Show Host Seen Dancing, Drinking Less Than a Year after Wife's Death!*

"Or we could hit up the jam session at Bottle and Cork," Feltz further suggested.

"Ah, Feltz, no ... no, man ... no, thanks. I can't. All it takes is one asshole to recognize me, take my photo, post it to the internet, and the talking heads will have more ammo to judge me. They'll invade this place, and I can't ... I can't go through something like that again."

"I know you're goin' through a tough time ... but ... you just can't do what you're doin'."

"What's that?"

"You can't just show up here and make things only on your terms, ya know?"

"I ... honestly didn't think I was doing that."

"What else would you think? I mean, you don't come back here for, like, almost twenty years! Then, when you *do* come back, you only pop up when it's convenient for ya."

Tom was dumbfounded by Feltz's small outburst, but he couldn't blame the guy. Tom *was* taking advantage of the quiet state, and not exactly being a good friend or even a decent acquaintance.

"I didn't think—"

"Yeah," Feltz said solemnly. "You didn't think. Listen, I get it. I get wantin' to hide away 'cause of what happened on your show. And I don't pretend to know what it's like to lose someone like that.

"But you gotta get out there, man! I'm not trying to ... be insensitive or anything. But ... she's dead. You ain't."

"What do you think I should do?"

"I think you should live. And it doesn't have to be goin' out to bars and shit. I know it ain't for everyone. But ... be in the world, man! Don't just hide away, lettin' your life pass ya by."

"You're right. My brain knows you're right. And I'm getting there. I just ... I can't today. How's that?"

"That's better."

Feltz didn't want to push Tom anymore. He had said his piece, and he knew as easy as it was for him to advise Tom to just say "Live," it was another thing to be the one who actually had to do it after such a horrific event.

"Thanks, man," Tom said.

"No problem. But just remember what I said. You livin' like you're dead ain't gonna justify *her* being dead, 'kay?"

Tom thought about that for a few seconds. "Yeah. OK."

"Just give me a call if ya need anything."

"Thanks."

Tom hung up the phone and began wondering when his life may ever be at least somewhat close to normal again. The months he had spent mourning over Maggie had displaced him from life, and it had been easy for him to pore over their life together every day and try to examine all the minutiae to find out how, when and why their relationship had grown sour. The bad times they had were equal to the good times. It had taken all of those months in L.A. and upon his first coming to Delaware to come to the conclusion he had confessed to his parents. Nevertheless, he still couldn't help but feel some shred of guilt in it all. The more Tom pondered it, he guessed he had survivor's guilt since he was the only one still living and Maggie didn't have that benefit.

He realized that the crux of his guilt was what Mr. Russell had said to him: Tom would always have the option, the liberty, the opportunity to live on, but Maggie would not; and that fact was unfair, sad, and excruciatingly painful to all who loved her - including Tom.

He looked on the coffee table and his eyes moved from his failed brainstorming to Jade's paperback edition of *To Kill a Mockingbird*, then thinking, *What the hell? I've got the rest of the holiday weekend.* Tom picked up the book and opened to page one, soon reading about Scout, Jem and their small town of Maycomb, Alabama, in 1933. Throughout the book, he noticed yellow highlighter marks over what he guessed were, to Jade, the most insightful excerpts and her favorite quotes in the book. The next morning, he finished the book and it had shot up to be one of the best he had ever read, although *The Razor's Edge* still held the top spot.

Upon closing the book, he felt a nauseating churn in his stomach and realized he hadn't had any dinner the night before. Whereas in the previous months, he hadn't had any appetite, it felt now as if it were coming back with a vengeance, much like a person's sudden recovery after suffering from a stomach bug. It was the final day of the three-day weekend and even though some people would be staying in the area for the week, most people would be returning home as schools hadn't let out for the summer yet. He knew he could probably sneak into downtown Rehoboth, wearing a pair of big black sunglasses and a hat, so he could get something he had been craving for a long time: a chicken cheesesteak from Louie's Pizza. The sub and pizza restaurant was small, a few stores down from the boardwalk, and had been the usual meeting place for he and his friends to eat a quick dinner before their evening shift at Funland. Tom's worry he had just expressed the day before to Feltz about being recognized was far surpassed by his need to eat. Besides, if he were to be recognized, it was better to be in a daytime, innocuous setting like Rehoboth's boardwalk compared to some bar or nightclub. So he grabbed his Bethany Beach cap, his sunglasses and as many quarters as he could find, and went for a quick drive.

Monday may have been the last day of the holiday weekend, but the time of day being just after noon coupled with the weather being sunny had not diminished the visiting holiday crowds that much. He drove in the back way to Rehoboth. When he came to the first stop sign, he turned right and luckily found a parking spot right along front of the St. Edmond's Catholic Church. Tom knew the find was extremely lucky as once tourist season started, the chances of finding any parking space – let alone one so close to the main avenue – were slim to non-existent. As he readied to get out of the Jeep, his pulse raced faster, his breathing grew a little shallow and a strip of sweat instantaneously broke out across his forehead. He couldn't tell if his hands were slightly shaking out of nervousness or out of hunger.

Tom stepped out of the car, tightly affixed the ball cap to his head, pulling the brim down as far as it would go before hitting the top of his sunglasses, put a few quarters in the parking meter, and took a swift walk four blocks north toward the main avenue and Louie's. He had decided it was too risky to sit in the dining room portion of the restaurant which was a small sliver of a room to the left of the establishment. Its combination orange-red-Formica tabletops, tile floor, and varnished wooden décor and beadboard showed its age – like a classic 1980s pizza hangout – but it had not gone out of style to all of the faithful customers who made continuous pilgrimages to the family-owned business every year. Inside the establishment, booths aligned along the entire left side of the wall and the right side was filled with tables and chairs with a break for a doorway which lead to the kitchen and service area.

He stepped into the take-out portion of the restaurant and ordered a small French fries, large pink lemonade, and a chicken cheesesteak with lettuce, tomato, ketchup and mayo. Looking through the large windows, which served as a partition between the take-out portion and the dining room,

Tom looked upon the full tables and felt a wave of nostalgia, remembering his days at Funland ... and the nights after a full shift. Tom couldn't help but picture the faces of friends and acquaintances long gone from his life. He focused on a group of six teenagers sitting at a table, and could see he and his friends laughing over some inside joke one of them had just cracked.

After paying for his sub, Tom walked down the boardwalk, headed toward the place he had wanted to see since he first got back. Even though it was the last day of the long holiday weekend, and kids still had to return to school the next day, Funland was still considerably busy. He sat down on one of the white benches aligning the edge of the boardwalk and positioned himself so he could watch the goings-on of the boardwalk game operators. Their uniforms still hadn't changed: tan shorts and red work shirts. The season was just starting and all of the kids working the games were full of smiles and laughing at their co-worker's stories, catching up on what happened to them over their time away.

Tom hadn't thought of the amusement park in years, but lately, it was more and more at the forefront of his memory. What started it all was his having to think about meeting Maggie for the first time, but now he was beginning to remember the other friends and good times he had had there: the all-nighters; the days off with friends; the trips to take foreign co-workers to all of the many tourist traps in Washington, D.C.; the camaraderie of closing the park late at night and hanging out afterwards to unwind; the gossip; the hook-ups; the summer couples; the parties; the different personalities.

At the time of his last summer working there, he felt as if he'd always be in touch with those close friends he had made; they would be in each other's lives forever. But when he moved out to L.A., and Maggie started living with him, he heard less and less from them. Tom knew friendship was a two-way road and he was just as much to blame for losing touch as they were. Now he wished he could just see them all again.

* * *

Jade had followed her usual routine that morning, and when Katie woke up and came down the steps, into the kitchen, Jade was surprised to see her friend had her bags and luggage with her.

"What's this?" Jade asked.

"It's been two weeks. I figure it's time to leave the beach life, get back to real life."

"But, what about Bryan? Are you finding a new place to live?"

Katie grew withdrawn and oddly quiet, giving Jade all the answer she needed.

"Wait. You're *not* going back to him, are you!?"

"Jade ... I—"

"—*Ughhh!*" Jade made a sound like an angsty teenager. "Katie! You don't have to do that! He *cheated* on you!"

"I *know*, J. I don't need any judgement from you right now. I already feel mixed up enough about all this. To be honest, I don't know what I'm gonna do."

Jade could tell by her friend's body language that she was confused and upset, so she figured the best thing to do was simply be there for her. She softened her tone, saying, "I told you you could stay here with me as long as you needed."

"And that was sweet of you. But I can't avoid my life anymore. I can't avoid Bryan. I know I should be able to just get over him like that," she snapped her fingers. "But I can't. It's something I just ... can't control."

"All I'm going to say is ... I don't think he's right for you. But ... that being said, I only want you to do what *you feel* is truly right for you. Just know you're not going to change him any more than I can change you about going back."

Jade had always been like a sister to Katie and vice versa; so they were both extra protective of each other, even more so than normal best girlfriends. Jade's words continued to bloom in Katie's brain, making her completely comprehend what she was saying, and tears began to fill her eyes.

Seeing her best friend tear up made Jade follow suit, with Katie crying over the uncertainty of her situation and Jade crying because she knew her friend was in a tough predicament ... as well as knowing there was nothing she could do about it. Mostly, their sadness was a shared understanding that even though they had lived away from each other for a while, this was the first time their lives were about to take an extremely dramatic turn to somewhere they truly didn't know - and it scared the hell out of both of them.

Katie took her friend's face and cupped her cheeks in her hands, looking her directly in the eyes, and said in a sisterly, appreciative tone, "I love you. Thank you so much for letting me stay."

"If you ever need me ... I'll be right here."

The two embraced in a big hug and Katie spoke with a lighter tone. "Thanks."

"Oh! Before I forget ..." They backed away from each other, each wiping the tears from their eyes and cheeks, and Jade ran upstairs then returned and handed the thin CD case to her friend. It was a blank CD with black Sharpie pen writing on it that read: **Jade's Jukebox.**

"A mix CD," Katie laughed at her friend. "I swear, you're, like, thirteen."

Jade laughed. "I know."

"I know I don't have to worry about you."

"Why's that?"

"You're happy," Katie plainly stated. "I can tell. I've never had to really worry about you ... as long as I've known you. You just ... seem to find your way. Plus ... with Jimmy taking you out, I'd say you're doing pretty well."

Jade rolled her eyes, pretty annoyed just thinking about it all. "I'm not sure that will last long."

"Enjoy it while it does, then."

"Katie?"

"Yeah?"

"Did you ever watch the footage of what happened to Tom and his wife?"

Katie's mouth started to form an "O" as if she were discovering some juicy secret. Her eyes widened and she said, "*Ohhhh* ... so *this* is what it's about."

"What?"

"Are you starting to like this Tom guy?"

"No. I just ... I'm just curious if you saw it."

Katie knew she could continue to tease and playfully harass her friend for an answer, but she didn't want to scare her from the prospect.

"Of course I saw it," Katie said. "Who hasn't!? It's all over the news, YouTube."

"I haven't ... seen it."

"I'm surprised you haven't seen it just by going on the internet. Then again, there's not much to see, really. It's just ... it's sad."

"Yeah. I just ... I feel bad for him. He's a nice guy. He doesn't deserve all the stuff people are saying about him."

Katie remembered how Tom was the one to pick her up when she was in her drunken stupor, and how he carried her to Jimmy's truck. "Yeah. He is nice. And you know more than anyone, Jade, not to take what those people in the media say seriously."

"I know." Jade's thoughts turned to her friend. "Are you going to be OK?"

"Yeah." Katie knew she was heading into unknown territory, but she knew she had support. "I think I am."

"Call me when you get there." Jade imitated a parent giving a stern lecture, pointing her finger at Katie.

Katie's smile made her mouth stretch as wide across as possible. "Count on it."

The two hugged again, this time a little longer, each giving an extra tight squeeze. Jade walked her friend out to the curb, to Katie's Audi, and helped put her luggage in the car trunk. Katie slammed the trunk closed, turned around, slid her sunglasses onto her face and held her arms out for another hug. Jade laughed at Katie's sweeping melodramatic movements, thinking of when they had first met and how Katie hadn't changed all that much. Jade upped the melodrama, throwing her arms open and practically dropped into Katie's arms. The two laughed, giving another tight hug.

"Love you," Katie endearingly said.

"Love you too."

Katie backed away, turned around to walk to her driver's side door, and raised her arm halfway, shaking the mix CD like a winning lottery ticket. "Thanks."

Katie opened the car door, slipped in and drove away. Jade watched the Audi drift to the stop sign, through the intersection and toward the town's exit. She hoped Katie wouldn't go back to Bryan, but it seemed more than likely that was exactly what her friend was going to do. After her own experiences following her friend's death, Jade had learned to not judge people so easily. She also learned that the press got things wrong more often than not.

"Hey," Tom's voice said from behind her. "I thought that was you." Jade turned toward the end of her block to see him, smiling, walking toward her. She returned the smile.

"Hey!" she said. "Did you park down this way?"

"In front of the church. I was walking by and thought I saw you out here."

"Where have you been?"

"Sorry. I just ... I sorta lost it after that news segment."

"Don't worry about it. Besides, I wouldn't exactly call *that* news. It's merely opinion."

Tom wasn't sure what to say but he was starting to like Jade more and more. He had always felt like it was too early to talk about Maggie, and he didn't want to talk about her or the incident just for hollow sympathy.

"What brings you out here today?" Jade asked.

Tom held up the other half of his sub.

"Let me guess," Jade said. "Louie's?"

"You got it."

"That's quite an outing just for a sub."

"I guess you could say my hunger just returned with a vengeance."

Tom would think that at his age, after all the women he had met and dated, that he would not still be so intimidated or baffled by women; but the truth was that women's enigmatic ways had not become any less of a mystery to him since he was a kid. It was right about now, staring at Jade, that he wished he had the superpower of reading people's minds.

"Is your friend still here?" Tom asked.

"No, she just left."

Tom thought for a couple of seconds about what to say next. "I finished *Mockingbird.*"

"*Ohh*! Wasn't it *so* good!?"

"Pretty amazing. I can't believe I'd never read it before."

Tom could tell the momentum of conversation topics was going down fast in an excruciating ball of flames. "I'm sorry I left so abruptly at Hammerheads."

"You *don't* have to apologize. I get it."

"Yeah, well ... thanks. It's been a while since I've had ... *any* company."

"Just so you know ... I didn't watch it," Jade said. Tom lost a breath or two and his heart felt like it had stopped. "The video. Of your wife. I didn't watch it. I just ... wanted you to know."

With that, Jade held her breath, anxiously awaiting what Tom would say. She could tell her admission had caught him off guard. Tom didn't feel any animosity at her admission, but the conversation had taken an awkward turn.

"You're probably the only one," Tom said.

"If you don't mind me asking ... how long has it been ... since ... it happened?"

"It's only been about ... seven months."

"Have people suggested to you yet that you 'should move on?'"

"Not many, but ... yeah."

"It's always the people closest to you that, when they say it, it hits you the hardest."

Tom wondered how she was able to know how it felt. Was she just guessing? Was it something she read in a magazine or some college textbook? The more he thought about it, the more pissed off the idea made him. But his anger faded as quickly as it had arisen because he knew she was simply trying to help. Tom nodded his head in agreement to what she had just said.

"I know they mean well," Tom said, "but ... it's ... just ... not what I need or want to hear right now."

"What sucks about it all is that, in the long run, you know you should be thankful for having even just one person who cares enough to try and help you ... even if it is in a screwed-up way. But you just can't help it that most times ... you wanna be left alone."

"Maybe that Will guy was right. Maybe I ended up in the Forgotten Mile for a reason."

Jade rolled her eyes as a sly smile crossed her face, trying to suppress a laugh. "Oh, c'mon! You don't believe in what he told you, do you?"

"Maybe. I don't know." Tom thought for a moment. "I mean, I punched my former best friend in the face, got arrested for it and didn't fight the assault charges. I alienated myself from pretty much everyone back in L.A. who was a friend to me. Who does that?"

"Why did you punch him?"

"He lied to me about some papers I signed. They were ..."

"They were what?"

"They were the papers that allowed to have my wife on the show."

Jade knew this was serious and she was, in some weird way, honored he would admit this to her. But she also didn't want to feed his melancholy or the belief he was too far gone with issues to live a normal life again.

"Maybe I've just got too many issues to work out to be around anyone right now," he said.

"Maybe. But ... don't we all? Have issues? I mean ... if any of us was looking to be around, or with, someone who has no issues – someone normal? – we'd all be alone."

Tom thought about what Jade had said and her rationale seemed correct and an outlook worth having, but living that way, when someone was feeling the way he was feeling, was nearly impossible. It wasn't that Tom was looking for someone with no issues, but rather he was thinking *he* was the one who'd be no good for anyone.

"I was just about to go somewhere—" Jade started.

"Oh! That's cool. I can get going."

"No," she had to stifle a laugh. "I was wondering if you wanted to come with me."

"Where are you headed?"

"Right up a few blocks. I wanna show you something."

"I have to get this in a fridge," Tom referenced the other half of his sub.

"No problem. I'll put it in mine and you can get it when we come back."

He handed her the sandwich and waited as she ran in to drop it in her refrigerator. Watching her small jog back to her place, Tom felt his first twinge of joyous anticipation ... immediately followed by guilt for having such a feeling.

Jade jogged back. "Are you ready?"

"Sure. But where exactly are we going?"

"You'll see."

She led him up Laurel Street, toward the boardwalk. "I'm not a big fan of surprises," he said as she walked slightly ahead of him.

"Don't worry. It's completely harmless. I promise."

"So you pretty much know how I got here. What about you? What brings you here?"

"You're the first person who's ever asked me that since I moved here." She looked into his eyes and he gave a flash of a look as if to say, *Go ahead, explain.* "Honestly? I needed a change – just like you.

"I told you I was a lawyer before this. Wasn't very good at it. I got into it for all the wrong reasons."

Tom watched this woman speak with so much conviction, as if she'd told this story many times before ... or practiced saying it. He was in awe of her willingness to be vulnerable to someone she didn't know very well. He still couldn't understand her connection between her reason for coming here and his. There was also no way of him knowing that while Jade appeared calm and carefree on the outside, on the inside, she was a storm of nerves and anxiety.

"I tried to make it work ... but, you know, it's funny ... there's a time when you realize that what you're doing is not just a hardship that you think you must push through; but you realize that ... what you're doing is ... not productive to anyone. The term 'soul-sucking' may seem drastic but it's the closest explanation for wanting a change. Every day of that job seriously felt like it was sucking out my soul, changing me into someone I didn't like.

"And, as I said, the city was *not* for me," Jade continued. "The cost of living in the city got to be too much." Her tone and manner of speaking reminded Tom of a way someone would speak who was trying to convince themselves of their own explanation. "Tell me, did you ever talk to your parents?"

"Yeah."

"Did you confront them?"

"Actually ... yeah."

"And how were they? Was it what you expected?"

"There was a lot less yelling than I thought there would be," Tom said, ending the sentence as if there were still hope to his situation with them.

"That's good," she smiled.

"Yeah ... well ... since Maggie ... and moving here ... I figured I've been given some weird kind of second chance. A new life. I figured I might as well start being more emotionally honest with my parents. I don't think I was being that way for anybody for a long time."

"What? Emotionally honest?"

"Yeah. And I learned my parents - especially my dad - just mean well. They tried so hard to ... build this protective wall around me that they couldn't see they were also building that wall between me and them.

"I'll tell ya ... I know our little talk isn't going to change my dad or even how they necessarily treat me. But I've aired my feelings and I know they still love me. I guess that's what I needed to let sink in."

Jade looked upon this man and an intense admiration grew for him – not any kind of romantic admiration but rather a bit of an envious admiration. Tom had confronted his parents with the person he had become – a man, from how he made it sound, that they might not necessarily like or approve of. And he had still come away with their love.

"What about you?" he asked.

"Me? No. I haven't spoken to them yet. But you kinda give me some encouragement to."

"So why did you move here exactly?" Tom asked. "'Cause I'm having a hard time making the connection to my situation."

Tom hadn't realized that they were up to the edge of Funland. Jade looked at him, smiled and said, "I'll tell you in a minute. First, come with me."

They went and sat on a bench across the boardwalk, near the edge overlooking the beach. They faced toward the amusement park, watching the kids having fun, smiling, laughing, and even some crying because they hadn't won a prize at one of the games or weren't ready to go home. In full sight, the bumper cars did their uncontrollable dance around the circle with the occasional kid moving in the wrong direction and the one token annoying jerk who insisted on using the ride as his personal bullying device disguised as fun. There was another entrance which brought you into the park and the skee-ball alley, where adults spent hours trying to get the highest score possible, which often meant spending insane amounts of quarters to trade up from the small prize to the jumbo size.

Families and couples sporadically passed by as the two continued to watch the playful fracas before them. "I know this is nothing new to you." She motioned to Funland. "But I wanted you to see this."

"Why?"

"This helped me a lot when I first moved here and I was going through my ... issues. Seeing these people happy. It reminds of my childhood ... a simpler, carefree time – you know? – all that kind of stuff."

"Did you vacation here when you were younger?"

"A few times. I'd come here with my best friend, Aishwarya. We had a lot of good times here. Just a couple of kids." She took in all of the people's laughter and smiles, then asked, "How was it? Working here?"

"It was ... a job. I mean, it definitely had its bad days but the good times outweighed all that." Tom thought about it as he looked into the park. "Of course, it was the *first* job I ever had, so setting the bar that high right out the gate probably isn't the best thing. Working at a place like that definitely gave me high expectations when it came to the type of people you work with." He thought about his times there more before staring down at nothing in particular and saying in a dream-like state, "That place changed my life."

It only took a few seconds for his reminiscing to end and he abruptly snapped out of it, his voice taking on a new life. "But ... again, there definitely were many moments having to deal with stupid tourists and difficult co-workers. I guess you get that anywhere, huh? Still, I can say it was probably the best job I ever had. I guess admitting that is either very sad or very endearing."

Jade, still looking on with a serious face at Tom's profile, nodded her head and said, "Both."

Tom laughed at her small joke and looked over to her just in time to see her serious scowl melt into a smile and laugh. After their brief laughter had died down, they both looked back toward the amusement park, almost losing themselves in the people-watching.

"Wanna know why else I moved here? I had this friend in high school. My best friend, Vanessa," Jade's voice cut the silence. "We roomed together at college and ... not long into our freshman year ... she was killed ... by her dad." The mere memory of it sliced Jade on the inside, but the pain was one she had been used to for a long time. What scared Jade the most now was admitting next what she hadn't told anyone since she moved to Delaware. "She and I had already been in the news. At our senior prom, there was a school shooting. Kids died. Some of the administrative staff died." She cleared her throat. "Anyway, when Vanessa died, the news came calling - looking for some sound bite or video clip to further their ratings. I was lucky, though. I was only the friend. Her mom got it much worse.

"By the time I decided to move, I still had press, occasional freelancers, still contacting me about Vanessa, the school shooting. It was especially bad come every May 'cause it would be the anniversary of the prom. Crime shows would want to do retrospectives ... things like that." She looked back to Tom and flashed a timid smile. "I just wanted to be left alone, y'know?

"Every year, with the approach of the anniversary, there was always this nagging feeling in the back of my mind - sort of like a splinter buried just enough below the skin that you can't get to it yourself." The thought of it nearly gave her a panic attack, but she began to regulate her breathing more, trying to be as inconspicuous about it as possible. "You think that living in the city, you'd be lost in the crowd. It wasn't that way for me."

Tom was racking his brain, trying to recall the incident she was talking about. It didn't take long before he remembered it due to his writing a senior college thesis on the tragedy. The press had dubbed it the Roosevelt High School Prom Night Massacre. It was one of many in a long line of school shootings but this one had been different because there were more than one or two shooters; hostages were taken and there were reports of some vigilante fighting off the shooters. The tragedy had been one of the biggest stories of the year.

"I'm sorry, Jade," Tom said, not wanting to mention his familiarity with the massacre.

"It's OK. I guess I did move here to forget. I was hoping others would forget too. But the thing is ... you don't forget. It stays with you. You know that by now." A nervous smile crossed her lips and she continued, "You move on because you have to. But it's always there."

Jade's story made Tom feel something he didn't think he would ever feel: a connection. He could tell that Jade wasn't trying to compare her situation to his, and she wasn't pretending to know what kind of pain he was going through. But she did know what it's like to be a survivor, to have the guilt. He knew what made her so damn strong was that she experienced this loss and she still could smile and laugh and appreciate the good things in life. The way he knew this was the mere fact that she still took joy in something as simple as visiting an amusement park and watching the enjoyment of others.

"You wanna go in?" her question broke his concentration.

"What?"

"Do you want to go into Funland?"

"Um ... yeah. Sure," Tom was a bit flummoxed. They got up, walked in and Tom was happy to see that the holiday weekend crowds had drastically thinned out due to it being the last day of the long weekend. Nevertheless, the frantic energy and fun still electrified the place. Tom could feel it in the air. It was still the same after all these years.

"So are there any tricks to winning any of the games?" Jade asked.

"No."

"C'mon! I always love playing this one!"

She led him over to the game where you buy rubber green frogs to try and, using a mallet, catapult one of them into one of the flowers floating along in a small water tank. They both bought a dollars' worth of frogs and Tom said, "OK. Well, there sort of *is* a trick with this one. What ya need to do is—"

BAM! Tom saw the frog fly through the air in a huge arc, almost joining the few other frogs resting atop the game's lighted sign, before coming down, just missing one of the flowers, hitting a green, plastic lily pad and slipping into the murky water. She kicked her foot at nothing in particular and made an "Aww!" sound like a little girl who had just lost.

"There actually is a trick to this one. You have to fold up the frog like this." Tom placed the frog on the catapult as if it were kneeling on top of its legs, shifted the catapult to aim it and waited for one of the flowers to make its way around. "But you don't just smack the hell out of it. You have to hit it ... just ... right."

Tom brought the mallet down swiftly but not strong enough. His frog lunged forward as if it had broken legs, not even making it into the tank. Jade let out a loud, hard laugh, trying her best to talk between each bellow. "I thought you said there was a trick with this one."

"That's not how it used to work," Tom pouted, but his determination swiftly rebounded. "Let me try again."

He set his next frog down the same way, but this time brought the mallet down with a little more force. The frog glided along and smacked down in one of the flowers.

"Hey!" Jade shouted. "You got it!"

The young Funland worker asked Tom which prize he wanted from the small size selection. As he picked, Jade plopped her frog down on the catapult and smacked the launcher, sending the frog smacking into one of the flowers. Jade couldn't help but shout out in excitement. "Yeah!"

Tom picked a small plush frog wearing glasses. The worker turned to Jade and asked her what she wanted from the same selection. Jade picked the other small prize - a plush owl.

"Oh," she said, holding up her prize to Tom's face. "It kinda looks like you."

She laughed at the likeness even though Tom didn't see it. She said, "Man, I love this place."

They walked away, further strolling into the park. Tom stared at his plush frog, and it made an uncontrollable smile break across his face. "Yeah. I had a few laughs."

"How many summers did you work here?"

"Four. What about you? What was your first job?"

"I worked part-time at a pizza place."

"Did you like it?"

"Not really. It was just a job, money in my pocket. I went, worked and left. Was that how it was working here?"

"No. I loved the people I worked with. But that's easy when you're a kid." He wanted to tell her more about those people who were some of the best he'd ever met; about the work ethic that was instilled in him because he worked there with the wonderful family who owned the place; and about how now that things were the way they were, how being in this place was beginning to make him feel like a complete and utter failure.

"I think you're lucky if you can find people you love to work with ... at *any* age. Most places you go, there aren't many people you can even agree with, let alone like or love." They walked up toward the kiddie rides then made a left in front of the Paratrooper ride. "Do you still keep in touch with any of them?"

"Um, no. No. I ... I haven't talked to any of 'em in quite a while. Feltz and Sprenkle are the first ones I've seen or talked to in a long time."

"Why not?"

Tom shrugged. "Don't know. No real reason, I guess. I just ... once I moved out to California, we kinda just ... lost touch. Grew apart."

"Do you miss them?"

"Ya know, I honestly haven't thought of it lately ... but ... now that you ask ... yeah. I do."

They made a left turn, walking between the Gravitron – a ride that looked like a big silver spaceship, where people went inside it, stood up and the ride spun so fast, the seats rose up and the riders stuck against the wall. They walked back the way they had come in and walked down the boardwalk, back toward Laurel Street.

"Do you miss your friends in New York?" Tom asked.

"I didn't have that many. The only one I really miss is Katie."

"Do you miss your friend? Vanessa?"

Jade grew alarmingly quiet and her face dropped, reflecting her sudden shift in mood. "Yeah, of course. When I think about her now, I just get sad. Not so much because of our friendship or having her in my life. But more because of her just not being in the world anymore. She was a wonderful person and a great friend. She was just ... a kind person."

"That's how I feel about Maggie." Tom couldn't believe he had just said that out loud. He figured he might as well go with it. "She certainly had her flaws ... but she was ... a good person."

"If you don't mind me asking ... do you ..." Jade wasn't sure she wanted to ask what she was about to ask, but she couldn't resist. "... Do you ... hate her? I mean ... for cheating on you?"

"No. Well ... yes ... and no." Tom was taken aback by Jade's question but he gave her credit for being honest. She was only asking what everyone was wondering. "Of course, I'm mad. But she certainly didn't deserve what happened to her. It's sort of funny we're talking about this now 'cause when I confronted my parents, we talked about this." He thought more on it for a few seconds. "I loved her. But that life ... is gone now. I wasn't really there for her ... not that that excuses her for having an affair.

"Our life together is over. It was over before that asshole pulled the trigger. It just took me this long to start recovering from that truth."

"But you still gotta have bad days."

"Yeah. I'd be lying if I said I didn't. Right now, I'm feeling the way you are about Vanessa - just sad that she's not ... in the world anymore."

Jade didn't like where the conversation was going. Tom was beginning to become more withdrawn. While she had thought it was important and necessary for him to open up about Maggie and the incident, she didn't want him dwelling on it for too long. So she decided to take their talk in another direction.

"Hey!" she snapped him out of his thoughts. "I'm sorry if I pried, made you go somewhere you didn't want to."

"It's OK. What happened to Maggie and me – it's not something I want to define my life."

"I think I'm in touch with that emotion."

Tom smiled at Jade's response. She was one of the few people who knew how to talk to him. He realized it wasn't some special talent she possessed, but rather just having an open mind about him and giving him a chance to speak out when he wanted. They turned down Laurel Street and the end of the first block came quick.

"You wanna go to Browseabout?" she broke away from the subject. "I finished *Shutter Island*. I could use something new to read. It's one of my most favorite spots in town."

Tom almost laughed out loud at her non-subtle way of changing the subject, but he kept his amusement contained. "Sure."

When they reached the end of the block, Tom looked to his Jeep and saw a familiar female standing next to it. She wasn't wearing the usual professional outfit Tom was used to seeing her in, but shorts, a t-shirt and sunglasses.

"Hey," he said to Jade. "I just remembered. There's something I gotta do real quick. But I ... can we meet up later?"

"Sure," Jade said, a bit suspicious of his sudden change of mind.

"I'll call you soon," Tom's voice had grown distant, like he was somewhere else.

"OK. See you later." Jade left and Tom's pace grew slower as he walked to his Jeep. Jade only hoped she hadn't scared Tom or said something to offend him. Either way, she carried on as if she were unaffected.

When Tom was close enough for both he and the woman to recognize each other, he let out a weary, silent laugh. "What are you doing here, Jen?"

Jen took off her sunglasses, exposing her different-colored eyes and a smile. "She's pretty."

"What do you want?"

"I waited two months before I came over here."

"You've known for that long, huh?"

"Yeah. I almost didn't think you'd come here, though. Last time we talked, you didn't exactly get along with your parents."

"Well ... what can I say? Things change."

"I'm happy for you, Tom."

"If you're so happy for me, then why did you come here? Why couldn't you just leave me alone? And how did you find me?"

"Even cash deposits leave a paper trail." She was proud of her tracking skills, but, looking at Tom, he was nothing but annoyed, and she could tell. "Maggie's parents set up a charity in her name, and I was thinking—"

"I mean, how did you find me right here, right now? How'd you know this was my Jeep?"

"I figured you'd be back in the area. But not with your parents. I have contacts here. So I—"

"How long have you been following me?"

"A little over a week."

"Unbelievable," Tom mumbled.

"You didn't actually think that by coming here you were going to escape all of your troubles, did you?"

"Don't the lovely people in the press have more important stories to cover than a seven-month-old has-been story?"

"You're the story, Tom. I don't pick the story. I just go where they tell me so I can report on it."

"Oh, so you're just doing your job?"

"Yes."

"Were you doing your job when you aired that audio clip of me? Were you doing your job when you didn't play the entire tape? I guess that wouldn't be a real attention-getter if people knew the entire story, would it? Wouldn't grab enough ratings?"

"I had nothing to do with that! That was my producer's call."

"Oh, so your *producer* was the one who made the decision to edit it! What about recording me without my knowing? Was that your producer's call? Or was it yours?

"What about handing over the recording? Was that your producer's call?" Tom waited for a reply but her silence was all the confirmation he needed. "Or was that yours?"

"I didn't plan on it all going down like that."

"What *else* did you think was gonna happen!?"

"I ... I ... I came to make it right."

"How do you expect to do that, Jen? It's done. It's already been all over the news, the internet!" He gathered his nerves enough to calm down. He took a deep breath, released it slowly. "I think you've done enough."

"I just ... I want to be there for you."

Tom began laughing. The idea that she was wanting to help him was hysterically amusing. It took about a minute for Tom's laughter to die down before he spoke again.

"Ya know ...," he said, "... when you dumped me, I honestly wasn't mad at you. I was actually thankful to you for being honest with me. Besides, if it weren't for that ... I probably wouldn't have reconnected with Maggie, or pushed myself to get the internship at the studio.

"But this ..." Tom grew more silent as he peered downward and steeled himself for what he was about to reveal. "How I've been living? This is ... what *you* did ... I can't trust you." He looked up into her eyes. "How can I trust you?"

"I understand what you must be feeling."

"No! You don't! You couldn't!" Tom yelled, then calmed himself. "Have you been afraid to go out because you were afraid someone would recognize you? Have you not been able to truly talk to anyone because of it? Have you not been able to even go outside for fear of being constantly judged? Did you ... did you honestly think that I would agree to have my wife on my show?"

"Tom." Jen had begun to cry.

"Did you?"

"Your signature was taken into evidence at court."

"*Did* you!?" he shouted louder.

"No."

Tom's face twisted from shock to a horrible, betrayed expression. "Then why did you go along with everything? Why did you take that recording of me?"

"I have to be able to do my job before I can help you. But, trust me, I'm here for you now."

"You weren't there for me when I needed you most. I could've used a friend, Jen. Not a PR agent. When Maggie died, I couldn't mourn the way most people get to. From the start, the press constantly put me under a microscope.

"I'm not naïve. I knew it was coming. But I honestly never thought you'd be ... I never thought you'd do what you did." Tom realized he was done with Jen. He didn't care what she had to say; whatever it was, it was inexcusable when it came to what she had done to him. "Go home, Jen."

"Tom, I know everything seems bad now, but I can help you get through this. I *want* to help you get through this. No strings attached."

"I doubt it."

"Do you know who that woman you're hanging out with is?"

Tom gave a nod.

"That's Jade Saha. She *survived* the Roosevelt High Prom Night Massacre!? You know!? The one you did your senior thesis on!? Her best friend who survived with her was gunned down a few months later!"

For once, Jen was telling Tom something he already knew. But he wouldn't give it away to her. "What does this have to do with me?"

"I talked to my producers and they're willing to hire you if you can get an interview with her."

"Interview? About what?"

"About the night of the massacre! To get her perspective on all of it. They know your experience with the story, plus the anniversary just passed, so it's still timely. But not for long." Jen could see the clueless expression on Tom's face. "*Tom!* This is your shot at getting your foot back in the door! I mean, she's just a rebound! This story could relaunch your career!"

Tom thought about Jen's and his romantic relationship, about how the great moments were great but the bad moments were completely disastrous. Jen was a passionate, exciting woman to date, a great woman to introduce to friends and family; but when it came to actual emotional support, Jen's acumen was sorely lacking. Her tunnel vision of simply kick-starting Tom's career, and dragging Jade back through the emotional turmoil she was trying so hard to move on from, was sickening to Tom.

He had dreamed of getting back into his career ever since he left L.A., and now the opportunity was here. But the idea of getting back into TV no longer appealed to him. The more he thought about it, the more he realized the passion he had once had for it had dried up. It wasn't that he was scared to get back into the field; he simply had no desire for it anymore. Tom knew it was time to try something new. He had no clue what that would be – which was nerve-racking – but he knew it would be better than how he felt with the likes of *Heartbrakers*. Besides, he thought, if just getting his foot back into the door of show business meant having to exploit Jade or *anyone*, Tom had nothing more to say than ...

"There's no more story here, Jen. No more sound bites or juicy quotes."

"Didn't you hear—?"

"Goodbye." He moved past her and got into his Jeep.

Jen recognized the look on Tom's face. When they were dating, he would show the same expression when he had absolutely made up his mind. She knew there was no talking him down from his position.

"Will I see you again?" Jen asked.

Tom started the engine and put on his sunglasses. "Does it really matter, Jen?"

He looked into the rearview mirror, saw no one coming and backed out of the parking spot, taking off without saying another word. Tom meant to press the "on" button on his radio, but hit the tape button instead, and the mix tape, which had stopped working on his trip over the Bay Bridge, suddenly switched over and started playing side B. Tom made a point not to look in the rearview as he drove around the curve, leaving downtown. The only slight relief was that he had made his decision about his career change. Hollywood and the media were as far behind him as Jen was in his rearview.

20.

"My yellow in this case is not so mellow
In fact, I'm trying to say ... it's frightened like me
And all these emotions of mine keep holding me from
Giving my life to a rainbow like you
But I'm bold as love"

--Jimi Hendrix
"Bold as Love"

It had been just about three hours since Jade last saw Tom. She didn't know why, but she was nervous he wouldn't call. There was some kind of unspoken attraction between them; Jade could tell Tom felt it too. It was all in the look. She wasn't sure how to feel about it because it wasn't the most convenient of feelings to have for someone like Tom, especially with what he was going through. On the other hand, the attraction in and of itself wasn't all too bad either. It had been a long time since Jade felt a connection ... to anyone. Nevertheless, she made a conscientious decision to be wary of her feelings. She turned on her radio and out came the soulful wail of the female singer for the band Houndmouth, singing about the legendary Georgian soul man, "Otis." Whereas most people called James Brown the godfather of soul, to Jade, Otis Redding was the king!

She picked up around the house and mid-way through, got a sudden urge to make some art. She went upstairs, picked up her sketch pad and pencil, returned downstairs, opened the house door, stepped out to the screened porch, slumped down in one of the plastic chairs and dove right into drawing. She made sure to leave the house door open so she could hear the music as it wafted through the house and outside. On days like today, it was nice to enjoy the warm weather with its occasional breeze ... and the drawing was taking her mind off of Tom and all the questions which had crowded her head within the past few hours.

Jade became absorbed with her drawing – a portrait of her grandmother that she was sketching from memory. Before the song was over, she heard her cell phone sound out a pinging noise and she knew it was a text message. She got up and got her phone. The message was from Tom: "Still wanna go to one of your favorite spots in town?"

"Where are you?"

"Out front."

She hurriedly put her sketch pad and pencil on the kitchen table, turned off the music, grabbed her wallet and keys, checked her look in the mirror, and closed the locked door, sweeping toward the street.

Jade walked a few houses down from her place and found Tom standing across the street, parked in a metered spot. He was leaning against the side of his Jeep, looking like that scene out of the movie *Sixteen Candles*, at the end, when Jake Ryan is standing against his red Porsche, waiting for Molly Ringwald's Samantha Baker to come out of the church. The only difference for Jade was instead of having the Thompson Twins' movie song playing in her head, she was hearing the opening guitar strumming of Tegan and

Sara's song "Underwater." She flashed a smile at him and Tom smiled back.

"I wasn't sure you were coming," Jade said as she approached him.

"I'm sorry. I remembered I had to go home 'cause I had an old friend coming to visit."

"Must've been a good visit."

"Not exactly. But it was one I had to have."

Jade's curiosity was really peaked now. She could only imagine what he was talking about – must've had to do with his wife and what happened to her. As much as her curiosity was screaming at her mind to ask Tom about what happened, what kept her from doing so was the small reminder in the back of her mind of her own experience of wanting to keep her secrets, her past, her pain, to herself. The least she could do was show him the same respect.

The both of them started their walk by agreeing to get to the book store by going the long way – up toward the boardwalk and walking with the ocean breeze sweeping their faces. They took the time to stop and use some ride tickets Jade always kept in her wallet to ride the bumper cars at Funland, played a game of skee-ball, Whac-a-Mole, and the horse race derby game before continuing their journey. They got soft serve frozen custard (which most people often mistook for ice cream) at Kohr Bros. and shared their personal stories and experiences about the town. Jade found out that Tom was actually funny although his humor was very dry and a bit dark; but she figured that was no surprise after what he had recently been through. Nevertheless, as she watched him talk about the town and share his Funland stories, stories of his friends, of growing up and the aspirations he had before leaving for L.A., she was impressed that he sounded so positive.

When they arrived at the book store, Jade had taken it upon herself to assist Tom with stocking his bookshelves with more contemporary novels. As they walked the store, the speakers were playing a live, acoustic version of Howard Jones singing his 1980s hit "No One is to Blame." Tom had picked up Stephen King's *The Stand* because he had always wanted to read it but never got a chance to on account that, at about twelve hundred pages, it was a bit too long for him to ever commit to reading it. When he told Jade how he had nothing but time now, she knew she had to give him some more light-hearted books. Between each book she suggested, she asked Tom if he had read the book yet and Tom would tell her each time that he hadn't. The pile in his arms consisted of Nick Hornby's *High Fidelity*, Sherman Alexie's *The Absolutely True Diary of a Part-time Indian*, Stephen Chbosky's *The Perks of Being a Wallflower*, Paulo Coelho's *The Alchemist*, and Jane Austin's *Pride & Prejudice*. When she laid Austin's novel on his small pile, he let out an exasperated sigh.

"What is it with *Pride and Prejudice*?" he asked.

"What do you mean?"

"It seems like every girl I've ever known *loves* this book. I mean, is it really *that* good?"

"Yes, it is ... smartass." She flashed him a sly smile. "It's one of the first romantic comedies ever written. The way Austin writes ... it's ... there's just something ... captivating about it." She looked to him and he gave her a look, cocking his one eyebrow up, as if to say, *It's total chick lit!* "Just promise me you'll give it a try ... if you have time."

"Sure. I'll try 'em all."

Jade smiled at her conquest of introducing someone to the books she loved so much. She always felt a connection to fiction – the written word. There was a kind of magic to its simplistic power of teleporting her to different worlds, different times, as well as its transformative power of giving her the opportunity to take on someone else's life. Since she had been able to read, Jade consumed the words of as many writers as she could. Men had come and gone, but books had remained her first true love.

"Listen ...," she said. "When I told you about Vanessa ... I didn't mean in any way to one-up or downplay what you were going through."

"Oh, no." Tom didn't think that at all, but he wondered if his long absence from seeing her today had caused her to think that. "Honestly ... I hate to admit that it helps. Knowing I'm not the only one with a tragedy. I mean ... I'm not so narrow-minded or shallow to think what happened to Maggie and me is some cruel injustice that's only privy to me. I know there are tragedies out there – millions – and they make what happened to Maggie and me seem miniscule in comparison. But even though I know this, it's easy to forget, get lost in the moment. So when I heard your story ... it was some kind of ... comfort, for lack of a better word. Does that make me a bad person?"

"No. I'd say it makes you human."

The next thing Tom knew, he saw a glimpse of something in Jade's gaze which he hadn't seen in a while. She had a face of respect, a face of excitement and attraction, which he recognized as the same face he saw on Gracie Bennett's face in eighth grade when she revealed she had a crush on him. He wasn't sure if she was making that face because he had made the same expression, or if there was something actually admirable that he had said. Maybe he had touched upon a feeling with which she could sympathize. Either way, he couldn't suppress his smile so he let it go, instantly feeling awkward about it. Whether it was a nervous reaction or she truly felt that way, Jade returned the same type of awkward smile, having to bite her lip to try and quit it. It wasn't long before Tom realized what was happening – or, what he *thought* was happening – and he shut off his smile as if someone flipped a switch.

"Do you *ever* see the negative in people?" Tom asked.

"I could. But writing people off is a hell of a lot easier than to see the good in them." She looked away for a few seconds before turning back to him. "I guess I'm just always up for a good challenge."

"Or you're a masochist." Tom let out a single chuckle. "You gotta admit: life can get pretty shitty."

"Sure. But every new day is a chance to start all over again. I know some people consider that a hassle, a burden. But I don't."

"Wow," Tom gasped, more out of wonderment than surprise. That was the moment – the watershed moment when he knew he was in trouble. He had feelings for this woman. Feelings he dared deem stronger than just friendship. Most of him felt horribly guilty for the feeling of it all. But it was unmistakable and there it was. He could contain his feelings by not telling her but they were still there, constantly churning just under the surface.

His thoughts raced to the press and how they would have a field day with the story of Tom starting a romantic relationship so relatively soon after Maggie's death. Conspiracies and scandal would abound, and Jade's name and reputation would be dragged through the mud.

Tom ran ideas through his mind, trying to think of what he could say to stop any more romantic sentiment.

"So ... did you ever go out with that guy? Was his name Jimmy?"

"Yeah," Jade said. She awkwardly broke her stare, turning her head to look at one of the bookshelves, and Tom knew his ploy had worked. "Uh, we ... went out on a date. But it didn't exactly take." Jade knew Jimmy's reputation. He was like most of the guys around the area: he downplayed his looks, spit out a few seemingly funny (to him) one-liners, and puffed up his chest by sporadically throwing in some quaint nuggets of fortune cookie wisdom here and there in a conversation. This pathetic scheme worked on about ninety-nine percent of the women of whom he used it on. For once in her life, Jade was proud she was a part of the minority. "Maybe we shouldn't talk about ex's and failed relationships. Reflection is one thing, obsessive dwelling is another." She thought for a moment, closed her head, trying her best to pick the right words out of her memory, then said, "'You are what your deep, driving desire is. As your desire is, so is your will. As your will is, so is your deed. As your deed is, so is your destiny.'"

"Who *are* you? *Yoda?* Did you just ... did you come up with that?"

"No," she laughed at the idea that he would think her so wise as to come up with something so profound. "It's from *The Upanishads.*" She could tell he wasn't understanding. "It's a book of Hindu philosophy and scripture."

"So are you a Buddhist?"

"Not practicing. But I agree with a lot of it."

"A Buddhist in Sussex County!? Who would've thought?"

"You'd be surprised."

Tom thought about all of what she said about dwelling, and her reasoning was right. But it still didn't alleviate the pain and guilt he felt over Maggie as he still felt his life, his choices, had inadvertently caused her death.

Jade could tell what Tom was thinking but she didn't want him to dwell on it anymore. Not today. She understood that he had to go through what he did after what he experienced in order to accept it and move on with his life, but he also couldn't move on with life unless he stopped focusing so extremely on what happened and actually lived. It was a fine line he had to walk and she knew he still had a long way to go.

"You ready to get out of here?" she asked.

"Sure."

They paid for their books and left. When they got outside, Tom pointed out a store a few doors down and talked about how it used to be an under-21 dance club called XLR8 back when he was in high school, and how he would sometimes go just to stand around and socialize. The two of them walked back toward the boardwalk, stopping at a nostalgia shop that sold records and pop culture items from the 1980s and older. One of the vintage record players in the store was playing Sharon Jones and the Dap-Kings' soul romper, "Let Them Knock."

Jade rushed over to the record shelves like an excited child running across the parking lot to get to a toy store.

"I'm so happy vinyl is making a comeback!" she said.

"I didn't know you had a record player."

"Oh, yeah! It's part of my system at home. What's your favorite music?"

"What's your favorite music?" he heard Maggie's voice.

436

Tom shook his head a few times as if he were trying to get some water out of his ears. This time he knew how to answer the question. He held up his pointer finger as if to say, *Wait and see*, then searched through the "S" section of the records. He grabbed out an album with a black and white cover and handed it to her: Bruce Springsteen's *Born to Run*. He walked around to the "B"s and handed her The Beach Boys' *Pet Sounds*. Next was The Gaslight Anthem's *The '59 Sound*, then Bob Dylan's *Blonde on Blonde*, then Jimi Hendrix's *Are You Experienced?*, then Tom Waits' *Closing Time*, and Otis Redding's *Otis Blue*. Upon his last pick, she let out an excited moan. "Just to name a few."

"*Oooooooooohhhhhh!* Otis Redding! *Now* you're *talking*!"

"What are yours?"

She mimicked his move with her finger and went throughout the two small aisles picking up albums and handing them to him. Amy Winehouse's *Back to Black*, Alabama Shakes' *Boys & Girls*, Nina Simone's *Silk & Soul*, Tegan and Sara's *Heartthrob*, Billy Joel's *Turnstiles*, and Kate Nash's *My Best Friend is You*. Then she said, "And some fifties and sixties girl group stuff. Oh! And I love this band called Postmodern Jukebox!"

Jade poured through Tom's choices and had to contain a laugh. "I think I'm noticing a pattern here. She motioned to the Springsteen album. "This one is about escape with a cast of desperate characters." Then she thumbed through the Waits, Redding, Beach Boys and Dylan albums. "These are all great! But they're also a bit ... morose. Don't ya think?"

Tom's face contorted as the truth of her observation hit him. "First off, Springsteen's album is about the great hope in the open frontier, featuring a cast of rebels. Secondly, since when are the Beach Boys *morose*!? I mean ... 'Wouldn't it be Nice!?' 'God Only Knows!?' How are *those* morose?"

"'Wouldn't it be Nice' is probably one of the only upbeat songs on the entire album ... even though 'God Only Knows' is debatable. Have you ever listened to the lyrics to the other songs!? The music may be their usual cheerful sound, but the lyrics can be pretty ... glum. Don't get me wrong! They're great lyrics! But they're definitely not the most cheerful. It's basically an unrequited love album."

"What about 'Sloop John B?'"

"What about it? It's a sea shanty—"

"Yes!"

"—about how the singer just wants to not be there! He even says over and over, 'I wanna go home!'"

"Well, I like 'em!"

"I do too! It's just ... interesting – your take on it."

"Wow. I didn't think I'd be getting some free psychological session today."

Jade laughed at Tom's dry tone, then said, "At least you can see the goodness in the music."

Tom ran the lyrics through his head, singing to himself, and he realized she was right. Maybe she was right about the nature of the lyrics, but he still loved the music just as much.

"What about your love of girl groups?" Tom asked.

"What about it?"

"Don't you think those songs are a little ... dated? I mean, they're mostly women just singing about the men they love. Not very feminist."

Jade nodded at his suggestion. "I can see your point. Although, I'd argue the feminist aspect. One could say those women are taking charge of their lives. Plus, there are a lot of songs about other real issues. The Crystals' 'He Hit Me (And It Felt Like a Kiss)?' The Exciters' 'He's Got the Power?' Those deal with physical abuse in a relationship. The Shirelles' 'Will You Love Me Tomorrow?' That's about pre-marital sex. And The Lovelites' "How Can I Tell My Mom and Dad?' That's teenage, unwed pregnancy! This is all before Madonna or Lady Gaga. Plus, you can't beat the soul in the vocals."

"OK. I get your point."

"But, mostly, it's the style of music I love – the Wall of Sound that Spector created. Brian Wilson used it to make one of your favorite albums. And Springsteen had it in mind when he recorded *Born to Run*." She turned to continue looking through the albums. "But I also love the soul of it. It's not so much the surface of the lyrics as it is the deep emotion in the song as a whole ... the yearning ... the passion. It reminds me of ...," her eyes drifted away, as her thoughts wandered. "... the exhilarating, bittersweet passion of life."

Out of anyone else's lips, her words may have sounded pretentious, but Jade had a way of speaking that removed any air of fallacy, and Tom could feel it.

"Well ...," Tom said. "Since you put it that way ..."

Jade let out a few low laughs. "Ya know ... you remind me of this character from one of my favorite books."

"Really? Who?" Tom asked. "And please say it's not Lassie or the Little Prince or something."

"No. Yorick Brown."

"Who!?"

"Yorick Brown is this character from a comic book."

"A ... *comic* ... book?"

"Yeah! It's called *Y: The Last Man!*" she said as they started putting their albums back where they had found them. "Remember that guy you met when we had lunch a while back? Will?"

"Oh yeah."

"He told me about it. Thought I might like it. In fact, he practically forced me to read it."

"And ... did you ... like it?"

"Yeah. It sort of has an open ending, but I really enjoyed it. It's how it sounds. All about this one day on earth when all of the males – and I mean every male, from fetuses to animals – die. All except this one guy and his pet monkey. I know. It sounds hokey ... but it's not.

"Anyways, the guy's name is Yorick Brown and he starts off going to find his girlfriend but he's swept up in this mission to see if he holds the key to bringing back male life."

"Almost sounds like a porno I watched one time," Tom said.

Jade stifled a laugh. "Quite the opposite. It's really a good story. And Yorick reminds me of you."

"How's that?"

"Well ... he's kind of self-deprecating but also full of hope. As for the rest, I can't tell you without spoiling it."

"I'm not exactly into comic books."

"That's a shame. You should read it. I think you'd love it."

By the time they were done with the albums, Jade was still holding The Gaslight Anthem, Tom Waits, and the Beach Boys albums. She stepped up to the counter, paid for them and left with a smile for the clerk. As they left the store, Tom said, "I thought *Pet Sounds* was too morose?"

"It is. But that doesn't mean I don't like it. Besides, it's not necessarily bad to have some melancholy in your life from time to time. It reminds us to be more appreciative of the happy times. It reminds us we're alive."

"You're a bit weird," Tom said playfully. "Anyone ever tell you that before?"

"Thanks. But, no, seriously ... what would life be without the down moments? We wouldn't be able to fully appreciate or relish the good ones." She noticed him giving her a funny look and her insecurity got the best of her. "What!?"

"Nothing. It's just ... your ideas, your way of thinking ... it's quite revolutionary nowadays. Especially after what you've been through."

Thank you was all she could say to his compliment, then she promptly changed the subject. "So you said you made some peace with your parents?"

"Yeah."

"How did you do it? I mean, you said your father was a real tough case."

"I yelled at him. Not exactly the best approach, I know. But, as weird as it sounds, I almost *had* to do it that way so I could get out what I've been wanting to say for so long."

"What's kept you from saying it?"

"Believe it or not ... his health. I wasn't worried that he'd disown me. But he's had a bad heart for quite some time. I didn't want to give him a heart attack and have him keel over and die. It'd be just like that old, stubborn S.O.B. to die just to win an argument.

"Also the fact that I know, deep down, that, even though he's got the most rotten way of showing it, he loves me. So whenever I'd get frustrated with him, I'd just think: *Is*

it really worth blowing up at him about something like this?
The answer was always no. It's kinda funny. For all children
who feel loved by their parents ... no matter how much you
want your life to be your own when you grow up, you're
always ultimately still looking for some level of ... approval
or acceptance from your parents."

"Yeah. I'd be shocked if my parents suddenly approved
of my choices since I left New York. Maybe I need to blow
up at *my* dad and see how it goes."

"I know it's gotta be rough for them, though. I mean ...
your life changes when you have a kid and you do everything
– give them your all to raise them for at least eighteen years.
Then they leave and you're expected to be completely
unaffected by their wanting a life of their own. Even if their
life doesn't agree with what you think – or know – is best."

The more Jade talked with Tom, the more she was
impressed with his insight, as well as the fact he had been
through so much lately and still held out for some hope,
some optimism. "I guess when you put it that way ... it's a bit
easier to see where they're coming from."

"When my parents and I had our talk, my dad said
something to me that I've mulled over since. He said there is
no manual to being a parent, that you do the best you can.
Now ... I know a lot of parents say that. But the more I
thought about it – I mean, *really* let it sink in – I realized he
was just going by what he truly thought was right."

"Aren't we all?"

"Heh. Not *all* of us. *Trust* me."

Tom need not say another word as Jade had heard of
his experiences with his former friend and their court case.

"I take it you're speaking from personal experience?"

"Yeah."

By the time they made it back to Laurel Street, the time on Tom's parking meter was just about to run out and expire.

"I guess this is my cue," he said, motioning to the two minutes remaining on the meter. "Besides, I didn't think it was five o'clock already."

"Oh, OK."

"Listen ... I think I've O.D.'d on pizza and take-out. So if you have any ideas of places to try for dinner, I'm open for suggestions."

"So you're actually going to go out somewhere?"

"Yeah. Figured I might as well get used to living in the world again."

"Well, if you stay in town, the good news is you can park in a permit spot 'cause they stop checking for 'em after five. What kind of food do you like?"

"I'm up for anything. But I'm kind of in the mood for seafood."

"Go to Jake's on Baltimore."

"I haven't been there in years. The seafood bisque still great?"

"Oh, it's *heaven!*"

Jade felt her stomach rumble at the mention of the locally famous soup. She didn't want to impose but her hunger trumped her modesty.

"Would you like to come along?" Tom asked.

"That would be great. It seems my stomach likes the idea of the bisque."

"I'm gonna move my car to a permit spot."

"While you do that, I'm just gonna get changed real quick."

"OK."

Jade rushed to her place, threw on a long, flowy skirt and a black shirt. She went back upstairs to her bathroom mirror to make sure she looked somewhat decent, ran a brush through her hair and left.

She liked the fact that there was no expectation tacked onto this outing. Her outing with Tom was not a date, which was fine by her. She enjoyed his company. He may have been serious and glum, but that was to be expected. Still, he had a dry sense of humor she found amusing and he was surprisingly easy to talk to. Plus, she hadn't been to Jake's in a long time and was craving that bisque, so what the hell could it hurt?

Jade saw Tom's Jeep parked on her street, not far from her place, and he jogged up to meet her. When Tom saw her this time, he felt a bit underdressed. She once had worn a t-shirt and shorts with sneakers, but now wore a skirt, fancier shirt and dressy sandals. It wasn't anything too fancy but it bested his shorts, flip flops, and polo shirt.

"Wow!" Tom said under his breath so as to make sure she couldn't hear. It was difficult not to notice Jade's beauty even if she didn't accentuate it with make-up and fashionable tight-fitting clothing.

"Are you ready?" she asked, a smile sneaking across her lips.

"Yeah." He smiled back.

The four-block walk to the restaurant didn't take long, even though Tom remained quiet as he listened to her talk about different things: stories about dumb customers, as well as the little kids she loved teaching and how it changed her into a better person. In the middle of one of her stories, they already found themselves at the restaurant entrance.

Jake's Seafood had a long history stretching back to its original roots in Baltimore, making it all the more fitting that the name of the street on which the restaurant was located was the same as the city of its birth. The entrance was located on the corner of Baltimore Avenue and First Street, and when they went inside, a decent-sized bar area welcomed them with a hostess stand to the left and a few tables against the windows on the right. Tom told the teenage hostess they'd like a table for two. The evening before a regular school and work day had driven away most of the tourists and locals, leaving plenty of tables to choose from and getting seated immediately. The waiter came quickly, as if they were his only table for the evening. They both decided to share a bottle of pinot noir.

"So you were saying ... about the kids you teach?" Tom said.

"Oh, yeah! So, I think I've decided what I want to do – as a career."

"What's that?"

"I want to teach."

"Teach?"

"I've really enjoyed substitute teaching this past year, but I've never been quite sure what exactly I wanted to teach. I really like teaching music to the kids, but I feel like I'm not knowledgeable enough to teach it."

"Do you know how to play an instrument?"

"Yeah. The guitar. I also played in band all throughout high school and did two years of marching band in college."

"Doesn't that mostly qualify you?"

"Not ... exactly. But I was still not sure if I wanted to teach it or not. Then, today, going through the records with you. It helped remind me of just how much I love talking about it - and teaching it."

"Don't you need to get your teaching certification for that?"

"Yeah. That's the thing. I've already gotten it."

"So you've known for quite some time this is what you want to do?"

"Yeah. I applied for it after the first day I taught music class."

"Damn. So what are you doing still substituting?"

"Well ... first, I wanted to tell my parents—"

"You haven't *told* them yet!?"

"I'm *working* on it." She playfully threw a piece of bread at him and he put up a hand to shield himself. "Besides ... I wanted to make sure it's what I wanted. And I was hoping to get a job at one of the local schools around here."

"You love it here that much?"

"Oh, yeah. Why? You don't?"

"I don't know." Tom looked off at the other diners surrounding them. The waiter brought their bottle opened it and poured a glass for each of them. After he left, Tom immediately took a drink. "When I lived here ... all I could think about was getting the hell outta here."

"High school wasn't so fun for you either?"

"Oh, no. The opposite, actually. I had a good amount of friends. Played lacrosse, went to all the dances and the other social stuff. I just ... it wasn't my scene ... is all I can say." He thought about his former life for only a few seconds. "I guess I was just so caught up in the usual teenage yearning - being so damn eager to get out of this town, out of this state, away from my parents. I wanted to move to a big city, make something of myself, prove to the world and my parents I could succeed on my own."

"So what made you decide to come back here?"

"I thought this could be a place where I could hide away for a while, plan my comeback. But after this O'Leary commentary, I don't think there's going to be one." He waved his hand dismissively. "Shit. I don't even wanna be in it anymore."

"Are you sure about that?"

"What?" Tom almost laughed at her incredulous question.

"I'm only asking because you seem to be sulking quite a bit about it."

"It's all I've known. I guess ... it's just hard to let go."

"How can you expect to move to the next phase of your life without letting go of the old one?"

"I think that's a little easier said than done," Tom's tone began to flare.

"Of course!" Jade picked up on his tone and immediately wanted to let him know she wasn't trying to be harsh or overly-critical of him. "I'm not trying to downplay what happened to you. In my own weird way, I'm just trying to be supportive."

"No, you're right. The first step to solving any problem is recognizing there is one. It's time to move on."

"That simple, huh?"

"Well ... no. But it does feel good to say it out loud."

"What are you gonna do, then?"

Tom thought of his earlier confrontation with Jen and how he had rejected the offer to interview Jade, then chuckled a bit, took a sip of wine, and said, "Long-term? I don't know. But right now, I'm gonna sit here and hang out with you."

"Sounds good to me."

The waiter came and took their food order, and the dinner came and went with the both of them laughing and talking about their old jobs, college experiences, friends, and other light-hearted stories.

When they were done, Jade suggested going out for a drink or two. Tom agreed and they walked along the boardwalk. The sun was just starting to kiss the watery horizon, leaving the air a hazy golden color, almost making the moment feel like an aged developed photograph from the 1970s.

"So where do you want to go for a drink?"

"Someplace small."

"I think I've got the right place."

They headed south, as if they were walking to Shorebreak, even turning down Wilmington Avenue, although they went down the right side of the road rather than the left. They only passed two or three storefronts before they came to the small entrance to Zogg's Bar and Restaurant. The entryway felt as if you were entering someone's tucked away, private beach bar. There was an outside tiki bar for the nice summer days, with the actual building consisting of two sides, each being in the shape of an equidistant ninety-degree angle. The longest part of the establishment had a pool table and video games, with a smaller L-shaped bar. The other side was devoted to seating with booths lining the walls. The speakers were in the middle of screaming out The Vaccines' "All in White," when the pair approached the bar and each straddled a bar stool.

"I was here not too long ago," Tom said.

"Really? When?"

"The first night I was back. Came here with Feltz."

"Well, then. What do you say we do a shot?"

"Sure. Suggestions?"

"How about Fireball?"

Tom wondered what the local fascination was with this particular liquor. He thought it tasted like the Red Hots candy and it wasn't strong at all, but if it's what she wanted, he'd go along.

"Sure."

They ordered a round and held up their shot glasses for a toast.

"Cheers to ...," Jade began trying to think of how to phrase what she wanted to say. "To confronting the things for which cause us the greatest turmoil."

"Well put. I guess."

They both whipped their heads back and let the amber alcohol slide down their throats. The warm cement filled their chests before dissolving into the rest of their body parts.

"You think you could do better?" Jade asked. "Let's do another and you can have your chance."

Two more shots of Fireball were set down in front of them and they raised their glasses. She made sure she widened her eyes and stared intently at him to show him she was at full attention for his wise words.

Tom knew he had screwed up. He thought, *Who am I kidding? She had a great damn toast.* He straightened his posture and thought, *Hell, I'll wing it!*

"Clear eyes. Full hearts. Can't lose."

Jade giggled a bit, recognizing the catchphrase from the NBC series *Friday Night Lights*, but she let him have it, and they each drank their shot. This time the sting in their throats wasn't so severe and the warmth lasted a little longer.

"That's a good one," she said. They both ordered a Yuengling draft beer and took in the song for a moment.

"So what's the thing you have to confront?" Tom asked.

"Me?" she almost cringed. "I'd have to say my parents. Telling them what I want to do."

"What's keeping you from telling them?"

"Basically, I'm scared. Scared they won't approve of what I've chosen. Scared my choice will cause them shame."

"I can get that."

"I know I'm almost thirty and I should be able to just make a decision on my own and not care about what others think – even my parents. But it's just ... they're a major part of who I am. I respect them. I don't want to say hell with them just so I can get my way. It's," she let out an annoyed single laugh, "really annoying how much I let that stand in my own way. But I can't help it."

"Do you think you'll ever be able to just throw caution to the wind and tell them about teaching?"

Jade pondered the question for a few seconds, trying to suss out the complicated situation in her head as quickly as possible. "At the rate I'm going, I think, yeah, it's inevitable. I just don't know when."

Tom thought about asking her what she was waiting for, but he knew the answer. When you're in a predicament, you hope that time will alter your situation, resolve what you're so scared of resolving yourself; but time just prolongs and enlarges the fear and the uncertainty.

"What about you?" she asked.

"I, ah ... I think I have too many to name."

"C'mon, then. I told you mine."

"The death of my wife. A wife who cheated on me. The death of my career. A career which I was beginning to not be very proud of but it was all I knew. Yeah. That about sums it up."

He took a swig of his beer and she followed suit.

"Do you miss her?" she asked.

"I wish she wasn't dead. As for us being married ... I've been mulling that over and over in my head. And all I can think of is ... what if she hadn't died? What if we did the show, I found out she was cheating on me, and the rest of the show went on in its normal way? Would I have left her? Or would I have tried to work things out? For a long time, it was difficult to find any of those answers ... because ... the 'what if's are meaningless. She's gone and that's the way it is.

"Though, I'm realizing more and more lately that ... we were done. Our marriage was over before we taped that episode. I guess now ... it's just a matter of living in the world again ... getting back to normal."

"I think 'normal' is overrated. No one's normal. Normal is some kind of tourist souvenir society tries to package up and sell. We all have our ... eccentricities which make us special. Why try to hide them for the sake of being normal?"

"Well, what if your eccentricity is going on a murdering rampage?"

"That's the wrong kind of special."

The music had changed to Bleachers' "I Wanna Get Better" and they both slowed their drinking as both of them felt a buzz and neither one of them wanted to get too drunk. When they left the bar, the music still echoed in their ears as the alcohol in their stomachs was catching up to their heads.

Tom volunteered to walk Jade home and their walk had slowed down as their heads weren't the only body parts affected by their drinks. As it often does late at night, after a few drinks, time seemed to race by, making their walk a short journey with hardly any words exchanged. When they came to Jade's small screened porch, Jade asked, "Would you like to come in for some tea?"

"Sure."

They both walked in and Jade asked what kind of tea he may like, adding she pretty much had every kind.

"Any kind with caffeine," Tom said.

After she had made the tea and served it to him, she suggested some music and he acquiesced. She approached her radio and pressed play on the attached iPod. Bob Dylan's deep country-sounding voice sang out "Tonight I'll Be Staying Here with You," and she returned down to the kitchen where Tom was sipping his drink.

"Thanks for the tea," he said. "It's really good."

"You're welcome. I'm glad you like it. So ... you said you moved here to get back to a normal life. Do you think confronting your parents was part of that?"

"Whoa. You certainly don't pull any punches with questions, do ya?"

"Nope." She sucked in her lips to suppress a smile.

"Well ... it wasn't at the forefront of my mind, but ... maybe ... yeah, it could've been. All I was really thinking at the time was that I needed to get as much distance between me and L.A. as possible."

"You're not gonna escape your problems just by moving across the country to some small, unknown area. They'll follow you wherever you go."

"Oh, I know. That O'Leary segment proved that."

"I'm sorry. I don't mean to sound—"

"No. It's OK. I know what you mean."

Jade felt a little bad for making such a bold statement. She didn't want Tom to think she was looking down on his choices or lifestyle. She figured she had to change the course of this conversation.

"Hey," she said. "Can I show you something?"

"Yeah."

"Come on up." She motioned to the upstairs sitting area. They both grabbed their tea and climbed the stairs to the open sitting area. Tom had noticed Jade had designed the layout of the room to be as warm, inviting and comfortable as possible – a place where Jade could lose herself in when she needed some alone time. There was a small couch and a plushy sitting chair – sitting on it, Tom noticed an old Funland game prize, a small stuffed pink flamingo wearing sunglasses. Both pieces of furniture were set around a small flatscreen TV, which had a very thin layer of dust on it. Tom looked at the framed photos set up around the room and was in awe of all the happy moments captured in each picture. Some were with her parents and some were with friends, maybe a few of boyfriends past. Then he noticed a framed photograph set apart from the others. It was of Jade and a pretty young woman with auburn hair, brown eyes and a big smile.

"That's Vanessa," Jade said.

"Oh," Tom snapped out of his stare of the photo. "Yeah."

Jade walked up beside him and opened the small photo album she was holding. Tom diverted his attention to the album and noticed all of the artistic-looking shots. The pictures looked like they belonged in an art gallery in New

York. There were also personal, candid shots of family, friends, and beautiful settings.

"Wow. These are ... pretty amazing."

"Really?"

"Yeah."

"Thanks."

"Have you thought about starting a photography business?"

"In *this* area? I'd be one of hundreds! Every woman and girl who picks up a camera and takes a few artsy pictures around here considers herself a photographer."

"So? Just because there are millions of writers in the world, it doesn't stop new ones from writing and getting published, does it?"

"Yeah. That's true. I guess I should take my own advice when it comes to taking a chance."

"Why not?" Tom asked.

Jade looked to him with a look of admiration as he continued to look through her photographs; she liked his support of her. It was more than most had given her when they saw her photos. A particular picture caught Tom's eye: it was of a little girl facing the ocean.

"Wow! This one is great."

Jade looked down to see which one he was talking about and it struck a chord of her memory. "Oh, yeah! I was on the beach last spring and this little girl sort of just wobbled up to the shoreline. There was something about the simplicity of it that I just found really ... enviable."

"Enviable!?"

"Yeah. I can't remember what it was like to be *that* young. I wish I could remember."

"You don't remember anything from your childhood?"

454

"Well, I don't remember most of it. I remember bits and pieces. I know I had a good childhood." Jade grew silent, looking downward, as if she were heavily contemplating what to say next. "I miss it. I wish I had ... relished it more, taken it all in."

Tom could sympathize with her. He believed nearly everyone who had a good childhood probably felt that way. Nina Simone's smooth, silky voice accompanied the strings and piano on "Turn Me On."

"But now," she continued, then looking into Tom's eyes with a hopeful glare. "Now I fully know the importance of every day. Every day is my chance to make a better life. Not just for me, but for those I care about."

Tom didn't know if it was Jade's admirable optimism or Nina's sexy crooning, but, looking into Jade's eyes, he saw a look he hadn't seen since he was a young man: a look of admiration, a look of yearning and passion. For once in his life, he didn't take caution. He didn't consider what the press may say, what people might think or how his own family may feel. He just went with his own emotion, there in that moment. He leaned in slow, his lips first hovering softly over her pillowy lips before landing upon them for a sensuous kiss. Her body welcomed him as his body drew closer to her and they wrapped their arms around each other. Then a quick urgency hit her. She moved her head back.

"I'm not going to save you, Tom," she said.

"What?"

"I'm not some woman who has all the answers to your life, and I'm not the woman in your story who's gonna struggle to make you a better man."

"I don't expect you to be."

"Good. Just so you know." She lunged her head forward and continued kissing him, their bodies continuing to be swept up in a passionate dance of sweeping arms, exploratory hands, heavy breathing and a spark which had ignited deep within them both.

Jade felt comfort in knowing she had said what she wanted to say. She knew her attraction to Tom wasn't some juvenile urge to change or fix him or his problems. All she could think of regarding her slow, growing attraction to this man was how he had helped her to see a side to herself and her life she hadn't seen before; and she wanted to know more about him. She believed him to be a good man and didn't want to think any more about it. She went with her heart and her heart screamed at her to make out with this man.

Their entanglement was driven by Jade toward her bedroom, where she grabbed her shirt and peeled it off over her head, revealing her darker caramel skin almost clashing against her Wonder Woman bra. Her eyes smoldered with sexual desire, staring at him like a woman on a mission, seeing her target directly in front of her.

Tom couldn't believe this was happening. Being with someone, whether exclusively or sexually, was the last thing he thought he would be doing any time soon. Jade was a woman he didn't ever plan on meeting, let alone thought ever existed. She threw him for a loop and left his head in a haze of wonder.

They had both been physically attracted to each other since they first saw one another. As much as people try to sell the notion that you notice and are first attracted to a person's sense of humor or intelligence or some other inner quality before their looks was a lie. We all notice a person's physical attributes first. However, they both knew that the physical should only be the starting point of the attraction. What should truly seal the deal of any relationship are those inner qualities which truly matter and make up a person: intelligence, humor, compassion, understanding, patience, and so on. It was those same qualities which attracted Tom and Jade to one another. They saw it in each other and it was the driving force behind their current heavy make-out session.

The song switched to Otis Redding's "Come to Me," and they removed the rest of their clothes before falling into an intimate dance on her bed. They kissed for a while longer as if the next big step would be all the more explosive if they waited just a little longer.

Jade moved onto him and they both shuddered from an ecstasy that started from deep within them both and rippled throughout their bodies, expanding outward to their arms, legs, hands, feet, fingers, toes, necks and minds.

As Otis crooned his soulful love ballad, their bodies moved in sync with the music, as if they had been doing this dance with each other their entire young lives, even though the excitement of a new love and desire dwelled within them both.

They both knew that finding someone physically attractive was a hell of a lot easier than finding another soul who was just as mutually accepting of you as you were of them. Every new introduction, every date, every fling, was an act of exposing your true self and willingly making yourself vulnerable. Tom and Jade both felt that vulnerability with each other as they continued to make love. The vulnerability was the one thing still pushing at the panic button in the back of their minds, but they were too enraptured in their current physical comfort to stop. The rest of the night blurred with sensuality building to a euphoric release, their bodies then slipping into a peaceful, exhaustive sleep.

21.

"Your masquerade,
I don't wanna be a part of your parade
Everyone deserves a chance to
Walk with everyone else"

--Family of the Year
"Hero"

Two-and-a-half weeks after their first official date, Tom had grown very happy with being around Jade, and she was beginning to have feelings she wasn't sure she still had left within her: romantic feelings. This thing with Tom was more than just a casual affair. She usually was scared to put her heart out there, leaving it vulnerable, and most men she had met were not worth it. On paper, he was not the most likely man she thought she would feel comfortable around, but her feelings had no logical explanation or reasoning. All she knew was she liked this man. A lot. She got nervous at the thought of seeing him – the good kind of nervous. And she hadn't felt this way about a man – or anyone – since college, so she knew this kind of feeling when she had it and she knew it wasn't something to take for granted.

Before she could move forward with Tom, however, she had to confront her parents. So she got in her Volkswagen Rabbit, turning on the radio to Florence + The Machine's "Ship to Wreck," and drove to Washington, D.C. She had made the trip enough so that the time went by fast. She would have rather been thinking about Tom or *anything* else, but her thoughts were uncontrollably focused on her parents and what she was going to say to them. The panic almost overtook her a few times throughout the drive, but her breathing exercises helped keep her emotions from turning her legs and arms to Jell-O. Most of her drive, her mind raced to piece together what exactly she was going to say to them. When she entered D.C., a recent, warm memory finally played in her mind.

* * *

A couple of nights after her first official date with Tom, she was lying in bed when she was awoken by a brief blast of running water from the tap in her bathroom. She sat up and rubbed her eyes to see the first glimpse of daybreak peeking through the window blinds. The light was a dull gray, barely lighting enough of her bedroom. She looked beside herself to see the other side of the bed empty.

She stood up and crept toward the bathroom, the light shining through the crack at the bottom of the door. She peeked her head into the doorway, slowly tiptoeing into the small bathroom like a child checking early Christmas morning to see if Santa had visited or not.

"Hey," she said. She wore a white halter top and blue cotton underwear.

He was dressed only in a pair of jeans, sitting on the floor with his knees almost up to his chest. He looked to her and she instantly saw the trepidation flooding his face.

"Hi," he gasped.

She came and sat to the right of him, sort of cattycorner, squeezing them both in the small bathroom.

"Are you OK?" she asked.

Tom took a gulp, unsure whether to ask Jade what he had so desperately wanted to ask her since that day they had lunch. He figured he had nothing to really lose, so he went for it. "You never asked me."

"Asked you what?"

"Whether I did it. Whether I intentionally signed that release form to have Maggie on the show. Why?"

"Honestly?"

Tom nodded his head.

"In the long run, it's none of my business. I don't want to force you into telling me something you might not want to tell me. I mean, if you—"

"I didn't," he interrupted. "I did ... sign a form. It's customary to fill out insurance forms before every taping and when Dylan came up saying it was legal stuff ... I thought ..."

The statement was too painful for Tom to finish, knowing what ultimately resulted because of his own assumption. Jade felt horrible, knowing what he must be going through.

"It's OK," she said, a sincere look in her eyes. "I believe you."

He looked her in the eyes. "Good."

She cracked a small smile, thinking this was a start for him, maybe for both of them. She leaned into him, resting her head on his bare shoulder. Tom could only look forward, his intense gaze practically burning a hole into the floor. It took a while, but after a minute or so of feeling her warm head against his skin, hearing each of her inhaled breaths like a soft sigh, his intense stare slightly cracked with a smile of relief and hope.

* * *

Before she knew it, she was pulling up to her parents' Chevy Chase home. The affluent D.C. neighborhood and home had been the ultimate symbol of success to Jade's parents – proof of a good, meaningful life. For the longest time, she had wanted those same things and she took every step toward that goal. Somewhere between law school and beginning her career, that goal changed. It wasn't that she didn't want to be successful or even not satisfy her parents. Jade's concepts of success changed. Being successful in life and in your career didn't mean you had to be a doctor, lawyer, or any other high-paying, well-respected, society-lauded profession. To Jade, being successful meant finding something you really loved doing, getting paid for it and doing it the best you could.

She took a deep breath and threw herself out the car as if she were diving into some inevitable, painful experience she wanted to hurry and face and be done with. Each step seemed to pull her heart further down so by the time she got to the door, the rapid beat felt as if it were on the tops of her feet. The panic attack was building deep inside her but she swallowed her fear down as best she could and knocked on the door.

The door opened and her mother appeared in front of her. Jade had always believed her mother to be beautiful in every sense of the word. She just wished her mother wasn't so traditional in her marital role, allowing Jade's father to speak for them both even though her mom worked, provided, and contributed as much to the family as him. Jade wondered if her mother was truly happy in the role she had chosen for herself all those years ago on the day of her traditional marriage.

"Hello, sweetie," her mother greeted. "This is a nice surprise! What are you doing here?"

"Hi, Mama." Jade embraced her mother in a tight, loving hug. "Is Papa here?"

"Yes. He is in his study. Come in!"

Jade came inside, closing the door behind her. Mrs. Saha led Jade back into Mr. Saha's study. The room's walls consisted of bookshelves full of books of all sizes – mostly non-fiction – and his desk was the picture of neat and tidy. Mr. Saha sat in a leather-cushioned chair, his legs crossed, a book in his lap. For once, Jade didn't try to sneak a peek at what title he was reading.

"Hello, Jade," her father said as he bookmarked his latest read and set the book aside.

"Hi, Papa."

"It has been a while."

Jade rapidly nodded her head, choking back tears.

"What brings you here?"

She took a breath and looked over to make sure her mother was still standing in the doorway. She was.

"I wanted to speak with you and Mama about something."

"What about?"

"I know you've been wanting me to pick up my career in law again." She looked him in the eyes, over to her mother, then back to him. "But that's not going to happen, Papa."

The hope which had just been in his eyes – a hope of his daughter's announcement of her return to law, to the city – was now gone, the smile running down his face, turning into disappointment, as if her statement were water capable of washing it away.

"So what are you going to do?" his tone grew terse and agitated.

"I want to teach."

"Teach what?"

"Music."

"You don't know anything about music," her father said. "How do you expect to teach a college course on music when you know nothing about it?"

"It's not college, Papa. There's an opening for a music teacher at an elementary school a few miles from Rehoboth."

"Elementary?"

"Yes. In a town called Ocean View." She looked away from her father's puzzled, shocked expression, toward her mother, hoping for either of them to say something supportive.

"I thought you were going back into law," Dr. Saha said.

"I never made that promise. What I said I wanted was to find something I loved doing. And teaching is what I love."

"Teaching music? What do you know of music?"

"I know how to read it. I play guitar. In fact, I've gotten a master's in music history and my teaching certification."

"When did you get your certification?"

"Just a few months ago. Which you'd know if you ever visited ... or at least called."

"Jade," her mother interrupted. "Don't speak to your father that way!"

"Do you think this job will be a breeze because you get your summers off? Or because you work with little kids? Because, first of all, your time off is not as much as you'd think. Second, working with kids will get very old very fast."

"I'm not doing it because of the summer. And, even if I do grow tired of it, what is wrong with pursuing what I have a passion for right now?" Before he could speak, she continued. "I'm not passionate about financial law. It's not what I want to do."

"Not what you want to do? It's a secure career with some of the best benefits and pay today. It will provide you with a good, secure life."

It dawned on Jade that her father was, as Tom had said, just wanting what was best for her – even if his way of showing it was screwed up. Regardless of his intentions, however, Jade knew she had to speak her mind and communicate to them what it was she wanted to do, but without being disrespectful.

"I'm not going to be a lawyer, Papa. At least, not any time soon."

"So you admit you may still do it?"

"I'm *saying* ... it's not what I want to do with my life ... for an indefinite period of time. Who knows where life will lead me? Never say never, right?"

"Jade—"

"I'm not looking for any kind of blessing or approval from you ... even though it would be nice. Regardless, I love teaching and it's what I'm going to do."

"But it's not what you *should* be doing," her father said. "Teaching is an admirable profession, but you're smarter than that. You could—"

"What!? I could *what?* Make more money? Be worthy of your praise when you're socializing with your friends?"

"Jade!" her mother interrupted.

"The money doesn't matter to me. If it did, I'd still be in New York."

"I still don't agree," her father said. Jade could tell his voice was straining and he was getting as emotional as she had ever seen him, which wasn't much. "Teaching is a waste of your talent."

"I'm sorry you feel that way," Jade said. She had to swallow down the enormous cry forming in her throat. "But I've already submitted my resumé and application, and it's what I'm doing."

She waited for her father to say something but he simply stared at her, his expression a mix of disdain and bewilderment. Just then, when he looked like he was about to speak, Dr. Saha picked up the book he had been reading, opened it back up to the spot he bookmarked and proceeded to read as if she weren't there.

"So that's it?" Jade asked.

"You have already made up your mind," Dr. Saha said. "You're nearly thirty. You can make your own choices. There is nothing more to say."

"Our talks really are so sentimental. I don't know why we don't talk more often," Jade said with sarcasm. She left the study and stormed back out to the hallway.

"Jade," her mother's voice rang from behind her. "Wait."

Jade turned and her mother was right in front of her.

"He's impossible!" Jade shouted. "How do you live with that man!?"

"He's your father!"

"And I love him! But it's awfully hard to like him!"

"Why are you so angry?"

"Because, all my life, I've done what you and Papa have wanted! I've gotten good grades, graduated valedictorian in high school *and* college, went to law school, started work at a prestigious firm right after. And now that I want to do something *I* really want to do, you both don't support me!"

"You did those things because you wanted to, Jade."

"Because I knew you wouldn't love or support me if I didn't!"

"Jade," her mother breathed. "Why do you think we wouldn't love you?"

"I think the proof was just displayed in the study."

"Jade. Just because he doesn't agree with your choices doesn't mean he doesn't love you. And we'll always support you."

"He? Does that mean you agree with my being a teacher?"

"It's what you love. It's what you want to do. Of course, I do."

"Then why do you not say anything? Why were you giving me the third degree a few weeks ago?"

"I didn't know this was what you really wanted to do."

"And what convinced you?"

"What you just did in there. Confronting your father."

"Well, if you don't agree with him, then why don't you say so?"

"Jade. I've known your father many, many years. And I know how he works. I know he's wrong in not supporting you on this. But neither you nor I will convince him of it. He is very stubborn. He needs to learn for himself. And he will."

"How do you know?" Jade asked with worry.

"Because he loves you. He misses you. Your father is just like anyone else, Jade. He needs to learn things on his own, in his own time."

"You could still speak up to him."

"I could," Mrs. Saha admitted. "And now that I know your plan, I will."

Jade still had her doubts about whether her mother fully supported her, but she could only take her for her word, so she was going to trust her. "OK."

"Were you planning on staying for a while?"

"Not really. I do need to get back. I may have to work." She looked to her mother and noticed she was beginning to silently cry. "Mama. Why are you crying?"

"I ... I miss you."

"I promise I'll be back to visit after the school year is over." She hugged her and they stood there, both relishing the sweet moment. They both didn't see Dr. Saha standing in the doorway of his study. He cracked a smile and went back in, silently closing the door behind him.

"There's someone I want you to meet," Jade said.

"Who?"

Jade felt foolish, at her age, labeling someone her boyfriend, and she wasn't exactly sure if Tom was, but their relationship did seem that way. "I met someone."

"Who?"

"His name is Tom."

"Tom who?"

"Tom Frost."

"Why does that name sound familiar? What does he do?"

Jade knew she was going to catch more disapproval from her parents when they found out it was the man with the reality show, the one whose wife was killed live on television. However, she wanted to be honest. "He used to be the host of a reality TV show."

A lightbulb turned on in Mrs. Saha's mind and she knew exactly of whom Jade was speaking. "The one whose wife was killed?"

"Yes."

Jade didn't need to further explain what had happened because Mrs. Saha had seen the footage. She knew it wasn't Tom Frost who had murdered his wife but she wasn't sure he hadn't inadvertently caused it.

"Jade," her mother scolded. "What are you thinking!? Seeing a man like that?"

"A man like what!?" Jade incredulously asked. "He is a good man who had something very bad happen to him."

"Something bad which his creation had caused. Have you seen the footage?"

"No."

"You haven't even seen it!?"

"No, I didn't. There's no reason to."

"You think there is no reason to see a seminal moment in this man's life? A man you're exclusively dating?"

"What about me, Mama? Should he dig into my past and look at the footage of my prom!? Or how about the interview footage of me after Vanessa was killed!?"

Jade's question had forced quiet into Mrs. Saha's mind. She searched for the right words to express her concern to her daughter, but found none before Jade spoke again.

"He had nothing to do with his wife's death. You know he didn't shoot her, he certainly didn't know she was going to be on that show, and he doesn't need another person digging into his own personal tragedy."

"How do you know for sure he didn't know she'd be on that show?"

"He told me."

"Don't be so naïve, Jade." She took her daughter by the hand. "Come here. I want to show you something."

"What?" Jade followed.

"I think you need to see the video."

"Mom, I don't want to."

"If you truly care for this man in any way, you need to face what he's been through, what he's seen."

Jade hesitantly allowed her mother to bring her to the home computer, which was already on. Mrs. Saha pulled up YouTube and searched for "*Heartbraker* tragedy." The video popped up and began to instantly play. "Now watch."

Jade sat down in front of the screen and watched the entire video clip, each minute causing her to tear up more and more, until the moment when Maggie was shot and the tears overflowed from Jade's eyelids, cascading down her cheeks.

When the video ended, Mrs. Saha closed the internet window and said with a hushed voice, "I just don't want you to get hurt."

"Where you see naivety, I see faith," Jade said. "But not simply faith in him. Faith in myself. Faith in my judgement. Faith in facts. If he willingly signed away his permission to have her on the show, why would he be fired and not given some kind of promotion or severance?"

"And why did he choose to remain in jail?"

"He was arrested for punching his friend, a producer on the show, and if you ask me, the man had it coming to him." Jade could tell by the look on her mother's face that she was still skeptical and Jade couldn't blame her. "I'm not trying to fix this man. I'm not trying to turn him into something he's not. If he screws up with me, I have no problem showing him the door."

"That's easy to say now ... before you're more emotionally invested. What happens when you have fallen in love with this man and he does something—"

"Does what!? Something wrong?"

"Something that gets you hurt! Whether it's an accident or not."

"I'm not in any physical danger, Mama. As for getting emotionally hurt, I don't even know for sure things will get that far. But if they do, that's just the chance you take when you open your heart. And it's the same chance you take with *anyone* you have feelings for!"

"Remember what I said just now about your father? About his stubbornness and having to learn for himself? Well, the apple does not fall far from the tree. Like him, I love you enough to have you make your own decisions."

"Thank you. All I want to know is ... if you will support me."

"Of course, I will."

"I promise ... it'll all be fine. I'll be fine."

The two embraced and Jade said her goodbyes to both her parents before leaving to return to Delaware. Upon entering her car, she noticed the fear was gone. A calm washed over her that she had not felt in a long time, and Jade wondered if her confrontation had something to do with it. She turned on her car radio with the Mumford &

Sons song "Broad-Shouldered Beasts" playing, and sat, listening to the song crescendo as butterflies fluttered up a small storm in her stomach. This time, though, the butterflies were the good kind. The kind which came when she thought of Tom.

* * *

"I know what you're saying, man," Will said. "But, I'm tellin' ya ... each of the seven deadly sins is represented in *Willy Wonka and The Chocolate Factory.*"

Tom came into the comic book store to see Will, who had told him about the Forgotten Mile back at Hammerheads, working behind the sales counter, talking to a customer. From out of the small computer's speakers, Of Monsters & Men's song, "Black Water," was blaring.

"Wait," the perplexed customer said. "Are you talking about the book or the movie?"

"The movie!"

"Wilder or Depp?"

"Wilder! The *only* good adaptation!"

"Then how are the seven deadly sins in it when there are only five kids?"

"A common mistake. OK. So Augustus Gloop is pretty obvious."

"He's the fat boy, right?"

"Yeah. He's gluttony. Then you've got Veruca Salt. She's greed."

"Yeah! Yeah! The 'I-want-it-now' little bitch."

"Violet is pride."

"She turns into the blueberry, right?"

"Yeah! Mike - the kid who watches all the TV? He's wrath."

"See! You're outta kids and ya still got three more sins."

"Not so fast. Charlie is envy."

"Wait! You're saying the main character, the protagonist, the kid everyone loves, represents a sin!?"

"Think about it. He wants more than anything to win that golden ticket! Throughout the entire story, he's not as outright bad as the other kids, but he's awfully damn envious of what Wonka has. And when everyone's buying up Wonka bars, all he does is make a whiny face 'cause he can't buy any."

"OK. What about sloth and lust?"

"Easy. Charlie's Grandpa Joe is sloth. Old bastard just lays around in his house all day. Then, when he hears there's a chance for a prize, and his grandson invites him along for a shot at that prize? He miraculously leaps up and dances about like some silly, damn fool. Even sings a song called "*I've* Got a Golden Ticket." He didn't get anything! It was Charlie's ticket!"

"Whoa, whoa, whoa!" the customer had to stifle laughter. "So who represents lust then!?"

"The only one left."

"No way!"

"Willy Wonka!"

"Get the *hell* outta here!"

"Seriously! Think about it! First off, lust isn't just sexual. It's a deep desire or strong craving for something. What's more craved for than chocolate? Also he's got those little men working for him? Who knows what he has them do! He opens his contest to tour his factory to an audience which he knows mostly consists of children. He's known as the 'Candy Man,' *and* he offers to give away a lifetime supply of his chocolate bars."

"What's so lustful about that?"

"Are you *kidding* me!? OK. Chocolate is known for having some property that releases endorphins. Even though I hate it, it's even mentioned in that Depp version! And who mentions it?"

The answer dawned on the customer. "Ho-ly *shiiiit.*"

"*Willy Wonka!*" they both shouted.

"Exactly!" Will said.

The two busted out laughing as Tom stepped forward and mumbled, "Excuse me."

"Oh, hey, man," Will greeted, his laughter dying down. The other guy said his farewell and left.

"Next week," Will shouted to the leaving customer, "I'll tell you about how Springsteen's 'Born to Run' is a contemporary retelling of *Peter Pan!*"

"Hey," Tom said.

"Oh! You're Jade's friend! Forgotten Mile, right?"

"Yeah."

"What can I do you for?"

"I'm looking for this book Jade was tellin' me about. *Y ... the Last ... Man?*"

"Oh yeah! Got the first two collected volumes over here." Will stepped out from behind the register and led him to the corner of the store, where racks lined the walls, showcasing both paperback and hardcover collections of every comic from *The Avengers* to *Wonder Woman*, as well as more independent, lesser known collections. At the bottom of the last rack near the left corner was a couple of paperback comic collections for *Y: The Last Man.* Will swiped them up and laid them in Tom's hands, all in one motion.

"Here are the first two volumes of Brian K. Vaughan's *Y: The Last Man*. These are the deluxe editions, so there are still three more volumes you need to complete the run."

"Three more!?"

"Yeah. Didn't Jade tell you?"

"She told me it was involved but ... I didn't think comics were *that* involved!"

"Yeah, man. This ain't kids' stuff."

They walked back toward the checkout register, located in the center of the store, against the left-hand wall.

"I guess this may not be a good time to see if you're hiring."

"I could use someone part-time," Will said. "You don't seem to know shit about comics, but, hey ... we all have to start somewhere. Besides, you know Jade, so ... you can't be all *that* bad." Will reached behind the counter and brought out a single paper application. "Fill this out and get it back to me as soon as you can, 'kay?"

"Sure. Thanks!" Tom took the paper. "So ... how long have you known Jade?"

"I met her soon after she moved here. I was out to dinner at Shorebreak one night and she was working. We sort of bonded over our mutual love for comics and pop culture, you could say. How about you?" Will rang up the sale. "That'll be thirty-eight dollars and ninety-eight cents."

"It hasn't been long." Tom handed Will two twenty-dollar bills. "We've ... uh ..."

"Oh, I know." Will handed Tom his change and the bag with the books.

"Know what?" Tom grabbed the bag and slipped the application in.

"You like her. And I don't mean in a friendly way."

"That obvious?"

"Not obvious. Inevitable. She's the kind of woman that you fall in love with just talking to her. She's a real Iris Lemon."

"A what now?"

"Iris Lemon? She's one of the character's from *The Natural*. Ya know? Malamud book? The baseball movie? Robert Redford?"

"Oh yeah! *The Natural*! Wait. Which character is Iris?"

"The Glenn Close character ... Iris Lemon." Will immediately could tell Tom had no idea what he was talking about so he shot directly into an explanation. "There are three main women characters in the film version of *The Natural*. There's Close's Iris Lemon, Kim Basinger's Memo Paris, and Barbara Hershey's Harriet Bird. They represent the three different kinds of women there are in the world."

"Oh, I don't know if I wanna get into that—"

"Wait. Wait. Hear me out. So Bird is the purely evil woman. She's a femme fatale who uses her wiles, sexuality and feigned innocence simply for destruction and emasculation. Paris is the kind of woman of whom most young women nowadays consist. She's the mix of good and bad. She's complicated to a fault – almost damaged. I mean, in the book, she even describes herself as a 'dead man's girl' ... and not just 'cause she was the ex-girlfriend of the baseball player who died. Even though Roy Hobbs – the Redford character ... even though Hobbs loves her and treats her nice and is pretty much her savior, she still only uses him as a means to an end. She just cares about money and living a comfortable, wealthy lifestyle, but tries her damnedest to be a good woman for him. Hell, even her uncle talks bad about her! Says she's 'always dissatisfied and will snarl a man up in her trouble.'

"Then, there's Lemon. She represents the true good. And it's not 'cause she's perfect. I mean, she's given birth to Hobbs' illegitimate son. But she's caring, selfless, humble, and, near the end of the movie, when Roy sees her in the baseball stands, she's standing up and the sunlight hits her brim hat just so that it looks like a halo is over her head. She's like an angel. She's the one who reminds Roy who he truly is and that he can always choose what's best if he wants.

"So ... that's Jade. She's an Iris Lemon."

"Wow," Tom said. "How do you think of this bullshit?"

Will chuckled and said, "It's a gift, I guess." His voice grew a little more serious as Andy Burrows' slow song, "Hometown," started playing through the small speakers near them. "So ... are you two ... in the beginning stage?"

"The ... beginning stage? Yeah. I ... guess?"

"Ya know!? The beginning? When you hate to put a label on it for fear it may jinx the whole damn thing?"

"Yeah. To be honest, I don't even know if we're *that* far or not."

"I can tell the way you two were around each other a few weeks ago. There's a spark there."

"Yeah. Well ... I don't know if it'll pan out."

"What do you mean?"

"You know who I am, Will. My story. My wife's death. For some insanely strange reason, I'm still in the press coverage. If I show up dating some woman not even a year after my wife's death, there's gonna be so much stupid rumors and drama goin' around."

"Yeah," Will said, an exasperated sigh escaping his mouth. "I get it. I was married once. She's gone now."

"What happened? If you don't mind me asking."

"Used to live in Jersey before I moved here," Will said with a jovial smirk and a reminiscent tone. "She and I had just celebrated our four-year anniversary. Still just kids. She had to go to work early that morning to file some paperwork. Then I get a call from her."

Will took a deep breath and his usual cheerful visage had grown solemn real quick. "She didn't know a plane had hit the building. I didn't know. I was sick so I had called out that day and was sleeping when she called. The only reason I woke up is 'cause I could hear her voice on the machine. It was panicked. When I picked up, and she asked if there was anything going on in the news, I turned on the TV and I saw it. That big, black trail of smoke coming out of her building. I saw the plane smash into the other building.

"Anyways," he cleared his throat. "I was told later that her tower had no ... no means of escape. All the stairways around the impact zone had been destroyed. And she was above that zone, so she had no ... no way of ... getting down. I didn't know that then. But I think there was some small part of her that knew when we talked. We both kept saying 'I love you' to each other. The last thing she told me, besides that she loved me, was that she and some co-workers were gonna try to make their way down. So I knew ... at least she died trying to get back to me."

Will drew in a sharp breath, as if gasping for an intake of air after being underwater for nearly too long. "After a couple of days, when I knew she was gone for sure, the press contacted me. I didn't want to speak to them. I told them to talk to her parents, her family. I shut down. When I lived back there, I worked for a bank. But after all that, I couldn't do it anymore. I took the money I had and decided to do something I'd always wanted to do. Opened this store.

"I know how you feel about havin' a life after your wife. I didn't date, couldn't even open my heart to that possibility after Sophie. At first, I did it 'cause I felt like I'd be betraying her. I also did it 'cause I felt like her family and our friends may not like me ... moving on. Now, I feel like I'm some freakin' cautionary tale. I know she loved me. And I know she'd want me to be happy. But I feel like I'm too ... set in my ways. Too scared."

"I'm sorry to hear about your wife." Tom said as Will waved off his condolences as if to say, *It's OK.* Tom looked away and asked, "So what do you do now?"

"Now? I just read Batman number forty-one," he held up the comic issue, "finish my shift, go home, maybe drink some wine, and continue living my life, taking pleasure in the small things: the smell of the salty ocean air, a good book, chocolate-peanut butter milkshakes, introducing people to new comics, walkin' my dog on the beach."

"What if I can't ... be with her?"

"Is it *you* who doesn't wanna be with her? Or is it what you think everyone around you wants?"

Tom shot Will a look that gave him the answer.

"See," Will said. "That's gonna get you in trouble – kowtowing to what people want ... or what you *think* they want. Take it from someone who's already made that mistake. Being alone may satisfy everyone else, but it only leaves you lonely. If you don't ever fall in love with someone again, that's fine. But if you find yourself getting a special case of the feels for someone, the last thing you should be worryin' about at your age is whether the public agrees or not. Those people who claim to truly care about you, over time they'll weed themselves out on whether they honestly do or not."

"And what about family?"

"Well, family's different. They mean a lot. What they say holds a lot of weight. But you're not some damn teenager fallin' for the girl on the wrong side of the tracks. Jade is sweet, so damn funny, and smart as hell – smarter than you and I combined! And you've got eyes! You *know* she's pretty. I mean, have you even introduced her to your parents yet?"

"We just ... got together."

"Then at least wait to see what happens after they meet. But you know damn well that your family's gonna love her."

"I just don't know if I'd want Jade to get any media harassment or backlash just from us going out."

"She's a big girl, ya know? Shouldn't *she* make that decision?"

"Yeah." Tom considered that maybe he was more interested in her than he thought. He let out a chuckle. "If things do work out, let's hope she doesn't have to meet my folks for quite some time."

Will let out a single laugh and Tom asked, the thought finally coming out, "If there are three types of women and they're in *The Natural*, what are the different types of men?"

"That's easy," Will said. "There are three types, and they're in *American Pie*."

"The teen movie? About high school boys?"

"Yeah! There's—"

Tom's cell phone rang and he noticed the call was from his mother. He shot Will a look as if to say, *Hold on.*

"Hello?" Tom said. "Mom? ... What's wrong? ... Dad? ... Wait. Where?" Tom listened as his mother rambled. "Where are you, Mom?" He waited as she tried to get her words out. "Beebe? OK. I'll be there in about twenty minutes!"

Tom hung up, slipped the phone in his pocket and practically ran to the door, only able to say "See ya, Will," as he left.

Will said goodbye but Tom didn't hear him. He was already in his Jeep and backing out of the parking space. He knew where the hospital, Beebe Medical Center, was in Lewes. The bad news was it was about thirty minutes away. But, true to his word, he was there in twenty.

* * *

The hospital's chapel had seen many visitors since its dedication back in 2012. Today, one woman sat alone amongst the empty seats, grieving over the man she had just lost. Her tears were some morbid baptism for the life she would now have without him. It was a situation no one envied but which everyone would inevitably come to know. Tom rapidly walked by the small window in the chapel's door, seeing a flash of the woman sitting in there, taking a brief comfort in knowing that would not be his mother, or him, in there today.

He found the room where the nurses had told him his father would be resting. As he came into the room, he saw his father sleeping, a bandage over one of his eyebrows, some of Mr. Frost's blood showing through the white gauze. The song he had just heard on the radio in his Jeep, You + Me's "Open Door," still played in his mind. Mrs. Frost stood up when she saw Tom in the doorway. She met him with a tight, long hug, and her wails of sobbing finally released into his chest. He wondered if she had been waiting all this time to finally crumble. When she collected herself enough to be able to sound coherent, she spoke, still embracing him.

"He'll be fine," she said, not only assuring Tom, but also reassuring herself. "The doctor said he'll need to step up his heart medication."

"Was it a heart attack?"

"No. He fainted. I swear, the man's as stubborn as a mule! He hasn't been taking his medication enough!" She backed away and looked Tom in the eyes. "They want to keep him overnight for observation. But he'll be fine."

"How long has this been goin' on!? I mean, I didn't know—"

"He's been this way since right before you moved to L.A."

"Are you OK?" he asked her.

"I'm fine." She cupped his cheek with her hand.

"I'm fine too," Mr. Frost's scratchy voice sounded out from the bed.

Tom and his mother turned to see the man awake, looking at both of them with what Tom thought was pure love. Tom pulled up a chair beside his father's bed and Mrs. Frost sat beside her son.

"I told your mother to call you here," Mr. Frost said. "I've been thinking a lot about you lately, about what you said a few weeks ago."

Tom was worried he had a lecture coming but the least he could do was hear his father out.

"I wanted to tell you I was sorry," his father said.

"For what?"

"For making you feel like I didn't care about your opinion. I should've told you that day we talked."

"It's fine, Dad."

"No ... it's not. I just wanted you to know that ... no matter what you do, I believe in you."

Tom thought this didn't seem like his father to sound so emotional and introspective, and he noticed his father's voice slightly slurring, some of his words nearly running together, so he jokingly asked, "How much drugs are they pumping into you?"

"A *lot.*"

Tom smothered a laugh, not sure whether his dad was joking or not. "I just want you to know, Dad, that I completely understand your intentions, and I know you and Mom love me. It's why I couldn't ever hate you."

"You seem like your ... mind's ... somewhere else."

"I want to be honest with you. I've met someone. Her name is Jade. I didn't plan on meeting her ... or having any feelings for her. There's just this one thing."

"What's the one thing?"

"I think I know the real reason I've felt I've ... never seemed ... right."

"What do you mean 'never seemed right?'"

"Ever since college, I've always felt like I've been ... going through the motions with my life. Faking everything I can just to get by. It's as if ... there was some ... moment in my life I forgot to experience, some road or distance I forgot to take. I know I did everything I was supposed to. But it felt ... empty. Maybe that's why Maggie and I never ended up working."

"I'm not sure about all that with Maggie. All I can say is that you never rebelled as a kid. But, being your father, I was happy you didn't."

"Maybe that's a part of what was missing. I don't know. But I can tell you ... coming here? Talking to you and Mom? I think it's helped. I feel like I'm doing something I never did before."

Even if Mr. Frost's head hadn't been all muddled from the drugs, he still wouldn't have been able to make much sense of what Tom was trying to say.

"I guess what I'm trying to say is ... for the first time, I think I'm finding my way, and I'm opening up more."

"What about this girl you met? Jade? Where is she?"

"She's visiting her parents in D.C."

"Is she a part of it?"

"Yeah." Tom cleared his throat. "I'll tell you all about her after I get a drink."

Tom got up and went out into the hall. He looked down to see how much money he had in his pocket then his sight moved up to focus on Jade standing a few feet in front of him. He stopped dead in his tracks.

"Hey," he said.

"Hi."

"How'd you know I was here?"

"Will called me. Is your dad OK?"

"Yeah. He wasn't taking his heart medication and he fainted."

"When are they letting him go?"

"Tomorrow. Just keeping him overnight to keep an eye on him."

"Good." Jade smiled and stood around, waiting for Tom to say something.

"Would you like to meet him and my mom?"

Jade didn't focus on the awkwardness of the fact she was meeting his parents so soon after just getting together with him. All she focused on was that before any romantic feelings she had for Tom, he was a friend. She wanted to be there for her friend. She smiled. "Sure."

Tom led her into his dad's hospital room and introduced them all. An hour went by all too quick and Jade said, "I'd love to stay but I have to work tonight."

"Oh, yeah," Tom said.

"It was nice meeting you, Jade," Mrs. Frost said.

"It was nice meeting you both, too," Jade said. "I hope you feel better soon, Mr. Frost."

"Thank you," Mr. Frost said with a smile.

Tom stood up with Jade and said, "I'll walk you out."

They both left the room and Tom's thoughts turned to how her being with him would most likely cause her some strife.

"So, that went really well," Jade said. "Your parents are sweet. Oh! Speaking of parents, I want to tell you all about the talk I had with *my* parents. Can you come meet me after I get off work tonight?"

"Yeah. Sure."

"What's wrong?"

"It's ... nothing. I just ... I like you. A lot. And I just ... don't want the things that've happened to me to ..."

"Tom. I like you too. But, like I told you, I don't want to fix you or change you. I knew way before we spent the night together what your life was like as far as public perception goes. 'Cause I've had some experience with that too."

Tom thought about what small hell her life must have been like after her friend's death, plus the fact she and her friend had both lived through the shooting at their school. He didn't want to frighten Jade off with his worry or insecurity, but it was there. He figured that maybe that worry and insecurity would always be there until he was no longer a target of the gossip blogs, tabloids and news networks' talking heads – but he wasn't sure.

"But," Jade said, "I can't be that one person who believes in you. You have to do that for yourself." Tom nodded his head in silent agreement. "Will you come see me tonight?"

Tom knew her question wasn't merely some informal invitation; she was asking him if he was willing to believe in himself, believe in them.

"Before I do anything. I just ... I wanna be honest with you. I want you to know I wrote my senior college thesis on what happened at your school. The prom massacre? It was big news at the time and I needed a big story to write about. Of course, at the time, I didn't know you were involved, but ... when you brought it up to me, I knew what you were talking about. I ... just wanted you to know that."

"While we're admitting to things. I have to tell you ... I watched the video of your show. My mother just showed it to me a few hours ago. I hope that doesn't change anything between us ... because ... it doesn't for me."

Tom smiled at Jade, admiring her honesty and caring. "I'll ... call you tonight."

"OK." She released a small smile, gave him a kiss on the cheek, and turned to leave. He watched her as she left and, just before she reached the elevator, she turned to get another look at him. He lifted his hand in a motionless wave and beamed a small smile.

After he got a bottle of water, he returned to his father's room and sat with his parents. It wasn't long before his mother excused herself to go get something from one of the vending machines nearby. Tom and his father remained in their seat and bed, respectively, pretty much quiet for the first time since Tom had gotten there. After a few minutes, Mr. Frost broke that silence.

"What's going on, Tom?"

"What do you mean?"

"With Jade. I know I just met her, but I can tell she really likes you."

"Really?"

Mr. Frost laughed at the absurdity of his son's question. "Oh, *son!* Are you *kidding* me!? The way she was looking at you?"

"Dad. It's not a good time. With what happened to Maggie and it hasn't even been a year! I just don't think ... I'm ready for that."

"Are *you* not ready for Jade ... or are you only going by your fear of what everybody else will think?"

"I ... I—" Tom remembered Will had posed almost the same question to him just a few hours earlier. He realized there was definitely a pattern with his train of thought lately.

"Do you honestly care about her as more than a friend?"

"Yes."

"Then to hell with what everybody else will think."

"That's easier said than done."

"You're right! It is. So are you gonna go down the easy path and be alone just to appease everyone else? People who aren't even in *your* life?"

"I don't know."

"Ya know. A wise man once said, 'Life can put the brakes on love ... but never let love ... put the brakes on your life.'"

Tom's head perked up at the quote he used to repeat at the end of every broadcast of his show. The surprise was overwhelming because he had always thought his father never watched.

"I thought you didn't watch my show. You called it trash."

"I didn't really care for it. But, of course, I watched it. It was yours. And I wanted to support ya."

Tom had to choke back tears. "It was really just something to say."

"I should've told you this weeks ago ... when we had our talk."

"What's that?"

"What happened to Maggie. It's not your fault. And those who *truly* love you know that. *I* know that."

Tears began to moisten Tom's eyes and his fight to prevent any sobbing made them grow red as he looked down from his father's gaze.

"And that saying of yours? It goes both ways, ya know?" his father continued. "If you let any love get in the way of living your life, then it's not really love. 'Cause love is supposed to inspire and lift you up; not hold you back.

"So if you let that love - or guilt - you had for Maggie get in the way of your love for Jade, you're going to be putting your life on an indefinite hold. And not just for any future relationships ... but also from being able to move on at all. Is that what you want?"

Tom thought about the unfairness of Maggie not being able to move on and how he could. He knew what had happened to her was unfair, but he also knew not living a full life would make it so he may as well have died too. And that wouldn't justify what happened to Maggie. It wouldn't justify losing his job or the public scrutiny or the loss of his friends. It wouldn't justify anything. He looked back up to meet his father's eyes. "No."

"Then what are you waitin' for, ya damn fool!? Go to her!"

Tom's worried look slowly transformed into a smile. The smile grew bigger as he thought more about what he and Jade had just discussed.

"Thanks, Dad." Tom stood up, bent down and kissed his father on his forehead. He flashed the older man a smile, noticing his father had tears in his eyes. "Didn't think you'd go getting emotional on me."

"What? Oh ... well ... *Brian's Song* was on the TV right before you got here."

Even though his father wouldn't admit it, Tom knew his dad was crying for him. Not tears of sadness or anger, but rather tears of joy. The feeling filled him with confidence and elation as he sprinted to the door, looking back one more time at the man with whom, just a few months ago, he couldn't even be in the same room. His father raised a weary hand and gave a wave. Tom waved back and ran toward the elevator.

When he got in, he pushed the button to try and get the contraption to move as fast as it could. As the doors started to close, he noticed down the hall his mother standing, watching him. He raised a hand to say goodbye and, with tears of joy in her eyes, she raised one of her wrinkled hands to her mouth and gently blew him a frail kiss, silently wishing him luck.

The drive to Shorebreak seemed to take longer than the twenty minutes it usually took, and the Alabama Shakes song, "Be Mine," fueled by soulful lead singer Brittany Howard, didn't help calm his nerves.

The guitar, drum and piano tempo grew, making an intense crescendo which began to match his heartbeat. When he did reach downtown Rehoboth and found parking, he ran the four blocks all the way to the restaurant, hoping she was not too busy to see him. He nearly tripped up the few stairs to Shorebreak's entrance door, pulled it open and stopped, catching his breath. The Alabama Shakes song continued to play over the restaurant speakers.

Jade stood behind the bar and gave a couple some drinks. After ringing up their order, she surveyed the length of the bar to see if anyone else needed something. Looking to the right, her eye caught a familiar person standing at the restaurant's main entrance and exit. It was Tom. She smiled.

As soon as he saw her smile at him, the gesture pushed his body forward to the opposite entryway to the bar.

Tom got to the end of the bar and she turned to him. "Hi."

He didn't say anything back, but just grabbed her, pulled her close and gave her a long, passionate kiss. Jade wouldn't have usually liked the public display of affection, but she recognized this was a big deal. She knew he was making a statement to her.

The few people who noticed - those sitting at and working around the bar, including Sprenkle - began to smile and taunt the new couple with a smattering of *woo*s and whistles, turning the once passionate moment into a public, comedic one. Neither Tom nor Jade joined in on the laughter, or noticed the song ending, or people staring at them. As they looked into each other's eyes, all they could do was uncontrollably smile, and, for the first time, both of them were unafraid of anything life would throw their way.

22.

"Try and sometimes you'll succeed
To make this man out of me
All of my stolen, missing parts
I've no need for anymore
I believe
I believe 'cause I can see
Our future days
Days of you and me"

--Pearl Jam
"Future Days"

The two sixteen-year-old Indian girls covered themselves with t-shirts, left the beach and walked up onto the boardwalk. The August weather was hot but the breeze coming off the Atlantic Ocean was cool upon their warm skin. Since they arrived, the girls had noticed a cute young man working at Funland, so the draw of seeing him won out over the beach. Fortunately, they didn't have to go far into the amusement park. They recognized him working one of the boardwalk games – the one with the squirt guns.

"C'mon," the taller girl told her friend. "Let's play!"

"I don't think so," the shorter girl said.

"*Pleeeease!*" the tall girl whined. "He's *so* cute! Just once!"

"Fine."

"Yay!"

They walked up to the game and picked a squirt gun.

"Where am I supposed to shoot?" the tall girl asked to no one in particular. Her friend rolled her eyes. They had played this game enough times to know how it was played.

The young man stepped toward her. "You, uh, just aim the gun at that bullseye right there," he pointed to a small orange dot, "and it makes your balloon race to the top. Whoever's balloon gets to the top first, wins."

The young man kicked the pedal activators near the ground, arming their squirt guns. He shouted, "OK! At the sound of the bell ... here we go!"

The bell rang and the water stream erupted from both girls' squirt guns, each hitting the bullseye. Both balloons glided up the track. When the taller girl knew she wasn't going to win, she redirected her gun to the young man, drenching him with water. Before he could retaliate, the bell rang, cutting off the water. The shorter girl had won. She cracked a smile while her friend giggled at the sight of the wet guy.

"Which one would you like?" the young man asked, still laughing, pointing to a small stuffed pink flamingo wearing sunglasses and a small white teddy bear wearing sunglasses.

"I'll take the flamingo."

He grabbed a flamingo from a prize bin and handed it to her. She couldn't repress her smile, beaming from the win.

"Here ya go, crackshot," the young man said. "Thanks for not drenching me."

"I was thinking about it. But the flamingo was way too sweet to pass up."

The young man smiled. "I like a woman who knows her priorities. I'll have to keep my eye on you when you come back."

"Who says I'll be back?" She cocked an eyebrow, taking a verbal jab at his flirtation.

"You can trade up your smaller prizes for a bigger one."

She looked up to see what the bigger prize was: a pink, fuzzy gorilla wearing sunglasses. She said, "I think I'll keep this one. He's cute. Besides, who says, if I come back, you won't get drenched again?"

"It's worth the risk."

Her friend was right. He was cute. The two looked at each other, sharing a romantic spark. Still, she didn't fawn over boys the way her friend did.

"Jade!" her tall friend, who had already moved on, called. "C'mon!"

Jade didn't break her stare but shouted back, "OK! Coming!"

"Maybe I'll see you around?" the young man asked.

"Yeah. Maybe." Her smile grew as big as it could get.

She turned and left to catch up with her friend. The young man watched her until they turned the corner to go into the park. Just as the girls turned, he swore he saw her briefly pause and stare down the way at him.

"Frost!" a voice shouted. Tom Frost saw Neal, one of the adult Funland workers, coming toward him. "Stop watching girls and watch your game."

Tom hadn't noticed a few customers waiting for him to start. He snapped out of his hoping to see her and went down the counter to take money from the next players, kicking on the activation to each of their squirt guns. As the afternoon waned, he thought he may get another glimpse of that girl.

He never did ... that day.

* * *

Jade stood in front of her vintage-looking radio, plugged in her iPod, hit the "RANDOM" button, followed by the "PLAY" button. A rolling piano riff sounded, beginning one of Jade's favorite covers of The Beatles' "Let it Be," a live version by Claudia Lennear from Joe Cocker's *Mad Dogs & Englishmen* album. Lennear's classic soul voice came in as if she were singing in the gospel choir, and it filled every room of the sixteen-hundred-square-foot home. A year-and-a-half after that kiss at Shorebreak, they were kissing at their small wedding ceremony in Annapolis, Maryland, on the water.

The blue-gray Craftsman home – they fell in love with three years ago – was located in a small town called Millville, about fifteen miles south from Rehoboth and five miles west from Bethany Beach. Jade smiled at the sound of Lennear's rendition and placed her left hand on her protruding, pregnant belly. She only had two more months to go until the due date and she couldn't wait for baby girl number two to become a part of their lives.

Jade moved into the living room, picked up a book and eased down onto the couch, next to Tom, who sat with his laptop, writing an article. Tom had found he loved writing and wanted to use it to try to bring something positive into the world. When he came across a Web site devoted only to good, cheerful news, he was ecstatic the site hired him as a major contributor and editor. After reading *Y: The Last*

Man and a few other recommendations from Will, he had also found he loved comic books, and started part-time work at Will's comic book store. Tom's money from his previous life had gone into buying the house and helped pay the bills, and he was the happiest he'd ever been. He moved his laptop onto the coffee table before their little girl, Molly, age three and looking like him, ran and jumped into his lap, and he instantly began frantically tickling her, igniting a laughing fit in them both.

Their wedding group photograph hung on the wall in their dining room, showing Tom and Jade with their guests, all with big smiles: Tom's and Jade's parents; Jade's friend, Katie; Tom's lawyer, Bob; Will, from the comic book store; and a few other local Delaware friends, including Feltz and Sprenkle. The other framed photographs hanging and sitting throughout the home were taken by Jade. Since confronting her parents, Jade's panic attacks had become few and far between until they were barely recognizable, and she had left teaching after having Molly. It wasn't long before she began her own photography business, which earned them a good amount of extra money, doing something she loved.

Tom had seen Dylan's name as the producer of a popular network reality competition dance series while the show was on the TV at a friend's house a few weeks ago. Feltz told him that Jen Desmond had made it to a major cable news network – the same one with "The Douche," Jim O'Leary and Kimberly Carlton – becoming a well-known talking head host on her own show called "On Point with Jennifer Desmond."

Tom and Jade had both received calls of offers to be interviewed regarding their respective tragedies, especially around the anniversary of the events or when a network was producing a compilation "Worst Tragedies" documentary program. They always just courteously turned down the offers. The charity Maggie's parents had set up in her name gave funding to a major science scholarship for high school students throughout California. Tom never spoke to Brenda and Eddie Russell again, but he made anonymous donations to their charity whenever he could.

Tom and Jade had found a small piece of land where they could make a peaceful, good life together. It wasn't perfect. They still got into the usual arguments and disagreements a majority of married couples found themselves in; they still had their personal issues which could cause the other much aggravation. They both had times they didn't communicate as well as they could or should, and they had the usual nitpicky pet peeves which are universal in all married couples. At the end of every day, though, neither of them doubted they were still crazy in love with each other.

Tom and Molly's giggling had settled down, and she asked him to read her a story. He told her to go get a book from her room. She ran toward her room, giving Jade enough time to move from sitting beside Tom to snuggling into him. The Lennear song ended and a song by Scars on 45, "Take You Home," began playing. Tom put his left arm around his wife and looked down at her as she read, then kissed the back of her head. It wasn't long before he saw his daughter, her favorite book in hand, come bounding down the hallway toward him. When she climbed into his lap, sitting on his right leg, and opened the book, he took in the moment: the smell of his wife's hair, her soothing, slow breathing, her warmth and comfort; and his daughter, whose laughter was the best elixir for any bad mood, grabbing his right hand and wrapping his arm across her midriff, making him pull her closer to him as he began reading.

Tom Frost didn't quite know how he had gotten here. He couldn't write a how-to book or devise a life plan about it to give anyone any kind of special advice, nor could he tell if there was any special, precise decision, move or path he had taken. Maybe everything that had occurred to him had led him to this place. All he knew was ... he was now here. He was happy. He was home.

FORGOTTEN MILE

MATT AMERLING

SONGS

1. **It's Hard to be a Saint in the City** – Bruce Springsteen
   Good Time – Leroy
2. **Tangled Up in Blue** – Bob Dylan
   Pauper – Love Seed Mama Jump
   Crush – Dave Matthews Band
   Blurred Lines – Robin Thicke
3. **A Matter of Trust** – Billy Joel
   Rocks Off – The Rolling Stones
4. **Better Days** – Bruce Springsteen
   Synthesizers – Butch Walker
   Take on Me – A-ha
   One Night Love Affair – Bryan Adams
   Modern Love – David Bowie
   Purple Rain – Prince
5. **Already Gone** – The Eagles
   In a Big City – Titus Andronicus
   I'm Goin' Down – Trampled by Turtles
6. **And So it Goes** – Billy Joel
7. **Tomorrow is a Long Time** – Bob Dylan
   Devil Town – Tony Lucca
8. **Who Knows Where the Times Goes** – Nina Simone
   Be Not Afraid – John Michael Talbot
   Feel it Now – Black Rebel Motorcycle Club
9. **My My, Hey Hey (Out of the Blue)** – Neil Young
   Better Than Sleeping Alone – Amelia
10. **National Anthem** – The Gaslight Anthem
    Say Something – A Great Big World w/ Christina Aguilera
11. **After Los Angeles** – Joe Firstman
    If You Could Read My Mind – Gordon Lightfoot
    Thunder Road (live) – Bruce Springsteen

SONGS (CONT'D)

12. Another Story - The Head And The Heart
Everything is Everything - Lauryn Hill
Bye Bye Baby - Mary Wells
Sweet Darlin' - She & Him
Great Expectations - The Gaslight Anthem
Better Days - Edward Sharpe & The Magnetic Zeros
13. Power Hungry Animals - The Apache Relay
14. Still Fighting It - Ben Folds
Burn - Postmodern Jukebox
Do-Wah-Doo - Kate Nash
15. Something To Sleep To - Michelle Branch
16. Running On Empty - Jackson Browne
Wake Me Up - Avicii
I Stay Away - Alice in Chains
17. Keepsake - The Gaslight Anthem
Fake Your Death - My Chemical Romance
Glycerine - Bush
Wait So Long - Trampled by Turtles
Same in the End - Sublime
Bleed Out - Blue October
18. Shadow of a Man - Neulore
19. Girls in Their Summer Clothes - Bruce Springsteen
20. Bold As Love - Jimi Hendrix
Otis - Houndmouth
Underwater - Tegan & Sara
No One is to Blame (live) - Howard Jones
Let Them Knock - Sharon Jones & The Dap-Kings
All in White - The Vaccines
I Wanna Get Better - Bleachers
Tonight I'll Be Staying Here with You - Bob Dylan
Turn Me On - Nine Simone
Come to Me - Otis Redding

SONGS (CONT'D)

21. Hero – Family of the Year
Ship to Wreck – Florence + The Machine
Broad-Shouldered Beasts – Mumford & Sons
Black Water – Of Monsters and Men
Hometown – Andy Burrows
Open Door – You + Me
Be Mine – Alabama Shakes
22. Future Days – Pearl Jam
Let it Be (live) – Claudia Lennear
Take You Home – Scars on 45

MATT AMERLING

ACKNOWLEDGMENTS

First off, it goes without saying that I wouldn't have been able to do this without the support of my family – particularly my beautiful wife, Erin, who's not just a great inspiration to me, but also an invaluable editor, artist and confidant! My daughters, Molly and Kara, make me the best man I can ever hope to be, and their intelligence, humor and love have helped me in ways which they may never fully know. For the rest of my family, especially my parents; my sister, Christina, and her family; my nephew, Brandon, and his family; my in-laws; and the rest of my extended family – thank you for being so supportive of my writing. To my niece, Samantha, and my nephew, Matthew, the dancer must dance, the musician must play music, and the writer must write – there is no greater joy than what we work so hard at to create.

Also, I want to express my thanks to the real Rich Feltz and Matt Sprenkle, who both allowed me to use their names in this piece of fiction. You guys are good friends, and I hope you know how grateful I am for your cooperation! To my friends not mentioned in the book, your spirit still resonates throughout the story and in my writing!

ABOUT THE AUTHOR

Matt Amerling was born in Washington, D.C., raised throughout Maryland and currently lives in Delaware with his wife and two daughters. Matt received his Associate's Degree in Communications in 1997 and his Bachelor's Degree in English in 2014. He worked for the *Delaware Coast Press* from 2000 to 2002, and was a former employee of the federal government before coming to his senses and deciding to live closer to the beach.

This is Matt's second book. His first book, *The Midknight,* was first published in 2005 by PublishAmerica, and a second edition was released in 2014 by CreateSpace. When not working on his next novel, he spends as much time with his family as possible; goes to the movies; reads a steady mix of genres including nonfiction, fantasy, suspense/thriller, science fiction, pop culture and comic books; continues to master his talent for making mix tapes and CDs; and writes articles for his blog – *The Amerdale Review* – as well as a pop culture blog named *The Culture Cave,* which he co-founded with a friend.

theamerdalereview.blogspot.com
theculturecave.blogspot.com
facebook.com/forgottenmile
facebook.com/themidknightbook